BESTIALITY, PARTHENOGENESIS AND WOMEN'S UNDERWEAR:

ASPECTS OF SEX IN MAYHEM PARVA AND PULP CITY

Andrew Taylor

Andrew Taylor has won the John Creasey Award and been shortlisted for both the Gold Dagger and the Edgar. His latest books are The Office of the Dead (Roth Trilogy) and Death's Own Door (Lydmouth Series). His web site is www.andrew-taylor.co.uk.

Well, I must admit I was flattered. An issue of *Crime Time* devoted to sex. And the editor thought of me. I imagined him sitting behind his great mahogany desk, its top scarred by the buts of innumerable cigars, in his editorial sanctum sanctorum. I saw him flicking through his little black book and murmuring, "Sex. Sex – Sean Connery? Too old and known to own a toupee. Colin Firth? Can't spell. Hugh Grant? Overrated and overexposed. Ah – the very person – Andrew Taylor."

We can all cling to our dreams, eh? And sexually, by and large, we do. Crime fiction holds a mirror to the society which produces it. What the mirror reflects these days is sex – lots of it, whether explicit or implicit. We crime writers live in the post-*Hair* era. We know what cunnilingus is. We even know how to spell it. Crime writing caters for a wide variety of sexual tastes. The modern crime writer and reader benefit from a groaning smorgasbord of sexual activities. But things were not always like this. Sometimes it is instructive to cast our eyes back to earlier, simpler days of the genre. Nothing so points up the differences in the past between British and American crime fiction as their differing treatment of sex. The view from Mayhem Parva was very different from the view from Pulp City.

By and large, the traditional British authorities of crime fiction tended to disapprove of sex among their corpses. Conan Doyle was a married man with children, but Sherlock Holmes left the messy business of marriage (and presumably sex) to Watson, not just once but twice. Irene Adler hardly counts as a girlfriend. Somerset Maugham believed that a love interest had no part in the detective novel, let alone sex. As for W. H. Auden, he thought that, "In his sexual life, the detective must be either celibate or happily married." In 1928, Dorothy L. Sayers published her first anthology of crime stories, prefaced by an influential introduction surveying the history and current condition of the genre. This is one of the points she made: "One fettering convention, from which detective fiction is only very slowly freeing itself, is that of the 'love interest'. Publishers and editors still labour under the delusion that all stories must have a nice young man and woman who have to be united in the last chapter. As a result, some of the finest detective stories are marred by a conventional love-story, irrelevant to the action and perfunctorily worked in…" Pretty damning. But the really significant point is that Sayers doesn't even mention sex. Yet only two years later, the lure of literary love – with

more than a hint of sex – must have become irresistible: Sayers suffered an apparent change of heart and published *Strong Poison*, the first of the Harriet Vane novels.

Here's another, perhaps more objective view from Colin Watson. Watson was the author of the brilliantly amusing Flaxborough novels. He also wrote *Snobbery With Violence,* the equally brilliant account of English crime stories and their audience. Incidentally it was he who coined the phrase 'Mayhem Parva'. He had this to say about the uncomfortable role of the heroine – a.k.a. the sex interest – in crime fiction, particularly in crime stories before the war: "She tends to be an encumbrance. Until very recent times, it was deemed that women could not run fast enough nor hit hard enough to keep up with the male characters. Their parts were passive. A woman might inspire and, within limits, sustain a hero – perhaps cut a bond or two for him at an opportune moment – but she was barred from violent intervention on his behalf. In return, she enjoyed immunity from vulgar assaults such as kicks, punches and blows on the head. Being locked in cellars, attics and crypts was in order; so was abduction by homicidal maniacs. But no matter how desperate or unprincipled her captors were supposed to be, it was never suggested for a moment that sexual conquest figured among their plans…" All this suggests that sex in pre-war British thrillers and crime fiction was characterised by a powerful strain of sado-masochism. Watson quotes a passage from a pre-war crime writer, Lynn Brock, which shows the exacting role that women had to play: "From the tip of her sprucely-waving golden head to the toes of her smartly-sensible shoes, her orderly

FROM THE DESK

Outrage is back. As media hysteria reminiscent of the darker days of the Thatcher era grips the less enlightened dailies and tumescent organs fill the cinema screens of the nation, the British are back doing what they're always comfortable with since the days of Mrs Grundy (and, latterly, Mrs Whitehouse): getting hot under the collar about sex. Actually, the written word has escaped the latest censures of our moral guardians – after all, who reads books these days? Books are only considered dangerous by some of the more illiberal world religions, and crime novels are a particularly unthreatening genre, unlikely to upset either the editor of The Daily Mail or the Ayatollahs. So will CT's sex issue generate any spleen? Unlikely – if you're reading this, you're unlikely to be the delicate type. If, however, you are that one shockable Crime Time reader, I advise you to steer clear of anything connected with Maxim Jakubowski in this issue. And that nice Andrew Taylor… who'd have thought it?

The team has excelled themselves this time… funny how easy it was to get them all talking about sex. But the hardest task was mine – coming up with a cover image that was erotic rather than gynaecological. Associate editor Judith Gray was bemused by the sight of me cutting into small pieces pictures of naked flesh from top shelf mags to come up with a subtle come-on. The final image came from Vogue…ah, well.

Now – if I tell you that the next issue is a Sherlock Holmes special, please don't say: haven't we visited Baker Street once too often? Not in the company of Crime Time writers you haven't – and there are many new things to say about our favourite substance-abuser. No, not Mark Timlin.

Now, I must write a letter to the Telegraph about these depraved Crime Fiction magazines on open sale at Waterstone's and other respectable bookstores…

Barry Forshaw

Publisher
Crime Time
7a King Henry's Walk
Islington
London N1 4NX
Fax: 020 7249 5940
e-mail: editor@crimetime.co.uk
Website:www.crimetime.co.uk

Distribution
Turnaround

Printing
Omnia, Glasgow

Editor
Barry Forshaw

Associate Editor
Judith Gray

Production editor
Paul Brazier

Film editor
Michael Carlson

TV & music editor
Charles Waring

Advertising
Philomena Muinzer
Tel: 0208 964 9106
Fax: 0208 881 5088

Subscriptions
£20 for 4 issues to
Crime Time Subscriptions,
18 Coleswood Road, Harpenden,
Herts AL5 1EQ
www.crimetime.co.uk

CRIME TIME ON THE WEB
Looking for that particular
review or feature? Visit our website on www.crimetime.co.uk –
up-dated weekly, and easier
than looking in your cherished
back issues!

CONTENTS

CRIME TIME

2001 **Nº 25**

freshness and daintiness were without blemish – an estate of jealously guarded, minutely vigilant propriety – sweet, sound English womanliness, scrupulously groomed, meticulously decked for the afternoon." Steamy stuff, indeed. One has only to join the Crime Writers' Association to meet many contemporary examples of sweet, sound English womanliness.

To return to Sayers: in *Strong Poison*, as in *Trent's Last Case* and indeed *The Moonstone*, the love interest is integral to the crime plot because of course Harriet Vane is on trial for murder. In terms of Britain in the 1930s, Harriet reeks of sexuality. She has lived with a man (a bounder, too) outside the bonds of matrimony. She is also an independent woman, used to making her own decisions; she's educated and highly intelligent; she has a career. Nevertheless, there comes a moment in *Have His Carcase* when she sees Wimsey in what is to her a new and indubitably sexual light: "...he had not so far produced in her that crushing sense of utter inferiority which leads to prostration and hero worship. But now she realised that there was, after all, something god-like about him. He could control a horse." So Harriet wants to be dominated? And as well as the masochism, can the modern scholar also detect a tell-tale hint of bestiality? In fact horses in *Have His Carcase* seem to bring out the worst in Wimsey, and in Sayers. He tells Harriet in one of his more jocular moments, "You miserable little cockney... Your knowledge of horses is comprised in the rhyme which says, "I know two things about the horse and one of them is rather coarse". Wretched girl – wait till we are married. You shall fall off a horse every day until you learn to sit on it."

More bestiality, of course. Its footprints – or hoofprints – are everywhere. Perhaps the sexual mores of Mayhem Parva were more advanced than modern readers tend to think. No wonder Harriet resisted her fate for as long as possible.

In *Have His Carcase,* we also learn that Harriet can vamp with the best of them, if only in the line of business. In this case she needs to extract information from a suspected criminal – at a picnic with the suspect's mother, so the decencies are preserved. First she has her hair done in a bunch of black ringlets – according to Colin Watson, long hair was associated with moral laxity. Then she chooses "a slinky garment...with a corsage which outlined the figure and a skirt which waved tempestuously about her ankles... high-heeled beige shoes and sheer silk stockings, with embroidered gloves and handbag, completed this alluring toilette..." She also wears an enormous hat and makes up her face "with just so much artful restraint as to suggest enormous experience aping an impossible innocence." It would be interesting to see a visual demonstration of this. Obviously, there's more to the art of cosmetics than meets the eye. Her unfortunate victim is so bowled over by this display of rampant sexuality that he parts with the information she wants without getting anything other than visual stimulation in return. When he tries to kiss her, the hat gets in the way, and then she shrieks and gives him a box on the ear. The victim's misfortunes aren't over. Later he has the temerity to complain in Wimsey's hearing that he's been short-changed, and he's soon taken to task. "Manners, please!" said Wimsey. "You will kindly refer to Miss Vane in a proper way and spare me the boring nuisance of pushing your teeth out at the back of your neck." No doubt Lord Peter's caveman behaviour was one of the characteristics which attracted Harriet – which woke what she coyly refers to elsewhere as her "shabby tigers". Here we have yet another hint of that recurring bestiality motif.

Where Wimsey and Vane led, others followed. Many other writers allowed love to rear its head among the corpses. Among them were Margery Allingham, Michael Innes and Ngaio Marsh. One by one, their sleuths fell in love and married, though the evidence for sexual attraction is generally scanty at best. None of the women was portrayed as obviously beautiful, let alone sexy; instead, they are people with style and intelligence: it is their personality that attracts, not their looks. But in all these cases the unions were blessed with children. The conclusion is obvious, and no serious modern scholar would quibble with it: either sex followed marriage or parthenogenesis did. But change was in the air, wafting across the Atlantic, where hard-boiled writing was beginning to provide an alternative to Mayhem Parva. American pulp crime writing rarely touches on parthenogenesis.

The obvious place to start is at the top, with Dashiell Hammett and *The Thin Man* (1932). Nora and Nick Charles are equals; they are several times larger than life and they have an awesome capacity for alcohol. They have something else, too. Julian Symons told the story of Dashiell Hammett introducing Ellery Queen to a lecture audience with the words, "Mr Queen, will you be good enough to explain your famous character's sex life, if any." The question sums up the difference between

love in Mayhem Parva and love in Pulp City. Nora and Nick Charles obviously, almost blatantly, have a sex life. (Given Nick's intake of alcohol, his continuing potency must in fact rank as a miracle on a par with parthenogenesis.) Interestingly enough, however, there's no evidence of bestiality. But before one cheers too loudly, it's worth remembering that the Pulp City branch of the genre was potentially as narrow-minded and restrictive as that of the classic whodunit. Like so much noir crime fiction today, pulp and hard-boiled fiction fifty years ago had its own conventions, which were often as cripplingly formulaic as those of Middle England and Mayhem Parva. Pulp City had its own sexual quirks.

Consider, for example, the rules which the publishers of a magazine called *Spicy Detective* laid down for their contributors on both sides of the Atlantic: "In describing breasts of a female character, avoid anatomical descriptions. If it is necessary for the story to have the girl give herself to a man, or be taken by him, do not go too carefully into the details... Whenever possible, avoid complete nudity of the female characters. You can have a girl strip down to her underwear, or transparent negligée or night-gown, or the thin torn shreds of her garments, but while the girl is alive and in contact with a man we do not want complete nudity. A nude female corpse is allowable, of course. Also a girl undressing in the privacy of her own room, but when men are in the action try to keep at least a shred of something on the girls. Do not have men in underwear in scenes with women, and no nude men at all. The idea is to have a very strong sex element in these stories without anything that might be interpreted as being vulgar or obscene."

Quite a challenge. I came across a copy of one of the regular monthly features from this magazine. It was a comic strip called Sally the Sleuth. And the word 'strip' seems particularly appropriate since the story line was designed so that most of the pictures could show her in her underwear, though not of course in a way that could be labelled vulgar or obscene.

Sex leads to another complication, which the later career of Raymond Chandler neatly exemplifies. The Marlowe books have plenty of glimpses of sexuality, albeit from a viewpoint not a million miles from that of *Spicy Detective*. But in fiction if not in life, Chandler was wary of love. This was the man who wrote: "Love interest almost always weakens a mystery because it introduces a type of suspense that is antagonistic to the detective's struggle to solve a problem." It's certainly true that *Poodle Springs*, Chandler's last, and unfinished, novel shows the real danger a writer of quality can face when sexual love runs away with him and his characters. Linda Loring, the woman with eight million dollars, meets Philip Marlowe in *The Long Goodbye*, and proposes to him in *Playback*. In *Poodle Springs* they are married, but the combination of her wealth and his pride seems a recipe for divorce. The bride's present to the groom is one million dollars, which he refuses. He turns down the Cadillac, too. No wonder Chandler didn't finish *Poodle Springs*. He had two problems to solve. First, his leading characters were incompatible in almost all areas of marriage. Second, there was an enormous technical challenge: as the protagonist of a crime series Marlowe Married was an entirely different animal from Marlowe Single. Marital sex seems inevitably tame in

comparison with the gamier flavours of the illicit or at least novel varieties which were available to Marlowe in his bachelor days. If only Chandler had enlivened *Poodle Springs* with a hint of bestiality.

So much for sex and crime fiction. What about sex and crime writers? Let the facts speak for themselves. Colonel Christie failed to last the course, though Agatha Christie made a better choice with her second husband. Margery Allingham married a man who in the language of the day seems to have been rather a cad and a sponge, though not an unmitigated one. Mr and Mrs Chandler did not have an idyllic time. Dorothy L. Sayers fell unsuitably in love, had a fling with a motor mechanic, and finally married a man whose main qualification seems to have been that he was the motoring correspondent for *The News of the World*. (Perhaps she had a penchant for the internal combustion engine, as well as the horse?) Hammett's marriage ended in divorce, though he did sustain a long-term relationship with another writer, Lilian Hellman. Ngaio Marsh and Josephine Tey stayed single. Out of all these authors, the one who wrote the most perceptively about sex – and in many guises – was Josephine Tey. *To Love and Be Wise*, for example, as Catherine Aird has pointed out, is "almost an essay on its title". Tey was neither a prude nor a fool, and her characters in this book hint at an astonishingly broad range of sexual and emotional behaviour. Oddly enough, though, Tey doesn't address those central sexual themes in Anglo-American crime fiction – bestiality, parthenogenesis and women's underwear. Only *Crime Time* does that.

Andrew Taylor

AN INTERVIEW WITH ANDREW TAYLOR

Adrian Muller

2001 will be a year of old beginnings and new endings for Andrew Taylor. Almost twenty years after its first appearance, the author's first novel, Caroline Minuscule, *is being republished this autumn by the Poisoned Pen Press in America. Meanwhile, in Britain,* Death's Own Door, *published in June, could be the last instalment of his popular Lydmouth series… or is it? In the following interview with Adrian Muller, Andrew Taylor looks back on the past and into the future.*

"Like many clergyman, he's always had a taste for crime," Taylor says, blaming his father for his early interest in crime fiction. "I have a clear memory of my father handing me *The Adventures of Sherlock Holmes* with the words, "You might enjoy this"; I was eight." Though the young Andrew didn't restrict himself to the world of crime – "I read just about everything as long as it was fiction" – he does admit that the family home was well stocked with Gollancz yellow-jackets and old green-covered Penguins. In a nice twist of fate Taylor's first crime novels would also be published in the Gollancz series.

Taylor decided he would be a writer at an early age. As well as an MA in English, he also got an MA in librarianship, archive and information science. Yet, like many aspiring (and professional) authors, he admits to adopting increasingly sophisticated tactics to avoid writing. "Like working", he says. Some of his jobs included wages clerk, teacher, librarian and boat-builder. Boat-builder? "Much of it involved driving tractors into walls, cleaning the tea machine, risking death in the sawmill, advising workmates on means of contraception – the blind leading the blind – and reading Dostoyevsky in my lunch breaks while enjoying that feeling of being a doomed intellectual", he recalls cheerfully.

So why did he turn to crime fiction when he finally did start writing? "A whole raft of reasons. Among them the old fashioned pleasure of stories with beginnings, middles and ends; characters you care about; narrative tension that makes you read on; the need to set crime and punishment into a moral and social context; and hell, most of all, I enjoy it." He adds, "I didn't – and don't – tend to set out to write 'a crime novel', which sounds like one those self-limiting labels. I prefer to think I write novels with crimes in them." Andrew Taylor's first novel, *Caroline Minuscule*, was published in 1982. Shortlisted for an Edgar by the Mystery Writers of America, in Britain it won the Crime Writers' Association's Creasey Award for best crime novel by a previously unpublished writer. The opening scene immediately sets the tone for what was to follow:

> Typical, *William Dougal thought. How bloody inconvenient. He was standing just inside the door of his supervisor's room in the History Department. Three yards away, a corpulent, tweed-covered shape sprawled on the oatmeal carpet, to the right of the desk. The eyes and the tongue protruded from its bloated face towards Dougal in the doorway.*

His supervisor strangled, Dougal is next in line to tackle Caroline Minuscule, not some notorious femme fatale but a style of medieval script. The script is the key to a cache of diamonds which, together with the promise of adventure, are the few reasons he needs to ignore the obvious dangers. It is easy to describe William Dougal as pleasing-

ly amoral, but Taylor feels this does his character an injustice. "Amoral implies psychopathic", he says. "A willingness completely to ignore the needs, desires, claims of other people; to be utterly selfish. I prefer to think of Dougal as having low moral fibre. He slides into things. He likes easy money. He's not good at saying no. He probably falsifies his tax returns. But there are people he cares about, sometimes without wanting to, and I think he has an idiosyncratic sense of fairness, a private justice." The explanation is just one clue that Patricia Highsmith's Ripley novels may have been of some influence. A fair assumption? "Well, there were the dead greats like Doyle, Sayers, Allingham, Tey, Chandler, Hammett. But yes, Highsmith was the biggest influence of them all", he acknowledges. "Reading *The Talented Mr Ripley* made me realise for the first time that

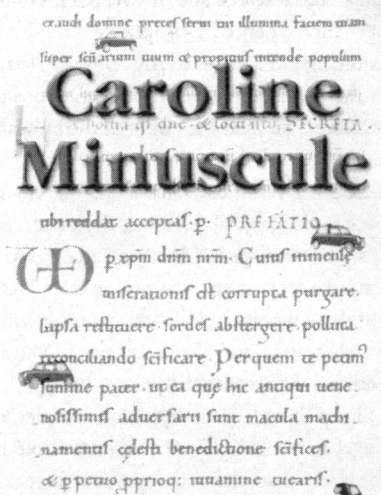

you could do anything you wanted with crime fiction, that it could liberate a writer as much as confine him. With *Caroline Minuscule*, one of my aims was to see if I could transpose Ripley into a British key. I couldn't, of course, but the result was William Dougal."

If William Dougal has low moral fibre, another character in the series more than gives him a run for his money. Dougal first meets James Hanbury in *Caroline Minuscule* when the latter hires him to translate some text. He subsequently lets Dougal do all the running, largely to avoid any danger himself. Did Taylor ever consider making Hanbury, rather than Dougal, the main character of the series? "When I started *Caroline Minuscule*, I had no idea whether I could write one book, let alone a series", the author says, "but having finished the book, I did a little research and discovered it would have more chance of acceptance if I billed it as the first of a series in my approach letter to the publisher." The hunch turned out to be correct because the editor at the publisher later admitted that she probably wouldn't have taken it if it had been a one-off. Going back to the original question, Taylor continues, "I'd forgotten it but, yes, years ago I started a story in the first person from Hanbury's viewpoint." He is still uncertain why it didn't work out. "Perhaps I need Dougal, who maybe is something of an alter ego."

Even though Hanbury didn't take centre stage, he would play an important role in the books that followed. A problem in many long-running series is inventing new ways for the protagonist to become involved in new investigations. "There's a dreadful tendency to have series characters who always stumble on a corpse when they go on holi-day, poor things", Taylor says. "I wanted to avoid that. So, after the fourth title, when it became clear that I wanted to carry on with Dougal, I gave him a way of coming across crimes in the future: I had Hanbury become a poacher-turned-gamekeeper when he buys into the security firm Custodemus."

Taylor has said that the Dougal books "vary considerably in tone and preoccupations". Does this imply that plot comes before character? "No", he answers resolutely. "Characters almost always come first. Reg Hill once said that plot was something he put in afterwards, and I know what he means." Dougal develops considerably throughout the seven novels. Starting out as a bit of a chancer, he later marries and becomes a father. "I think he's changed as I have", Taylor says, "though not in the same way. I wanted a character who aged naturally, unlike so many series' heroes who stay forever thirty-five. Now with at least one child, he's had to face the choice: either he ignores fatherhood and carries on as a bachelor, or he recognises he has to handle that responsibility, albeit in his own feckless way." Will Dougal ever return? "I hope he will", Taylor responds. "As a character he's alive and well in my head."

The manuscript for *Caroline Minuscule*, as well as those for all other novels by Andrew Taylor, have found their home in America's Boston University Library. The library has a policy of collecting manuscripts, "Presumably," Taylor says modestly, "on the principle that in a hundred years time, the work of one in a hundred authors will turn out to be incredibly valuable." So does the library have any of his unpublished efforts? "I have one or two scraps of juvenilia," he says, "with the emphasis on the juvenile – and none of it's in Boston University Library. Nor is an unpublished novel I wrote immediately after *Caroline Minuscule*. Not crime, and best forgotten."

When asked which of his colleagues he reads, Taylor initially is wary of naming any of his contemporaries. "There are plenty of longer-established authors whose work I rate very highly indeed. It's invidious to name names, because I'd have to leave so many out which should be in." Instead he says, "I'm in my fourth year as a Creasey judge, and I've had huge pleasure from each intake of new, inventive writers. Some of them awe me, too. Out of last year's crop, I particular enjoyed Joolz Denby's *Stone Baby*, Stephen Booth's *Black Dog*, Andrew Pyper's *Lost Girls* and Boston Teran's *God Is a Bullet*." Then, feeling more comfortable, he says, "One of my definitions of literary hell is being deprived of the novels of Frances Fyfield and Reginald Hill. No one is a better guide than Fyfield to the strange and sometimes wonderful landscapes of the human heart, and she writes beautifully, too. Hill's novels look with both wit and compassion – a difficult combination – at the world we live in; and he makes me laugh."

Does Taylor think much has changed since he won the Creasey, and has he detected any recent trends in crime writing? "It's harder for mid-list authors to make a living by writing fiction – crime or any other type. A recent Society of Authors survey showed this beyond reasonable doubt. On the plus side, crime fiction as a genre has opened up: it's much more varied than it was when I started. I think it has become critically more respected, too." As for trends, he says, "At worst you get literary authors playing coyly with the conventions of crime fiction, and often doing so very badly. Also, ironically, despite their pretensions, they lack the literary skills needed for good crime fiction, like the ability to plot coherently." However, Taylor is heartened by the new writers who show that crime fiction can be more than good entertainment. "An increasing number of Creasey submissions have serious literary qualities", he says. "At best this results in excellent novels which happen to have crimes or damaged people in them, which throw shafts of light on the world we live in." The latter sentence perfectly describes Taylor's own novels also.

Intermittent with the Dougal books Taylor wrote three novels that are now referred to as the Blaines Trilogy. Linked by Eric Blaines, a shadowy figure in the British espionage community, the Blaines books are a trilogy only in an informal sense. Having

ANDREW **TAYLOR**

'There's no denying Taylor's talent'
TIME OUT

DEATH'S OWN DOOR

THE LYDMOUTH SERIES

first appeared in the third Dougal novel, *Our Fathers' Lies*, and subsequently in a Lydmouth, in the trilogy Blaines is sometimes central to the story line, sometimes barely visible on the periphery. The three espionage novels were a departure from Taylor's previous work. What caused this sudden side-step? An idea for a book, or a concern of being pigeonholed? "Yes to both those", he replies. "Sometimes you see an opportunity and go for it. Also, it's very easy to get stale. I enjoy enormously tackling a new type of book." One aspect Taylor wanted to examine in the Blaines novels was how private actions often affect public events. "I was also interested at that time in the private lives of intelligence operatives: we tend to think of them as spooks on a 7/24 basis. But they aren't of course." Both the Dougal and Blaines series have been described as taking sharp but humorous looks at British institutions and sensitivities. Does he agree and, if so, did he do so with disdain or a mocking affection? "A bit of both", he says. "I didn't set out to look at them, it just seemed to happen. Crime fiction can be a great way to offload one's anger, by the way. One day I'll write the great Foot and Mouth novel in which the sheep and cows and lambs and calves gang up and fire bomb the Ministry of Agriculture." Taylor lives with his family in a small town in the Forest of Dean on the Welsh border. Many of the healthy sheep, who for centuries wandered about the area unrestricted, were culled as a precaution to contain the viral outbreak. It is obvious that Taylor is angry at the possibly unnecessary slaughter.

As well as adult fiction, Andrew Taylor also has written a number of novels for teenagers and children. "I like reading children's books", is his simple explanation for doing so. "And", he adds, "because writing for younger readers was a challenge." The novels for younger readers are more clearly issue driven, dealing with such varied topics as the animal rights movement, illegal immigrants, nuclear power, etc. Stressing that this was unintentional, he explains, "Exploring an issue isn't the same as having a moral, a message." The cross-over effect of minor characters also applies to the novels for his younger readers. "I like the idea that all my fiction is cut from the same piece of cloth, whatever it is and whenever it is set", he says. "Almost all of these books have something to tie them into the adult ones. Usually it is a very small detail like a minor character or a location. So the Youlgreave family appear in the Roth Trilogy, their eighteenth century ancestors get up to things they shouldn't in the teenage thriller *Double Exposure*, and another resident is one of the churchwardens in Lydmouth."

Before starting his Lydmouth series, Andrew Taylor wrote two psychological thrillers: *The Raven on the Water* and *The Barred Window*. These stand-alone novels resulted in an effort to develop his writing skills. "Highsmith says somewhere that writers should work out what gets their creative juices flowing", Taylor explains, "and the double narrative device is definitely something that titillates mine. I tried it out first, in a big way, in *The Raven on the Water*, which has a lot in common with *The Barred Window*." Something else both books share, something that would become predominant in the Roth Trilogy, was how distant and recent past unfold together until they converge in the present. Why is this device, used to great effect in many crime and suspense novels, so popular? "I think it is because we are fascinated by causes of crimes as well as their effects. The investigative process, in fact and fiction, is almost always a quest which takes the investigator back into the past. In a sense the structure of the Roth Trilogy was a way of formalising that." Another theme in *The Barred Window* was the blurred dividing line that sometimes exists between predators and victims. The resulting ambiguity of the characters, together with many Gothic elements, suffuses the novel with a sense of claustrophobia. Agreeing that this was one of his intentions, he adds, "I think each of my characters is a varying shade of grey. It's often hard to predict how they will behave in any given situation, until it actually happens." Explaining how this uncertainty about character development affects his writing he says, "I usually – but not always – have an idea of where a book is going, though not always a very clear one. Occasionally I plot in detail, but whatever degree of planning I do, characters grow on the page in a different way from in the mind. On several occasions, as I've neared the end of a first draft, I've changed the murderer."

After *The Barred Window* came the first of the Lydmouth series. The books are set in and around a fictional town on the Anglo-Welsh borders in the decade after World War II. Each book is an independent mystery novel, but the series as a whole is designed to create a picture of an entire society in a time of change. There are many recurring characters from all levels of society, but the two main protagonists are both outsiders. With the reader, they gradually discover more and more about Lydmouth. Jill Francis is a journalist from London, running away from sad

secrets in her past. Detective Inspector Richard Thornhill comes from the fens of East Anglia; his inclinations are permanently at war with his puritan inheritance. Appropriate for its time setting, the romance that develops is vaguely reminiscent of Noel Coward's *Brief Encounter*. "It's turned into quite a long encounter", Taylor responds with good humour. "Obviously the relationship develops. But it has done so organically; I've never planned it, and I don't know how or when it will end." Clear from the outset was Taylor's intention to use the poetry of A. E. Housman for the series' titles. "When I put together a proposal for the first three Lydmouth books I was reading *A Shropshire Lad*. Many of the poems have a similar setting on the Anglo-Welsh borders – Lydmouth is south of Shropshire – and the titles leapt out at me." These also changed, however. "I wanted to call one book *Wholesome Flesh*", he says, "but Hodder thought it might give the wrong impression. I wanted to call another *A Dead Man Out of Mind*, until I realised I'd read Kate Charles' excellent novel of the same name a few years earlier."

Unless paying particular attention, readers may not have realised that the sense of time in the Lydmouth books was created without referring to any particular dates. Again setting himself a challenge, Taylor had more practical reasons too. "It lessens the risk of anachronisms creeping in", he admits. "Though in fact there is an exact chronology, and the dedicated PhD student, should there ever be someone studying the Lydmouth series, will probably be able to work it out." The author takes the historical context in the books very seriously. "Almost obsessively", he says. "For example, before I print out the final draft I spend a day or two with the Oxford English Dictionary, checking the dates words were first used. And I still make mistakes." After completing the first three novels, Taylor was pleased to be asked to revisit Lydmouth for a further three instalments. *Death's Own Door* is the sixth in the series and Taylor doesn't rule out a return. "The Lydmouth series is open-ended", he responds, concluding, "One intriguing option is to visit Lydmouth at another point in its history."

Started and completed during the Lydmouth series was the acclaimed Roth Trilogy. Intended as a one-off thriller centring on a kidnapped child, Taylor encountered difficulties during his initial efforts. "Then", he says, "there was one of those flashes that sometimes happen. I saw it as the first of a trilogy which would move, layer by layer, into the past." The three books – which can be read as independent novels – strip away the layers of a psychopath's history. Even more chilling is that the serial killer has the face of an angel and a fondness for little children. The novels were written in reverse order, each discreetly modifying its predecessors. Uncertain why, the author knew this was the only way he could write them. "The answer must have something to do with the quest-into-the-past idea we were talking about earlier." Listing Lawrence Durrell's *Alexandria Quartet* and Robertson Davies' *Deptford Trilogy* as examples, Taylor says, "I like series where the whole is greater than the sum of the parts. I wanted to see if I could write three very different crime novels. Each tips its hat to a different area of the genre." Since the books examine the relationship between crime and evil or, as Taylor puts it, "Between secular and religious views of what's morally wrong", the

titles have religious references. *The Four Last Things* (in Catholic theology heaven, hell, death and judgement) is a psychological thriller complete with kidnapped child and severed body parts; *The Judgement of Strangers* – "a phrase from the service of commination, which is a heavy duty piece of cursing in the prayer book" – is a village mystery parody; and *The Office of the Dead* refers to a traditional service when someone dies, and is a Gothic novel with a young woman stumbling in where angels fear to tread. "I'm delighted that HarperCollins are going to issue all three in one volume in Spring 2003", says Taylor, "because that's how I – and they – saw it: as one big novel, not as three separate ones." The tentative title for the trilogy in one volume is *Requiem for an Angel*.

American fans of Andrew Taylor will be delighted to know that he will be one of many British authors attending the Washington Bouchercon this November. The Bouchercon is the world's largest crime fiction convention, and he will be appearing there with his fellow Unusual Suspects: crime novelists Natasha Cooper, Leslie Forbes, Manda Scott, Michelle Spring and Laura Wilson. They fashioned themselves after the Murder Squad, a band of crime writers made up out of John Baker, Chaz Brenchley, Ann Cleeves, Margaret Murphy, Stuart Pawson and Cath Staincliffe (they too will be at the Washington convention). Following their February launch party – on the anniversary of the St Valentine's Day Massacre – at London's Crime in Store, the Unusual Suspects can be booked for readings and library talks, events in bookshops, to provide after-dinner speakers, and much more. When asked how the Unusual Suspects came about, Taylor affably replies, "I blame Murder Squad myself. They showed to brilliant effect what a small group of crime writers could do, if they set about organising their own events and trying to promote themselves and their books. It's a dirty job, but someone's got to do it."

These days it is the Internet that provides Taylor with the excuse to avoid writing. "The website is wonderful displacement activity", he admits. "When I set it up, I asked advice, mainly from those splendid people at Tangled Web [a link can be found on Taylor's site]." Taylor designed and maintains the webpages himself and says, "I try to keep it simple, without too many large images. I hate websites where you spend ten minutes waiting for a page to download, and then you can't read the text because of the swirling multicoloured background." Then he cheerfully admits, "I lack the expertise to make it complicated, in any case." Fans eager for more news of future novels are most likely to find the information on Taylor's website. When asked what readers can expect next he leaks only a few tantalising clues. "At present I'm working on a novel set in the early nineteenth century, the first time I've written something set in a period before the lifetime of the living. It starts from the fact that Edgar Allan Poe was partly educated in England." When pressed for more details, Taylor smilingly responds, "I don't mean to be cagey! It's really that I'm deep in researching the early nineteenth century at present. The story line is gradually emerging by fits and starts. I'm at the stage where anything may change."

Adrian Muller

The Great EC Crime Comics – 1

In our homage to the most sophisticated work ever done in the medium – the much applauded, much-condemned EC comics masterminded by publisher Bill Gaines and editor Al Feldstein – we present more classic covers throughout this issue: two by Johnny Craig and one by master draftsman George Evans. *Crime SuspenStories* (note the usual dropped "e") #11 by Craig features a favourite EC visual motif: the foregrounded large object – in this case the frozen feet of suspended cadavers. The tale illustrated ends with the customary poetic justice meted out to the criminal protagonist.

LUST MURDERS

Carol Anne Davis

Sex rarely features in crime novels – but I didn't know this when I started writing them. And so far no one has complained.

I was curious about the subject from an early age, probably because no one would tell me anything. At eleven the nurse gave us a little blue book about periods and told us to ask our mothers if we had any other questions. I had lots – but my mother would turn a glowing red and change the subject, whilst my father only communicated with his fists. So I turned to the library, seeking out the sex scenes in mainstream books and, for some unknown reason, westerns. When the librarian refused to let me borrow these adult books on my child's ticket, I simply read them within the library itself. Sex seemed to offer a different kind of life to the one I was living or rather enduring. People who had sex on the television looked relaxed and happy. At least they did in the few seconds before my parents exchanged horrified looks and switched off. A friend's dad left Harold Robbins style novels lying around and I

read them avidly. They confirmed my suspicions – people that were good at sex were invited to parties on tropical islands and on private yachts.

At thirteen a local boy dared me to go to the indoor market and buy a top shelf mag. Worried about being challenged, I dropped some of the coins so was a few pence short but the shopkeeper gave me the magazine anyway. The boy and I went back to my bedroom and looked at the pictures. He lifted my top and immediately the room was heavy with the scent of ejaculate. I didn't fully understand what had happened but I had a feeling that I'd soon know a damn sight more than my repressed and puritanical mum. And so, when I came to write my first novel I just assumed that – amongst other things – it would explore sexual acts and the psychology behind them. Publishers said they were only taking on unusual books so I chose necrophilia as my subject. I'd always wondered why some men (and occasionally woman) desired a corpse rather than a receptive and responsive partner. After researching *Shrouded* I understood a lot more. The book reviewed very well – but I still met with some resistance from potential readers who seemed to think that the entire book was about sex with the dead. Trust me, I'm not fixated. One fan had a friend who refused to read it. The fan said, "Just read that section when Marjorie's having a discussion with a near stranger. Isn't it exactly how you've felt at times?" The friend agreed and read the book then went on to buy her own copy and another as a gift. *Shrouded* is about the legacy of abuse, about loneliness, about feeling different. The scenes set in the mortuary with Douglas, the necrophile mortician, are only a part of that.

I went on to write *Safe as Houses* and it also contained lots of sex – but this time it was both non-consensual and strongly sadistic. My main protagonist, David, is a sexual sadist who keeps girls captive. He's incapable of having ordinary sex with his wife. Strangely, it wasn't the extreme flagellation that upset one journalist but the masturbation scenes. "I think", she said coyly, "that some of our readers would find it difficult to read the scenes in which he has sex with himself."

My third novel, *Noise Abatement,* attempted to show how a rational man can be driven to kill by persistent unwanted noise. Stephen is a caring, straightforward man before he's driven mad by the neighbours from hell, so I made his sex life entirely normal. He and his wife enjoy the kind of erotic role play that thousands of long-term marrieds employ to keep their sex lives interesting. I thought that I'd made these sex scenes entirely legitimate but one reviewer referred to them as 'kinky and surreal'.

My fourth book, *Women Who Kill: Profiles of Female Serial Killers* is true crime and shows that fact is stranger than fiction when it comes to sex. Several of the women trembled with ecstasy whilst slowly strangling, injecting or poisoning their anguished victims. One woman undressed and sexually molested a girl during her death throes. Another videoed herself assaulting her younger female victims over several days. Those who killed as half of a couple clearly used the killings as an aphrodisiac, both during and after each deadly event.

I never want to be one of those writers who puts in gratuitous sex scenes to pad a book out. But I don't think there's anything wrong in exploring arousal within a realistic crime novel or a true crime text. Many crimes are classified as sex crimes, though the motive is usually power as well as lust. After all, in physiological terms most people obtain as much pleasure from masturbation as from intercourse. Sex with a partner is desired for all sorts of other reasons – to alleviate loneliness, to conform, to share pleasure, to feel superior to others who aren't enjoying a similar congress. Or, in the case of a serial killer, sex can be used entirely to debase the victim, which is why they prefer sodomy to vaginal intercourse.

My next novel looks at sex as a weapon and deals with an often-misunderstood type of crime.

Carol Anne Davis

Carol Anne Davis dark crime novels Noise Abatement, Safe as Houses *and* Shrouded *are all published by the Do-Not Press. Her true crime book* Women Who Kill: Profiles of Female Serial Killers *is published by Allison & Busby.*

THE CHELSEA GIRL, THE PLAYBOY, THE HONEST COP AND THE PROVEN LAWYER

Anthony Frewin

The author of London Blues *tells a strange (and true) tale of sex and death...*

I t started with a photograph. A photograph on the back of a book's dust jacket. The photograph on the facing page. Saturday on the King's Road, Chelsea, in 1967. Ground-zero for Swinging London. A local photographer out for a walk snaps hither and thither. He stops outside the Picasso coffee bar and knocks off a shot. A moment is captured for all eternity. A single, discreet moment that had already become history when the shutter closed. The photographer moves on. There's more to shoot. He's been photographing his beloved Chelsea for nearly twenty years. One day he'll put a book together. But we'll stay at the coffee bar. Stay at the Picasso. Look carefully at the faces. With a photograph you're God, because you know what happens next. You know how the story develops. The faces here, of course, had no idea what would happen next, but within twenty-four hours or so one of them

would be dead. But not just dead – murdered. Look carefully at the faces again. Is there one that says, "I am a murderee?"

Every so often I'd buy a book or two on the local history of a London neighbourhood I knew. I bought a couple on Chelsea through the Automated Book Exchange (abe) on the net, a wonderful source for second-hand books. The two I got were a 1970s off-set reprint of Alfred Beaver's standard work, *Memorials of Old Chelsea* (1892), and John Bignell's *Chelsea Seen from its Earliest Days* (1987) because of the sub-title *A Collection of Photographs and Engravings*. Older histories tend to be stingy with illustrations, though Beaver, an accomplished artist himself, ensured his was better than most. But Bignell's book is a particularly rich source of pictures. I kept it by my bed. Over the next few weeks I'd open it at random and explore a Chelsea that no longer exists. One photograph I kept returning to was the one taken at the Picasso. On the front jacket flap it merely said "The Picasso Café, 1967". Nothing else.

The photo started to haunt me. I had some strange, almost 'occult' feeling. I kept looking at it in the hope of discovering something I hadn't noticed, something hidden that would be the key to understanding what was going on. It was a crazy and irrational feeling that persisted. The eight people were beginning to seem like old friends and I even gave them names, or rather titles. Starting with the girl crouching on the right and moving clockwise: White Hat or Gazelle Babe, Felt Hat, Black Girl, Popinjay (he with the floral waistcoat and shirt), Blonde Curls, Guy in the Shadows, Scarecrow Hat and, lastly, Granny Glasses. There are some ghosts here too. A face behind Blonde Curls that might be a reflection of someone in the street and a face to the right of Scarecrow Hat that could be a customer inside the coffee bar. *And* there are the woman's feet in buckled shoes underneath Black Girl's chair. Nothing else is seen of her. She's not in the script. The photograph was taken thirty-four years ago, in 1967. Where were these eight figures now? What had become of them? I began to put together imaginary histories.

A month or so went by and I took the book into the office to photocopy some photos of Cheyne Row for a girlfriend who used to live there. I was flicking through the pages when I came across a spread I hadn't seen before, which surprised me as I thought my random raids had eventually exhausted the book. Actually, I was doubly surprised because the back cover photo was included here, in a

spread devoted to the Swinging Sixties. But when I looked a little closer it wasn't the back cover photo, but a shot that had been taken either immediately before or after, and it had been cropped. It showed White Hat, Felt Hat, Blonde Curls who was now looking apprehensively into camera, Scarecrow Hat, and Granny Glasses behind whom was hidden Guy in the Shadows. I read the accompanying caption. I read it again and immediately reread it a third time. There had been some mistake. Some alternate reality had made an unheralded and unwelcome incursion into the King's Road:

> *Below*: People on parade and sitting outside the Picasso Café. Life may have seemed like one long game but it wasn't: not anyway for Claudie Danielle Delbarre (with the blonde curls), an eighteen year old French au pair girl who was murdered in her Walpole Street bedsitter the weekend this photograph was taken in September 1967.

Well, hold on. This just wasn't right. People don't get murdered in Swinging London photos. This is the frothy, good times end of reality. They live for ever. But there it was. So, that was the secret of the photo on the back cover. We are looking at someone enjoying her last hours. We are sharing what little remains of their life before that exit to oblivion. She had a name, Claudie Danielle Delbarre. She also had a mother and father, aunts and uncles perhaps, certainly grandparents and she may even have had a brother and sister. She had a bedsitter, a blonde curly wig (it must have been), a coat with a fur collar, and a truncated future. All at the end of September 1967 when Tom Jones was somewhere in the Top Twenty singing *I'll Never Fall in Love Again*, and Engelbert Humperdinck was at

Espresso GAGGIA Coffee

ISBN 0-7090-3109-2

9 780709 031093

No. 1 with *Last Waltz*...

Little Claudie, dead at eighteen. No more hanging out at the Picasso. No more parading up and down the King's Road. No more anything. Who? Why? How? What did she do to be murdered? If anything? If indeed one has to *do* anything to be murdered? I thought there might be more details of the crime elsewhere in the book. There weren't. Bignell says she was murdered and that's it. He isn't going to hang around in this neck of the woods. I found another of Bignell's books at the abe site, *John Bignell: Chelsea Photographer*, a self-published chrestomathy of his pictures that came out in 1983. I thought it might contain something. There was nothing. The back flap had some biography of Bignell. He was born in 1907, had worked in the family concern of manufacturing chemists, and hadn't seriously taken up photography until he was made redundant in the early 1950s, when he went to live in Chelsea. Would it be worth trying to contact him? I could try. He would now be ninety-four.

I read and re-read the caption wondering if I had overlooked some important piece of information. Claudie was eighteen. An au pair girl. Murdered in her bedsit. In Walpole Street. And where was that? I know Chelsea pretty well, but I couldn't place Walpole Street. I went to a street map site on the net and keyed in the address. A coloured map appeared to the scale of 10,000:1 and there it was. The second street on the left when you're walking down King's Road from Sloane Square, just after the open space of the Duke of York's Headquarters. If she was an au pair girl, what was she doing in a bedsit? Au pairs live with a family, they don't live out. Or was she between jobs? I also did a net search for John Bignell and came up with two hits. The first was a brief notice of *Chelsea Photographer* in a column that Christopher A. Long had written for *London Portrait Magazine*, a glossy give-away of the 1980s. In the May 1983 issue he had recommended the book and noted that Bignell had recently had a successful exhibition at the Ebury Gallery. The other hit was a "Tribute to John Bignell, 'The Chelsea Pho-

tographer'" put up by Kensington Central Library advertising a free exhibition of his works that would run at the library from 3 July to 29 July 2000. Which was good to know, except it was now six months after it closed. Amongst the photos on display were ones of David Hockney, Dylan Thomas, Sybil Thorndike, Jayne Mansfield, Diana Dors and Julie Felix (who she? Try this: a 'protest' folk-singer from the USA who went out with David Frost. Yes, sir.). The page noted that Bignell had died in 1997 (late again) and his photographs "were offered to the Borough by his long-time companion Catherine Grant". The Royal Borough of Kensington and Chelsea acquired the lot with the help of the Victoria and Albert Purchase Grant Fund.

There were two leads here: the collection would be worth visiting to see whatever other photographs there were in the sequence, if any, and Catherine Grant might be of help. Both leads would eventually become redundant. I checked a couple of reference books on crime, but there was nothing on Claudie. She never made the big time. It wasn't a murder that captured the public imagination. She was no Maria Marten *de nos jours*. I walked down Walpole Street late on a rainy Thursday night. The south side is one long mid-Victorian terrace: open basement, mezzanine, then three floors above. I didn't know Claudie's address but I felt this was the right side (I later learnt that it was). The terrace had been freshly painted – a bright white that looked bright even at night, even in the rain. The street had decidedly gone up-market. If there were bedsits here in the 1960s they had metamorphosed into studio flats now with a corresponding hike in price. Some were even single dwellings. The facing side was a reflection, the same terraced houses, but they stopped abruptly two-thirds of the way to King's Road and there sits a massive, bulwark-like block of flats rising to some eleven storeys, dating from the 1930s. I didn't get any vibes in Walpole Street. Any spirits had long been exorcised. Later I drove down the King's Road and saw the coffee bar, the Picasso. The frontage had changed, it had been refurbished, looked a little smarter, but there it was, a station on Claudie's last journey to her heavenly translation. And no vibes here either.

My brother, Mark, was doing some research at the British Library in Colindale and I asked him if he had a spare moment to check out the *Chelsea News* from the beginning of September 1967 onwards. A week later he gave me a folder of newspaper photocopies. The first report in the *Chelsea News* was on Friday 22 September 1967. It was the lead story on the front page:

Girl not seen around for two days
leads to grim find
MURDER IN BEDSITTER LAND
Police visit King's Road haunts
for clues to killer

Her body was discovered on the Tuesday by a Mark Shaw Lawrence, the landlord. She had lived in a bedsitter at 17 Walpole Street since July. She was face down on a divan, naked except for a bra and a pyjama top. Dr Donald Teare, the pathologist, after a post-mortem on Wednesday said that death was due to "suffocation following cerebral haemorrhage as a result of blows to the head". Claudie Danielle, as she was known, a French girl, was said by a neigh-bour who didn't want to be named to have "masses of boy friends". And "her clothes were so extraordinary. She wore long vests like skirts and sombreros". The police were visiting clubs and discothèques (then a word just coming into English usage) in Chelsea with photographs of Claudie. A 'vital clue' taken away by the police from the bedsit was a bundle of some 200 letters and cards, many from boyfriends. No murder weapon had yet been discovered at the crime scene. A description of a man in 'a red military tunic' and 'mod gear' and with long blond hair had been given to the police. He had been seen waiting outside Claudie's room at 3am some two weeks earlier. A description that must have fitted half a million guys in the London autumn of 1967.

The first and last sub-head in the article now appears, "Might have been deterred". It reports a letter sent to the *Chelsea News* by Louis Fitzgibbon, secretary to Duncan Sandys, the Tory MP, and an individual not slow in seizing an opportunity: "Your readers will not need to be reminded of the dreadful murder which has recently been committed in your area. Many of them may feel that the perpetrator of this tragic crime might have been deterred if the death penalty had still been in force." Fitzgibbon was also secretary of the Capital Punishment Petition, one of the many groups that felt it was a bad day for England when hanging was abolished. To the left of the lead article were a couple of paragraphs headed: "Yard asks – did you see her?" Scotland Yard would like to interview anyone who had seen Claudie after Friday, also any of her friends. She was reported to have been seen in the Chelsea Potter pub on Saturday night. "One who

The Great EC Crime Comics – 3
Later in the run of *Crime SuspenStories*, one of the finest illustrators in the medium came on board: the highly talented George Evans. Note issue 23's almost abstract composition with the concentric circles in the water around the central act of violence.

knew her as a passer by" was Fred Hillsdon who sold flowers at Wellington Square. Fred vouchsafed that she "was nearly always with long-haired men and wore bright clothing". Her skirts were short "even for Chelsea".

What else was on this 1967 front page? The London Rent Assessment Panel had increased the yearly rent on a luxury flat in Cadogan Square from £750 to £800, eight artists and students were busted in Milner Street for cannabis possession, and there is a photograph by John Bignell of a photographer on the King's Road taking a photograph of a pretty girl. Snapper snapped. Bignell, it appears, was a regular contributor to the *Chelsea News*. So, he may have seen a photo of Claudie at the newspaper and realised this was the girl he had seen on Saturday or, indeed, he may actually have known her.

The following week, Friday 29 September 1967, the *Chelsea News* again led on the front page with the murder:

Claudie: Police net closes
'CHELSEA SET' MAN SOUGHT BY MURDER SQUAD
Men named in diaries interviewed: questions at 'swinging' club

"The net was closing in", stated the article. Detective Superintendent Fred Lambert described a man he wished to interview. "When he was last seen he was wearing a blue jacket, grey trousers, a light coloured shirt open at the neck, and he needed a shave." He was now missing from the Chelsea 'circle' in which he and Claudie moved. The police were also after a taxi driver who took the man to a hotel in Knightsbridge early on Monday 18 September, the day before Claudie's body was

discovered. Sixty detectives were now working on the case and a Murder Squad headquarters had been set up in a local police section house (essentially a bunkhouse for single policemen). The GPO (the General Post Office, the forerunner of BT) had even laid on three extra phone lines with extensions. The 'swinging' club mentioned in the headline was the Speakeasy Club in Margaret Street, near Oxford Circus, which I remember well, a psychedelic disco. A mobile police station was set up and the club's clientele interviewed, some of whom remembered Claudie. An inquest was opened but adjourned until 15 November. Evidence of identification was given by Detective Superintendent Lambert who said Claudie was identified by her father in his presence and that arrangements were being made with the French Consul for the body to be returned to France for burial. Lambert didn't describe Claudie as an au pair, but as a club hostess. Club hostess?

A boxed insert within the article is headed CHECK ON BUSINESSMEN. Nine 'high-salaried' businessmen whose names were found in Claudie's address book were asked to come forward voluntarily and assist the police, otherwise "detectives would have to visit their homes". A photograph appears on the left of the front page and is a *third* photograph taken by Bignell outside the Picasso coffee bar on the Saturday. Above it is the heading "Last Picture Taken?" The caption states that this was amongst other photos Bignell had earlier passed to the *News* for use in the paper when Claudie "was unknown outside her circle". Also in the folder my brother had given me were photocopies from the national papers that pre-dated the first appearance of the story in the *Chelsea News*. The *Daily Telegraph* ran a small item hidden away on page seventeen on the Wednesday, the day after Claudie's body was discovered, headed "French girl found dead in Chelsea" which at least had the virtue of getting the basic facts right. On the same day the *Evening Standard* had a full-page article:

LOVE LETTERS CLUE IN CHELSEA MURDER HUNT

Diaries may name girl's killer

The article by Roger Bray and John Ponder describes the murder scene, the post-mortem and the police's hope that the diaries and letters will soon lead them to the killer. According to the writers she had been in England on and off for about two years and was 'well-known in Soho' – probably a coded reference to some vice connection that Bray and Ponder could not then substantiate. The man in the red tunic is mentioned again by an unidentified informant (presumably the landlord or a fellow lodger at No. 17) who is quoted as saying, "He seemed irritated that she hadn't turned up – he appeared to be a bit of a nut and was considerably older than her." Police had visited the 'restaurant and bar' in Romilly Street where Claudie had been working for three months. She was also on the books of a model agency in Kensington, Rose Enterprises, and the eponymous Mr Ken Rose said he had taken her along for an 'interview' with *Penthouse* magazine, a London-based glossy men's glamour mag for blokes who thought *Playboy* was a bit too intellectual. Rose continued: "She came to me about two weeks ago and said she wanted a job modelling. I immediately

recognised she had fantastic potential. She was a lovely girl and she would have done very well. She told me she had been painted by Salvador Dali. The news of her death has come as a shattering shock. I was to take her back to *Penthouse* next week where she was to be photographed."

Rose had last seen her on the Thursday before she had been murdered. She called to collect some photographs he had taken of her. The final paragraph notes that Claudie's father had been told of her death while at work in what was presumably her home town or village, Tourcoing in Northern France (near Lille, on the Belgium border). Neighbours there said her mother had been dead for some years. A photograph in the top right hand corner dominates the page. A waist-up photograph of Claudie semi-sideways looking over her left shoulder into the camera. She wears a bikini top and her hair is shoulder length blonde and straight (the blonde curls were a wig). There is a look of sultry, knowing sexuality to the picture which was absent from the Bignell photographs, and it isn't posed or contrived either. She may have been an au pair once, but this is most certainly the club hostess. Beneath the photograph is a heading, ONE DAY OF JOY IN THE SAD LIFE OF A CLUB GIRL, that banners an interview with Claudie's best friend, Lucy Cardovillis, "a twenty-one year old coloured girl", from Kenya: "She [Claudie] won a competition in a Chelsea Boutique and was to get £30 worth of clothes from any boutique in the King's Road. Her picture was in the local paper." Lucy and Claudie had worked together a year ago in a Soho bar: "We were allowed to keep the £5 hostess fee for which we had to ask the customers with whom we sat. We could come in any time we liked. I don't go to the West End any more now. But Claudie and I remained close friends. She was round almost every day." Claudie told Lucy she had come to England about two years ago as an au pair after her mother had died. She never wanted to return to France. She was originally an au pair then she worked as a waitress, but what she wanted to be was a model: "She was always in the boutiques in the King's Road. She loved buying clothes. She never had a boyfriend for more than a few days as far as I know. She always got fed up with them. I told the police I knew of no steady boyfriend. I once lived with her in the same house in Cornwall Gardens, and she loved parties but the wish to be a model was the most important thing in her life."

Was Lucy the black girl in the Bignell photographs? She certainly looks the right age. By the side of the item about Lucy was a column-wide photograph of 17 Walpole Street captioned "Arrowed: Claudie Delbarre's bedsitter". It was on the third floor, the window on the left, directly above the front door. The *Telegraph* ran a follow-up piece the next day, Thursday 21 September, noting that Claudie was last seen at the Speakeasy Club on the Sunday morning before her death, and that she was paying £6 a week rent for the bedsit (some accounts said £8). No small sum in those days. The *Evening Standard* had a small piece the same day about the police going through the names and addresses in two brown pocket books she kept. Claudie, the paper said, jotted everyone's name down "even those men who paid 'a hostess fee' to sit with her in the bar where she worked". Accompanying the piece

was a small, column-wide close up of a sultry, kittenish Claudie, probably taken by that agent with a nose for talent, Mr Rose of Kensington.

My brother said that he had checked all issues of the *Chelsea News* through to the end of December 1967 and there was no mention of Claudie's murder again after the 29 September issue. So, had the police found the murderer? They certainly hadn't found him in that period. I wasn't sure what to do next. Neither Mark nor myself had the time to sit at the Colindale newspaper library going through back issues of newspapers hoping something would eventually appear. It may be that the police never found the murderer, that the case was unsolved. I asked Martin Short, an old friend who has written books and made documentary films on crime and police corruption, what he would do. He said my best bet was to write to one of the police divisional PR offices and see if they could be of help, but he wasn't hopeful. Or I could try contacting one of the officers who was on the case. The weeks went by and I did nothing until one afternoon I thought I'd try something else, the Hans Tasiemka Archive in North London.

Hans Tasiemka was a journalist who fled Germany in the 1930s. He was always collecting and filing away newspaper clippings and these became the basis of what must be the largest private clippings library in England. His widow, the sprightly Edda, has administered it since his death. I phoned Edda and on the off chance asked her whether she had a file on Claudie's death? She said murders are filed under the murderer's name and did I have that name? I told her that I didn't even know if the murderer had been discovered. "Oh", she said. However, Claudie Delbarre's name seemed to ring a bell. She would check and call me back. And she did. She had found a file. The murderer *had* been discovered. I asked her to photocopy the clippings and a couple of days later I got them in the post. I carefully arranged them in date order while assiduously avoiding reading them. I wanted to follow the story as it developed. But before I did that I received a copy of Claudie's death certificate in the post. I had asked Stephen Wright, a genealogist, to get me a copy. The Certified Copy of an Entry of Death was dated 1968 (not 1967, the year she died) in the sub-district of Chelsea First (whatever that is) in the Royal Borough of Kensington and Chelsea. It stated that Claudie Danielle Delbarre had died on the "Nineteenth September 1967" at 17 Walpole Street. She was a female, of eighteen years, and was a 'club hostess'. It further noted: "Certificate on Inquest adjourned and not resumed, received from G. Thurston, Coroner for Inner West London. Inquest held 22nd September 1967 and on 16th October 1968" which would explain the 1968 date at the head. Under cause of death is recorded the following: "Suffocation following cerebral haemorrhage and blows to the head. Defendant convicted of manslaughter." The suffocation, I was subsequently to learn, was having eight inches or so of bed sheeting stuffed down her throat. I read the cause of death again. Suffocation? Blows to the head? *Manslaughter?* Manslaughter is, essentially, unlawful killing without malice aforethought. Well, there may have been no aforethought malice, but suffocation, blows to the head? There was certainly

some malice abroad. But who? How? Why? The clippings I had received from Edda would have the answer.

The *Daily Mirror*'s front page on Wednesday 20 September 1967, declared MODEL IS MURDERED IN HER BEDSITTER. The *Daily Express* on the same day ran as their front page lead CHELSEA PYJAMA GIRL MURDER accompanied by a photograph of Claudie in the street wearing a top and looking as though she had forgotten to put a skirt on. The *Express*, ever mindful of its Middle England readership, helpfully explained: "The flat is on the fourth [*sic*] floor of a house in Walpole Street, not far from the King's Road, centre of the so called "Swinging London" scene." The *Evening Standard* revealed the next day that Claudie had a number of 'sugar daddies' and that she had a "fantastic number of boyfriends – more than 300"! Huh? The sleuths at the *Express* hadn't been idle and on the same day devoted almost a page to "Secret life of model Claudie": "By day she was a 'swinging chick', a hippy with the miniest mini-skirt in Chelsea. A world of psychedelic gear, tinkling bells and candle-lit discotheques. By night she lived in the shadows of Soho, a lonely girl seeking 'friends' with fat wallets in West End clubs. Only her very close friends knew the secret of Claudie's double life." Accompanying the article were two 'modelling' photographs of Claudie. One of her looking demure in what appears to be a velvet evening dress, ankle length, and the other a white bikini shot with Claudie pulling her hair across her face and attempting to look provocative. She looks amateurish and gauche in both pictures, but this may not be her fault. It is more likely to be down to the photographer, and who might that photographer be? More than likely it was Mr Ken Rose of Rose Enterprises (Models) in Kensington whom we have met before, *or* someone associated with him, as Mr Rose is quoted at length in the article and had supplied to the paper Claudie's file card from his agency. This is reproduced between the two photographs. It is headed rose enterprises (model) [sic] and is a printed card with spaces given for information to be written in. It gives Claudie's Christian names, her surname, 'nom de plume' (Claudie Danielle), her address and telephone number, her age as nineteen (she upped it a year), her marital status as single, and her occupation as student, which wasn't quite true. The following is also given: "Height: *5ft 3*. Bust: *36"*. Waist: *25"*. Hips: *36"*. Hair colour: *blond*. Eyes: *blue green*. Shoe size: *4_*. Glove size: *6_*. Foreign languages (if any): *French Spanish German*. Other Talents and Abilities, i.e. singing, dancing, etc.: *dancing singing*." One line hasn't been filled in or, if it had, the information has been deleted and that is the penultimate line: Escort Services.

Now, this puts a slightly different complexion on Mr Rose's little operation. Would a reputable modelling agency be offering *escort* services? One also looks again at the heading and wonders why *model* is in the singular. Were there other divisions of Rose Enterprises? The *Express* reporters didn't tax Mr Rose about any of this. The *Sunday Mirror* on 24 September reported that the police were seeking 'nine rich men' who knew Claudie and that she may have been involved in a blackmail racket. She made periodic weekend trips

to the country but would never tell her friends where she was going. A girl friend said she received large sums of money from time to time. Over the next couple of weeks several photos of Claudie surfaced and appeared in the national press and even overseas magazines, but there was no news, just recycled police briefings and rumours. Then it went dead. In late November 1967 there were reports that an American citizen the police wanted to interview concerning Claudie's death was in a mental home in New York. The FBI's help had been solicited by Scotland Yard and the Feds had traced the man to a hospital. He had been identified as going to a party with Claudie in the West End and flying back to the States immediately after her death. His name was not given. When he arrived in New York he had been admitted to St Luke's Hospital in great emotional distress. Later he transferred to a private mental institution. Detective Chief Superintendent Lambert, who had been promoted in the meantime, was having talks with the Director of Public Prosecutions. At the end of January 1968 a warrant was issued in London for the arrest of the American citizen in connection with Claudie's murder. The extradition process would now begin. The man Lambert sought was not named until the beginning of March. He was Robert 'Bobby' Lipman, the thirty-seven year old son of a rich New York property developer. Lipman had an apartment on Central Park West. He seemed to live a drug-fuelled existence flitting about the international circuit and not doing much else. He was currently in an 'exclusive' psychiatric retreat in Hartford, Connecticut "used by

Hollywood and Broadway stars". But exactly who was this Bobby Lipman or, more interestingly, who would he *become*?

Towards the end of March a United States district judge in Hartford, after hearing numerous legal arguments, ordered Lipman to be extradited to Britain. This order was subsequently confirmed by Dean Rusk, the US Secretary of State. The *Evening News* on 1 May had a front page photograph of the 6' 6" Lipman being led down the steps of a BOAC VC10 at Heathrow with a coat over his head by Fred Lambert and Detective Sergeant Robin Constable (misidentified as Detective Superintendent Robert Huntley, I later learnt). Lipman was taken to Chelsea police station and charged and later remanded in custody at Marlborough Street magistrates' court. A week later the *Evening News* ran a story headed CLAUDIE: MY CLIENT IS INNOCENT – SOLICITOR. And the solicitor in question was none other than the illustrious David Napley, later to become Sir David, a future President of the Law Society and chiefly remembered now for representing Jeremy Thorpe when he was accused of conspiring to murder the male model Norman Scott in the late 1970s. The *News* told how Napley at Marlborough Street had successfully applied for the immediate lifting of restrictions on reporting the case as his client "vigorously protested his innocence" and it was hoped the widespread publicity would result in people coming forward to assist in his defence. What was the script Napley was working from? Was the vigorous protestation of innocence regarding the charge of murder as opposed to manslaughter or what? But who were the people they were hoping would come forward? Where were they?

What could they say?

The trial at the Old Bailey began in early October 1968 and was widely reported in both the tabloids and the broadsheets. Lipman pleaded not guilty to murder. Michael Eastman, QC, the defence barrister, invited the jury to step into a world of "grossly excessive drinking and the world of taking hallucinatory drugs". His client, he continued, had become an alcoholic and drug addict by 1967. He continued by saying that Claudie, possibly because of her profession as a prostitute, was already on hard drugs (methadone actually; this had been established at the autopsy): "It is not my function to blacken her name but it is right you should know this because this is not the case of an older man trying to seduce an innocent girl and trying to persuade her to take drugs." Eastman recounted Lipman's activities on the Saturday 16 September 1967. In the morning he had smoked opium and cannabis and took some amphetamines and in the afternoon he was a little restrained and merely did some hashish, though he was also drinking alcohol throughout the day. In the evening he said he took some LSD at a friend's place in Chelsea and this was where he met Claudie for the first time. He went with Claudie to her flat at around 4.15am. Lipman explained: "We went into the living room. She said she would put on the kettle, and I was to make myself comfortable. I asked if I could put on some records. She made some tea. She asked me if I wanted an orange. She was eating an orange and I had a piece of it. After that I put on the records and settled down. I think she then brought the tea in. I was sitting on the bed or the sofa or whatever you call it. She said she was going to change into something more comfortable, which she did. I took off my shoes, socks and suede shirt. We listened to the music. She said, 'Let's take the acid.' We went into the kitchen. I think the suggestion about taking acid was made before she changed." Lipman had, in his own words, "some great acid from America". They dropped it together and shortly after began to make love, but their lovemaking hardly got going because, in Lipman's words, "the LSD turned me on and I went on a trip".

Lipman continued: "I felt myself speeding through space and I felt the earth opening and I went right down to it, into the centre of the earth, and found myself in a den of monster snakes which I was fighting off and battling with. They were [a] huge prehistoric type, scaly and with fire shooting from their mouth [sic]. I felt I was fighting for my life. I am not sure how I dealt with the fire coming from their mouths." Lipman claimed that when he came out of the trip he saw that Claudie was dead and could not understand how or why. He left the flat immediately and was seen running down Walpole Street. He returned to the hotel he was staying at in Knightsbridge, gathered some things together, settled his bill, checked out and flew out of Heathrow, cutting short his two-week stay. Eastman said there was "no ground for not believing" Lipman may have "thrashed about" trying to kill his imaginary assailants. However, "thrashing about" is a random activity and would hardly account for numerous blows all limited to the head *and* the stuffing of some eight inches of sheeting into Claudie's mouth. Lipman admitted to tak-

ing LSD "fifteen to thirty times" between 1965 and September 1967. On none of those occasions had he ever been violent, either towards another person or himself. The pathologist, Sir Francis Camps, appeared on behalf of the defence and suggested that Claudie may well have killed herself! Three other expert defence witnesses, all doctors with knowledge of LSD, including one from the National Institute of Mental Health in Washington, were in accord on the view that Lipman would have had no awareness of killing Claudie. One of them also agreed with Camps.

John Matthew, QC, for the Crown told the jury that there was no doubt Lipman murdered Claudie but that he might not be guilty of murder. "He would not be guilty of murder on the basis that he was under the influence of the drug [LSD] and unable to form the necessary intent." The jury was out for nearly four hours. They found Lipman guilty of manslaughter and Mr Justice Milmo sentenced him to six years' imprisonment. The reason the jury gave for finding him guilty was that he knew that it would be dangerous to take the drug and this constituted grossly negligent and reckless behaviour. To be guilty of murder one must commit a wilful or dangerous act with the intention of killing or, at the very least, causing serious bodily harm. If you do not know what you are doing the act cannot be wilful, neither do you have the necessary guilty intent. Jurists argue that if a man does not know what he is doing *that* is what is of importance, not the *why* of him not knowing. Lipman argued that he didn't know what he was doing and the jury believed him. But he was caught by the fall-back line in

The Great EC Crime Comics – 2

Crime SuspenStories #13 by Johnny Craig shows a rare period excursion for the title; Lizzie Borden's axe-wielding spree is given the EC touch. Despite the company's reputation for explicit violence, we are spared the sight of what Lizzie's axe has done to her parents' heads.

English homicide law: manslaughter. To be guilty of manslaughter, intent does not have to be shown. The mere committing of the act is enough. As Mr Justice Milmo observed in his summing up: "An unlawful act does not become lawful because it is done by someone who has rendered himself intoxicated by drink or drugs."

Lipman's defence was that he had taken acid and didn't know what was going on while on the trip. A smart defence as it turned out, but we only have his word for it that he took the substance. A further factor is that in the literature on LSD this is the only case I've come across of a murder being committed while under its influence. There is no evidence that the drug induces violence towards others. What 'violence' there is is restricted to the drug *taker* and arises from the hallucinatory experience itself. For instance, persons jumping from buildings in the belief that they can fly. Another suspicious circumstance is the alleged duration of the acid trip. Lipman said he arrived at Claudie's flat around 4.15am. Shortly after they took the acid. Yet by about 7.30am Lipman was aware of what had happened and was fleeing the scene, rushing back to his hotel, catching a plane out of the country. He wasn't on any trip then. Three hours seems a suspiciously short time for an acid trip. Lipman admitted to smoking opium, cannabis and hashish in the twenty-four hours before Claudie's murder and he also took amphetamines, and the only drug that does regularly induce violence towards others – alcohol. The guy was a walking pharmaceutical cabinet. It may have been this mixture of substances and a certain character predisposition that resulted in Lipman murdering. My own

feeling, which I cannot substantiate, is that he was aware of what he was doing, but the *why* will forever remain a mystery. It may have been some psychopathic episode. It could have arisen from sexual inadequacy – he admitted that their lovemaking was uncompleted (but blamed the acid). Perhaps Claudie taunted him? Perhaps, fuelled by the drugs and alcohol, it drove him into a rage? The perhaps' are endless.

As I read and re-read the clippings I wanted to talk to Fred Lambert, the Detective Chief Superintendent in charge of the case. This was presupposing Lambert was alive, traceable and contactable. But before going down this avenue I want to return to the playboy, Bobby Lipman. In the early 1990s the marriage of the Duke and Duchess of York, Andrew and Sarah, was over and the formal separation was under way. Fergie had strayed, and strayed big time. Here's what Allan Starkie, a one time confidant of the Duchess, writes in his memoir of the period, *Fergie: Her Secret Life* (1996): "The truth was that the love of Sarah's life, always, was not John Bryan [of the famous toe sucking photographs] but Steve Wyatt. It was with Steve Wyatt that she broke her wedding vows, while pregnant with her second child and with her marriage barely three years old. And since her real affection remained with this other American, the stepson of Houston oil magnate Oscar Wyatt, Jr, it made what happened next...all so futile [the relationship with Bryan and what followed]." Fergie had first met Wyatt on an official trip to Houston, Texas, in November 1989 while staying as a guest at the River Oaks mansion of Wyatt's mother and stepfather. She later met him in England and the rest is royal history. Right royal history. Steve's mother was a New York socialite named Lynn Sakowitz who in 1954 had married Bobby Lipman. She had two children by him, Steve and Douglas, the latter a member of Eternal Values, a gay Nazi group. She had walked out on Lipman in the early 1960s and subsequently got a divorce before marrying the Texas oil and gas billionaire, Oscar Wyatt, Jr, who formally adopted the two boys. Sakowitz claimed that neither of the two boys had seen Bobby since they were under seven years of age.

Wyatt, understandably, has been reticent about discussing his father in public. He claims he was killed in a train crash in Austria soon after he got out of prison in the early 1970s. This would be an effective way of heading off any inquiries. Nigel Dempster, the London gossip columnist, believes that Bobby is still alive, as do a number of other journalists. Bobby, who would now be fast approaching seventy-one if still alive, probably assumed another name and with the backing of his wealthy family set up shop somewhere that he wasn't known. And that was the Bobby who was – or is.

Now, how to contact Fred Lambert? Martin Short suggested I send a letter care of the Metropolitan Police pensions fund. They'd pass it on, supposing Lambert was still alive. I wasn't hopeful, I don't know why. I did nothing for several weeks until it occurred to me that there might be a simpler way. I phoned Jim Smith, a retired CID officer I know, and asked him if he knew Fred Lambert. He did, he had worked under him at Scotland Yard in a lowly capacity back in the early 1960s when he first joined the force. Did he know where I could contact him? Give me five minutes, he said. Three min-

utes later he phoned back with an address and phone number in South Africa. Fred, as I'd come to think of him, was alive and a mere phone call away. I stared at the number, a little nervous about calling. Would he want to discuss a murder that took place over thirty years ago? Would he regard my call as an intrusion? Any misgivings I had about phoning Fred were dispelled in the first couple of minutes of our conversation. He had a warm, youngish-sounding voice that belied his seventy-nine years. His manner was relaxed and affable. He was happy to talk and I was eager to listen. And – this was a bonus – his memory was as sharp as when he was a detective. We talked for about twenty minutes that first time and our conversation encompassed matters other than Claudie's murder – modern policing in London, corruption at Scotland Yard, the hijacking of football by showbiz and the middle classes and, as it turned out, a mutual friend, Martin Short. (When I had asked Martin about contacting retired CID officers I hadn't bothered to mention Fred's name. I should have done.) The circumstances in which Fred knew Martin arose out of the reason why Fred had left the police force and this is detailed below.

Fred Lambert was born in rural Norfolk in 1921, the son of a miller and baker. He was in the army during the Second World War and joined the Metropolitan Police after demobilisation in 1946. His first station was Commercial Street in the East End, G Division. He was only in uniform for eleven months before he became an aide to CID. Two years later he was a detective at Rochester Row, A Division, and soon after that was posted to the Flying Squad, the 'Sweeney', where he remained for eight years. It was a swift rise through the ranks and reflected Fred's dedication, application and intelligence. He was involved in many cases including that of Guenther Podola who shot and killed Detective Sergeant Raymond Purdy in Kensington in 1959. It was Fred's detective work that identified Podola as the murderer and led to his arrest and subsequent execution. When Claudie was murdered Fred was Detective Superintendent at Chelsea and was responsible for the seven stations within B Division. On Tuesday 19 September 1967, around 1pm, Fred was just about to leave his office and go to lunch when a sergeant came in and told him that the dead body of a woman had been found in Walpole Street and that murder was suspected. Fred went straight up to the bedsit and found Claudie on the bed. Rigor mortis had passed so she had been dead for some hours. Fred noticed that her nose and ears had been bleeding and there was haemorrhaging in her eyes, sure signs of a fractured skull. Sheeting was stuffed into her mouth. Nothing was touched. The two rooms were dusted for fingerprints and scene of crime photographs taken. Fred found several address books, letters and postcards. The local PC knew Claudie by sight and told Fred she was on the game. It was reputed that her earnings were often as high as £500 per week, a fortune in those days. Many of the names in her address books were clients and these included some high-flying figures in the City and even a bishop.

The murder of a prostitute, because of the very nature of the job, frequently presents the police with their most difficult cases. Fred thought this was likely to be a headache. At the autopsy Donald Teare, the pathologist, confirmed to Fred that she had a fractured skull but attributed the actual cause of death to suffocation. Teare said she had been hit with something wide (or thick) and heavy. The only items found in the room matching this description were a couple of heavy glass tumblers that had been sent to the forensic lab. Fred quickly built up a picture of Claudie's somewhat compartmentalised life. A mobile police inquiry unit was set up at the Speakeasy Club and all of its patrons were interviewed. This is where the first break in the investigation came. Claudie had left the club with a tall American, around 6'6", in the early hours of Sunday morning. They were going back to her place. Meanwhile fingerprints other than Claudie's had been found on one of the heavy glass tumblers. A search was done in the fingerprint records and a match was made. This was the second and triumphant break in the inquiry: the fingerprints belonged to an American, Robert Lipman, who had been arrested in London only a week prior to Claudie's death for possession of cannabis. Fred checked the hotel in Knightsbridge that Lipman had given as his address and found that he had hurriedly left on the Sunday morning within hours of Claudie's death. Inquiries soon revealed that Lipman had caught a flight out of Heathrow to Amsterdam and, later, had flown to New York. Liaison with the Federal Bureau of Investigation led to Lipman being run to ground in St Luke's Hospital in New York where he was in a psychiatric wing. Later Fred flew out to interview him.

Lipman was not going to return voluntarily so the long drawn out process of extradition began, with Fred shuffling between the Home Office and the Foreign Office. This was eventually granted and Fred flew out to bring him back. What was Lipman like? Fred says he had dried out when they collected him. He was off the drugs and the booze. He was a decent fellow, reserved, well spoken, easy to get on with. There was nothing mean, let alone evil, about him. He wasn't a bastard, he was a tragedy. He was from a rich and privileged background and there were conflicts within him that had made drug abuse an easy and welcome option. How did Fred greet the verdict? Six years for manslaughter? He thought it was fair and just. On 10 October 1968 Lipman was sent to Her Majesty's Prison at Wormwood Scrubs. An appeal against his conviction was dismissed on 28 July 1969. Within a year of Bobby Lipman being sentenced a sequence of events would begin unfurling that would force Fred Lambert to quit Scotland Yard ahead of his retirement age. Fred was the right guy in the right place at the right time, but that wasn't how some of his governors saw it. Most certainly not. Fred's 'downfall' was merely to be the next name on a duty roster *and* an honest cop.

On Saturday, 29 November 1969, *The Times* ran a story headed, "London policemen in bribe allegations. Tapes reveal planted evidence." This small story would, eventually, engender three major inquiries into corruption in the Metropolitan Police, the biggest shake-up in London CID's history, the gaoling of five detectives, the dismissal of many others, and the trial of the two most senior Scotland Yard officers ever to find themselves in the dock, ex-Commander Ken Drury and ex-Commander Wally Virgo. The inquiries were popularly known as the 'Porn Trials', after the lucrative Soho pornography trade that was generating enormous cash profits, and they revealed widespread and systematic corruption at the very heart of the Met that surprised even the force's severest critics. Two *Times* journalists, Gary Lloyd and Julian Mounter, had secretly tape-recorded a small-time South London crook and three detectives in conversations that left no doubt as to the extent of corruption that existed. *The Times* rightly feared that the allegations would be brushed under the carpet if they went straight to the Yard with them, so publication was seen as the only way of ensuring the story came out into the open. The material the newspaper had, including some thirty hours of tape recordings, was duly handed over to Scotland Yard and Roy Yorke, an acting Commander, appointed Fred Lambert because he, Fred, was 'top of the frame', waiting at the cab rank as it were for assignment. Fred was left alone to head it for the next six months working under Frank Williamson, Her Majesty's Inspector of Constabulary (Crime), whom James Callaghan, the Labour Home Secretary, had appointed in response to demands that there should be an independent element to the investigation. It could not have been easy for Fred investigating fellow officers, many of whom he knew, over allegations of corruption, but he did the job to the very best of his ability and was zealous in following up all leads wherever they might go. And that was Fred's undoing. On 21 May 1970 Commander Virgo, Fred's boss, took him off the inquiry and gave him a desk job handling his correspondence, an effective demotion. Virgo's chilling words were, "You have backed the wrong horse. You have backed Frank Williamson against your own senior officers." Virgo was mouthing what *his* boss,

John du Rose, had told him to say (du Rose, as corrupt as his underling, miraculously escaped prosecution).

Who was to replace Fred? Easy! Virgo appointed his fellow crook, Bill Moody. This was an officer who didn't have to be told what belonged under the carpet. But Fred's troubles were not yet over. Virgo was displeased with his conscientiousness in handling police reports and he was transferred to Interpol liaison, a dead end job if ever there was one. That was it for Fred. In September 1970 he went on permanent sick leave and quit the Met completely in March 1971. At the 1977 trial of Moody and Virgo, Fred's dismissal surfaced and was examined. Virgo declared that Fred was incompetent, a drunk and that he was removed from the *Times* inquiry because he knew one of the officers being investigated. Unfortunately Virgo could produce no paperwork from the time that would substantiate such serious charges. Peter Brodie, the former Assistant Chief Commissioner at the Met, appeared in court and said Fred was removed because Frank Williamson requested it. He claimed that Williamson said the inquiry was not going fast enough and Fred was the reason; aside from that, Brodie said Fred was having domestic problems (a divorce) which Brodie himself felt was reason enough to remove him, though somehow the Assistant Chief Commissioner never quite got around to discussing these matters with Fred at the time, which he should have done. Unfortunately, Williamson appeared at the trial, dissed what Brodie was saying and said that he had no criticisms whatsoever of Fred's work. It is hard now to imagine what power these corrupt officers had within the Metropolitan Police force. If your boss is bent and

your boss' boss is also bent, who do you go to? At the top of the totem pole was the Commissioner, Sir John Waldron, and his number one, Peter Brodie. They had no practical policing experience between them, no understanding of what it was like *out there*. They were essentially ex-army officers. Their 'NCOs' pulled the wool over their eyes. They were a pushover. Fred cheerfully confessed that one of the greatest days-and-a-half in his life was appearing in the box at the Old Bailey for the prosecution at the trial of Virgo and Moody, who got twelve years apiece for corruption. It was a personally satisfying ending. And dramatically satisfying too. Fred was out of the Met through no fault of his own. Twenty-five years abruptly ended. A career officer out to graze. No hope of ever returning now to his home county constabulary, Norfolk, at a senior level. All gone. He was devastated. But the Fates had kept an eye on him. He was snapped up by Mecca/Grand Met and for the next fifteen years was their director of security and personnel, flitting about the world keeping an eye on night-club, casino and cruise operations and earning three times what he did as a detective. He now lives with his wife, Judy, in South Africa, enjoying the sun, gardening, listening to and playing music (he is an accomplished organist) and collecting porcelain and glassware. That's the copper's tale.

In 1982 the memoirs of Sir David Napley, the proven lawyer (to borrow a line from Peter Cook), were published under the title of *Not Without Prejudice*, a dense and bulky book riddled with measured and cautious judgements, the deadening 'humour of the bench', and archaic phraseology, but not entirely without interest. There's a chapter on drugs and the law largely devoted to the case of little Claudie. Napley presents a detailed account of the trial and the background, even if he does get her age wrong and claims she lived in Knightsbridge. He scrupulously avoids any discussion of the innocent plea at the committal proceedings. He resurrects the argument that Claudie could have been the author of her own death. Even if she wasn't, he continues, the conviction of Lipman for manslaughter was unfair as he did not know what he was doing. Had there been a law regarding 'dangerous intoxication' Napley feels he should have been convicted of *that* rather than the greater crime of manslaughter. So, you take some intoxicating substance, get out of your mind and commit a crime. As you are not aware of committing that crime you cannot be held responsible, Napley argues. You are only responsible for *taking* the substance. As nice a legal argument as ever was put forward by the legal profession on behalf of a client, and one that ignores the consequences of an individual's actions. But this is Napley's fee talking. Hasn't little Claudie got lost in the shuffle here? There *was* a dead body in Walpole Street, lest we forget. A life *was* extinguished. Napley's book is essentially an *apologia pro vita sua* and should be regarded as such. He wasn't going to start revising opinions in his twilight years, rather this was his last chance to buttress those iffy arguments of his professional career. There was something else in the book that I found more disturbing. And poignant. And obscene, almost: a scene of crime photograph taken in Claudie's room soon after she was found. There is the divan pulled out from the wall with some cushions on it next to her body, face down and naked below the waist. There's a little square coffee table with angled wooden legs and on it two cups and saucers. Against a wall, a 1960s chest of drawers supported by four spindly legs. A calendar or print on the wall above the *bed* and next to it a narrow mirror with what looks like the blonde wig Claudie was wearing when we first met her outside the Picasso. Napley credits the photograph to the Director of Public Prosecutions, which is incorrect. Even if he thought the DPP owned the photograph he did not apply for permission to use it. The Commissioner of the Metropolitan Police has the copyright – it was one of his officers who took the photograph. Fred Lambert couldn't recall seeing any similar Met photos being reproduced outside of forensic textbooks. He thinks Napley's use of it is unwarranted and cheap sensationalism. He also thinks it demonstrates a gross disregard for any surviving members of Claudie's family. And there is also the question of how Napley obtained the picture. There would have been no reason to supply it to him during the case as the facts regarding how Claudie was found were never in dispute. So where did he get it?

Claudie was a young French girl from a working class background who worked as a prostitute, therefore, one must assume Napley reasoned, it was OK to use the picture. But ask yourself this: would he have done the same had the victim been the daughter of, say, a Member of Parliament or a High Court judge? Claudie wanted to be photographed and she was, right up until the end. The manner of her death has given her the fame she craved. *Requiescat in pace.*

Anthony Frewin

London Blues, Sixty Three Closure *and* Scorpian Rising *are published by No Exit Press*

FATAL WOMEN IN THE HARD-BOILED FIFTIES

Lee Horsley

The author of The Noir Thriller *spills the beans...*

The fatal woman poses seductively on hundreds of mid-twentieth century pulp covers, the immodest icon for a period during which sex became one of the major ingredients in the paperback boom. This is the decade that saw the beginning, both in film noir and crime fiction, of a great outpouring of femme fatale plots. Changes taking place in the representation of women had been visible in the pulp magazine illustrations of the previous decade. *Black Mask* covers which in the 1930s had depicted women as helpless victims were by the 1940s as likely to picture an aggressive dame shooting a .45 or even a submachine gun, or stamping with her spiked heel on a man's hand. In the 1950s, this iconography was made still more provocative in the cover art of the host of new paperback originals being published by Gold Medal, Lion and others. The elements of the image are a kind of visual shorthand for perilous attraction and steamy corruption. Sometimes the dangerous woman is simply a sexual predator who tempts and weakens a male protagonist; sometimes she actually imitates male aggression and appropriates male power. On the pulp cover she perhaps holds only a cocktail glass and a smouldering cigarette, or she might hold a gun and might by the end of the narrative have pulled the trigger.

But if you look beyond the boldly clichéd cover art you see a much wider range of representations. Many of the hard-boiled thrillers of the 1950s not only reproduce but rewrite and challenge the stereotypical image of the sexual, aggressive, independent woman. Constrained by the Hays Code, Hollywood tended to package the femme fatale narrative in ways that ensured the defeat of the independent female and the reassertion of male control. The novelists of the time, however, were free to play much more extensively *against* stereotype. They often, for example, set up plots that initially lead us to judge according to stereotype and then make us reverse our expectations; they establish strong female figures who, though sexual, are admirable and/or indomitable. The literary as opposed to the Hollywood femme fatale is less likely to be repressed, killed or otherwise punished for her strength and transgression.

The tough tart who seems able to survive in a male world better than most men in fact becomes a familiar figure in both American and British pulps of the time. She can be seen in her most caricatured form, for example, in a British gangster novel of the 1950s, *Yellow Babe*, by 'Ace Capelli' (Stephen Frances). Lotus, a Chinese singer, is a 'reign-

ing moll-in-chief' who has lived 'with one gangster lover after another and always the minks that go with them and the emotion growing cold inside her...' When she and her lover are caught by the gang boss ('Johnny was in a pair of shorts... She wasn't dressed as formally as Johnny'), Johnny is emasculated, but, tough as ever (and with no more use for the unfortunate Johnny), Lotus emerges in one piece, eventually becoming 'a famous girl in her own light'.

The toughness and staying-power of the powerful woman are even more evident in a 1950s series of British gangster paperbacks that featured the character of Miss Otis, who happily indulges her proclivities and seems to regret very little. Ben Sarto's (Frank Dubrez Fawcett) Miss Otis novels started with *Miss Otis Comes to Piccadilly* in 1946. From a male point of view, they can perhaps be seen as over-the-top and therefore fear-free indulgence in the 'forbidden' fantasy of the powerful and indestructible female with all her erotic allure intact. In American sensationalist and erotic paperbacks of the same period, there was a distinct market in lesbian fiction and it seems clear that Miss Otis had something of the attraction of a leather-clad dominatrix, the same kind of 'strong woman' appeal to be found in the pulp erotica of the time. The opening description in *Miss Otis Throws a Come-Back* (1949) captures Mabie Otis in all her glory: nearly six feet tall in her high heels, full-bosomed, posing with a 'cat-like voluptuousness... with an underlying suggestion of strength and cruelty', the silk of her dress stretched tightly over her thigh, 'making the limb look as if tautened for a spring. An experienced dame, you would say'. In this novel, she is in business with an ex-FBI officer who has become an entrepreneur with 'the many bucks any clever cop can get on the side', but who isn't man enough to satisfy the Otis, who longs for a man who can 'ride up rough with her on occasion'. 'The Otis' is a kind of Thatcherite gangster's moll, running her own business and more than a match for the men who try to take her on. This tough broad is the femme fataleError! Reference source not found. given 'hero status', unashamedly sexual, dominant, hardheaded, smart and calculating, manipulative – and hugely popular.

British gangster paperbacks of the 1950s were, of course, at the less subtle end of the pulp fiction spectrum. In many of the best American crime novels of the period, the figure of the femme fatale is a much more complex creation – often seen through the eyes of a heavily satirised male protagonist whose own views are presented as warped or even deranged. The effect is to undermine the stereotype, which is revealed as the product of male fantasy, desire and the will to dominate. Some of the most interesting hard-boiled fiction of the time focuses our attention on the male need to control women's sexuality in order not to be overwhelmed by it. The angle of vision is not unlike that of numerous neo-noir filmsError! Reference source not found. of more recent decades (for example, *Vertigo*, *Chinatown*, *The Grifters*), in which the female threats posed to a man's welfare or psychological stability are represented as the projection of male anxieties.

The narrator of Gil Brewer's *Nude on Thin Ice* (1960), for example, begins by abandoning Betty ('a forget-yourself machine') in the hope of acquiring money and Nanette ('a satisfactory form of entertainment'), but is soon in the arms of Justine, the femme fatale he deserves, 'an amazing creature' who ensnares men in 'the wild tumble of her thick pale-blond hair'. It is entirely appropriate that his punishment at the end is entrapment with a Justine who has ceased to maintain herself as an imitation of male fantasy, instead reverting to the antithesis of the blonde, sylph-like ideal – 'that short fat girl with the oily black hair'. By the mid 1950s, methods of ironising misogynist conceptions of women were becoming well-established in pulp crime novels (other notable examples are Charles Willeford's *High Priest of California*, published in 1953, and Harry Whittington's *Web of Murder*, which came out in 1958). Unquestionably, though, the two writers most fully identified with this type of satirised protagonist (generally though not invariably a first-person narrator) were Charles WilliamsError! Reference source not found. and Jim Thompson.

One of Williams' most gripping pieces of male self-exposure is *Hell Hath No Fury* (1953), probably better-known as *Hot Spot*, the title chosen for Dennis Hopper's quite faithful 1990 film adaptation. The descriptions of the femme fatale, Dolores Harshaw, all suggest over-ripe sexuality. With her 'bos'n's vocabulary', her drinking and her vacillation between being kittenish and belligerent, she is a caricature of woman as sexual predator: 'God knows I've always had some sort of affinity for gamey babes, but she was beginning to be a little rough even for me'. Although Dolores can objectively be said to possess many of the attributes of the spider woman, Harry Madox, the narrator, makes judgements of her that are put into perspective by his ready categorising of all the other women he thinks have bedevilled his life ('What was my batting average so far in staying out of trouble when it was baited with that much tramp?'). His own complete amorality and self-interest are revealed throughout to be the actual cause of his troubles, and are abundantly apparent before he has anything to do with Dolores. Like the protagonist of *Nude on Thin Ice* (or of Whittington's *Web of Murder*), he happens upon the femme fatale he deserves: '"We belong together... We need each other. You said I was a tramp; well, did you ever stop to think you're one too?"' Her 'snare' is her knowledge of his guilt, and Williams devises a nicely ironic reworking of the eternal devotion theme: '"You said nobody could ever take my place, and you'd never be able to leave me. I thought that was awful sweet. Don't you?"' It is crucial to the plot both that she is triumphant and that she is, for Harry, a dreadful fate – and it is arguably a weakness in Hopper's film that for Harry to drive away at the end with a Dolores played by Virginia Madsen seems too little like a punishment. In the novel, the grim ironies of the end are made painfully clear: 'I've found my own level again, and I'm living with it'.

In *A Touch of Death* (also 1953) Williams creates a narrator who, like the protagonist of *Hot Spot*, claims a certain amount of sympathy. Again, though, we become very aware both of his own uncertainties in judging the femme fatale and of his corrupt and mercenary motives. He not only loses the contest with the femme fatale but ends confined in a lunatic asylum, her schemes having so entirely discredited his narrative of events that he is deemed crazy. The woman, Mrs Madelon Butler, is the classic spider woman. She is also, however, allowed enough latitude within the narrative of Lee Scarborough to establish a conceivably sympathetic explanation for her conduct, and, like the femmes fatales in such neo-noir filmsError! Reference source not found. as *Body Heat* (Lawrence Kasdan, 1981) and *Last Seduction* (John DahlError! Reference source not found., 1994), 'ruthless and amoral' though she is, she has some admirable strengths – intelligence, sophistication, cool determination – and uses these to safeguard her own interests. The narrator's attitudes towards women are established from the outset as blithely exploitative. She asks, "You take women pretty casually, don't you?", and he replies, "There's another way?" His obsession with money becomes overwhelming, ultimately itself arousing sexual passion, as when Madelon 'stirred the loosened bundle with a caressing slowness...' The effect of her poise and skilful self-fashioning is that the narrator never knows whether she is acting or not, whether she's teasing and mocking him. He feels he has the upper hand and will literally and metaphorically screw her, but she turns the tables by simply walking away with money that he ultimately realises she has been carrying all along. What finally unhinges him and makes him 'wake up screaming' is his uncertainty to the end about what her real intentions were, and we, as readers, are left equally in the dark.

Another Williams femme fatale who resembles the potent women of neo-noir movies is Mrs Cannon in *The Big Bite* (1957). Like *Touch of Death*, this is a novel with a mercenary hard man as narrator, himself satirisedError! Reference source not found. as he judges the femme fatale, displaying even more obvious male prejudice than

Harry Madox and Lee Scarborough. Mrs Cannon, represented as much the more intelligent of the two, not only is able to out-manoeuvre the protagonist but is capable of seeing through to the real implications of the position she is in. Although she is doomed at the end, she takes ample revengeError! Reference source not found.. With considerable poetic justice she leaves the narrator, John Harlan, trapped by his own arrogance and scheming. From their early conversations we see Harlan's judgements as over-confident and dangerously mistaken. Williams drives the point home-Error! Reference source not found. by having Mrs Cannon match his macho comments with little parodies of male sexism, as when she puts him down by returning his own insult, telling him, "Just don't be an egg-head. You're stacked all wrong." In the end, she sees to it that he receives both the money and an exactly appropriate revenge, rectifying his emotionally barren life by bequeathing him '"the only emotion – besides greed – that I believe you capable of feeling. Fear."' It is a sophisticated torture, allowing him to 'savour [his] emotion to the fullest.' As in *Hot Spot* and *Touch of Death*, Williams leaves his protagonist tortured with ironic appropriateness for his greed and stupidity, outmanoeuvred by a woman he has underrated and treated with condescension.

Jim Thompson often exposes the self-deluded ways in which even quite ordinary men (like Roy Dillon in *The Grifters*) judge the mothers, wives and girlfriends in their lives, but when he pushes the characterisation of his protagonists further towards the psychopathic, he creates a sense that stereotypical representations of women are not just reflections of male greed and self-satisfaction but projections of deeply disturbed minds. From 1949 on, with *Nothing More Than Murder*, Thompson created a succession of off-beat and subversive portraits of psychologically disturbed protagonist-murderers. *Nothing More than Murder* was followed by *The Killer Inside Me* (1952), *Savage Night* (1953), *A Hell of a Woman* (1954), *The Nothing Man* (1954), *A Swell-Looking Babe* (1954) and *Pop 1280* (1964). All but *A Swell-Looking Babe* are written in the first person, and all use the form for savage satiric exposure. Of these, the novel most fully engaged in dissecting the dementedly misogynist mind is *A Hell of a Woman*, in which the narrator is the door-to-door salesman, Frank 'Dolly' Dillon, whose nick-name captures something of the inadequacy of a man who is forever failing to assert himself in the male world. Thompson gives Dolly, who is very evidently responsible for his own failures, free rein to rant against the women in his life, creating with cumulative force the image of a mind possessed by hatred. As the novel progressively distances the reader from his self-pitying, self-justifying voice, it becomes clear that to Dolly *every* woman is 'a hell of a woman', an emasculating tramp he can blame for his troubles in the world. So, for example, when he hits his wife, he adopts what to him is a reassuring manner: 'I leaned against the door, laughing... I hadn't really hurt her, you know. Why hell, if I'd wanted to give her a full hook I'd've taken her head off'. After she throws him out, Dolly begins to tell us about how he got married to Joyce: 'No, now wait a minute! I think I'm getting this thing all fouled up. I believe it was Doris who acted that way, the gal I was married to before Joyce. Yeah, it must have been Doris – or was it Ellen? Well, it doesn't make much difference; they were all alike. They all turned out the same way.' It is characteristic of Thompson's darker novels that, towards the end, almost every view Dolly expresses has acquired ironic force. In the sections written by 'Knarf Nollid', Frank Dillon reveals still more about himself than he does in the other narrative, composing, 'Through thick and thin: the true story of a man's fight against high odds and low women...' As the narrative becomes increasingly surrealError! Reference source not found., and Dolly's murders do not enable him to 'depart this scene of many tragic disappointments', he drifts on to an even more symbolic woman, 'the lovely Helene, my princess charming', at which point narrative coherence breaks down altogether:

'And right at the start it made me a little uneasy; I got to wondering what was real and what wasn't. And maybe if I saw her as she really

one more bag like all the rest

was, I wouldn't be able to take it. But that was just at first... I mean she had to be

a bag in a fleabag, for Christ's sake, and I couldn't go any

beautiful and classy and all that a man desires in a woman...'

One line of narrative recounts Helene's (the emasculating harpy's) castration of Dolly, another (which we take to be reality) his self-mutilation and suicide, the culmination of Dolly's self-destruction – '*and she didn't want it, all I had to give...*'

Lee Horsley

SEX AND SAVAGERY

IN PULP CRIME PAPERBACK COVER ART

Gary Lovisi

In the cover art of the pulp crime paper-backs of the 1950s, sex and savagery went together like peanut butter and jelly. Paperback cover art from the 1940s, 1950s and 1960s relished the sexy, the lurid and often the sleazy to make a sale. Mystery and private eye novels especially were packaged by combining crime with sex. Paperbacks evolved from a pulp magazine heritage; not only were many of the writers and artists originally from the pulps, but so were many of the editors (Leo Margolies, Sam Merwin) and publishers (A. A. Wyn of Ace Books and Ned Pines of Popular Library). Paperbacks of this era had a particularly strong connection with sex, mostly images of scantily clad women in pulp-inspired cover art used to sell copies. After all, they sold to a predomi-nately male book buying public at the time. Publishers knew what book buyers liked back then and gave it to them. Today, these old paperbacks often send modern feminists shrieking while sophisticated readers shake their heads in disapproval. But to those who understand and appreciate them, the cover art on these old crime paperbacks is beauti-ful and fascinating.

Some of the most egregious examples of sex and savagery in pulp crime paperbacks also turn out to be some of the most hotly desired and collectable paperbacks today. No surprise there. Covers showing so-called 'bad girls' (you can tell them because they almost always are blondes holding a cigarette), and femme fatales (dangerous homicidal women) are inextricably linked to noir, hard-boiled and tough-guy private eye mysteries. A beautiful woman with a gun is a pulp and paperback staple, and if she's scantily clad – all the better for most male book buyers of the era. Interestingly

enough, even traditional mystery novels suffered from this packaging. For instance, *The Doll's Trunk Murder* (Popular Library #211) by Helen Reilly received the sex and savagery treatment with a particularly brutal bondage cover by pulp art great Rudolph Belarski. Here we see a beautiful woman bound with rope, her mouth taped, and her dress open to strategically expose as much breast as was permissible in the era. As if that's not enough, she's also menaced by a man's gloved hand holding a knife at her throat. This was an extreme example, but even mainstream mysteries were given the sex and savagery cover art treatment to make them more saleable. However, most books just had the generic sexy girl, or femme fatale cover without the savagery of bondage or violence. The violence was implied, not shown on these covers. One good example is the Veronica Lake look-alike on *A Dame Called Murder* by Robert O.

Saber (Graphic Book #111). This is an outstanding cover by Walter Popp. Here we see a doll get the drop on a two-timing jewel thief. Somehow we know she's not playing, and that she will very efficiently shoot the man in the back. A classic sexy femme fatale on a crime paperback cover.

To be sure, certain authors, or certain publisher runs, had a near lock on sex and savagery in the paperbacks. They seemed to specialize. Mickey Spillane's hard-boiled Mike Hammer paperback reprints from Signet Books showcased some brutal bondage cover art by Lou Kimmel that oozed sex and violence. In *One Lonely Night* (Signet Book #888) Hammer fights commie spies in the 1950s and comes upon a woman stripped naked, tied and hanging by her wrists. Luckily, Hammer is there to save her. On the cover of *The Long Wait* (Signet Book #932) it is Mike Hammer himself, bound and beaten, shirt torn and tied to a chair

with a disheveled women in the foreground. What is her connection to the scene? Is she Hammer's captor or companion? Other crime authors like Jim Thomspon, David Goodis, Charles Willeford, Bruno Fischer, Richard Prather, John D. MacDonald and more in their early books for Lion, and later Gold Medal, benefited from sexy cover art. Sometimes violent art as well.

In England, James Hadley Chase (beginning with his savage and violent opening opus) *No Orchids for Miss Blandish* (a 1950s paperback reprint from Harlequin Books #108), set the tone early in the 1930s and 1940s. When these books were reprinted in the 1950s, the sex and violence oozed out of the cover art based on events in the story. For instance, in *No Orchids*, we have the story of Slim Grissom – homicidal maniac and kidnap rapist of the innocent Carol Blandish. It's a brutal crime novel with a high body count. The book horrified the critics of its day in the 1930s and 1940s; much as Spillane's Mike Hammer would do so with critics in the 1950s. What do critics know, anyway? Chase continued with many other hard crime novels, including a sequel, *The Flesh of the Orchid* (Harlequin Book #111), where the 'bad seed' from an unholy rape becomes a beautiful and sexy female homicidal maniac. Chase was a staple of the UK tough-guy and violence crime school that imitated American hard-boiled private eyes – specifically Spillane's Mike Hammer. In American and Canadian reprints he became popular on this side of the Atlantic in the 1950s and churned out numerous tough crime novels. Many of these had the prerequisite sexy girl with a gun on the cover or the female victim being menaced by a male criminal with murderous intent.

However, the genre reached its nadir of sex and savagery (or it's heights according

to some collectors today) in England with the cover art on the early Hank Janson crime digests. These were small magazine-size paperbacks, written by Stephen Frances with cover art by Reginald Heade. Heade's exquisitely sexy women were pin-up art supreme, such as the cover he did for *Lola Brought Her Wreath* (Gaywood Press, 1950). Later the books became so hot the publishers were raided by the police and some copies were banned. Others were destroyed. Heade himself went into hiding for a period, and afterwards did paperback cover art under a pseudonym, as by 'Cy Webb'. By that time about fifty Hank Jansons had been published and more would come later – albeit toned down in context and with cover art by different artists. One of these later Jansons with an excellent 'bad girl' crime cover is *Come Quickly Honey* (Roberts & Vinter, 1960). Meanwhile, all the Hank Janson sales success spawned an

entire genre of imitators, called today 'British gangster digests'. They were written by a host of authors under tough-guy, Americanized pseudonyms and with great campy titles. Examples are: *Unhappy Hophead, Floosie on the Run, I Like My Women Tough,* and *Rebecca of the Snatch Racket.* They featured sexy, often undressed women, sometimes violent content, cover art by a host of Heade wannabes, mostly near-hack pros such as Perl and Ferarri. Ferrari on a good day: *Tomorrow – The Chair* by Ross Angel (Scion Books), with the typical half-naked girl with a gun. On a good day the gangster artists could turn in an adequate cover. On a bad day: you had to wonder what they'd been drinking.

Back in America, the digests also contributed to the crime scene. Phantom Books published an excellent private eye novel by Joe Barry, *Homicide Hotel* (Phantom #500), but the cover art shows one of the most

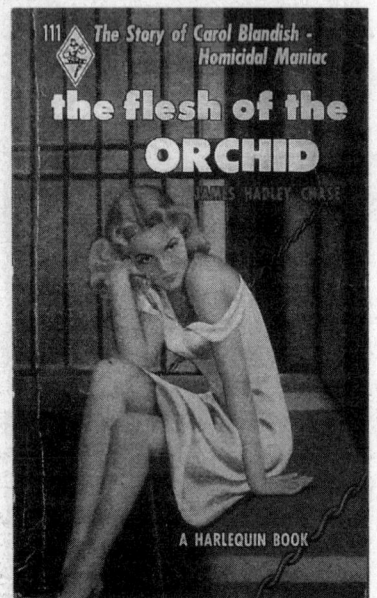

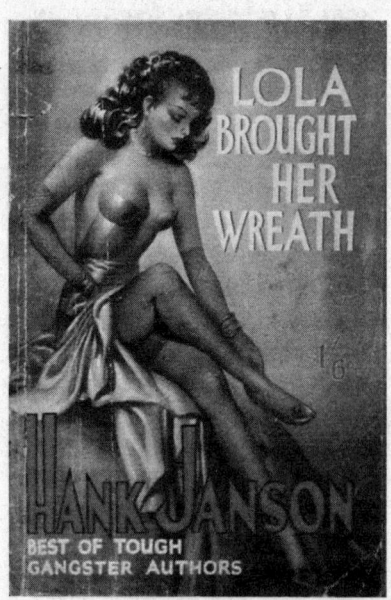

brutal sex and exploitation scenes ever. On it we see two double-Y-chromosome thugs chloroforming a woman tied with rope to a chair, as they pull her hair and terrorize her. You know she's a goner. I think it's one of the most brutal covers ever to appear on an American paperback. Just as a side note, the image on the cover has absolutely *nothing* to do with the book, a situation not uncommon between the text and cover art on many of the books of this era. A runner-up in the violence-against-women category would be another contribution by British author James Hadley Chase and his American publisher Eton Books (#E112, which was an imprint of Avon Books). It had the charming title of *Kiss My Fist*. It shows a man roundhouse punch a woman in the face, literally knocking her block off. It's a cover that packs quite a wallop. Guaranteed to get all kinds of people upset today for all kinds of reasons.

Not to leave it with the girls always getting the rough end of things, there were also various American crime digest magazines in the 1950s and 1960s – lesser sisters of *Manhunt* and *Ellery Queen's Mystery Magazine* –

much lesser. They went by names like *Guilty, Trapped, Two-Fisted, Hunted, Saturn Web* and *Sure-Fire*. On the covers of many of these the women turn the tables on the men, showing they can be just as violent and brutal. The cover for *Guilty* (July 1958) shows a woman garroting a police detective from behind as he tries to make a report at a street call box. An incredible scene. More savage yet, the cover of *Trapped* (August 1960), where we see a disheveled, almost stripped naked woman getting the drop on her attacker with a particularly long pair of nasty scissors as she tries to push him out a window. Many of these magazines had particularly sexy and savage art. In fact, one cover art motif on most issues seemed to be to show ever more violent and imaginatively graphic ways for a woman to kill a man. Or vice versa. Covers showed femme fatales, or 'wronged women' getting their revenge by garroting, death by stabbing

with a knife, axe, scissors, ice-pick, shot with gun, pistol whipped, whipped with a whip, choked, and more. Liberal doses of sex and flesh were thrown in the art. Some covers had girl fights with the inevitable cat fight tearing of clothing. Some showed two girls ganging up to kill a guy. These were all lower rung magazines full of crime stories, but sex and savagery were the selling points. In truth, crime is a nasty, violent business; and murder, often committed from reasons of passion or jealously, inevitably has a sex and savagery angle to it. However these digest magazines, and many of the most egregious examples of the books in this article, in their cover art only exacerbated and exploited the situation for a sale. It's all crime sleaze. It's also avidly collected today.

Falcon Books, another 1950s digest outfit mixed hard-boiled crime with outstanding sexy cover art. Books like *Girls Out Of Hell* by Joe Weiss (Falcon #28) told the sordid story of girl-gang crime – a classic of the

juvenile delinquent genre. In *The Evil Sleep* (Falcon #40) by crime legend Evan Hunter and *Dagger Of Flesh* (Falcon #31) by Shell Scott creator Richard Prather, we have two early crime novels by modern day legends in the field still active today. This entire short-run series of about two dozen books is a collector's dream with something in content or cover art for everyone. In the US many mainstream paperback publishers also specialised in crime, such as Lion Books, Monarch Books, Graphic Books, Gold Medal, Popular Library, Avon, Eton Books and Ace Books with their 'double novel' books. All featured very sexy cover art, updated images based on the old pulps. They even used covers painted by pulp greats like Rudolph Belarski, Earle Bergey, Rudy Nappi, Walter Popp, Robert Maguire, Norman Saunders and others.

Signet Books, the company that boasted it's motto, 'Good Reading For The Millions'

(which translated to the proletarian 'good books for the masses'), was nevertheless built on the sex of their Erskine Caldwell early paperback reprints (*God's Little Acre*) and the savagery of the early hard-boiled Mickey Spillane paperbacks (*I, The Jury*). They also published a long run of hard-boiled crime in the Spillane mold with sexy and sometimes violent cover art. Writers such as Adam Knight, Charlie Wells, Jack Webb, Sam S. Taylor, Mike Roscoe and more gave us Spillane-like classics, many with glorious sexy cover art by veteran paperback master Robert Maguire. Two good examples of Maguire's art: *So Cold, My Bed* by Sam S. Taylor (Signet #1247) where a bad girl does in a guy; and *Slice Of Hell* by Mike Roscoe (Signet #1216) where a guy gets a drop on a girl. Maguire's women stand alone as pulp noir femme fatale icons on the paperbacks of the 1950s. He did many great covers in this style for Signet

Books, Berkley Books, Pyramid Books and others. They're exquisite. In fact, the sex and savagery shown in the cover art of these early crime paperbacks of the 1950s and 1960s is what mostly sold these books. It's what helped make some of these authors successful, and in some cases, household names. It ensured publisher sales and company success. It's also what has made the books so avidly collected today – in a world where no contemporary mainstream books offer anything to rival this incredible artwork. The best examples of these covers are just wonderful, showing very sexy and beautiful women often involved in the height of passion or crime. The worst examples are savage, brutally sadistic images of violent crime. Each is a snapshot frozen in time of our collective historical tapestry, from an era of less pretensions, no political correctness, and few if any sensitivities. That's the way it was back then. Sex and savagery in paperback cover art often mirrored life. The anger, the hatred and passions were all there, displayed as colorful images to entice the reader and book buyer. These covers, for the most part, showed crime as the ugly and nasty business that it is. Today, we can enjoy these books in our more enlightened era for what they are. They're history. The cover art is outstanding and often fascinates us. These books are fun. Sometimes, they're even *cool*.

Gary Lovisi

Gary Lovisi has been a paperback collector for the last thirty years and is editor of the field's leading magazine, Paperback Parade. *His latest book is* The Sexy Digests, *a survey, checklist and price guide to the good-girl art and exploitation digest paperbacks of the 1950s. Visit his web site: www.gryphonbooks.com*

SEXY CRIME – NOT!

Russell James

Crime fiction is sexy? No way.
Back in the golden days – yes, back before most of us were born – as twentieth century crime fiction struggled to throw off the stilted legacy of Wilkie Collins and Arthur Conan Doyle, it stumbled onto sex – and what did it do? It reacted like an errant preacher falling for a wicked woman's easy charms. After a few hot and sultry encounters the black-coated preacher ran cursing for the pulpit.

For a short while, in those first few encounters brazenly proclaimed to a startled congregation from wonderfully lurid pulp fiction paperback covers, our sobbing preacher buried his head in the warm and fragrant bosom of the blonde on the street corner – but all too soon he repented, and the come-hither blonde, the evil sex of womankind, the fearful praying mantis of sex itself all became abominations to be denounced.

He left a long legacy. In how many crime books since the Second World War has any crime fiction character enjoyed a prolonged period of enjoyable, uncomplicated, reciprocal sex? Too few, my brethren. Those that the most well-read can dredge up will simply exemplify the old nostrum that a rare exception proves the rule. For decades, the sex that crime writers have laid before us has been perverted, the crimes that they have written about have been sex-based, and in crime fiction novels even legitimate sex has been taken to distorted extremes: sado-masochism, snuff killing, bondage, fetishism and fisting. What happened to that Sixties Grail, the *joy* of sex?

Do crime writers hate sex?

In recent years we've seen one or two women writers try to lighten up a little – but all too soon the men in their beds turn back into bastards. Gay writers too have tried to play down the kinkiness – but gay writers haven't yet made it into the sunlit uplands of pubic acceptance: if a gay writer rhapsodises about good sex their publisher grows nervous. Overall though – and swamping these tiny messianic minorities – is a vast foetid lake of crime writers who describe sex as sin.

How did we get so uptight?

Back in the 1930s when sex first forced its way into crime fiction, the workaday hack writers gave us brassy blondes and tough heroes – fast and sassy, engaged in sexual contests and sexual tests – but after the watershed Second World War the writers returned more misanthropic, or perhaps plain misogynous. No, let me not blame the Second World War: no sooner had the sexual genie escaped from the Spanish Fly bottle than crime writers' inherent prudery rose up to shove it back. Even in the 1930s, women and sex itself were labelled evil, diabolical and insatiable. Lurid covers screamed of Evil Love, Satan's Temptress and The Mistress of the Grinning Corpse. When David Goodis, for example, got a come-hither glance on the first page of *The Blonde on the Street Corner*, he spent the rest of the book gibbering in fear that he might be asked to follow up. He knew about sex – it was something to fear.

As the war faded and writers grew older, sex and sexual attraction began to be seen through more wistful eyes. When those same writers moved into their fifties, their heroes slid correspondingly from their late twenties to their mid forties – though the women stayed young. A world-weary seen-it-all cynicism came in – to be blasted aside by a new breed of hard young writers for whom sex was part of the sin, the cause of it: Ellroy and the corroded city of Los Angeles; Harris

and the warped psycho-killer who flayed a woman so he could dress in her skin.

Some wistfulness remained. Ageing authors like Charles Willeford and Walt Mosley allowed their heroes to age. They wrote about sex as an occasional and welcome visitor to their heroes' lives. But they're exceptions – most writers slate sex. As an ageing writer myself (you'll never know how much courage it takes to say that) I too am guilty. Not in my early books, perhaps (the Gollancz trio all place their hard-boiled heroes in romantic relationships) but later, when I brought a paedophile into two of my strongest novels. In defence, I'll point out that I could never be bothered to make perverts central to my stories. In *Painting in the Dark*, indeed, I let my eighty-five-year-old heroine reminisce fondly about her earlier and rampantly healthy sex life (at eighty-five, of course it was an *earlier* sex life) – wistful writing again, but how much easier to read than the parallel modern track in that book depicting the tribulations of a paedophile and an astonishing young rent boy. How have my readers reacted? They prefer the eighty-five-year-old. They can relate to her. They enjoy her memories of straightforward, enjoyable sex. But they shudder at the rent boy.

Looking back at the twentieth century, we see crime novelists getting almost everything right – everything except sex. Sex isn't dirty. Sex isn't evil. Sex does not lie at the base heart of wickedness. It's time we crime writers shook off this 'given' that sex is dirty and at the root of all crime. It isn't. Money is at the root of most crime. Sex is fun. Sex is life. Sex is not a crime.

Russell James

MAXIM JAKUBOWSKI

FILTH PEDLAR OR EMPEROR OF EROTIC NOIR?

Jim Driver

Of all the authors published by The Do-Not Press, the one who excites the most attention and controversy is Maxim Jakubowski. The world seems split on whether his fiction exists purely to shock and corrupt, or whether he's a genius, pushing hard against what is acceptable and comfortable in modern literature. Opinion is divided, with two threatening letters ("he has a sick and depraved mind and should not be allowed to corrupt our bookshelves with his perverted rantings... if he ever shows his disgusting face in Florida I would be proud to shoot him down like the dog he is..." and "Your throat was made to slit, you pornographic sick fuck") – both bearing US postmarks, not surprisingly – perhaps tipping the balance in favour of the sane but depraved.

For those not in the know, Maxim Jakubowski wears more hats than a troop of Village People tribute bands. He owns and runs London's Murder One specialist crime bookshop and mail-order business, is literary director of the Crime Scene convention held annually at the National Film Theatre, is an advisor for the London Film Festival, reviews crime fiction for The *Guardian,* BOL Online and this very organ, as well as erotica for *Time Out*. He has edited many fiction collections including *London Noir*, the *New Crimes* series and co-edited the ground-breaking *Fresh Blood* series of British crime anthologies, plus a

BECAUSE SHE THOUGHT SHE LOVED ME

MAXIM JAKUBOWSKI

raft of erotic work, including the *Mammoth Books of Erotica*, *International Erotica* and *Illustrated Erotica*. He founded Virgin Books and edited Black Box Thrillers and Eros Plus. Maxim was born in Barnet, but raised in Paris. A man of many parts. As with the author, Maxim Jakubowski's fiction doesn't fit easily into pigeon holes. It unashamedly crosses genres and carries themes and characters that permeate the books like silver thread. The first slice of Jakubowski we ever published was *Life in the World of Women* (1996), a collection of almost-connected short stories that were classified (by the author) as "dangerous and erotic stories of war between the sexes". It was one of those "boy meets girl, boy and girl make love, boy loses girl, girl turns to prostitution, boy kills girl, boy commits suicide" tales. There were rumours that certain of the scenarios pertained to real life events, and one female crime writer called the collection "the most elaborate literary revenge", but nothing was proved and no charges were ever brought.

In *Locus*, Edward Bryant dubbed the collection "as hardboiled as Hammett" and Ed Gorman, writing in *Mystery Scene* highlighted: "the hard sexy edge of Henry Miller and the redeeming grief of Jack Kerouac." He summed it up as: "A first class collection". Others weren't quite so fulsome in their praise and at least one well known critic refused to review *Life* for his revered organ on the grounds that it "glorified violence and depraved sex". Pretty hard to deny that charge. As ever, you pays your money and you takes your choice. *Life in the World of Women* was followed by *It's You That I Want to Kiss*, subtitled *A Deadly Romance of the American Highways*. This was either a thriller

with pornographic elements or erotica peppered with thrills. Jacob and Anne meet in Miami Beach, but soon they're on the run from bad boy Teddy Caliban and his aptly named hardman, Evil. The violence is extreme, the sex hard, and in the background, crossovers with the earlier stories are subtle and maddeningly nebulous. A Katherine appears who may or may not be based on (one of?) the central character(s) in *Life in the World of Women,* whilst Jake has much in common with the stories' leading men. And he, too, is fleeing Britain and the memories of an affair gone wrong. *Time Out* called the book "an unholy mixture of Jim Thompson and *American Psycho*", whilst the USA's *Library News* amazed everyone by decreeing it "literate, sophisticated prose; recommended".

The sado-masochistic, voyeuristic sex themes of *Life in the World of Women* and *It's You That I Want to Kiss* were expanded in the next novel, *Because She Thought She Loved Me*. It begins:

> The wind was howling like an apprentice banshee outside the hotel windows. The Bloomsbury pavements were wet. It was dark and cold, a Dashiell Hammett kind of night. Completely wrong weather for the season.
>
> 'Are you sure you want to do this?' Caitleen asked me.
>
> The warmest place was between the sheets.
>
> 'Yes,' I told her. 'I haven't come this far to just stand and shiver.'
>
> 'Undress me then,' Caitleen said.

Joe the accountant is having an affair with the wife of an Internet porn baron. The obvious solution to their problem of their not being together as much as they'd like is to remove the problem, and that's just what they decide to do. But, as you might expect, things don't end there. Abby Ehman gets it dead right in *Extreme Fetish*: "This isn't a junk novel designed to be a highbrow version of a jerk-off story, it's only reason for being to provide the necessary stimulation to inspire foreplay. No, this is a novel that depicts sex as it is in reality, raw and vibrant and pungent, all of it described in electrifying detail. No cutting away to babbling brooks or crashing surf here. This is a Silhouette Romance with every thrust, grunt and explosive cum-shot lovingly scripted."

To be honest, *Because She Thought She Loved Me* isn't a personal favourite. But it was the first to inspire a death threat, so maybe I'm missing something. To my mind, the succeeding *The State of Montana* was a far better novel. As *Montana*'s back cover blurb has it, echoing and expanding on the book's opening line: "Montana has never been to Montana but often dreams of its open skies and chilly valleys. Montana is

the name Adrienne selected from childhood movie memories for her Internet handle." This was one of the first, possibly the best, and almost certainly the most erotic of the rash of Internet love stories that still provides mainstream publishers with a complacency of innovation. Although Maxim may remember it differently, I helped give him the title (the *The State of* part, that is – I can claim no shares in the clever Montana idea) and I think that his idea of producing a novella that's half the size vertically rather than in thickness was new and clever. It was so new and so clever that a high proportion of booksellers rejected the book on the grounds that it may be confused for a children's title, or that it was too easy to steal! Now that a hundred or more novels have followed us into that format, it's almost become a cliché.

Adrienne is possibly Maxim's most endearing female character and she seems to have more say in her fate than maybe his earlier heroines managed. Seven years married, one child, bored, she heads off on a series of bizarre encounters with men in

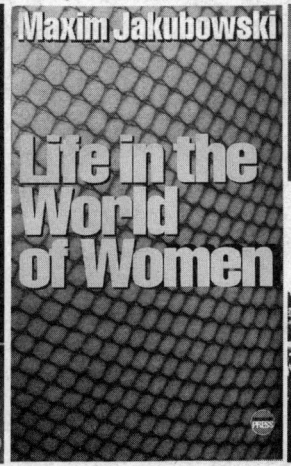

motel rooms that culminates in a week at a New York mansion that provides her with serial sodomy, cunnilingus and more S&M activity than you'll find in a hundred London suburbs. As Brian Case summed up in his *Time Out* review: "Phew!"

Then there followed Maxim's long-awaited private eye novel. But being Maxim Jakubowski, all was not what it seemed and although Philip Marlowe rarely achieved a hard-on in print, we don't have to wait long for hard, steamy sex – this time literally, in a men's sauna. Philip Oakes hits the, er, nail pretty much on the helmet in his *Literary Review* piece when he says: "Hard-boiled, proudly pornographic thriller concerning London shamus's search for two missing women, taking him to Amsterdam and New Orleans in cahoots with a glamorous stripper-cum-hit-woman who murders only to finance her passion for rare first editions… Probably the most comprehensive rendering of S&M variations ever to make it mainstream fiction." Can Maxim Jakubowski's writing now be described as 'mainstream fiction'? Maybe the mainstream has caught up with the man. It's certainly very worrying.

All of Maxim Jakubowski's books are on sale in Murder One. Crime Time has got together with The Do-Not Press to offer the five books mentioned in the article for the unbeatable price of £20 (including UK postage and packing). Send your cheque for £20 (payable to The Do-Not Press together with your name and address to: Maxim Book Offer, The Do-Not Press Ltd, 16 The Woodlands, London SE13 6TY. Please allow 14 days for delivery.

Jim Driver is publisher at The Do-Not Press and variously writes on crime fiction, booze and Indian restaurants for Time Out *and* Bizarre *magazines*

69 LOVE SONGS

Maxim Jakubowski

69 Love Songs *is a brand new story from the King of the Erotic Thriller which will appear in the Thomas M. Roche anthology* Noirotica 4 *towards end of the year...*

1 – It begins like a movie. With a white screen and a wash of music, massed strings or more likely synthesiser chords, rising to a majestic crescendo. Images coalesce and a melancholy melody emerges from the unshaped wall of sound... *Porcelain* by Moby maybe, or the soundtrack for an imaginary western whose ending will turn out to be particularly bitter-sweet. A tune that aims straight for the heart but hints at sadness to come. Sadness, yes; because tragedy is too strong a word. The credits roll and then shapes emerge out of blurry chaos throughout the rectangular geometry of the once silver screen. Panavision format. A woman's voice is heard, plaintive, across the fading sounds of the music. Is she singing? Has she a quaint, somewhat exotic foreign accent?

2 – Like all men with talent, he had many flaws. But his worse trait was how he romanticised over women time and again, never learning from experience. How the emotions they created inside his head and body skewered his perception of them and coloured all his relationships. He was aware of the fact, but knowing the existence of this Achilles' heel didn't help him avoid the same old mistakes over and over again. Was it the way he was brought up; the fact his father never had the guts to tell him all about the birds and the bees? How he mentally stored and interpreted the distorted facts about the way men and women coexist and war from tell-tale stories circulating amongst school kids? How he was savagely wounded by the unknowing betrayal of the first girl he felt longings for?

3 – Her presence in a world of men had nagged her from early teenage years. They fascinated and attracted her, but at the same time there was something fearful about these other creatures. They were different. She had always been accepted as a fun person by the groups she wove in and out of, at school, at play, mingling with her elder brother's friends. Always rough and ready for a game, a tumble, she was treated as an equal. Her breasts came late and were never quite as opulent as many of her girl friends. She would eventually grow into a B cup, barely. But from the moment those bumps made their bow inside her blue school shirt, the young men, the older men she would see in the street or in shops seemed to look at her in a new way. Thus did she discover lust.

4 – Catherine Guinard was not the prettiest young girl in the class during his first year in a mixed school. Nowhere near; Rhoona DeMole, Beatrice, Elizabeth and Jacqueline ruled that roost. But something about her touched him inside, where it mattered. Maybe that was his main flaw: he thought with his emotions, not with his cock. She was small, had thin, mousey light brown hair and slightly crooked teeth. But you know how it is, it's not just the way they look that does it; it's the way they laugh or their eyes sparkle at a given moment. He worshipped her from afar. Helped her with her class work. Then, one night, at a friend's party, Pierre what's-his-name in a game of Truth or Dare revealed he had already fucked her and, compounding the injustice, said she wasn't even that good in bed. His heart had dropped a thousand vertical paces to the ground at the unexpected news.

5 – Her parents were anything but intellectuals; her father installed shower units and her mother worked in a local government office, but they both loved opera. So she was called Mimi, in homage to La Boheme. It puzzled her for a long time. Nobody in Estonia seemed to be called Mimi apart from her. That's because you're special, her mum and dad would say to her. Which became, as she reasoned it out, a reason for great satisfaction: her brother was just plain Pavel. When unhappy days ended and she lay in bed listening to the silence invade the room and darkness take over, she would invariably remind herself that she was special. I am special. Then fall asleep with a smile on her face. That expression later became almost permanent, and her lips always appeared to be smiling, whether she was happy or not. That was one thing that attracted men to her like fireflies.

6 – Catherine Guinard was the first to carve a deep notch across his damaged heart strings. Others would follow. Over thirty-nine years, it became a gentle litany of hurt. Many of them were blonde. So he did learn to approach blonde women with the utmost caution. Maybe he wasn't good enough for blondes, he reasoned. Or they were too good for him. And sometimes, juggling memories tried to balance his past sexual statistics by hair colour. The results never made sense.

7 – Men liked Mimi. But they wanted more than she was willing to give them, she soon realised. As much as she enjoyed their company, dancing across the smokey floors of youth clubs and downing endless glasses of vodka, she knew that

the roving hands caressing her body, clumsily fingering her, were just an overture to fucking her. And she also knew she wasn't ready to be fucked. As much as sex attracted her, and mad thoughts of its horrors and delights flew across her dreams and nights, something inside also told her none of the callow boys she went out with were right for her yet. Sex must mean something.

8 – He also had dreams. Dark eyed, always elegantly dressed, Pierre was fucking Catherine. She lay passively on her back, legs held wide apart by the young man's weight while he thrust in and out of her. The scene was always silent. It brought tears to his eyes, but it also made him cock hard as he strained to move closer and observe the movement of the penis breaching her entrance. But he could never see enough. He would have to wait until his first trip to Scandinavia where hardcore films were legal to witness the copulation of others at first hand and on a large screen.

9 – He was not a violent person, but he reasoned Pierre should die. But at seventeen, you have neither the imagination nor the means. His betrayer being run over by a bus seemed to be the best option. But it didn't happen. Next time, he decided, maybe he should take matters into his own hands, and began noting methods of murder and execution in his notebook, gleaning necessary information from the crime paperbacks he was reading: James Hadley Chase, Brett Halliday, Peter Cheyney, Claude Rank, Jean Bruce. Although the latter seemed to be more interested in the minutiae of sexual torture. Which also provided him with regular erections.

10 – Catherine Guinard was quickly forgotten after the school year ended and she returned to France. He followed her to Paris a year later, but by then the world was full of blondes.

11 - At first, Mimi felt the men would be satisfied if she consented to let herself be kissed. Real kisses, of course, with tongues. It pleased them briefly, but failed to satisfy her. They tested of stale alcohol and tobacco and she found the experience of kissing her dance partners and boyfriends definitely unpleasant. And still their hands, encouraged by their locked lips would venture further and they would suggest full sex; almost demand it. She confided in friends and the consensus was, if she wished to retain her popularity within her circle of friends, that she should give in or at least accept to give the men and boys blow jobs.

12 – Elizabeth was the first blonde to break his heart. Well, you have to begin somewhere. She was much more sexually experienced than him, and years later, he would marvel how in hell he had managed to hold on to her for all of six months. Her pubic hair was short and curling, thus initiating another of his obsessions, and a shade or two darker than her mid shoulder length straight blonde hair, which puzzled him mightily, ignorant as he was then of hydrogen peroxide. They fucked like rabbits. She found him fun but he made the capital mistake of falling in love with her. One day while she was sleeping, he read pages from her diary and discovered to his disappointment that he didn't even rate very high in her sexual pantheon.

13 – Mimi had never before given too much consideration to men's cocks. She knew they had them; had seen enough of brother's dangling genitalia, even her father's. At first, the idea of taking one inside her mouth felt a bit ridiculous, but she was also curious to know what it would feel like to experience one swelling up and growing under her lips, tongue or ministrations. Would a penis have a specific taste? A particular texture? The thought intrigued her.

14 – When Elizabeth finally tired of him, she broke the news gently. After all, she had a good heart. Not ready for commitment and all that. Naturally, he took it badly and, melodramatically, a couple of weeks later slashed his wrists, cunningly arranging for her to discover him just in time. Which didn't bring her back to him. She even left the country to avoid seeing him again. Another lesson learned.

15 – So, while some of her girlfriends were losing their virginity time and time again in the back of cars or in the badly lit backyards of local jazz clubs or in the fields that bordered the fun fair near the chemical plant, Mimi became the blow job queen of their home town. After all, she reflected, it's only a piece of flesh, harmless in this form, and even though some men seemed overly keen on pushing their cocks too far and made her gag, she knew she was always in control. And however many cocks she sucked, she was still a virgin, waiting for the right man to come along. The one who would at last matter. Wasn't too keen on swallowing their cum though...

16 – Even though his attempt had been far from earnest, he also developed an unhealthy fixation on suicide and death. And years before Woody Allen came on the scene, already equated love and death in strange juxtaposition. Even began making listings of how famous people, actors, writers had committed suicide or been killed. Columns for poison, knives, guns (broken down into manufacturer and calibre of course), car and other accidents, etc. But then he was a far from cheerful young man. The gloom surrounding him would not dissipate much until he turned thirty and had made love to further blondes in various countries.

17 – Cocks had no taste per se; cum did. They came uncircumcised or cut, although the latter were few and far between since the local Jewish population had been decimated in WWII. Each one was different in length, thickness, appearance and smell. Mimi was unconcerned. It kept them out of her pants and, her nipples proving particularly insensitive, she didn't overly mind their rough, often drunken hands grazing, twisting her nipples or kneading her small breasts. It made her popular, paid for drinks or cinema or club tickets. A cock was a cock. In a way, she felt, it wasn't even connected to the man. Just a transaction. You want to be sucked; so okay, I'll suck you but don't expect any more. She had no regular boyfriend, just men whose cocks she didn't mind taking in her mouth for the comfort of their company.

18 – Beretta.
Sig Sauer.
Colt.
Luger.

Smith & Wesson.

Sawn-off shotgun.

Digitalis.

Cyanide.

Strangulation.

Smothering under a pillow.

Swiss army knife.

Asphyxiation.

Carbon monoxide emissions.

Death by drowning.

Methods of revenge.

In search of the perfect murder.

19 – She'd suck their cocks with her eyes closed. Almost pretending she was blind, her tongue moving over the head, licking the ridge, imagining the shades of pink, brown and purple of the aroused mushroom inside her cheeks. She would tease the opening, the slit, with the pointed tip of her foraging tongue, feel the tremor of lust surging through the man's body as she did so and retreat in time before he came so that the flow of hot ejaculate would either fall over her tongue or, preferably, outside her retreating mouth. Some guys came too fast, some couldn't and she would learn to finish them off by hand. But she learned to enjoy sucking cock. Even took some pride in her growing skills and the occasional compliment proffered.

20 – Then came Nicky. She was the sister of one of his best friends and they somehow drifted together. Light brown hair and cheekbones to kill for. Short and square-assed and prone to awful mood swings. At first, she was head over heels in love with him; he advised caution and patience. By the time he realised he loved her too, her own ardour had quietened and

they faded apart following summer holidays spent separated. Bad timing, he reckoned and began writing crime stories in which the perfect crime always came undone because of a lack of attention to small details and deep-seated psychological flaws.

21 – Of course, she pined for actual sex, but Mimi was determined to wait for the right man, the right occasion. She wanted it to be so absolutely right. Even a blow job queen can be romantic. And six years is a lot of blow jobs and cocks in your mouth.

22 – After Nicky, there were others. After all, he wasn't unattractive and was particularly fluent and articulate, even displayed a witty sense of humour when the darkness didn't dominate his soul. There was Marie-Jo, followed by Anne and then Danielle, who was absolutely wild and insatiable and even, one night, moved from their shared bed to join an ex boyfriend who was staying over in the next room where their noisy sex kept him awake for the rest of the night. His first two men a night woman. For weeks, he would mentally kick himself for not having joined them which he realised she wouldn't have minded. Another obsession took root of a threesome with two men both servicing the same woman.

23 – So Mimi drifted through the final years of her teens, desultorily moving from school to menial part-time jobs with a live now, pay later attitude to life and that infuriating smile ever draped across her face. Often doubting her purpose, neither happy nor unhappy, aimless in a quiet way. Somehow inside she knew there was something better waiting for her around the corner. So, she made her way down the road. Life wasn't bad after all: there was music, there was vodka, there was the flattering attentions of younger and older men, there was the beach at Nidas with its fine yellow sand, and the never unpleasant feel, texture and sensation of warm cocks as she swallowed them and offered a willing harbour to men's lust. Mimi was patient, seldom worried about tomorrow.

24 – He tried whores but they never engaged his heart and their embraces were too mechanical and unfeeling. He travelled. Prospered. Even one day married and settled down. The epiphany and beauty of babies briefly assuaged his unhappiness, but children grow and always disappoint to some extent, he discovered. And that hole in his heart, first opened by Catherine Guinard's treachery, kept aching and reminding him of all the roads never taken. Often, he would serenade himself to sleep with a monotonous litany that endlessly conjugated all the 'what if's' of his life so far.

25 – Mimi had been mixing with a group of friends attending the science faculty of the local university and, one balmy summer, met up with a group of young Belgian students who'd come to the city for exchange summer classes. Serge was the first man to make her heart leap. They paired off most evenings and she even introduced him to her family and he became a regular guest at their dinner table. She liked his cock, long and thin, somehow devoid of the rough vulgarity of most of the local boy's penises, she felt. One night, she invited him back to her room but somehow couldn't find the courage to go all the way with the Belgian boy, and after fellating him, found herself content with sleeping naked against him in the small bed, feeling his warmth permeate her to the core. Drifting off into the lands of sleep, she swore to herself that this was the first man she would let herself be fucked by.

26 – Serge returned to his studies in Belgium when summer ended and they began corresponding in broken English.

27 – She took a job in the administrative offices of the chocolate factory and took night classes in English in order to communicate better with her foreign boyfriend. She would still suck other men's cocks on Saturday night after the dance, if they really insisted, but Mimi felt detached from the act now, already planning a nebulous sort of future. Serge wanted them to spend the following summer together after his graduation. He wrote that he was saving his money up for this already. She had agreed.

28 – He drifted into his first affair almost by accident. Then further opportunities for unfaithfulness arose. An American tourist one night in Athens with whom he had anal sex (Danielle, albeit willing had been too tight). Someone at the office. Another woman at a trade fair. The satisfaction of illicit sex was transitory, and never lasted very long, but what surprised him most was that he felt no guilt.

29 – The Belgian boy sent her a plane ticket to London and met her at Gatwick. When she noticed him waiting for her outside the luggage hall, she somehow remembered him as sweeter and more attractive. Mimi sighed. But she was now committed to this holiday. He had liquidated all his savings and had arranged a package to a Thai beach. The plane to the Far East left in thirty-six hours; in the meantime, he had booked a hotel room in London. So, Mimi lost her virginity in Bloomsbury. She was too tight and screamed in agony as she lowered herself onto his jutting cock and tore herself apart. She bled profusely and felt no pleasure this time. The water in the bathroom when she washed afterwards was tepid. Sleeping against the snoring man, she felt no affinity with him any longer. He had already become a stranger.

30 – He dreams of death. In dark alleys, in western shoot-outs, in soiled beds. He remembers his mother's cancer and darkness like a cloud settles over him. Publicly, he is affable and successful, always has the right turn of phrase to make a woman smile and get into bed with him. But he's on automatic pilot, wanting ever more out of life.

31 – The beach was a sheer vision of paradise following the long, dusty journey by bus from Bangkok. Lying in the sun wearing the brand new green bikini he had bought her in London, Mimi lives again. The sex with him, every morning and afternoon and night, is relentless. She no longer feels pain, has been stretched enough to accept his cock inside her, but he is always the one to initiate it. At the end of the first week, her cunt is sore, inside and

outside from all the pounding she has to submit to. She realises she is now paying the price of the holiday. He seems happy, unworried that all his money has gone and has been spent on her and this tropical idyll. She knows she is using him, but the thought comes easy. He doesn't even want blow jobs, goes straight for the missionary position and fucking her.

32 – He meets Edwina at a professional function and, despite his better judgement, the uncontrollable lust he feels for her turns to head over heels passion following their first fuck. She is tall, blonde of course, also married, but the sex between them is both wild and tender and out of control. For the first time, he feels fulfilled and loses contact with the emptiness that was laying waste to his guts. She takes him into her mouth on the first occasion they go to bed; they make love on floors, tables and in hotel bath tubs. He ties her hands and she flushes with delight. He breaches her sphincter ring with two fingers and she squirms and moans like no woman ever has before for him. He makes plans. Wants to take her to Cap d'Agde, New York, Barcelona, Bangkok. Promises her the world and more. He loves to watch the scarlet pool of her orgasmic flush spread from cheeks to chest while she lies there still dripping his juices in the penumbra of the room, the smell of their exertions and the echo of their whispered obscenities still hanging like a stain in the atmosphere. He is reborn.

33 – Following Thailand, he accompanies her back to Estonia before returning to Belgium where he is due to begin his apprenticeship in a lawyer's office. Mimi's family are delighted by the fact he has a good-looking, responsible foreign boyfriend. Arrangements are made for her to visit him and his parents for the Christmas holiday. Mimi acquiesces, allows others to make all the decisions. When he is gone, she doesn't miss him and goes back to her routine of bestowing blow jobs on Saturday nights to her escort for the day. One Saturday, she drinks too much at a party and a Pole fucks her roughly in the tunnel near the railway station. But she goes to Bruges for the holiday. On Christmas Eve, her Belgian boyfriend introduces her to a Dutch friend of his. The next day, Mimi moves out of his place and follows the Dutch man back to Holland. He has a beard, works for a business magazine and is ten years older than she is. Six months later, she is pregnant by him. Even precisely remembers the occasion it happened: the day they were both drunk and he had mounted her at the bottom of the stairs and smacked her bottom until it hurt. After she announced her pregnancy to him, he would use this as an excuse to fuck her repeatedly in the arse. But she wanted the baby, she really did, so she kept silent and allowed Marcel, the Dutch man to dominate and use her.

34 – Edwina returns to her husband and breaks off the affair. He is gutted. Never even saw it coming, or rather intentionally misread all the signs. He drowns his sorrow by listening to melancholy music with the volume turned up to maximum, imagining a soundtrack for his imaginary tragedy and he dreams of death. Her death in a thousand and one circumstances, as he'd rather she was dead than

no longer his. Her husband's death in cunningly plotted scenarios. His own wife's, even. But the thoughts of revenge come to nothing. He is aware he is too much of a coward to do anything about it.

35 – Following the birth of her baby boy, Mimi declares to Marcel she is no longer in love or even in the least attracted to him any longer. She refuses all further sexual contact. The authorities give her Dutch nationality and a passport and benefits. Everything about Marcel now disgusts her and she sleeps with the child in the spare bedroom of his canal side house, half an hour's drive from Amsterdam. He has lost his job in a reshuffle and now pens freelance pieces from home while he attempts to start up a small business. He doesn't understand her change of attitude and resents it. Secretly she plots to leave the house they uncomfortably now share and applies to the council for her own place. He strongly opposes this.

36 – Still emotionally damaged by the affair with Edwina, he stumbles almost by mistake onto an Internet chat room and soon begins new affairs with women he meets there. He is a man to whom words come easily and his voice over the phone was knowingly seductive. There was an overweight opera singer in New York. Then came an American banker in Paris who delighted in cybersex of the highest and kinkiest calibre but lied about her identity and never turned up for their assignment before disappearing altogether from view. Later came a woman in the south of France, who had five children, no husband, but looked too much like his own sister for him to even contemplate seeing her again following their sweaty weekend together.

37 – Mimi loved her baby dearly but still she knew something was missing from her life. While Marcel was out, she would play around on his computer and, after typing in the words 'sex' and 'love' into a search machine, landed in an adult chat forum and began flirting with other men there. In her naivety, she never lied to them, always revealing who she was, her approximate whereabouts, even on occasion her mobile telephone number and the nature of her circumstances. They came running. Even faster once she scanned a colour photo of herself taken the previous summer on the deck of Marcel's canal boat.

38 – All the men Mimi met on the Internet wanted to meet her. Although her written English was halting and riddled by mistakes, she enjoyed cybersex and graded her suitors by the imagination they displayed in their virtual embraces and sundry penetrations and variations on positions. She had never realised before how much the power of words could affect her imagination, and was surprised how wet she would often become, sitting there at the keyboard, her mind racing from situation to situation, imagining what the sex would be like in real life. She met a banker from Zurich, in Switzerland. He was particularly imaginative. He amused her. He came to Amsterdam. She arranged to meet him, leaving the baby with Marcel. After dinner, she followed him back to his hotel room at the Krasnapolsky and they fucked.

39 – Muted rumblings from the brass section emerge towards the back of the normally plaintive melody, interrupting his smooth, sad flow. The pace of the song, the music quickens.

40 – They meet online. He is 'melancholy'; she is 'estonian girl'. He declines her offer to have cybersex. She is surprised. He explains how words alone don't make it for them. They talk. His curiosity is piqued. She tells him her story. He tells her his. They speak daily, although there are times when she ignores him when he pages her. No doubt too busy indulging in virtual sex with others to pull herself away. But the dialogue continues over several weeks. He is being cautious, doesn't want to run before he can walk. She is intrigued by his reticence. The day after her Hotel Krasnapolsky tryst, she reveals excitedly that the man in Zurich wishes her to come live with him in Switzerland, and she can even take the baby with her. Will she? he asks. Yes, she answers, no one has made a better offer and it's a chance to start all over again maybe. He nods, facing the lines on his computer screen scrolling up and up until they are out of reach. He wishes her good luck and absent-mindedly hopes they will somehow stay in touch. He files her photograph away in an old folder, believing this is the last he will hear of Mimi.

41 – Marcel is furious when she informs him she is leaving to live with another man in Zurich; he makes dire threats, forbids her to take their child. He hits her on the face in the heat of the argument. She waits until he goes shopping to leave and takes a cab to Amsterdam Central railway station. The apartment in Zurich is beautiful and for a few days Mimi feels she has taken the right decision to travel here. But soon, the sexual demands of the Swiss banker become more extreme the moment the child has fallen asleep. He wants her to become his submissive. This goes against her nature. He orders to her keep her sexual parts shaven at all time although it sometimes brings her out in a rash, and buys leather harnesses and enjoys taking photographs of Mimi in revealing positions. He wants her to wear a dog collar and announces he will take her to parties as his slave, and might actually allow her to be used by other men in his presence if he feels so inclined to share her. Reveals that her cock sucking talents are indeed superior and should be demonstrated to the world at large. He gets uncommonly angry when she moves furniture or things around in the apartment. She finds him increasingly petty, and dangerous. She leaves Zurich in haste and lands back on Marcel's doorstep in Holland only two and a half weeks following her initial flight.

42 – Severely addicted, he continues to haunt the Internet chat rooms. Fascinated by the number of people who profess to be bisexual online, his mind wanders over risky waters and, one day, out of sheer curiosity indulges in his first man to man oral experience. It is not totally unpleasant.

43 – Mimi apologises profusely to Marcel for her escapade to Zurich but stands firm when it comes to resuming sexual relations. Her ex-boyfriend and father of her child just no longer attracts her in the slightest. She will accept his hospitality until the day she is given her own accommodation by the authorities, and remain in his house for the sake of their little boy. His anger gets out of control. She has to flee his blows several times and one day, furious at having to listen to her flirt over the phone with an internet acquaintance, he attacks her and rapes her. Mimi stays passive and when he finally withdraws from her, Marcel is in tears and begs her to have another child with him. She refuses.

44 – Mimi sends an e-mail to the man in London. Somehow she still thinks of him warmly. Explains that Zurich didn't work out after all. He answers and they resume their conversations, online and over the phone. He makes arrangements to stop over in Amsterdam for a night and a day on his way to an academic conference in Warsaw. He books a small hotel by a canal near the station through his travel agent. They agree to meet for dinner nearby. He, naturally, hopes for more but doesn't count on it. Mimi tells Marcel she will be away overnight staying with a girlfriend.

45 – She is taller than he expected. Conversely, she finds him shorter than she somehow thought from their conversations and mutual self descriptions. She is also prettier. There is a delicacy about her, a gentle sadness also, which allied to her peculiar accent and ever-present smile, make him feel all shy. The meal comes and goes, spoiled only by the boisterous company of a large table of office workers nearby. They walk back to his

hotel. He doesn't ask her up, but she follows him silently into the lift. The door closes and he slowly moves his lips towards hers and they kiss. She remains standing as he undresses her, slipping off her panties and burying his nose and mouth in the short, matted hair of her cunt. He likes her taste. She thrills to the firm but gentle caress of his tongue opening her up. She comes. He is still fully dressed. They move to the bed.

46 – Her body is pale and her breasts slight. Her hips are high and firm like a Russian peasant's. He surveys the pale expanse of her flesh as he spreads her out beneath him, noting every mole and blemish scattered across the whiteness of her arm skin. A brown stain on the left side of her left breast, a hardened mole in the small of her back, a spot of darker pigmentation blending into the darker pink of her right nipple. He licks every exposed inch of her. She devours his cock with ardour but also delicacy, her clever tongue darting across his shaft, her hot mouth cupping and then swallowing his heavy, dark balls. He notes that her nipples are not overly sensitive. 'How do you prefer it?' he asks. 'Doggie style', she answers quietly. He turns her over, holds his cock aloft and directs it to her entrance. The view is breathtaking. The puckered hole of her anus darker, inviting, vulnerable. He positions herself at her lower entrance, parts her now wet lips as she raises her rump further upwards, face buried in the blanket, her breasts hanging firm from her supple body. He thrusts himself inside her. She holds her breath and exhales with a deep sigh of pleasure.

47 – He would later reflect how much she enjoyed taking her pleasure. He woke her in the morning by sliding inside the bed covers and waking her with his tongue and teeth inside her still damp cunt, in which he could still taste himself. Other women always washed themselves out after fucking; Mimi was the first since Edwina not to do so and keep his juices inside her. Her whole body spasmed and she came. He then rose up, pushed her legs apart and inserted himself between her swollen cunt lips. While he moved in and out of her, her eyes locked on his, imploring, screaming silently, watching him as he fucked her, both wordless. Something about her touched him deeply. Before they rose for breakfast, he managed another erection and she sucked him off to completion, his thin, tired cum jetting into her mouth. She said nothing and afterwards rose quietly to move to the bathroom where he heard her spitting it out and gargling.

48 – What affected him most about Mimi was the way she kept her eyes open throughout their lovemaking. A silent stare that spoke of a thousand words. And how she joked that her eyes were now all shiny and glazed and Marcel would know, without the shadow of a doubt, that she had been fucked. That it was written all over her eyes and would be like that for days. And reassured him by stating that it didn't matter in the slightest. She remained with him for the whole day, his guide to Amsterdam on a cold and windy December day. He remembered her in the throes of sex; she, cheerful that this man could make her laugh so much, with his dry, almost absurd jokes and wit. They parted at the train station, both refraining from any kind of promises.

49 – She had told the Englishman of her dreams and plans. She couldn't stay with Marcel forever. Maybe she should advertise herself as a potential mistress for a rich man to subsidise and keep in comfort. After all, it would only be sex. A commercial transaction, but not as compromising as being a whore. The way his eyes clouded when she said this, she realised he disapproved so she dismissed the idea as a joke. But she did put an advertisement in a newspaper a few weeks later

50 – She received a handful of answers to her advertisement. She met some of the men. A drink, maybe a meal, at worst a blow job, she reckoned, even if they were unsuitable. Kept her out of the house for a few hours, looking after the now growing baby, away from Marcel's clutches. There was another Englishman. Commercial traveller across northern Europe. He'd fuck her in his car, not even bothering to take her to a hotel room, but she kept on seeing him several times. The asshole, she kept on calling him, and afterward she would cry because she knew he was just using her, and treated her like dirt. Why was she punishing herself in this way? She confessed to the man in London. She knew it gave him pain, but he absolved her. So she saw the jerk again. He didn't even bother to undress her, ordered her skirt up above her waist, roughly pulled her thong off and indicated the back seat of the car to her. They were parked by the side of a small regional road. Anybody could have seen her moving bottomless to the back of the car. He posi-

tioned her on all fours and savagely entered her with no preliminaries. He grunted as he came, then, pretexting an important business appointment, excused himself from dropping her back to the bus station where he had picked her up and left her standing there in the countryside, his cum still dripping down her thighs and legs. Never again, she swore, but deep inside was uncertain how long her resolve would last. Maybe she needed this humiliation?

51 – He called her every week and told her how much he missed her and how he liked her and just felt so natural and comfortable with her. Mimi agreed: it wasn't just the sex, they did feel good together, walking by the Rijksmuseum, the canals, Kalverstraat and across town, smiling in front of the window of the Condom Shop or nervously giggling at the windows of the Red Light District. Yes, we must meet again, they both agreed.

52 – She had told him how the man in Zurich had insisted she shave her sex, and this thought obsessed him and kept him awake, and hard, at night. She has a lovely cunt, hair straight and brown and thick lips pouting through the growth. When she positioned herself with her rear thrust towards him and on her knees, the spectacle of her cunt was better than any porn movie. Straight gash punctuated lower down by little hills of darker, protruding flesh which he liked to chew on, pull gently, play with, opening her cunt like a flower, unveiling the nacreous pink of her damp insides.

53 – Through the ad, she also met a younger Dutch boy. He was too good looking by her standards but liked the baby and didn't mind her bringing him along when he took her for drives. They would help the child fall asleep and then would go to bed in his bachelor apartment. He worked in computers. The first time he undressed in front of her, she was shocked by the size of his penis. Seemed so enormous. She was really scared how much it would stretch her, but surprisingly he fitted inside her like a glove. However, he often had difficulty coming and would thrust away inside her for ages until she had lost all feeling and she would then have to tire herself out until her jaw ached helping him climax with her mouth.

54 – Her eyes, below me, inches from my own, as I move inside her. Watching me. Judging me. Asking questions I have no answer to. Listening to the shortness of my breath as my climax approaches. Glazing with joy, shiny, luminous. Moving the thousand shades between grey and blue. Mimi's eyes. She's getting to me.

55 – They decide to meet again and he FedEx's her the money for the train journey to Paris. They arrive at the same station a half hour apart. He has booked a small, picturesque hotel on the South Bank with a view of Paris roofs and migrating pigeons. They walk, see movies, shop on the Champs Elysees, eat too much and make love with great abandon when their stomachs are not too full. Enjoying ice cream at the Haagen-Dasz terrace on the Boulevard Saint Germain he cracks a joke, and Mimi laughs so much she pees in her knickers. Back at the hotel, he licks her clean. She is still laughing. The sound of

her happiness alleviates his darkness. But the weekend quickly ends and there are trains home for the two of them, separate trains, separate lives.

56 – He knows she is partial to words and whispers indecent suggestions and dirty deeds into her ear as they fuck and feels her whole body strain and react as her cheeks colour even further at the thought of what he is outlining. He intimates at another man joining them in their activities, watching this stranger mount her as she fellates him and then both males simultaneously investing her holes. He improvises a story in which they are both captured by pirates or gangsters and made sexual slaves and in which he has to suck to hardness the cocks of their male captors and then guide them manually into her and is made to watch as they despoil her repeatedly; to cap it all, he is then himself sodomised in her presence and gladly sacrifices his anal preserve out of love and affection for her. She listens in rapt silence, but the heat generating from her body, her cunt, her skin tells the story of her lust and her eyes acknowledge her increased excitement.

57 – He wants her again. By now, she has left Marcel's house and lives alone in a small cottage with the baby. A friend comes from Estonia to stay and arrangements are made to leave the little boy in her care. They meet up in the bright arrivals hall of a small airport by the Mediterranean. She has cut her hair shorter and coloured it auburn. She wears faded jeans and a burgundy chenille sweater. He hires a car and drive to a nearby port where someone has recommended a pleasant hotel. The room has a balcony overlooking the sea and he fondles her arse while they take in the view. He undresses her with all the slow, lingering ritual of a religious ceremony. He trims her pubes. Jokingly suggests she should not wear any underwear for the duration of their stay here. She smiles and agrees to his whim. They eat, they fuck, they talk, and neither of them wishes the week to ever end. One afternoon, he takes a short nap and she decides to go for a walk in the town. In her absence, he delves into her handbag and finds a photograph of her and another man, a good-looking younger man by whose side she is smiling blissfully into the lens of the camera. He knows it is not Marcel. Or the English asshole or the Dutch computer man. He guesses she is still seeing other men in the intervals between him. He says nothing to her.

58 – He knows it doesn't make sense and the relationship has no future. She is twenty years younger than him and there is no way he has the mental fortitude to even try and believe he could try and bring up another child, even more so that of another man. He knows she likes sex too much and will eventually tire of him. He knows she uses him, and the sex she grants him is her unethical, if Eastern European way, of paying him back for the gifts, the money, the travel. He often awakens at three in the morning in his marital bed at home dreaming of her, fantasising of the warmth of her body, of witnessing her being fucked by total strangers while he holds her head in his lap and wipes her feverish brow. He imagines taking her to a nude beach and exhibiting her to the unflinching gaze of others, her nipples and sex gash highlighted by scarlet lipstick, showing her off, maybe piercing her parts, and organising her ravishing in some sort of pagan ceremony. He plays with himself when he thinks of the way her eyes always betray her sexual pleasure. He pictures her with her erstwhile Dutch friend, he of the uncommonly large penis, and in abominable close-up watches the monstrous cock impale her to the hilt, stretching her apart like a peace of raw meat. In dreams, he has no shame.

59 – She sends him a birthday card in which she assures him he is special. You are my treasure, she says. Two weeks later, she calls him, desperate for some money. He obliges, relieved she didn't phone advising him she was pregnant. Apart from the first evening in Amsterdam, they have never taken any precautions.

60 – Christmas comes and Mimi has made arrangements to return for the festivities to her family in Estonia. She cannot afford to fly so is hitching a lift to the German coast at Kiel to catch a ferry with one of her girlfriends who married a Dutchman. Even though she hasn't asked, he sends her money and a gift for her little boy, whom he has never seen outside of photographs. The two year old is blond.

61 – He misses her intensely. Wants her like hell. Since she moved out of Marcel's house, she no longer has access to a computer so their rare conversations take place over the phone. In Estonia, her mobile is out of reach. Out of sheer stupidity, he logs on to their familiar Internet chat room under her old handle 'estonian girl'. Within minutes, he is deluged by calls. The majority of them are clearly just attracted by the reasonably exotic name, particularly the Yanks, and have no previous knowledge of her. It's been months after all since she had last been online. But some clearly know her. He improvises his way through a half hour conversation with an architect in Brooklyn who has seemingly extended her an open invitation to come to America. Visibly they have often spoken on the phone. As he probes further to unveil any possible intimacy, he is rumbled and the other man disconnects.

62 – He compounds his mistake the following day and assumes her Internet identity again. He gets a call from 'infinity and beyond'. Another man who knows Mimi, and through process of deduction he uncovers the fact they are still in contact and have exchanged pre-Christmas text messages on their respective mobile phones. The man has just returned from a trek to Tibet and wishes to meet her again. He blunders his way through the conversation by pretexting the mobile's battery is low and elicits more information. It is quickly apparent Mimi is fucking this guy on a regular basis; in a hotel in a place called Aalmark. He logs off angrily.

63 – He knew he wasn't her only man. How could he expect to be? But the smug assurance by 'infinity and beyond' that she was a great fuck and why didn't they have another session after Christmas, in the obvious expectation of an enthusiastic response, damn hurt. A lot. And made him so angry at Mimi.

64 – Between the rage, the haunting images of her with others. Men as well as women (although he'd never been the sort of man who gave undue thought to women together). He remembered how during the course of evening meals in restaurants on the Mediterranean port, she had often remarked on the sexual attractiveness of, one day, a waiter who limped and the next evening a waitress who enjoyed using her poor English while serving them but was otherwise dreadfully plain looking. She said she took pity on them, but he knew her interest was also to some extent sexual and her mind was still excited by their bedside patter about a third person between the sheets.

65 – Still under the empire of anger, he felt the need to confront her. Tracked down her parents' address through directory enquiries and booked himself on the first flight to Estonia. He just had to confront her. On one hand, something unhealthy buried deep within his heart or loins, hankered to share her touching beauty with others, but not this way. Not without him. The jealousy burnt a hole inside him.

66 – He'd kept watch on the apartment block for half day when she emerged. She held the little boy's hand and made her way, holding a heavy suitcase in the other, towards the nearest bus stop. He hailed a cab and followed her.

67 – Mimi and her son arrived at the docks, and, standing fifty yards back he observed her passing passport control and walking the gangway with another woman dressed in thick winter attire on to a large passenger boat. He checked the destination: Kiel. She was on her way back to Holland. He had over an hour to get his own case from his hotel room, check out and purchase a ticket for the boat. He saw her, the boy and her girl-friend eating at the ship's snack bar that first evening but decided against making contact. The next day, the ship held a large dance after dinner and, sitting in a remote corner, of the cavernous room, he observed Mimi from afar as she kissed the child good-bye and her friend returned to their cabin. She sat at the bar, alone, slow-ly sipping a drink. The music began, loud and formless, a frantic aggregate of beats and naked rhythm. A man invited her on to the dance floor. She was smiling. Damn, why did she always smile? Another drink, then another dance partner. Midnight came and she was visibly drunk. But happy. He watched as her last dance part-ner whispered something in her ear and took her hand and moved towards one of the doors to the lower deck. He followed. He was already seasick and what he saw didn't help. There was Mimi, in a dark cor-ner of the deck, on her knees, sucking the man's cock with an appetite that looked mighty indecent. The man gripped her hair between his hands, forcing her to take him ever deeper. From his hiding place in the shadows, he couldn't see whether she had her eyes open or not. He turned and vom-ited over the wooden deck.

68 – The man she had been voraciously sucking off had finally returned inside and Mimi stood on the deck, leaning over the guard rail, watching the sea at night, lost in her thoughts. What, he won-dered, was on her mind? Did she feel there was poetry in the landscape of the night? Sadness in the oppressive silence, broken only by the clapping sound of nearby waves? He moved quietly towards her, her silhouette highlighted against the brightness of the pockmarked moon. He gently put a hand on her left shoulder. She turned round to face him. Thinking maybe the other guy had returned for more. She was crying. 'You?' she gasped. 'Yes,' he answered, a knot gripping his stomach. 'What are you doing here?' The faint trace of a smile spreading across her cold lips. 'I loved you,' he said, 'didn't you know that, didn't you realise it by now?' She lowered her eyes, accepting her fate.

69 – He raised his other arm and pushed. Mimi offered no resistance. Her body toppled over the rail and disap-peared into the darkness and the sea. He looked at the illuminated face of his Tag Heuer: it was one in the morning. The dis-tant horizon was 200 miles off both the coasts of Denmark and Germany. A time and a place for love and death.

[I acknowledge stealing the title of this story from Stephin Merritt's and the Magnetic Fields' wonderful triple-CD set]

Maxim Jakubowski

HENNING MANKELL

SWEDEN'S PREMIER CRIME WRITER VISITS THE UK

Barry
Forshaw

He doesn't want to go in to the party being held in his honour. I sit in a quiet drawing room with Henning Mankell, author of such remarkable thrillers as *The Faceless Killers* and his new one, *The Fifth Woman* (Harvill). And all we can hear is the bustling of the caterers in the kitchen. Outside in the garden of a fashionable Islington house, the guests wait expectantly, including an urbane representative from the Swedish Embassy. But Mankell would rather talk to Crime Time. And that's fine by us.

How closely does he follow the translations of his books? As much as he can, Mankell replies. At least in those languages he's proficient in. He knows some authors regard a translation as no longer their property, but he feels he has a duty to turn out the best book he can for each country.

Chatting earlier to the man from the Swedish Embassy, he was talking about how welcome it is to have Swedes whose work makes them unofficial ambassadors for their country. Once it was the great director Ingmar Bergman – now it's Sven Goran Eriksson. I ask Mankell with some reluctance, if he minds being an ambassador for Sweden in the vein of Bergman. Well, he replies in his customarily dry manner, I am married to his daughter, Eva. So he supposes he's keeping up a family tradition – although (he admits) Bergman doesn't really leave Sweden these days… and Mankell is braving North London.

How does Mankell respond to such tired clichés as 'Nordic gloom' whenever the art of his country is mentioned? Every country has to put up with stereotypes, he supposes – look at the English! But he hasn't found the appellation applied to his work too often.

A KURT WALLANDER MYSTERY

"Inspector Wallander is one of the most wonderful creations in contemporary crime writing…A classic of its genre"
MICHEL ABESCAT, *LE MONDE*

HENNING MANKELL
THE FIFTH WOMAN

A key question for any crime or thriller writer: what are his favourite thrillers? He has two unorthodox choices: Shakespeare's *Macbeth* and (particularly) Conrad's *Heart of Darkness*. That follows all the rules, and explodes them, he says. The hero makes a dangerous journey to the centre of a mystery that ends in death. It's still the best thriller ever written.

Barry Forshaw

The Fifth Woman **is available from Harvill at £9.99**

K. C. CONSTANTINE ON *GRIEVANCE*

S ince *Grievance* is being published in the UK by No Exit Press, I guess I'm supposed to say something about it. I think the book's self-explanatory, but I did write it out of the sense that while we're entering this wonderful New World Order, it appears to be one where the emphasis and empathies have shifted away from the worker bees toward the investor bees, i.e. capital searches for cheaper and cheaper labour.

The fall of the Berlin Wall caught a lot of people by surprise, especially those in American government and media who made their careers by keeping alive the fiction of the Cold War – that the Great Russian Bear was a nearly omnipotent adversary, despite one fact the CIA and the news gatherers never seemed quite able to grasp, that the Soviets had to buy wheat

'Terrific...one of contemporary American literature's great masters of dialogue' *Washington Post*

from capitalist farmers to feed their own people. And if Westerners couldn't or wouldn't grasp that fact, what were they to do with the other unassailable fact that the Soviets were getting their collective ass kicked in Afghanistan? How to perpetuate the myth of the Cold War with those two burrs under the Western saddle? But perpetuate it our leaders did – until the Wall came down. Then what? Our leaders scratched around in the dirt like so many hens, found an oil rustler, and promptly turned him into the new Hitler, that's what. And then they went to work finishing the job of convincing the masses that capitalism is the best form of government, because it was the opposite of communism, which was the worst form of government. (Some day, some smart, courageous soul is going to examine in depth the propaganda techniques Western governments and news media used to turn capitalism from a form of economics into a form of government.)

I've been asked many times (okay, five times) who my influences were, who inspired my early efforts. I was influenced primarily by Eric Hoffer, whose *The True Believer* I copied in longhand to learn how to make a sentence, and by Flannery O'Conner, who demonstrated the power of the vernacular. They're the only two I still read for instruction. Of course, like many beginners I imitated a lot of writers; I think it's not only unavoidable but necessary to the learning process. Music students aren't asked to compose something different from Bach in order to practice scales and basic fingering; nobody chides them for their lack of compositional skills at that stage. And the same with art students who are sent into the museums and told to copy

the masters. It's only with writing that the old biddies who profess to teach it seem obsessed with the idea that students must submit original work. To turn in something they've copied – mercy mercy, that's plagiarism – hold their hands over the gas ring until they vow never to do it again. What horse shit. In America a football coach who tells his players they're either going to run a play until they drop or get it the way he drew it on the chalkboard – whichever comes first – is viewed as a fine taskmaster and disciplinarian. But God help the writing teacher who tells his students they're going to copy declarative sentences until their fingers go numb or until they grasp the concept that the pattern we're after in English is noun, verb, object.

A smart-ass once told me the reason I'd been published and he hadn't was that I'd been born with talent. This irritated me so much I immediately calculated for his benefit that I'd written more than a million and a half words before I'd sold the first one, thus demonstrating that whatever success I'd had was a result far less of talent than of bull-dogged determination. Most of my early writing was such sorry crap I hope nobody ever gets the idea after I'm dead that it should be published. I've pitched most of it already and will probably pitch the rest the next time I move. I raise this point because, with the exception of those rare geniuses who seem born to every art or craft or science, the rest of us have to work our asses off to get anywhere. To mollify students by telling them that writing, unlike football, isn't meant to stretch their boredom threshold does them no service at all. They need to hear that English is a hard language and that for all but a very few of us learning it has been anything but easy, and if they want to do it, they've got to do the drills – the boring, repetitive stuff which is no less boring or repetitive than the scales the piano student must do or the minute sketches in the live-model class the beginning painter must do.

I'm often asked (okay, five times) who I read, whose work I never miss. I used to read Simenon a lot – in translation of course – until I reached the point where I couldn't tell one of his books from another. I like Carl Hiaasen's stuff, for his outrage and for his wild sense of humour. *Native Tongue* and *Sick Puppy* come to mind. Larry McMurtry is a great storyteller, maybe one of the greatest in American English, though I haven't read more than a half dozen of his books. McMurtry almost killed me once. I took a sip of beer at the wrong time in a story of his, started to laugh, and very nearly choked because I couldn't swallow and couldn't stop laughing. Not many writers can make me laugh out loud, but he's one, and so is Hiaasen. I also think Jerry Doolittle's *The Bombing Officer* is a great novel.

Because I write novels about police officers and in which crimes happen and because I'm often chided about the profanity in my dialogue, I'm frequently criticised that I'm adding to the so-called 'coarsening of America' (as though no one ever cursed before I started writing). I will readily admit this is a problem for writers. But not for the reason most propaganda sellers on commercial TV want us to believe; like every other emotional hobbyhorse they like to ride while calling it news, they want us to believe it's got only two sides. You're either against explicit violence or explicit sex in the arts because they provoke or incite the same behaviour by the consumers of the art, or you're against censorship. And the propagandists always wind things up with a shrug and a wry, knowing smile that this either/or conundrum is one of life's insoluble problems that we'll all have to live with – until another misunderstood, bullied loner in high school drags daddy's pistols into school in his gym bag and shoots a half dozen of his classmates. Then the idiotic debate begins anew, followed by the smug preaching of the political hacks trying to suck up to the religious nuts decrying our lack of family values – at the same time of course keeping secure our God-given right to bear arms which we'll have to have – or at least know how to use – when we're called upon to crush our enemies, especially those intent on rustling the oil we need to run our SUVs.

There's an old joke about a father, mother and pre-school daughter moving into a house next to a vacant lot. Very soon a construction crew arrives and begins to build a new house on the vacant lot. The daughter is fascinated by all this activity and can't stay away. The tradesmen come to look out for her and give her jobs, like filling their water bottles, etc., for which they pay her. When she's accumulated a few dollars, her mother, who thinks this is a fine use of her daughter's time, takes her to the bank and helps her open a savings account with the newly earned wages. The teller approvingly asks the little girl how she came to earn the money. The little girl tells proudly what she's done. Then the teller asks, "Well, are you going to continue to work for these fine gentlemen?

And do you think they'll continue to pay you?" "Oh yes", the little girl replies with a bright smile. "If those stupid cocksuckers at the lumber yard ever get around to sending us the fucking wood we ordered."

Let me tell another story, one that took more than forty years to complete. When I was a marine recruit at Parris Island in the early 1950s, I was, like all the other members of my platoon, shown films of marines in combat during World War Two battles in the Pacific: Tarawa, Iwo Jima, Okinawa, etc. Oddly enough, when the combat photographers were hit by Japanese fire and the cameras tilted crazily as the photographers fell, that footage was left in. And while we saw many images of Japanese soldiers, sailors, and marines being killed, wounded, or set afire by flame throwers, or committing suicide by jumping off cliffs, I began to notice that we never saw a marine being killed. We saw lots of bodies floating in the water and saw the wounded bandaged and hobbling about and being helped by the Navy corpsmen or being carried on litters by their truly brave comrades, but it began to dawn on me that we never saw a marine being killed or wounded at the moment his wound happened. Now you'd have to be an idiot to believe that all the marines' wounds were flesh wounds, or that if they received a fatal wound – like John Wayne in the movie The Sands of Iwo Jima – it was the kind that hardly ever bled. Just last year however, and forty-six years after I survived boot camp, Steven Spielberg, et al., put together a story for TV distribution on the history and bravery of combat photographers, splicing their footage with the photographers' own commentary. Spiel-

berg was universally commended for his patriotic act of assembling the footage and the photographers (those still alive anyway) who took it. But as I watched one particularly grisly scene of a German tanker, his torso nearly torn in two by the shell which had destroyed his tank and killed all the crew, the photographer who took the film said very quietly (and I'm paraphrasing here), "We never took pictures of Americans like that. We were told not to. The officers told us that if Americans saw what actually happened to them in battle, they would refuse to serve." And then I knew for the first time in forty-six years why I hadn't seen a marine actually die in the supposedly real film of supposedly real combat on Tarawa, Iwo Jima and Okinawa. The truly explicit violence didn't have to be edited out because it had never been filmed in the first place. And we recruits were told – and doubtless believed – that we were seeing the real war that ordinary citizens never saw.

So how does this pertain in the so-called debate about whether explicit violence or explicit sex in the arts leads to actual violence or actual sex, especially in light of the US government's explicit orders that its combat photographers were not to film the physical destruction and disintegration of Americans dead as a result of combat in WWII? And where does it pertain in the filming of all those body bags in Vietnam that were shown on the evening news during that war? How often has it been said that TV in American living rooms did as much as anything to bring about the end of US involvement in Vietnam? And how often have right-wingers claimed that reporters in Vietnam who grew up to be celebrity interviewers like Mike Wallace and celebrity news readers like Dan Rather were living proof of the liberal bias of the Eastern news media? I don't have the answers. All I'm saying is that violence in the arts and news is not anywhere near as uncomplicated an issue as a lot of people want the rest of us to believe. Certain contradictions are inescapable: if you want soldiers to obey your order to kill your enemies, you have to convince them that they won't be blown to bits in the process because if you fail, most of them won't do it. So you have to keep at least three ideas in the air without dropping one of them: 1) the wrongness of the government's trying to take away US citizens' right to own firearms; 2) the greater glory of giving your life for your comrades in time of martial law (which is whatever the sitting executive says it is; they've become masters of avoiding Congressional declarations of war); and 3) the hocus-pocus of saying that killing your classmates or relatives or neighbours is forbidden by God's law, which law is of course the first to be repealed whenever the executive orders you to kill somebody he doesn't like.

There's one other troubling fact about our governments and our propagandists in regard to this question of violence: when was the last time anybody in the US or Britain took cameras into the veterans hospitals to show up close and personal the living victims of our wars, the ones who "fought for our freedom and kept us free"? I honestly cannot remember ever seeing such a program in my lifetime. That's not to say there hasn't been one, but is it just me? Can anyone else remember seeing

one? It would be interesting for some brave journalist to ask the network news directors if it's just this crank from southwestern Pennsylvania or if there's a reason nobody takes film of how our wounded vets are treated?

Certain other questions also can't be ignored: how many young men who saw *Taxi Driver* and lusted after Jodie Foster shot Ronald Reagan? How many young men who read *A Catcher in the Rye* shot John Lennon? And while I can't think of the name of the book Timothy McVeigh read which, it's alleged, incited him to blow up the federal building in Oklahoma City, so far he's the only one of many thousands who read that book who's actually done it. Whenever a commission appointed to study the effects of pornography declares that they can find no connection between pornography and any other sexual behaviour besides masturbation, the people who appointed the commissioners rise up and say something like this: "Of course reading bad books promotes bad behaviour, because if it didn't then what would be the point of reading good books in school?" That's actually not a bad paraphrase of what Richard Nixon said when a commission appointed by his predecessor found that they couldn't really make any connection between reading porn and bad behaviour. Which brings me to this curiosity: until slavery was repealed by Constitutional amendment in the US, teaching a slave to read was a crime. So it might be that the problem is not content at all. McLuhan might be right. It might be the act of reading itself that's dangerous to the established social order. And I'm sorry, but I have to ask: can any one of us describe how we learned to read? Or what goes on in our brains as we read? Damned if I can.

Now that I've got all that wind out of my fingers, I suppose I should say something about how I work, though I'm always puzzled that anyone else is interested. Oh well, if they are, here's what I do: I just type and revise it until it looks and sounds like it won't make me embarrassed to have my pen name on it. Not that it won't eventually be embarrassing, but at the time I'm working on it, I have to think I'm giving it the best I've got or what's the point? I used to ponder why so many writers continued to write as though cameras had not been invented. I quit trying long ago to compete with them. My stories are more and more becoming radio plays: I write the dialogue and let the audience fill in whatever images they choose. Is that a copout? Probably. Do I care? No. Regarding music, someone once said that all art aspires to music. Walter Pater? Can't remember. And who was it who said that without music life would be a mistake. Nietsche? Whoever it was, I couldn't agree more. At the same time I hate the false emotion that music provides in films. I keep wondering what kind of films Martin Scorsese or Quentin Tarantino would make if they were told they couldn't use music to tune up scenes. Here's the pitch I'd like to make to them: you can make any kind of movie you want but it's got to be exclusively visual and verbal. No music except where the characters have to dance. And the dance has to be integral to the plot. I'd really like to see what they'd make.

Sometimes I think I'm trying to write books without plot because I'm thinking

characters first, last, always. I just finished a book of about 320 typed pages where the only real action takes place in less than a couple of seconds. All the rest is talk and more talk.

Someone asked me recently (really) if there was a city that got my creative juices flowing more than any other. The only one I could think of was the one I was born and grew up in because I think you never truly escape from that one psychologically, no matter where it is. I also happened to have been born at the height of the Great Depression in an industrial town that nearly dried up and blew away as a result of it, and I'll never shake that experience.

I heard a really interesting question recently: Is reading important these days? Or is it a pleasant throwback to a vanishing past, hanging on by the skin of its metaphorical teeth? Well, what can I say? Every time we turn around these days we're being sold some form of electronic communication, and we're told it's as important as the invention of moveable type. I confess a computer makes my work immeasurably easier. How much easier? I honestly think I'd quit writing if I was told I had to go back to using a typewriter. But does that mean my writing's gotten any better? I keep asking my computer-worshipping friends these questions: tell me something that's come out of our national leadership in the time computers have been extant that will stand with the stuff that was written with quill pens, or tell me one speech written on a computer that can rival what Lincoln wrote with a pencil on the back of an envelope. That said, I'm very curious to see whether e-books fly. I've never even held one in my hand so I don't know how I'd react to reading a book on the screen. Of course I read my own stuff on the screen, but that's different. How? I can't say, or don't think I'll be able to say until I try to read somebody else's book on an e-book. But the idea that the entire OED, for example, is on one CD, as expensive as it is – and it's not nearly as expensive as the whole OED in twenty-six volumes – that idea enthrals me. I mean, to imagine that I can insert one CD in this laptop and be able to look up any word from that book in a matter of seconds is amazing. I have the two-volume edition, but even with the magnifying glass I find it cumbersome and awkward to use because my eyes, not good to begin with, are getting worse. But with the OED on CD – and I'm going to order one soon – I can, because of the computer's capabilities, display the definitions in whatever font and size I choose. And when I see myself doing that, I think, yes, computers *are* as important historically as Gutenberg's moveable type. But whether we're reading pages glued together along the spine of a book or on an e-book, we're still reading words, still going in our culture left to right top to bottom. And we're still having to try to find meaning in the arrangement of the words; that's the nature of English, American or British. Despite McLuhan's notion that the medium is the message, and despite the fact that computers have indeed changed the medium, it remains for someone much more astute than I to explain whether the message has been changed and how.

The same person who asked if reading was important asked me if writers need to be of this world or remote from it. I believe writers absolutely, definitely, positively need to be of the world. If you doubt that, just try reading the stuff that comes out of all those graduate writing programs. Yes yes, I too attended one of those programs. But when I went there were only three. Now, for Christ's sake, there are more than 250. Fortunately, I ran out of money and had to get a job to take care of my wife and brand new son. But until 1993 when I was fired from my last job, I always had a day job, and sometimes two. (And I've never applied for a grant either, from anybody.) What I'm trying to say is, what the fuck do you write about if you don't move around in the commercial and political world? How long can you keep writing about having your first sex or observing your first death or how your Uncle Buck's drinking spoiled your family holidays? Or God help us all, how many stories can you write about the politics in the English Department?

This same fellow, and a bright one he is too, asked if the religious sense was a help or a hindrance for a writer. I immediately thought of Flannery O'Conner, from whom I learned the power of the vernacular. She had as strong a religious sense as anybody I've ever read. She thought that any writer who didn't have a religious sense, and in her case, a Roman Catholic sense of the mystery of the Christian Resurrection, was hopelessly devoid of vision. I never shared her religious sense, either generally or particularly, but having said that, I can't explain where I get my sense of fairness about crime if not from the Jewish Commandments. I mean, where does Western law come from? You can talk Greeks, Romans and British Common Law all you want, but where'd they get it? I state emphatically that I'm out of my element here, i.e. I'm not a historian of the Western legal evolution. I'm just saying that anybody who writes about crime and punishment or the lack thereof or the injustice thereof has to get some part of his motive from a religious sense of right and wrong.

Same fellow asked if there was anything I didn't like about writing or publishing. And there is. There's the more or less constant effort by publishers to turn writers into commodities. I despise the effort. What's happened is a result of people in the boardrooms of these international conglomerates thinking that books are no different from aluminium siding. And what's required to sell siding to a housewife is a salesman with poise, charm, affability, congeniality and boyish good looks. So writers who fit that description, regardless of their sensibilities and technical skills, are marketed aggressively because they're seen – and therefore used – as their own best salesmen. I have none of those attributes, so my complaints can be called sour grapes. But I have a fantasy about writers and publishing: In my perfect world, every manuscript would be submitted anonymously and every writer who appeared on TV would have to wear a paper bag over his head and all the pictures of his lovely wife, delightful children and cuddly canine companions would be burned before he was allowed to speak from within the confines of his paper bag. And his voice would be distorted to sound like a guy who's kidnapped your daughter and wants all your tax-exempt bonds in exchange for her. I don't know that this would change anything about publishing, but I'd like to see it tried for a year or two.

And finally, I suppose the few hundred people who read my books want to know what's next. Well, the book I've just finished is about three patrolmen on the same 3-11 watch. All were characters in previous books in the Rocksburg series, but I decided to use them to try to tell a story about the tedium and danger of dealing with feuding neighbours, angry, bitter, and resentful over tree leaves, dog droppings, parking spaces and furtive glances. I have yet to hear my editor's reaction, but I liked it and so did my wife. My agent read only the first 165 pages or so and he liked that much. We'll see.

K. C. Constantine

Blood Mud and *Grievance* are published by No Exit Press

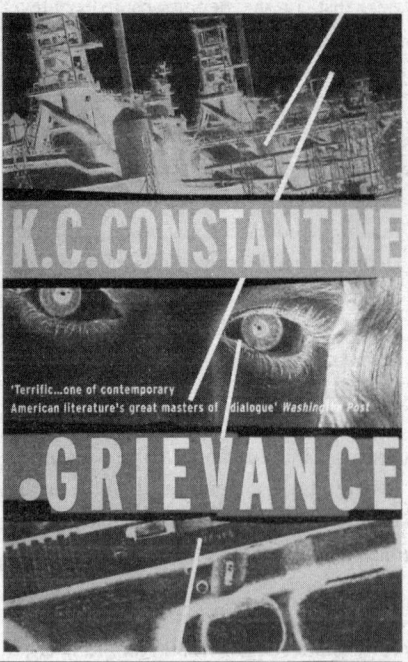

JEFFREY DEAVER: LET'S TWIST AGAIN LIKE WE DID LAST SUMMER

Michael Carlson

[Note: One of the questions below gives away a twist central to *The Blue Nowhere*, so read the book first if you're worried about such things.]

I met Jeffrey Deaver in the lobby of his hotel, where he was just checking in, after arriving from the States on an overnight flight. A few minutes later, we were in the hotel bar, and Deaver appeared remarkably fresh. Of course stamina is an obvious quality for a writer who can produce a steady stream of bestsellers, and Deaver has an uncanny ability to produce a thriller, full of twists, for every summer's reading. In the publicity material for The Blue Nowhere *(Hodder & Stoughton, £14.99)* Deaver says he was *"influenced by popular crime fiction writers like John D. MacDonald, Ian Fleming, Mickey Spillane, as well as more literary writers like Saul Bellow, Theodore Dreiser, John Irving, John Cheever and Paul Theroux."* It's an eclectic list, but the realism of Dreiser shows through, I think, as do the working methods of John D. MacDonald, who would work extensive research into his Travis McGee novels, and use such research as the basis for stand-alone novels, about, for example, Florida real estate swindles. So that's where we started...

How do you see your connection with John D. MacDonald?

We're still looking for that one! I still go back to him. I'm not a character-driven writer, I'm story-driven, and John D. told a story. So did Mickey, so did Ian Fleming. I read every Bond novel when I was younger. I've re-read them too, and they hold up well, but the sexy bits seem so modest now. In a way less is more. I hate writing sex scenes, mostly because they slow down the action. In my novels the action is fast, most take place within forty-eight hours or less. With so much mayhem and murder, nobody should have time for sex!

Your new novel is about a serial killer who hacks into his victims lives... how important is research in building the scope of the book?

Extremely. Writing commercial fiction is a left-brain activity, it's analytical. I have enough ego to want to please audiences who expect a certain kind of book, which I'm delighted to write. At the same time, interesting facts have a payoff – people often tell me they aren't aware at how they're turning the pages until after they've finished doing it. I work hard at giving them twists and good reversals, and they appreciate it.

One of the best moments in *Blue Nowhere* is the twist regarding 'Shawn', the accomplice, who turns out to be a computer.

I thought I'd get slagged for that... I thought I'd taken a real risk, but Shawn does nothing that can't be done with chatterbox, a programme that can mimic human speech and responses in conversa-tion. There's an Alan Turing Award, named after the British scientist, given to anyone who can write a programme that fools humans into thinking they're speaking with other humans. You speak to two humans and one machine and the judges have to decide which one is the computer.

Like a digital 'to tell the truth'!

Yes, but I'm not sure the computer is allowed to lie.

Do you do your research on the web?

I use the web all the time. There's such a wealth of information out there, particular-ly for this book [*Blue Nowhere*] because it is about hackers and computers. I'd visit chat rooms, and lurk, not participate. I'd read bulletin boards from usenet newsgroups about hacking, thousands of messages, some brilliantly written and some quite illiterate, almost scarily so. It gave me more of a sense of just who these people are. Researching *Blue Nowhere* I discovered that Cap'n Crunch has his own website – he's the hacker who discovered that the toy whistles given away with Cap'n Crunch cereal produced sound at the right frequen-cy to hack into the telephone system. Now he runs a hacking website! I'm writing the new Lincoln Rhyme novel, *Stone Monkey*, now, and I'm researching illegal immigra-tion from China. I found the website of the Taiwan National Security Agency, which describes in rather veiled terms all the good it does for the people of Taiwan. You have to read between the pixels.

Are you worried about someone hack-ing in to your own life?

Sure: my own websites (www.jeffrey-deaver.com or www.bluenowhere.com) aren't hacker proof – nothing is, as you know if you've read my novel. It's like a cop told me twenty-five years ago when my car was stolen in Chicago; "If they want to steal it they'll steal it." All you can do is make it so difficult they'll steal someone else's instead. But if they want to hack into your computer they will, unless you have a 'concrete firewall', really serious stuff with zero access to outside connections. I don't do anything sensitive, like cheque books or banking, by computer. I have ordered a few things via the net, but your credit card is out there so often anyway.

Your books have generated lots of interest in Hollywood. Have you been involved in that?

No, I'm a novelist. I sell a book and get on to the next book. I don't care to be that involved. I have no patience with writers who whine about what directors did to their books, failing them. If they don't like what happens when books become movies, they don't have to sell the rights.

Were you happy with the way *The Bone Collector* turned out?

I was generally pleased. There were things I would have done differently. My books are very plot-driven, tightly constructed, with no loose ends, at either resolution or red herrings.

Yes, needing to find a book to discover the pattern the villain is following, when Rhyme, as a historian, would know that already?

Yes, but they have different dramatic needs. I thought they did a great job of building atmosphere; it's a beautifully dark and threatening city.

You trained as a lawyer?

Actually, I got a degree in journalism at the University of Missouri first, then I went into law. It was good training for my organisational and research skills. I have a big criminal library and I research, research, research.

Why do so many lawyers seem to be writing crime novels?

Because we hate practicing law! But I work harder now than I ever did as a lawyer. Maybe it's because there's nowhere else you can tell stories and get paid for it. Though come to think of it, some lawyers get paid for making up stories too!

Michael Carlson

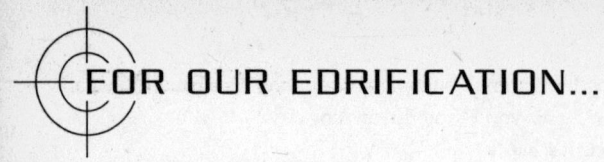
DARK SECRETS: ROBERT EDRIC

Barry Forshaw

The uncovering of long-hidden secrets is the mainspring of many a novel, and certain novelists handle this device better than most. With the appearance of *The Book of the Heathen*, we have a reminder that Robert Edric is nonpareil in this disturbing territory. In an isolated station in the Belgian Congo at the end of the nineteenth century, an Englishman awaits trial for the murder of a child, while his friend attempts to discover the circumstances surrounding the charge. Edric sets his remarkably impressive novel in a world that is undergoing constant change: the dark side of Colonial Africa is

becoming exposed to the world, even as its once endless bounty and wealth begins to dry up. But Eric is dealing with more than the death of a child at the heart of this novel. There are secrets involved that are far more complex, secrets that will destroy one man, and force another man to partake of the destruction.

There are, of course, echoes of Conrad in this riveting book. But Edric is very much his own man. Those who were lucky enough to read the equally disturbing *The Sword Cabinet* will know this is a writer who combines highly impressive narrative gifts with the kind of brilliantly ordered prose that is all too rare these days. Earlier books by the author, such as *In Desolate Heaven*, had marked him out as one of the most accomplished writers at work today, and *The Book of the Heathen* consolidates that impression. At present, such remarkable Edric titles as *Elysium* and *The Earth Made of Glass* are unavailable, and one can only hope that Black Swan will bring them back into print... and soon.

Barry Forshaw

Bibliography
Winter Garden
A New Ice Age
A Lunar Eclipse
In the Days of the
    American Museum
The Broken Lands
Hallowed Ground
The Earth Made of Glass
Elysium
In Desolate Heaven
The Sword Cabinet
The Book of the Heathen
Published by
    Black Swan & Anchor

ROBERT EDRIC
The BOOK OF
THE HEATHEN

'It will be surprising if this year sees a more disturbing or haunting novel'
Peter Kemp, Sunday Times

JAMES ELLROY
IN LONDON

Woody Haut

*I interviewed James Ellroy in London where
he was promoting his latest high-octane
installment of twentieth century America,*
The Cold Six Thousand. *Despite his reputation and the success of the film* LA Confidential, *Ellroy prefers to refer to himself,
not as a crime writer, but as a historical novelist whose remit is to document twentieth
century America. Even so,* The Cold Six
Thousand, *which begins in 1963 and ends
in 1968, deals with a number of large-scale
criminal events, from the JFK assassination
cover-up, the murders of Robert Kennedy
and Martin Luther King, to Vietnam and J.
Edgar Hoover's war on the civil rights movement. These days Ellroy appears calmer and
more serious than he was in days when he
was writing the* LA Quartet *and promoting
himself as the 'demon dog' of crime fiction.
Still, he has lost neither his sense of humour,
nor his singular perception of the world.*

One is immediately struck by the almost incantational style of *The Cold Six Thousand* which seems to be more in the mode of *White Jazz* than *American Tabloid*.

The difference is that the style of *White Jazz* was about omitted words, deliberate fevered dreams and concision. The style was suitable to that book, with its first person narrative, and a white racist cop whose life is burning down in the fall of 1958, and who paradoxically gets hooked on black bebop jazz. *The Cold Six Thousand* is written in a fully explicated, easy to follow style (once you get into the rhythm), which is directly suited to the language of the narrative, and the language of the inner and outer lives of the three main characters. I wanted to reinvent the American language. I wanted to reinvent narrative style. It is a tremendously urgent style. And it forces the reader out of their daily life and compels them to read the book obsessively in as few sittings as possible, which, in the end, aids them in their retention and comprehension of the plot.

It's an amazing feat to maintain that level of intensity over some 670 pages. Was it difficult to write compared to the other books?

Each book is always more difficult. If you get better as a writer, you bring greater and greater self-confidence and self-consciousness – self-consciousness in the true sense, that is to say, consciousness of self – to the work. I was striving for a style, but it took me about five drafts of the book to get it right.

You once told me that your writing consisted mainly of extensive outlining and note-making, but only one draft and a final polish. Could that really have been the case with *The Cold Six Thousand*?

In my very early stuff, I was that sloppy. Really from *LA Confidential* on, I've become more and more painstaking, both in the outline and the note-taking process, and in the writing of the actual text.

How long did it take to write *The Cold Six Thousand*?

I was on this book – with breaks, of course, for journalism and touring and other commitments – for over three years.

Does the promotion of your books and your various bits of journalism and such get in the way of writing?

Not if you allot the proper amount of time for a book. Not if you go back to it refreshed, invigorated and ready to go. I'm not trying to set a record. I'm never going to be Simenon – 6,000 women and 800 books, or whatever he did.

Even though you don't write crime fiction per se anymore, you're writing a kind of crime fiction, because you're writing about American history, which, in itself, is based on an assortment of crimes.

In that sense it's true. But I made a conscious decision after *White Jazz*, and concluding the *LA Quartet*, that these books wouldn't be crime novels. I think *American Tabloid* and *The Cold Six Thousand* are simply historical novels.

I was interested in reading in *The Cold Six Thousand* that you make real-life private eye Fred Otash a major player in all these events. Just the other day I was just reading Richard Ben Cramer's biography of Joe Dimaggio, and who should the Yankee Clipper hire to trail Marilyn Monroe, but Fred Otash. You knew Otash, didn't you?

I knew Otash in his declining years. I met him in 1989. He died in 1992. The story I heard was that he was having a heart attack and called a cab rather than an ambulance. It was an error. He was seventy years old when he died.

He was heavily involved in a lot of nefarious activities in Hollywood, wasn't he?

He was a shakedown artist. He was the guy who verified stories for *Confidential* magazine. He was about to be indicted for doping a racehorse, circa 1959. He was the guy who bugged Peter Lawford's beach front love shack at the behest of Jimmy Hoffa and the Teamsters in 1961. By the way, Otash didn't think that Robert Kennedy ever had an affair with Marilyn. And that JFK only met her maybe seven or eight times, beginning in 1957. But people will believe what they want to believe.

The narrative to *The Cold Six Thousand*, with its connections, seems all too plausible.

Yes, but it's a loosely shifting narrative. The cabals are very loosely formed.

The assassinations in *The Cold Six Thousand* are all connected. How much of that do you think is true, and how much did you create for the purpose of the narrative?

One question I never answer flat out is what's real and what's not. Because I'm trying to create a cohesive verisimilitude. I believe the theory, which I first encountered in Don DeLillo's wonderful novel *Libra* of the unholy alliance of renegade CIA men – not the CIA as an entity – Cuban exiles and the Mob killing John Kennedy. It was all for Cuba. Though this theory has become somewhat worn-out, with all these Kennedy assassination

books, it's still the most plausible, as well as the most dramatically viable theory.

And the connection between JFK's assassination and RFK's and Martin Luther King's, it's possible?
If your mixing of fictional and real life characters is plausible, then you'll believe it. You'll even believe that Sonny Liston met Sirhan Sirhan.

I liked Bayard Rustin's shakedown of Sal Mineo.
If it didn't happen it should have. Of course, Sal Mineo ends up getting murdered in 1976. On Holloway, or one of those streets off of Sunset. It was just a street robbery. There was a black guy who was in prison in Missouri who happened to mention it. I imagine the sheriff's department didn't investigate it. They probably

thought it was some kind of gay thing. It just turned out to be something else entirely. While Bayard Rustin, who was rousted in Pasadena in the early 1950s, showed quite a lot of courage given his situation.

Did you do a lot of research for this book?
I hired two researchers who compiled fact sheets and chronologies so that I would not write myself into factual error. Of course, it becomes a question of how you employ the research, how well you can extrapolate your information. The book covers the breadth of an era. There are seven or eight very solid historical elements there. You have Vietnam, the cover-up of the JFK hit, the FBI's war on the civil rights movement, the factionalisation of the Cuban exile cause, the deaths of Martin Luther King and Robert Kennedy, Howard Hughes' conquest of Las Vegas, and the doings of the Mob.

Did the era affect you as much as it did other people?
I was a kid with a kid's agenda. I didn't care about Martin Luther King or Kennedy or the civil rights movement or the Vietnam war. I was self-absorbed as only a conscienceless kid can be. But I sensed at the time that these were big events and that there was some sort of human interest structure attending them. So now I get to go back and plunk a fictional human interest structure down on these great events with these real-life people and create something out of it.

So the next volume is going to go up to Watergate?
Not Watergate. Chiefly because a) it bores

me, b) it's been done to death, and c) since it took place only twenty-eight years ago, most of the real-life characters are still alive, and can't be utilised fictionally. So the book is going to end in the summer of 1972, but it will steer clear of Watergate. I've always thought Watergate was a snore. The best thing you can say for it is that there were some Cubans involved. Then I'm going to do a novel about Warren Harding's presidency, and America in the 1920s. Because the grand design of the rest of my career is to recreate twentieth century American history to my specifications. Really, the first half of the century is a romance. For instance, there will never be a romance like World War Two. And there'll never be anything again like the first half of this century, because progress is marching on. It was the modern era, but it was pre-psychologised, and what a time.

What's interesting about Warren Harding?
He was the second most corrupt president of the twentieth century. But a good-natured man. He was put into office by the Ohio gang. Cut-throat politicians and presumably businessmen made him. They understood that he was personable and good-looking, had a certain amount of charm. He lasted three years. But first things first. I want to concentrate on the sequel to *The Cold Six Thousand*.

Will the sequel have some of the same characters?
It'll be a three man triumvirate, and one of the men will be Wayne Tedrow. All the threads are laid down in *The Cold Six Thousand*. Littel's foreign casino plan, which

takes us to Latin America, the continuing Cuban cause, Vietnam, Mr Hoover's continuing war on the civil rights movement and Howard Hughes' continued conquest of Las Vegas. So the books, from *American Tabloid* to the next the sequel to *The Cold Six Thousand*, will have gone from 1958 to 1972.

Which really will end an era.
That will be it. These books are huge, so this won't be a quartet. This trilogy is as far as it will go.

You've gone about as far away as possible from the Chandler paradigm of crime writing. Do you feel like you're out there on your own?
I think I'm my own man with my own style. There's never been anyone like me, and I doubt if there ever will be, frankly, because the books are so damn difficult to write, and I don't see people having the vision and concentration necessary to write them.

What's happening with the proposed film adaptation of *White Jazz*?
It's out there in the ether. Since in Hollywood, dysfunction rules, I would still be extremely surprised if it ever got made.

But you prefer to stay outside the project?
Well, I adapted it. So let's see what happens.

What do you read these days?
Very little. The last two novels I read and admired were DeLillo's *Libra* and *Underworld*. These days, when I'm not working, I just like to brood and spend time with my wife and be quiet in Kansas City.
                                              Woody Haut

CRIME TIME NEWS

Lawrence Block

Lawrence Block reports that he's finished the film script for *Keller*, the screen adaptation of his novel, *Hit Man*. "Patrick McGrath and Maria Aitken did a couple of drafts," Block told us, "and developed a solid structure for converting an episodic novel into a cohesive work for the screen. Then producer Richard Rubinstein decided the project needed a writer who could make the film more like the book – unheard of in the film industry! I got on board and wound up doing a top-to-bottom rewrite, and if all goes well we'll be shooting in the fall. Jeff Bridges will star as the stamp-collecting, dog-loving assassin, and Martin Bell will direct." Block added that he found film writing very different from novels. "It's easier," he said, "in that a film script is a third or a fourth as many pages as a novel, and there are fewer words on the page, and many of them don't have to be all that well-chosen, as they're stage directions. So there's less heavy lifting involved, but the concentration is at least as intense. I found I couldn't work more than two hours a day; after two hours my brain was fogged over."

Orion will publish Block's new novel *Hope to Die*. It's number fifteen in the Matt Scudder series, and about to get heavy promotion in the US and UK. The book to follow, as yet unwritten and untitled, will be a big multiple-viewpoint thriller set (no surprise here) in Block's beloved New York.

Edward Marston

Edward Marston is to be Guest of Honour at Malice Domestic XIV in 2002. Held near Washington DC, the convention follows the Edgar Awards. Marston has twenty-five titles in print, and his eleven Domesday novels are particular favourites among crime readers.

Danuta Reah

The film option for Danuta Reah's first novel, *Only Darkness*, has been sold to the French company, Escazal Films. The intended director is the award-winning Charlotte Brandstrom.

HIGH-TECH WRITING

Peter May

When I first started writing, more than thirty years ago, terms like 'zip disk', 'gigabyte' and 'firewire' would have meant nothing to me. Now I sit at a computer connected to the Internet, a picture in the corner of my screen replaying a crucial location on digital video, a piece of software telling me how many words I've written. I used to think the sentences I wrote flowed directly from me to paper through the pen in my hand. I didn't want anything to get in the way of that, reluctant even to use a typewriter. Then eight years in journalism turned me into a touch-typist. Words and paper became connected by a keyboard.

In the late 1970s I started writing television drama. Script drafts were laboriously hammered out on my battered old portable. I began to see the advantage of keying my words only once, being able to rewrite without having to retype. I bought my first Apple Macintosh. It had no hard disk (what was that?), and just 256k of RAM – which meant it could only hold half a script in its memory. But it seemed like a miracle. I could never have dreamed how rapidly that miracle would grow.

Research, however, was still time-consuming, expensive and often frustrating, limiting me to subjects relatively close to home – remember the old adage: write about what you know?

Then in 1996 I had an idea for a story that would only really work in a Chinese

Peter **MAY**

snakehead

The new all-action thriller featuring Li Yan and Margaret Campbell

setting. *The Firemaker* involved a smouldering corpse in a Beijing park, a Chinese cop and an American pathologist. I knew nothing about the Chinese police, or pathology, and had only been to Beijing once. But I had just made a very important discovery. The Internet. In just fifteen years the advances in computer technology had brought the world to my desktop. There did not seem any topic I could not tackle. Through the power of e-mail I made invaluable contacts around the world, gaining direct access to the arcane field of Chinese criminal justice. It was on the Internet that I 'met' my pathology adviser, a medical examiner with the US Armed Forces Institute of Pathology, who e-mails me all the information I require to make my novels authentic.

Whatever subject I am researching, I can access in minutes on the Internet information that might otherwise have taken months to uncover. When I make my research trips to China or America, I take my palm-sized digital video camera to shoot all my locations. Back at my desk, I edit them on my iMac computer and save them as files which appear as little television pictures at the top of my screen, giving me instant access to the sights and sounds of my trip to refresh my (not always reliable) memory.

The third of my China thrillers, *The Killing Room*, is out in paperback. The fourth, *Snakehead* is published in hardback at the end of the year. I could not have written any of them without the power of my computer – at least, not in the same time scale. Technology has truly empowered my writing.

Peter May

Peter May is published by Hodder & Stoughton

DARK... AND OTHER FIRST NOVELS

Barry Forshaw

There is so much sophisticated and intelligent writing around these days that it takes something special to rise above the fray. Kenji Jasper's *Dark* (No Exit Press paperback, 20 September) is just that: a haunting portrait of an urban generation, shadowed and often erased by violence, but determined to make its mark on the world. *Dark* is a fresh, evocative African-American coming-of-age novel that synthesises the caustic style of James Baldwin with the contemporary subject matter of rap and hip hop.

American Sarah Strohmeyer's *Bubbles Unbound* (Headline) aims at the Janet Evanovich market with a heroine determined to turn her taste for gossip into a talent for journalism. She soon discovers while brazen bravado gets results, some people will do anything to keep her quiet.

Adrian Flanagan's *Cobra* (Robert Hale) is a tough and involving thriller with the terrifying premise that nuclear weapons in the US have suffered major security breaches; the fact that all the background to this taut piece is authentic screws the tension ever tighter. A debut of real accomplishment.

There's a considerable buzz about *Dangerous Data* (Bantam) by Adam Lury and Simon Gibson, a highly persuasive thriller about the current fears we all have about data surveillance. The central character is a data detective, and this is a satisfying marriage of technology and the standard detective novel.

Cold Zero (Transworld) is the sniper's term for the one shot you get at finishing a job. Christopher Whitcomb's compelling book offers a stark first-person account from the front lines of violence. As an account of the silent battle America wages behind the headlines, this is visceral stuff. Snipers are surfacing in films and novels in quantity at present, but this is a distinctive entry.

Sally Spedding's *Wringland* (Macmillan) is a tale of chilling menace and powerful atmosphere set in haunted fen country. The heroine's job as a sales negotiator for a property firm takes her to the sinister Black Fen and a series of increasingly disturbing incidents. This is a ghost story handled with consummate skill.

Hugh Collins' *No Smoke* (Canongate) is a vicious, original and very funny crime novel set in 1976 in the author's native Glasgow. This was a time when flares, mullets and flick knives were the currency of cool, and the old criminal codes of honour had yet to be destroyed by the new breed of gangster. The language, humour and culture of Scotland's most violent city are captured with the skill of William McIlvanney.

John Colapinto's *About the Author* (Fourth Estate) has more than a touch of Highsmith and Hitchcock about it, and it's already been snapped up by Spielberg's DreamWorks company. A canny psychological thriller with a literary theme.

BACK TO GREENELAND

Barry Forshaw

Had Graham Greene not written his 'serious' novels (such as *A Burnt Out Case* and *The Heart of the Matter*) which marked him out as one of the greatest of all English writers, his entertainments (as the author rather dismissively described them) would constitute a body of thrillers almost without equal in the field. Early in his career, Greene introduced an element of the spy story into *The Confidential Agent*, in which D, the agent of a Latin government (Republican Spain in all but name), figures in a narrative that was clearly influential on such later writers as le Carré. The latter has long acknowledged Greene's influence on his work.

Greene's most celebrated crime novel, of course, is *Brighton Rock* (with its psychotic young anti-hero Pinkie), which the author moved out of his 'entertainments' category. This shifting of genres by Greene was always rather arbitrary: the moral concerns of the thrillers were often precisely those of the more serious books, while the pursuit narratives of the serious books (such as of the whisky priest on the run in *The Power and the Glory*) had precisely the same trajectory as the thrillers. But all the books have that dark and sardonic view of existence which quickly became identified as 'Greeneland', a queasy admixture of the seedy, the surrealistically funny and the dangerous.

The handsome series of reissues in trade paperback format by Vintage gives one a welcome chance to encounter again such superb books as *The Ministry of Fear*, which may be considered to be among the finest of Greene's thrillers. Despite the writer's long association with the cinema, the number of first-rate films associated with his work is relatively few (Carol Reed's *The Third Man*, of course, and Fritz Lang made a creditable stab at *The Ministry of Fear*), but re-reading such superbly written novels as *The Quiet American* (in which CIA double-dealing is the mainspring of the plot, and the Vietnam conflict was introduced to many readers for first time) is a salutary reminder that the best way to approach the writer is (unsurprisingly) through the books rather than the hit-and-miss films. The first film of *The Quiet American* downplayed the anti-American tone of the book, and while the forthcoming Michael Caine adaptation may be more faithful, there's no question that the author's tone of voice will be lost.

The Vintage reissues give us a chance to enjoy again the wonderfully mordant humour of *Our Man in Havana* (which drew on Greene's own experiences in the intelligence services), but almost without exception, all these novels remain as vivid and involving as when they were first published. Of course, there are those who find difficulties arising from the author's self-torturing Catholicism. But Greene was never an apologist for the Catholic Church. The acquisition of faith in such books as *The End of the Affair* is rarely a life-enhancing, positive thing. In fact, the overriding impression that one receives is that most his heroes (notably Scobie in *A Burnt Out Case*) would be far better off without the dubious consolations of Catholicism. And Greene himself was far too much of a sensualist to be at ease with the anti-sex asceticism of the Catholic Church (true also, it seems, of many priests, given a recent host of scandals). So the agnostic reader need not fear, and if such reservations stop a reader from tackling one of the most considerable bodies of work in English literature, they will be doing themselves a considerable disservice.

Other Greene novels in the Vintage reissues series include *England Made Me, Twenty-One Stories*, and the masterly *The Comedians*. In fact, the latter may be the best book for the novice Greenian to tackle – this is the novel that made Haiti's dictator Papa Doc Duvalier very hot under the collar – a testament to its persuasiveness.

Barry Forshaw

KEY CRIME SCRIBES
A RANDOM SELECTION

Eve Tan Gee

Dennis Lehane

When Dennis Lehane published his first novel, *A Drink Before the War*, in 1994, he received the American Shamus award and instantly became a crime writer of consequence. This was the first in a series set in the grim Boston community of Dorchester (a million miles away from Thomas Hardy's) with two series protagonists, private eyes Patrick Kenzie and Angie Gennaro. Of course, when every new hardboiled hero appears, the customary adjectives are wheeled out: Chandleresque, Hammettesque: but Lehane probably owes more to the richly textured novels of Ross Macdonald, in which dark family secrets cast a shadow over the present. As with so many male/female action duos (Steed and Mrs Peel, Modesty Blaise and Willie Garvin) the unresolved sexual tension gives the relationship between his characters a keen edge, and the astringent wisecracks are set against narratives that lay more stress on human feeling than is customary in the genre. Novel touches involve a detective with two distinctive cars (one of which is a Porsche Speedster) and a preference for a .44 Magnum (not to emulate Dirty Harry, but because his aim is too bad to use anything

but a man-stopping gun). The first book dealt with several serious topics (racial issues, child abuse, corrupt cops), and in 1996's *Darkness, Take My Hand*, Lehane's detectives are enmeshed in a narrative involving the Mob. This second outing was followed by the curious *Sacred* (1997) where the duo is hired by a millionaire to find his missing daughter. But although the plot may have owed something to Chandler, the sensibility was particularly modern. Subsequently, *Gone, Baby Gone* (1998) – something of a breakthrough book – had a kidnapping theme. Apart from the characterisation, Lehane's books are marked by an evocative sense of place, with his Boston as atmospheric as Chandler's Los Angeles.

Recommended titles – Dennis Lehane

Darkness, Take My Hand
Sacred
A Drink Before the War
Key title – Gone, Baby Gone

George Pelecanos

A native of Washington DC, George Pelecanos (born in 1957) has spent his whole life in the city. The author sold electronic equipment and worked in shoe stores before taking up his crime-scribe's pen But while other writers concentrate on the high-flying lawyers and corrupt politicians of the nation's capital, Pelecanos is more of Elmore Leonard's party: his concerns are with the poor and disadvantaged, as well as the African-American community (known in DC, demeaningly, as Chocolate City). Like George V. Higgins before him, Pelecanos is particularly adroit at handling the colour and rhythm of working-class speech, which he renders with the utmost felicity. And he differs from the conventional hard-boiled practitioners in another significant way: the violence in the genre is usually short and brutal, but Pelecanos ups the ante and dispenses fairly grisly mayhem in the fashion of the serial killer genre. Nick Stefanos is his customary gumshoe, and Nick (along with the brilliantly observed characterisation of the other figures) is one of the reasons that the author's stock is so very high. In fact, the word of mouth on Pelecanos has been strong enough to turn him into something of a cult writer, with each new book keenly anticipated. His detective begins his career as an appliance store PR manager in *A Firing Offence* (1997), where he is asked to trace the missing boy. Nick was firmly established by the time of *Nick's Trip* (1998) in which he takes on the job as bartender at The Spot and undertakes the odd case as unlicensed private investigator. Throughout these books (and the later *King Suckerman*) the stress is on the reality of the characters as much as the situations, and because the author takes time to involve us with his protagonists, the threat of the gang of psychotic killers (as in *King Suckerman*) has a particularly powerfully force. English readers are famously less keen on basketball than their American counterparts, but these aspects of the books (clearly a particular interest on the part of the author) can be ignored in precisely the same way that the Roman Catholicism of Graham Greene is often screened out by lovers of his writing. Certainly, Pelecanos is something special in the field.

Recommended titles – George Pelecanos

King Suckerman

A Firing Offence

Key title – Nick's Trip

Ian Rankin

In the UK, female crime writers have thoroughly colonised the psychological mystery, extending the innovations of such practitioners as Patricia Highsmith. But the master of the tough regional crime novel is Ian Rankin, who enjoys the kind of spectacular sales for his gritty Scottish thrillers enjoyed by more middle-class writers such as Colin Dexter. Rankin was born in the kingdom of Fife in 1960, and, after graduating from university in Edinburgh, undertook a bizarre sequence of jobs: grape-picker, swineherd, taxman, alcohol researcher, hi-fi journalist and even punk musician. His literary credentials were established by his poetry and short stories, but with the first of his Inspector Rebus novels, *Knots & Crosses* (1987), he began the sequence that has made his name. In an unflinchingly rendered Edinburgh, Rankin puts his beleaguered detective through some grim and convoluted narratives, always observed with the keenest eye for detail and local colour. Even such clichés of the genre as his detective's battle with alcoholism are handled in a fresh and innovative fashion, but in the same way that Colin Dexter thoroughly colonised Oxford for the crime genre, Rankin has made it difficult for other authors to utilise Edinburgh. Among the most striking of the Rebus books are *Let It Bleed* (1995), *The Hanging Garden* (1998) and *Death is Not the End* (also 1998). Rankin has also written as Jack Harvey (the impressive *Bleeding Hearts* appeared under this nom de plume), and even an indifferent TV pilot (with a youthful John Hannah miscast as the mature DI Rebus) made no dent in Rankin's phenomenal appeal.

Recommended titles – Ian Rankin

Set in Darkness
The Black Book
Mortal Causes
Key title – Dead Souls

Raymond Chandler

The most celebrated and influential of American detective writers, Raymond Chandler was born in Chicago but acquired his literary finesse when educated in Britain at Dulwich College. He fought with the Gordon Highlanders in the 1914-18 War, and received two decorations. A career as an oil executive in Los Angeles did not offer him the fulfilment he sought, although he made a success of it. But after losing his job in the Depression, he began to write the crime stories for such pulp magazines as *Black Mask* that consolidated the style which he was to make uniquely his own. The short stories from this period (often featuring John Dalmas, a prototype for Chandlers' definitive private eye Philip Marlowe) sometimes found their way, transmogrified, into the brilliant series of novels on which his reputa-

tion rests. The first, *The Big Sleep*, appeared in 1939, and marvellous though its successors are, this first appearance of Chandler's tarnished Knight Errant is still the finest thing he ever wrote. The mean streets of Los Angeles are conjured with an evocativeness never equalled since, and the tortuous plotting (which Chandler himself made fun of, but which is perfectly logical) allows his detective to encounter a series of grotesques, degenerate rich folks, thugs and (of course) femmes fatales. All the Marlowe characteristics are in this first book: his sardonic wit, his tenacity (Marlowe never gives up on a case, even when his clients ask him to), his wry toughness and vulnerability. In the seven Marlowe books, Chandler creates a Los Angeles that is corrupt and seedy but utterly fascinating, and such luminaries as W. H. Auden were fulsome in their praise. Chandler was friendly with Ian Fleming, and both enjoyed sending up the more unlikely aspects of their much-battered protagonists. But it is precisely the balance between humour and grim seriousness (particularly in the examination of treacherous human behaviour) that makes these astonishing books as readable today as ever. Chandler also wrote a much quoted essay, *The Simple Art of Murder*, in which he sets out his stall as a writer dealing with real situations rather than the more bloodless crossword puzzles (as he saw them) of the classic English mystery – murders committed for a reason, rather than simply to provide a body.

Recommended titles – Raymond Chandler

The High Window
The Little Sister
The Long Goodbye
Key title – The Big Sleep

Nicci French

There have been crime-writing duos before, but few as accomplished as the husband and wife team who, jointly, are the writer Nikki French. Journalist Nikki Gerrard and writer Sean French produce these superbly turned novels while pursuing their own writing careers and raising a family of four young children in Suffolk. The stress is on dark psychology, always explored in a cool, dispassionate tone. 1998's *The Memory Game*, dealing with false memory syndrome, established the duo's style, with the kind of steady accumulation of tension found only in the very best thrillers. In the same year, *The Safe House* had a similar electric charge, and by the time of *Killing Me Softly* (1999), there was an established and keen following for Nikki French titles. Particularly notable was *Crazy for Me*, showing a firm understanding of the fraught relationships between men and women, with the heroine Alice finding a chance affair with a stranger threatening both her subsequent relationships and her sanity. All of the above may have been said to be curtain raisers for the superb *Beneath the Skin*, a sophisticated and highly sensual thriller concerned with the vulnerability of all human life, no less. Three women in the suffocating heat of a London summer (Zoe, Jenny, Nadia) are connected only by the killer, obsessed by a demented love that can find only one outlet. These days, readers are said to consume books in bite-sized chunks – but it would be a strong-minded reader able to easily put down any of the titles bearing the Nikki French logo.

Recommended titles – Nicci French
  The Memory Game
  The Safe House
  Killing Me Softly
  Key title – Beneath the Skin

Patricia Cornwell

Her first book was the biography of an evangelist. Ironic to consider this now, when Patricia Cornwell is one of the world's best-selling crime writers, with a series featuring the tenacious pathologist Kay Scarpetta. Although Ed McBain has pointed out that he inaugurated the forensic as a key element of crime novels, it was Cornwell who virtually created a sub-genre in this arena, and Kay Scarpetta has to be the most imitated protagonist in the genre, her characteristics as a heroine ripped off quite as often as those of Chandler's Marlowe are by male writers. In the first book, *Post Mortem* (1990), we encounter Scarpetta, a medical examiner in Richmond Virginia, who soon plunges into a typical mystery in which her own life inevitably ends up on the line. This book won the American Edgar Award for the best first novel, along with the John Creasey Award from the British Crime Writers Association. Cornwell had worked as a crime reporter and also undertook technical writing and computer analysis in the Richmond medical examiner's office. This experience was, of course, heavily utilised within the books, and apart from the canny characterisation of her heroine, it is the unblinking examination of the horrors of Scarpetta's profession that have made an indelible mark on readers. But there is much more to the author than grisly thrills: the plots are usually extremely well engineered, and a recent period in which her talent appeared to stall is now, thankfully, over. Among the best Cornwell books are the compelling *Hornets Nest* in 1997, and the equally adroit *Black Notice*. Cornwell's other protagonist is police chief Judy Hammer, aided by officers Virginia West and Andy Brazil, with computer viruses, teenage gangs and threatening rednecks all part of the heady mix of elements. However often Cornwell is plagiarised, she remains the most consummate practitioner of the forensic thriller.

Recommended titles – Patricia Cornwell
  Southern Cross
  Black Notice
  Hornets Nest
  Key title – Post Mortem

Val McDermid

Few would dispute the fact that Val McDermid is one of Britain's finest crime writers, marrying a narrative skill with the kind of psychological acuity found only in the finest writers. Her private eye, Kate Brannigan, has become one of the best-loved characters in the genre: feisty, vulnerable and dogged in the pursuit of the solution to some often grim mysteries. And McDermid is not afraid to tackle serious issues within the context of the crime novel – never as a mere prop, but utilising the issues to make some sharp and valid points about social issues. McDermid grew up in a Scottish mining community, before reading English at Oxford. She spent sixteen years as a journalist, with the climax of her journalistic career being three years spent as the northern bureau chief of a national Sunday paper. But it is her crime writing that has made her a particular favourite for many readers. Her first detective, Lindsay

Gordon, featured in five novels, with *Common Murder* being among the most striking. But having a low boredom threshold, McDermid decided she wished to write more than one kind of crime novel, so she created the Manchester-based sleuth Kate Brannigan in a series of books that had a considerably grittier feel. In 1995, the Gold Dagger-winning *The Mermaids Singing* was yet another departure, but it is A Place of Execution which many consider her most radical innovation in terms of characterisation and style. The main part of the latter is set in an isolated Derbyshire community in the Sixties, and appears to be the true account of a landmark criminal case, related by a journalist who has persuaded the policeman at the heart of the case to open up after thirty-five years. But the final section of the book, set in the present day, produces revelations that leave the reader stunned. Following up this much-acclaimed novel was no easy task, but *Killing the Shadows* is McDermid firing on all cylinders, with Professor Fiona Cameron, an academic psychologist as the protagonist.

Recommended titles – Val McDermid
  A Place of Execution
  The Mermaids Singing
  Key title – Killing the Shadows

John Grisham

Few writers can be said to have virtually created a genre, and although legal thrillers existed before the advent of John Grisham's ventures, there's no question that his phenomenal success was responsible for hundreds of imitators. But very few of the latter have enjoyed the popular success (and highly successful film adaptations) that Grisham has had, and if the author has not always enjoyed critical acclaim, readers have made the appearance of each new book a cause for much excitement. It was recently estimated that Grisham books and films have earned in excess of one billion dollars, but this would have seemed ludicrous to the young law student at the University of Mississippi whose ambition was to play professional basketball. But when his success began in the early Nineties, Grisham never looked back, and his highly original thrillers began to appear with satisfying regularity. His formula is straightforward: persuasive courtroom action along with the dangerous shenanigans that accompany arraignments, all tied into well-plotted murder mysteries. His protagonists are usually high-achieving young lawyers (Grisham's characters are always high achievers) and his technique of conveying the authenticity of the legal world to the reader is reminiscent of such writers as Frederick Forsyth, who similarly freights in much authentic-seeming detail. His first novel, *A Time to Kill* (1989) was based on an actual rape case, and begins with a savage attack on a ten-year-old child, and established the page-turning, distinctly non-literary style of his subsequent work. He is always able to come up with a new twist in plot terms (*The Pelican Brief* in 1992 concerned the murder of two Supreme Court Justices with a female law student heroine sorting out the mystery) and his recent work has more than a touch of Graham Greene in its use of religious elements. Greene, however, never tried to persuade the reader of the virtues of religion (quite the reverse, in fact), but Grisham's sharp narrative skills will undoubtedly carry him through this particular blip in his career.

Recommended titles – John Grisham
The Firm
The Client
The Testament
Key title – A Time To Kill

Elmore Leonard

The term 'Tarantino-esque' conveys to most people brilliantly funny, sharply observed dialogue exchanges between low-lifes. But who actually invented this stuff? Quentin Tarantino would probably be the first to give the credit to the wonderful Elmore Leonard, whose series of utterly unique crime novels redefined the genre and placed dialogue centre stage in an even more forceful way than such Leonard predecessors as George V. Higgins. Born in New Orleans, Leonard attended the University of Detroit and graduated in the early Fifties. He decided to live in Detroit and subsequently made it the locale in which many of his books are set. His first publishing success was as a writer of Westerns (ironically, those Westerns are now keenly sought after by readers of his crime fiction). Although several of these books had been made into fine films (such as Paul Newman's *Hombre*), Leonard's career moved to another strata in the 1980s with such books as with *Stick, La Brava*, and *'52 Pickup* which crystallised the elements that defined his writing: quirky, often farcical plotting, a cool amoral tone and (most of all) an entrée into the world of petty criminals possessing an authenticity that no other writer had achieved. Films of these latter novels varied from the indifferent (such as Burt Reynolds' *Stick*) to the first-rate (as in John Travolta's *Get Shorty*), and the hallmark of his success was that many writers began to emulate his style, even in this country. Leonard has also written a sequence of novels set in south Florida, with the drifters, drug dealers and dodgy businessman that populate his other books. Recently, a certain repetition may have set in (probably inevitably), but the sheer skill of his work continues to amaze. He has won several awards, including a French Grand Prix for *City Primeval*.

Recommended titles – Elmore Leonard
Be Cool
Unknown Man Number 89
The Split
Key title – '52 Pickup

Dashiell Hammett

Before Raymond Chandler, there was Dashiell Hammett. America's first major private eye novelist was formerly an agent with the detective company Pinkerton's. He left the job in 1922, fearing that his days were numbered because of a lung disease contracted during the First World War. His pieces for the legendary *Black Mask* magazine quickly established his reputation, and by the late 1920s he had revised the longer stories as his first novels, *Red Harvest* and *The Dain Curse*, both written in 1929. His period as a powerful force in crime writing was short, and by 1934, he had ceased to write, despite many attempts to add to his canon (as with his successor, Chandler, alcohol cost him much serious work). But his influence is considerable. Many would consider him the greatest of the hard-boiled novelists, even more than Chandler, with a prose-style as lean and pared-down as that of Hemingway. Along with creating many of the conventions of the private eye genre, his work was shot through with powerful political undertones (*Red Harvest* is still one of the greatest studies of municipal corruption ever written), and a vision of existence that stressed the tenuousness of all human endeavour. His private eye Sam Spade was subsequently immortalised by Humphrey Bogart in John Huston's film of *The Maltese Falcon*. Sam remains the quintessential private dick, despite appearing in only one novel. He is tough, fallible and (like Marlowe) all too open to the possibility of corruption. But, like his successor, he usually resists, retaining a kind of honour. And Brigid O'Shaugnessy, the beautiful (and lethal) femme fatale of the novel is, similarly, the matrix for all similar temptresses. Hammett's other protagonist, the anonymous Continental Op, is deliberately left vague in order to act as a conduit for the narratives rather than as their instigator.

Recommended titles – Dashiell Hammett
Red Harvest
The Dain Curse
The Big Knockover
Key title – The Maltese Falcon

Agatha Christie

The most celebrated of British detective story writers (1890-1976), Christie's work is the epitome of the civilised and superbly crafted crime novel. No other writer brought the classic mystery novel to such a level of public acclaim, and she inaugurated several much-imitated innovations in the genre (such as the device of the murderer/narrator in *The Murder of Roger Ackroyd*). To this day, she remains the crime writer who has sold more books (and been translated into more languages) than any other writer, and her name is synonymous with the genre. She is often criticised for the straightforward language and cloistered settings of the books, but Christie transforms these limitations into shining virtues, with her narrative abilities paramount. Created a Dame Commander of the Order of the British Empire in 1971, her most famous protagonists are the Belgian detective Hercule Poirot and the deceptively diffident elderly sleuth Miss Marple. Poirot, most able member of the Belgian Sûreté, retired from the force in 1904 but enjoyed an unfeasibly long life subsequently tackling insoluble cases privately. Fastidiously turned-out (the waxed moustache is to him what the deerstalker and Inverness cape is to Holmes), Christie gave him a loathing of English tea and made him highly self-critical, despite his percipience. Jane Marple, a tall and thin old lady (unlike any of her screen incarnations) confounded the local constabulary with her razor-sharp analytical faculties right until the posthumously published *Sleeping Murder* in 1974. And despite her seeming gentleness, Miss Marple is (on closer inspection) a clear-eyed cynic with no illusions about human behaviour. But the mysteries about which Agatha Christie wrote were matched by one in her own life: she mysteriously disappeared for nine days in the 1920s and became the centre of a remarkable press furore. Love her or loathe her, few can ignore the influence of this remarkable writer.

Recommended titles – Agatha Christie

The Mysterious Affair at Styles
Death on the Nile
Murder on the Orient Express
Sleeping Murder
Key title – The Murder of Roger Ackroyd

Kathy Reichs

In an overcrowded field such as that of crime-writing, it's difficult to establish a solid reputation. To achieve the acclaim that Kathy Reichs has – and in a relatively short time – is quite an achievement. Reichs, like Patricia Cornwell, has utilised her medical background to create a series of tough and uncompromising thrillers. She was forensic anthropologist for the office of the Chief Medical Examiner of the State of North Carolina, and worked in a similar capacity in the province of Quebec. Her massive experience in the area of forensic science has been heavily drawn on, and at present she is one of only fifty people certified by the American Board of Forensic Anthropology, and very few of these individuals are women. As with her leading character, Dr Temperance Brennan, Reichs found herself obliged not only to function but also to distinguish herself in the male world of law enforcement. *Déjà Dead* established her reputation in 1998, and Temperance Brennan made an immediate mark as a solid and reliable heroine. Brennan was, of course, similar to Cornwell's Dr Kay Scarpetta, but Reichs nevertheless rendered Brennan a fully rounded character in her own right, and managed to build new elements through three successive books. The first novel had a relatively cool tone, but by the time of *Death du Jour*, Reichs had begun to consolidate and refine elements present in the early book (such as character interaction), and the emotional temperature was higher. This new level of energy and invention clearly established Reichs as a more impressive writer than had been originally thought, and decisively moved her out of the shade of Patricia Cornwell. With *Deadly Decisions* (2000), the consolidation process continued. The book begins with Brennan teaching a body recovery course in the FBI headquarters at Quantico, when she is called back to Quebec. Bikers are engaged in a war, and two of them appear to have blown themselves up. Brennan is largely unconcerned with what the bikers do to each other, until a nine-year-old girl is killed in the crossfire. What follows is a superbly rendered thriller, with a particularly acute sense of locale.

Recommended titles – Kathy Reichs
Death du Jour
Déjà Dead
Key title – Deadly Decisions

Carl Hiaasen

Born in Florida in 1953, Hiaasen customarily writes about those natives of the State who were not born there. His career as a writer began in journalism, and to this day he writes for the *Miami Herald*. But his name as a novelist was made by a series of books synthesising different elements of both the crime novel and the mordant social satire. His distinguishing feature is humour, and humour of a black and scabrous nature. For the *Miami Herald*, Hiaasen won several awards for his reporting, and was even mooted for a Pulitzer Prize. This crime reporting, of course, has been drawn on extensively throughout his career (in much the fashion that Kathy Reichs and Patricia Cornwell use their forensic knowledge), and his particular speciality has been marshalling a massive cast of crooks and heavies, quite as disparate in appearance and behaviour as those of Elmore Leonard. The comparison with the latter is instructive: where Leonard finds

dark humour in the double and triple crosses of petty criminals, Hiaasen moves in a world that would be recognised by English playwright Joe Orton, who similarly took cruel behaviour to bizarre and surrealistic heights. After three novels co-written with William de Montalbano, Hiaasen made his mark with *Tourist Season* in 1996. The basic theme was terrorist assaults on tourism, with the attacks on visitors to Miami centre stage. The final impression was beguiling in a grim fashion, even if the tone faltered on occasion. With *Double Whammy* in 1987, set in the bass fishing industry, Hiaasen utilised the conventions of the private eye narrative. His PI is an ex-photographer hired to take incriminating pictures of a cheating fisherman, but find himself in very deep waters. With 1989's *Skin Tight*, private eye Mike Stranahan is caught up in a narrative touching on plastic surgery and the world of TV celebrity. Surviving the debacle of Demi Moore's film of his novel *Striptease*, Hiaasen has continued to create his own brand of grim and bizarre crime writing.

Recommended titles – Carl Hiaasen
Double Whammy
Tourist Season
Lucky You
Key title – Stormy Weather

James Lee Burke

One of the most distinctive crime-cracking protagonists on the scene is James Lee Burke's quick-witted Dave Robicheaux, and *The Neon Rain* was a perfect calling card for a striking new writer. Burke had enjoyed only small success as a writer of non-crime novels, but his time had come once he fell into the genre which he quickly made his own.

Burke's novels are set on the Gulf Coast, where he grew up. Born in Texas, Burke ensured that the New Orleans and Bayou backgrounds his books were crammed full of authentic detail about Cajun culture. His books have also taken on board some cogent social issues: in *Heaven's Prisoners* (1988), a priest involved in the sanctuary movement is killed when a private plane crashes, and the narrative touches on US involvement in Central American terrorism. But *The Neon Rain* (1987) is Burke's most striking example of narrative and setting being married with consummate precision. Dave Robicheaux finds himself caught in a morass of violence in this darkest of novels, while the cast of characters Dave encounters (including drug pushers who target children and CIA agents prepared to provide weapons for foreign death squads) is drawn with particular richness. The truly interesting thing about these books is the level of ambitiousness, with such themes as redemption and the horror of the human condition treated with a surprisingly degree of seriousness. But Burke remains primarily an entertainer, and such books as *Black Cherry Blues* (which won the American Edgar Award) will continue to give readers great pleasure.

Recommended titles – James Lee Burke
> The Neon Rain
> Black Cherry Blues
> Heaven's Prisoners
> *Key Title* – Cimarron Rose

Jeffrey Deaver

Jeffrey Deaver is a former lawyer and sometime folk singer who lives in California and Washington DC. More and more people are investigating his Lincoln Rhyme crime novels, featuring a quadriplegic investigator assisted by a young policewoman who spends most of the novels in mortal danger. What makes these books so distinctive is the inauguration of a genuinely novel protagonist: Rhyme may sport elements whose lineage stretches back as far as the Master of Baker Street, but few crime writers seem able to shake off that particular strain. Rhyme is a very distinctive creation, and the puzzles that Deaver creates for him are usually grim serial killer pieces with no shortage of grisly details. One of the most striking is *The Devil's Teardrop*, which begins with a man getting onto a packed subway escalator and firing a machine-gun into the crowd. The narrative quickly escalates into a truly engrossing thriller. Deaver's cogent plotting and intelligent psychological profiling of his villains pays dividends here, but the Lincoln Rhyme novel which has acquired the most devoted following is *The Empty Chair*, published in 2000. Rhyme travels to North Carolina for some experimental surgery and is drafted in by the local police to help track down two women kidnapped by the psychotic killer known as Insect Boy. Some of the devices here are familiar (the brilliant maverick outfoxing the workaday efforts of the local police is, of course, a device patented by Conan Doyle), and the horrendous Insect Boy owes not a little to the most accomplished of serial killer writers, Thomas Harris. But Deaver is his own man, and brings a very individual strand to his quirky series of novels.

Recommended titles – Jeffrey Deaver
> The Devils Teardrop
> The Bone Collector
> *Key title* – The Empty Chair

Arthur Conan Doyle

By far the most influential and acclaimed writer to have worked within the crime genre, the creator of Baker Street's immortal Sherlock Holmes is a writer whose work has never been out of print since the nineteenth century, and remains as fervently loved by aficionados today as ever. Edgar Allen Poe may have created the first superrational detective in Auguste Dupin, but it was Doyle's refinement of the concept in his coolly brilliant Victorian sleuth that became the blueprint for so many subsequent characters (not least Christie's Poirot). Apart from the gaunt, charismatic Holmes (with such memorable traits as his violin playing and cocaine addiction), the inauguration of the narrator/companion in Watson may well have been Doyle's most canny invention. Through his chronicler's bemused eyes, we are treated to the astonishing displays of ratiocination that, however often they are parodied, never cease to afford immense pleasure. And in Professor Moriarty, Doyle created the definitive criminal mastermind – the cool, civilised confrontation between the two antagonists (far more like each other than either cares to admit) is as mesmerising as anything in literature. Having trained for a career in medicine, Doyle began to publish short stories in the *Strand* magazine from July 1891 onwards. His astonishing success led to *A Study in Scarlet* (1888), in which the great detective first appears. The novels, such as the much-filmed *Hound of the Baskervilles*, are remarkable, but it is the short stories which remain the key creations of this greatest of detective story writers. Towards the end of his life, Doyle (always keen to believe in the realities of spiritualism) was duped by the faked fairy photographs created by two schoolgirls – a gullibility that the brilliant Holmes would never have countenanced.

Recommended titles – Arthur Conan Doyle

The Adventures of Sherlock Holmes
The Memoirs of Sherlock Holmes
The Hound of the Baskervilles
The Sign of Four
Key title – His Last Bow

From Simon John...

I thought **Mark Campbell's** review of Jim William's Recherché was incredibly unfair. I felt that Mark was merely trying to 'pigeon-hole' the novel into a category that he felt safe reviewing and failed to recognise the novel for its intriguing and erudite existential qualities.

Of course Mark was **'reminded at times of John Fowles' *The Magus'*** as this is not only mentioned in the novel itself but also in *The Guardian*'s review (which can be found on the cover of the paperback). Indeed, most of Mark's review seems to 'rob the blurb' and 'prey upon the press release', leading me to believe that perhaps an in-depth read was sorely missing here.

Mark, in a literary environment of banality and mediocrity, please don't ask for writers to clasp to a genre (your final paragraph) and claim that matters are 'obvious'. Encourage and persevere.

And, for God's sake, read the end of the novel (again?) as the irony here is so pronounced that I wonder if Williams wouldn't laugh himself silly.

HOW I WROTE...

Top Scribes Tell Us How...

Foiled Again: **Peter Gutteridge**

Book titles, I love 'em. In fact for me I can't make much of a start on a novel until I've figured out the title. Not for me the apt quote from Shakespeare, though I do han-

Just don't mention the pelican...

ker to make use of the world's most unfeasible stage direction – "Enter the Persian Army" – from Christopher Marlowe's *Tamburlaine*. Give me a bad pun every time. I like the titles of all my books in the Nick Madrid/Bridget Frost satirical crime series but *Foiled Again*, the latest, is the first one to be a bad pun. The novel is, you guessed it, about fencing. (You have to imagine me miming a little swordplay when I write that word fencing, something I became conditioned to doing during my modest fencing career to head off the inevitable lousy gag from some wag about gardens and fence posts etc.) I'm embarrassed to say that skilled wordsmith that I am (ha!), I'll go a long way for a bad pun. In my second novel, *A Ghost of a Chance*, it's shaming to admit that I made one of the characters a short Greek man simply so I could have someone say "Beware of Greeks Wearing Lifts". And I've been patience personified trying to put together religious people and chilly weather so that I can write *Many are Cold but Few are Frozen*.

Whole Wide World: **Paul McAuley**

Inspiration for *Whole Wide World* (published by HarperCollins)? Not just Wreckless Eric's terrific tough and tender love song, but London, surveillance, Internet camera sites, and the problem of gaze. I've written about London before, in the near-future novel *Fairyland*, and I've used a variation of the chase-the-McGuffin thriller plot as a skeleton on which to hang the story of *Pasquale's Angel*, set in an alternate sixteenth century Florence transformed by the inventions of Leonardo da Vinci. But *Whole Wide World*, a police procedural set in London, is less fantastic and more particular than either. Although it's necessarily set just a few years in the future, it takes place mostly in the neighbourhood of Islington and Hackney where I settled. It's hotter, more hectic, and traffic is very much worse, but otherwise it's pretty much the London I've been exploring

ever since I moved here five years ago. One unmissable change I've noticed in those five years, the explosion in the number of surveillance cameras, was the seed for the novel. Walk or drive along any of London's main roads, and you'll see aluminium shoeboxes raised everywhere above the traffic. They festoon the exteriors of just about every office building; smaller cameras track you across lobbies and stare at you inside lifts; there are cameras installed on buses, in Tube stations, and, of course, cameras in just about every shop, from the multi-lensed flying saucers of the big supermarkets to astigmatic black and white Chinese knock-offs clinging above the doors of every off-license and every other corner shop. Their static, unedited gaze is exploited for tacky real-life clip shows, and invests the last moments of murderees with poignant significance. I've been using the Internet since 1991, and the same trend is evident in the proliferation of sites transmitting images from static cameras watching street corners, telephone booths, Scottish hillsides, coffee pots (yes, really, although the very first coffeecam, in Cambridge University, has now closed down) and, increasingly, the intimate lives of strangers. Tip in the RIP Act, face recognition software, dictionary computers that tirelessly scan electronic traffic for key words, employers monitoring employees' every key stroke, and you explode the notion of privacy. Up to this point, my novels have all fallen, more or less, into the science fiction genre, in which ideas and social trends are pushed to their extreme limits, but I wanted to explore and complicate the increasing transparency of the world in a more personal and particular way. I've read enough thrillers and noir novels to know that most fictional detectives have something of the voyeur in their psychological make-up. *Whole Wide World*, then, is about an online murder that isn't quite what it seems, and a detective who discovers that seeing isn't the same as understanding. It's also the first novel I've written in the first person. It was a technical necessity, allowing the reader to watch the story unfold through the eyes of a man who, because of vanity and desperation, doesn't grasp the significance of everything he sees, but I have to admit that it was also extremely seductive – an intimate form of voyeurism I'm very tempted to repeat.

The House of Dust: Paul Johnston

This is the fifth novel in my series set in 2020s Edinburgh, featuring investigator Quint Dalrymple. As anyone who writes a series knows, the challenge every time is to keep both writer and reader interested. In the previous book, *The Blood Tree*, Quint and his team spend over half the case out of independent, totalitarian Edinburgh – in the democratic paradise of Glasgow, would you believe? Having got our hero away from his home city once, I wanted to find another exotic setting for the fifth book. Let's face it, after you've done Edinburgh and Glasgow, you've covered quite a lot of Scotland – so I decided to be really daring and set the bulk of this one in Oxford. (Yes, there are references to D. L. Sayers, Colin Dexter and the like.) Apart from setting, ideas are what stimulate me during the writing process. The Quint novels all contain approaches to political and social issues (individual versus the state, genetic engineering, nuclear power, nationalism and so on). There are three main thematic concerns in *The House of*

PAUL
JOHNSTON

Winner of the Crime Writers' Association John Creasey Memorial Dagger

The House of Dust

'First-rate crime fiction with an original twist'
SUNDAY TELEGRAPH

Dust – imprisonment, education, and the artificial enhancement of humans (i.e. robotics). The action starts in Edinburgh where the Council of City Guardians is acting in its usual heavy-handed way and reopening a maximum security prison (earlier in the regime prisons had been done away with because crime no longer existed – ha!). But because of the guardians' lack of recent expertise, they've had to involve consultants from the university state of New Oxford in the planning process – and New Oxford turns out to be even more hardline than Edinburgh. Quint ends up in Oxford on the trail of a rogue killer. In the course of the investigation he sees the soft underbelly of a state that treats its citizens both as slaves and as guinea pigs in criminology research programmes. Needless to say, the university is the focus of the city, its research funded by multinational corporations. Students still go around in gowns, but their bicycles are gas-powered and they use mini-computers rather than books. If you can detect a satirical edge here, award yourself a first class degree. I've always found the tension between ideas and the technicalities of crime writing (plot, characterisation, motive and method etc.) very interesting. Creating and maintaining the right balance is tricky, but it's rewarding for readers as well as the author. Writers who underestimate their readers' intelligence should be banged up – as should those without a sense of humour.

Die Cast: Alan Dunn

I'd been writing for years. Mostly science fiction shorts published in friends' fanzines, the beginnings of a novel or two. Then I won second prize in the 1991 Ian St James Award with a vicious little murder story called *French Kisses*. At the awards ceremony I met an agent who asked to see what else I'd been writing. That something else was a part-finished historical novel set in the north-east, and it was duly published in 1993 as *The Collier and his Mistress*. So I was typecast, placed in a pigeon-hole with Catherine Cookson and others of that ilk, asked to produce more of the same. I did. It was called *The English Dancing Master*. Neither sold particularly well. But I was brought up on short fiction, the twist in the tale, and I found my gravitating naturally towards stories with an element of suspense, of mystery, and – almost inevitably – of crime. At the same time I was teaching creative writing night classes, and *Die Cast* began as a simple writing exercise. "Devise a character whose inner thoughts are demonstrated by his actions." And so was born the introverted, under-confident, neurotic ex-cop, ex-

drunk and ex-gambler, Billy Oliphant, a near bankrupt, a failed husband and father. He wasn't inclined to be cheerful – would you be? The setting? I'd been working for a double glazing company so decided to use that industry as the framework on which the story was built. The place? Rural Cumbria didn't seem quite right, so I fell back on my native Newcastle as the nameless city. Add drugs, arson, and a plot masquerading as a corkscrew, then see what happens. And that was what I did. I didn't have the luxury or the discipline of writing a commissioned novel; I was writing crime fiction but had no track record in that area; so I wrote for me. I wrote to please myself, and I wrote to keep my readers (that's my wife, my parents and my brother and sister) interested. And so the novel changed as I wrote it. I built in a few red herrings and, when I finished, I reread it and thought "that's quite good". I even enjoyed proof-reading it, and that's when you really become tired of your own writing, when you're rereading it for the sixth or seventh time. Piatkus said they'd publish, it's been kindly reviewed, and I've been commissioned to write another. It's called *Pay Back*, and in it Billy's as neurotic as ever. The plot? Forget corkscrews, think instead of the twists and turns of the Cresta Run. That might give you, if not the flavour, at least the temperature.

Autographs in the Rain: Quintin Jardine

Autographs in the Rain, the eleventh novel in the Bob Skinner crime series (Headline), is the concluding part of a loose trilogy built around the personal life of one of the chief supporting characters, DCC Bob Skinner's assistant Detective Inspector Neil McIlhenney. Parts of the book proved fairly difficult to create, while other sections virtually wrote themselves, as was the case with its two predecessors, *Gallery Whispers* and *Thursday Legends*. When one is involved with a long-running series, whatever the genre, the creative process is akin to spending time with old friends. If this sounds a little sentimental, it isn't. One of the first pieces of advice given me by my former agent was not to give up my day job. "Your work fuels your writing", she told me. While this advice was offered sincerely, I know now that it was a gross understatement. One's total experience fuels one's work, and influences what happens to one's characters, for good or ill... especially ill. If I met Neil McIlhenney in my local (improbable, even allowing for the fact that he's a fictional character, since he doesn't drink any more) he'd be unlikely to thank me for some of the things I've visited upon him. Tough luck, Neil; if you had a birth certificate like the rest of us, you wouldn't find any warranties or guarantees on the back. These three novels have been something of a watershed in the Skinner series; they're allowed me to stand back from the central character and develop other players. They've also given me room to look more objectively at Deputy Chief Constable Skinner himself, to give some thought to his career options, and perhaps to look more cynically at his personal relationships. Having spent eleven books building up his strengths, and establishing him as someone radically different from the stereotypical flawed middle-ranking detective, perhaps it's time to explore his weaknesses. When I want to get away from the telephone to work on a new book, I head for L'Escala in Spain. The place has a special significance for me; I started to write there, and even now, going on for fifteen years along the road, it's still my favourite creative environment. That's where most of *Autographs in the Rain* was written. I return there next week, to work on *Head Shot*, the twelfth Skinner novel.

The Bad Fire: Campbell Armstrong

All my career I've had one overwhelming obsession, the desire to write a novel set in my native city, Glasgow. I've lived away from the city for my entire adult life, so I had to go back to get all kinds of detail correct when it came to writing *The Bad Fire* (HarperCollins). I walked the city, and it was like strolling a haunted place, everything had changed, old friends had vanished from the phone book (casualties? absentees? where had they gone?). There were no familiar faces on the streets. The city, which I'd always remembered as dark, has been cleaned up and restored to its Victorian grandeur. The tenements, refurbished and scrubbed, have shed the standard black colour I was used to as a kid – they are pink, red, honey, ginger, so that on a sunny night certain parts of Glasgow emit a quality that is almost Mediterranean. It's not all terrific, of course. The housing schemes that ring the city are sometimes sad wastelands where the drug culture functions openly, and there is bleakness in abundance. Some of the old neighbourhoods close to the city centre are also badly rundown. Against this background, I set my story – an exile returns to Glasgow from the US to attend the funeral of his father, and gets caught up in a murderous situation, old crimes and family secrets. *The Bad Fire* isn't an upbeat suspense novel, but it's populated with characters that

I hope are as colourful and as idiosyncratic as Glasgow itself, and a mystery as complex as the heart of this vibrant, varied place.

The Singing Dead: Ron Ellis

On the evening of January 23 1963, after finishing a BBC recording session, The Beatles were driving up from London to play top spot at Liverpool's famous Cavern Club, when the windscreen of their transit van shattered. This gave me the idea of a plot for my new Johnny Ace book, *The Singing Dead*. Freddie Starr & The Midnighters were also on the bill that night but, as The Fab Four were late, I invented another group who would fill in the extra time, Bobby & The Voxtones. Bobby, being a car mechanic by day, offers to replace the said windscreen and comes across a reel to reel tape in the van's glove compartment, containing unheard songs performed by John Lennon with acoustic guitar. Bobby steals the tape, hoping it might be worth something one day. Now, nearly forty years later, he's ready to cash in on his find but he soon finds people are prepared to kill to get hold of a now highly valuable item. The plot was perfectly suited to the Johnny Ace series. Obviously, The Beatles connection would strike a chord with many potential readers, whilst the Merseybeat era of the 1960s has a unique place in the nostalgia calendar. But it is also a quintessentially Liverpool novel and that is what Johnny Ace is all about – the city of Liverpool. *The Singing Dead* is the fourth Johnny Ace book and many of the characters reappear as the series progresses. We have Tommy McKale, gangster friend of Johnny who owns the notorious Masquerade Club, where social deviants, prostitutes and racketeers are among the clientele packing the illuminated dance floor. The barman, Vince, is six foot four, sports designer stubble and pierced nipples, doubles as a ferocious bouncer, likes Noel Coward music and hopes to marry his friend Rupert. Then there is the dreadlocked Neville 'Badger' Mountbatten who has a degree in English Poetry, a Porsche and an undisclosed source of income; Johnny's partner, ex-DI Jim Burrows, who used to play bass in The Chocolate Lavatory in 1961 and wants to reform the band despite his angina; and middle-aged spinster Pat Lake, one of Johnny's tenants (he is also a landlord), who likes heavy metal music and sports a tattoo.

Johnny being a radio DJ means that music is always to the fore, both in the records Johnny plays and the fact that Liverpool is very much a city of musicians and entertainers. But there is also a controversial political agenda there as well. To the horror of Johnny's producer, Ken (Ågleather patches on his jacket and he's only twenty-nine!Åh), his on-the-edge phone-in show has listeners voicing outrageous ideas on the air like should the public pay to stone Dr Harold Shipman to death, a pound a stone, money to his victims' relatives. In the third book, *Framed*, Johnny acquires a new companion, a rascally brown mongrel called Roly whose saving grace is an irresistible smile. Judging by reactions from readers, he's come to stay. One of the features of the Johnny Ace series is the number of real life people who appear in the books as themselves with, as it were, speaking parts. There really is a café in the city centre called Lucy in the Sky (in Cavern Walks) run by the same lady called

Margie who chats to Johnny Ace. Spencer Leigh and Billy Butler are both presenters on BBC Radio Merseyside and, if you go along to the Plaza Cinema in Crosby, you are really are quite likely to see Jan Dunn in the paybox. Her husband, Rob, is the local vet who is called to Roly's aid in 'The Singing Dead. The Everton fanzine, *When Skies Are Grey*, regularly reviews the books but then, after all, it is always mentioned in them along with Johnny's comments on the club's progress (or lack of it!) in the Premiership. Unlike many crime novels of today, which seem to verge on the dour or gruesome, there is a lot of humour in the Johnny Ace books. Tommy McKale's eighty-four-year-old granny, Dolly, guards the door of his club and worries if the Queen Mother has the same trouble she does with her thong riding up her bottom. There is also romance. Of a sort. Johnny has two girlfriends, the long standing Hilary (blonde, bouncy and sexy) and the more recently acquired and ravishing Maria, who looks like Cher but who wants to settle down, something not on Johnny's agenda. So he is left to keep the two of them happy like a man juggling with a hand grenade, though he can always find solace in Shirley who looks like Mary Wilson of The Supremes. Which one will he end up with?

If I had to compare Johnny Ace to any current fictional hero, I'd put him as more like Lovejoy or Minder than Morse or Sharman. Yet, despite his sociability, he is still very much a loner. He has that quality of the outsider in him that can be found in Marlowe, Rebus and other noir heroes. One other controversial thing about *The Singing Dead*: at the time I was thinking about a secondary plot, a young Southport mother called Lynsey Quy had gone missing and Åg'Have you seen this woman?'Åh posters had gone up all over town. The police dug up the family garden and made it obvious they thought the husband had killed her and I got to thinking, Åg'What if he hadn't done it? To whom would he turn to help find her and so prove his innocence?'Åh Answer – a private eye like Johnny Ace. So, I had my other thread to the story and, to give a bit of publicity to my home town resort, I even had the police digging for the body under Southport's new roller coaster, The Traumatizer. But then, nearly eighteen months later, just as the hardback came out, the missing girl's body was found – in pieces- and her torso was buried near to the Cyclone, Southport's other roller coaster! In January, the husband was sentenced at Liverpool Crown Court to life imprisonment for her murder. Needless to say, in my book, the plot takes a totally different turn, but you can imagine the publicity locally on publication day as people made the connection. The next Johnny Ace book, *Grave Mistake*, is due from Headline in October. In this book, Johnny is asked to rescue a kidnapped girl abducted from Tesco's car park but things go wrong. He is also helping trace a missing footballer, last seen playing in goal for Wavertree Corinthians in 1979. The idea came from the Tony Martin case and the right of people to defend their homes and property. All the usual characters are back; there is music, football, romance and excitement plus a cameo appearance of my other series character, DCI Glass of Scotland Yard. And, of course, Roly!

The Noir Thriller: Lee Horsley

I first thought of writing *The Noir Thriller* when I was working on an article about Ellroy's *LA Quartet*. The label 'noir' was unavoidable, but I could find very little criticism that wasn't mainly focused on cinematic noir, often presenting it as a narrowly time-bound phenomenon (canonical films noirs, starting with *Maltese Falcon*, ending with *Touch of Evil*). I decided that a wide-ranging survey might make possible a broader understanding of twentieth century British and American literary noir – of its contexts, techniques, themes and protagonists (private eyes, transgressors and victims, strangers and outcasts, tough women and sociable psychopaths). Looking for both constant elements and changing patterns, I took the Black Mask boys as my starting point and ended with the 'future noir' of *Blade Runner* and cyberpunk. The research for the book involved some detection as well as criminally enjoyable months of reading pulp fiction. Since I was trying to cast my net as widely as possibly, I wanted to draw in many (getting on for two hundred) novels not currently in print. This meant a long period of hunting for old editions – searching out British dealers in second-hand and vintage paperbacks, attending London's paperback book fairs and making regular visits to Murder One. Each hunt was followed by the pleasure of reading battered copies of, say, Charles Williams, early Charles Willeford, David Goodis, Leigh Brackett, Margaret Millar and Harry Whittington, alongside Black Lizard reissues of Jim Thompson or the Payback Press volumes of Chester Himes' Harlem cycle. It would be nice to think that *The Noir Thriller*, when it eventu-ally emerges in paperback, might provide other readers with a rough guide for their own explorations of literary noir.

Dangerous Data: Lury & Gibson

True Crime? It's Just a Matter of Looking: Arthur C. Dogg

I'm going to let you into a secret. We can all be detectives now. Me, I'm a professional data detective. I work for clients who pay me to track down people. But the tools I use are open to everyone. All you need is a computer, a modem, a link to the Internet and a willingness to invest your time – which, after all, is a precious commodity. With these few tools you can track down just about anything you want to. You can find out about those cranky neighbours of yours; check out on an old girl- or boyfriend; or simply go after a bad guy. True crime is out there; all you need to do is start looking. All of this is possible thanks to our friends who built the Internet. The net isn't just some huge encyclopaedia. It links computers everywhere. And these computers want to talk to one another, share information. Or, as I say, "Information wants to be free". And there's a lot of it to free up: vast amounts of data on you, me and everyone. Just about everything you do is getting stored on a database somewhere: the phone calls you make, your credit card payments, your loyalty cards and your magazine subscriptions, your medical records – it's all there ready and waiting. Your personal life is held on databases that exist to talk to other databases; explosive combination huh? Too right. All the facts that a conventional detective spent hours on the trail uncovering, you can know from the comfort of your own front room. You can start right now, piecing the patterns of behaviour together; closing in on your quarry. You can pick your own subject and simply follow the leads. You could choose anyone – because if we're all detectives, we can all be suspects too. And you'll be amazed at what you'll find.

But before you get too carried away, do you really want to be a detective? The hours are long and the pay's not good, but that isn't what I'm talking about. I mean have you got the attitude? What do think about privacy for example? How valid is a notion like privacy in a world of integrated networks and instant communications? Here in Britain we have the Data Protection Act to safeguard our personal data. But they don't have the same law in the US or in many other countries. And since the World Wide Web is a global kind of thing, what use is a protection in one country when you can go to another faster than you can say Yahoo! And there are also good reasons why personal information should be made public. If you like reading crime stories you'll know that detectives are the good guys because they find out whodunit. They go on and on until they find out that little personal fact that fingers the criminal. The basic premise in any detective story is that getting the facts out into the open protects society. So a true detective doesn't get squeamish about privacy. He or she goes after the facts like there's no tomorrow – which of course there isn't for the bad guys. But not everyone is tough enough to think like this. Most people want privacy to work both ways: they want some facts to be made public, but not all of them. They tell you they should know if a paedophile lives next door to them, or an axe murderer or a member of some fanatic political party. But they don't want their own details to be made available. That's wrong, they say. "Imagine what might happen if someone unscrupulous got hold of my personal details, and sold them on! I could be going out for a date and the person I'm meeting for the first time could everything about me, right down to my medical records." (Yeh just imagine! Well it's happening right now!) These people want protection for themselves (privacy), but they also want protection from others (knowledge of those around us). The true detective doesn't worry about protection for himself – he says, "Welcome to the end of privacy". The knowledge that comes with the 'end of privacy' can only be tolerated by those with nerves of steel. Knowing things about other people is what gives detectives nightmares and turns them to drink. You have to be tough to know secrets. And you have to be tough to handle the addiction: you'll want to know more and more. So before you go on with quest to be a detective, ask yourself the big question: "How much do you want to know?" Only the true detective can answer this question and cope with all its consequences. If you are one of these few, then you have the right stuff. You can be a data detective. As a data detective you'll be able to go anywhere and find out anything and no-one need ever know you're tracking them. You do it all on-line. You assemble your own story from the facts. You can even try out what it's like to be other people, by 'borrowing' their data. All this is open to you. The facts of the case are there, just waiting for you to piece them together. Read my story *Dangerous Data* and it'll show you every move and every trick. And what if you find a crime? A true crime? If the data tells you so, then you'd better believe it.

The Chinese Girl: John Baker

I'd already written and published four Sam Turner novels and although they proved to be adequate vehicles for what I had to say there was still a niggling feeling that I would like to do something different. As a central character Sam Turner was suitably gnarled and worldly wise and a great mouthpiece for that healthy cynicism that allows us to co-exist with some of the worst excesses of our 'advanced' political system. But he lacked the dynamism and innocence of youth and for the novel that was slowly forming in my head I would need a character who would have both of these qualities. I wanted to write about masks, about their necessity and about how we construct and use them not only to hide behind but to project different facets of our character. The prison tattoos

THE CHINESE GIRL

'One of Britain's most

talented contemporary

crime writers'

THE TIMES

John

BAKER

on stone Lewis' face are of course a mask, but as they are slowly removed he comes to realise that they are only one skin of the onion. The Chinese girl herself uses her pancake makeup as a mask, feeling naked when she is discovered without it. The two of them together, and all of the other characters in the novel in their different ways, wear their masks to conceal identity and to proclaim it at one and the same time. So much for theme. What I also wanted to do was to see what happens when you come home one evening and find something exotic and beautiful and vulnerable and totally unexpected waiting for you. How do we activate and maintain our responsibilities for each other? And when the acceptance of those responsibilities means facing up to the evil in the world, how do we cope with that? Especially when that evil is manifest not only in the world that is external to us but when we come to perceive it as an integral part of our own lives. This was important for me, to try to distance myself from the concept of dualism. To dispel in some way the idea that there are good guys and bad guys and that the world would be a better place if we got rid of the bad guys. Life isn't that simple and books that suggest that it is don't really do us a service. Thirdly I wanted to experiment with the narrative by using an epistolary form for at least part of the novel. In the first draft the letters section was much longer. I cut it reluctantly because it was by far the best written section, but with hindsight it was a necessary sacrifice. *The Chinese Girl* wasn't an easy novel to write and in many ways it was good to get back to grips with Sam Turner and the crew in the next novel (*Shooting in the Dark*, Orion). But we haven't heard the last of Stone Lewis and his friends. They are scheduled to return in a second novel in the series (*White Skin Man*, Orion) next year.

The Month of the Leopard: James Harland

The forests outside Tartu, in the far north east of Europe just inside the Estonian-Russian border, are a place of pristine silence. Huge pine trees dominate the soft, rolling landscape, the distinctive, pungent fragrance of their needles filling your nostrils as you walk amongst their sturdy, ancient trunks. The scent of pine is instantly recognisable, although mostly in its manufactured, chemical form: it is used most heavily by the manufacturers of soap – washing up liquids, detergents, air fresheners and toilet cleaners all come in pine-scented formulas. That tells you something about pine – it is a good perfume for covering up nasty smells. That struck me as I walked through the Estonia forests, researching the history and geography of the area for my new book *The Month of the Leopard* (Simon & Schuster). If you wanted to bury something nasty, this would be the place to do it. There was no shortage of things to choose from. Estonia is one of those small, forgotten countries that emerged blinking like new-born puppies from the collapse of the old Soviet Union. We probably once knew more about it than we do now. Close to the docks of its capital Tallinn, there is a small, obscure monument to five British sailors killed in action in Estonia. They had been sent there to fight in the civil war that followed the Russian Revolution: hard to imagine British sailors sacrificing their lives for the freedom of the Estonian people anymore, which shows how much narrower our outlook has become and how slender our obligations to the rest of the world. What had drawn me to Estonia was the story of the *metsavennad*, the woodsman. The Cold War, like any war, has lots of forgotten stories, but the story of the *metsavennad* struck me as one that combined heroism and tragedy in equal measure. Estonia, which is only as far from St Petersburg as Edinburgh is from London, had been drawn into the Russian Empire by Peter the Great. Between the wars it had briefly been liberated from Russian control. When Russian rule was reimposed by the Red Army, thousands of young Estonian men fled to the forests that dominate their country. For thirty years, they fought a bitter civil war against the Red Army. It was not until 1978 that the last of their warriors, August Sabe, was killed by Russian soldiers whilst attempting to escape across one of the lakes that mark the Russian/Estonian border. It was a futile, hopeless struggle, of course: the West would not support them, and without foreign support they had no hope of ever liberating their country. Yet it was also heroic. These were men who preferred to burn up their lives in a useless battle than accept the enslavement of their country. It struck me that there might be something in their legacy that would make an interesting story with resonance for an audience today.

The inspiration for *The Month of the Leopard* came from a variety of different sources. The story brings together lots of different themes, in a way which, I hope, is exiting and challenging, and allows us to look at the recent history of Europe in a slightly different way. The fun of writing a thriller – and a conspiracy thriller in particular – is that you can take a whole group of things that interest you, and tie them all together into one story. Thrillers, at least the good ones, are about making connections. I started taking notice of hedge funds after George Soros forced the pound out of the European exchange rate mechanism in 1992; that seemed to me to be a lot of power to put in the hands of one eccentric individual. I became more interested after an American fund called Long Term Capital Management crashed in 1998 with debts of one trillion dollars. For a few weeks that fund seemed capable of plunging the world into the kind of recession it hasn't seen since the 1930s. I was fascinated by all the money that leaked out of the Soviet Union before that regime collapsed. Two years ago, reports surfaced of Red Army accounts in the Channel Islands. It seemed likely to me that what had been made public was probably just the tip of a very large iceberg. I was interested as well in the way that many of today's leading politicians had backgrounds in the radical, extreme student politics of the 1960s. Look at Lionel Jospin, the French Prime Minister, who has been forced to admit that he belonged to an extreme Trotskyite sect as a student. Or Joschka Fischer, the German foreign minister, who's involvement (even if it was tangential and accidental) with the extreme German left wing groups of the 1960s and 1970s was revealed in the trial last year of one of his old comrades. Those were strange times, no doubt. But I was intrigued how many of those former radicals had gone on to hold senior positions in government, in industry and in finance.

What debts might they still owe to their past? Then I was intrigued in what might happen to a guy whose wife vanished, then turned out to be a completely different person from the woman he thought he married. How would he react? What would he do? Try to forget her, or try to find her? *The Month of the Leopard* is really about historical baggage, how the past is always with us. That story is told through Tom Bracewell, an economist at a London bank, who comes home one day to find his Estonian wife Tatyana has vanished. It is also told through Jean-Pierre Telmont, a fantastically wealthy, powerful, forceful and corrupt financier who is bent upon destroying the economies of Eastern Europe. But it is told most forcefully through Tatyana, a woman who finds the past is something she cannot escape. Her attempt to shed an old skin for a new one is the central story of the book: an attempt that, in the story, provokes calamity for herself, for those she loves, and triggers a meltdown in the financial markets.

Pay Days: **Bill James**

All of my Harpur and Iles books are 'grey area' stories – police and criminals occupy very much the same world and at least in part share some views. That doesn't mean either Harpur or Iles is bent. They don't take money, but they do stray from the strict rules of policing occasionally – more than occasionally, especially Iles. I wanted to place this kind of behaviour in a wider context than I have tried before, and brought in the political aspect – itself quite a grey area as far as morality and ethics are concerned. *Pay Days* is published by Constable and Robinson.

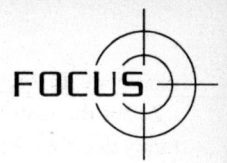

PERISHING TWICE WITH ROBERT B. PARKER

I haven't much to say about my most recent book, *Perish Twice*, which No Exit Press are publishing in the UK, except that it is really good, and currently for sale (with a dandy picture of me on the back).

As for influences, I suppose Raymond Chandler would be the most telling. Though in my formative years I read a ton of pulp magazines (*Black Mask, Dime Detective*, etc.). I am currently rereading all of Rex Stout and liking it very much (again). On the other hand I have a PhD in English Language and Literature and was, among many other things, a professor of English, and have in the service of those conditions probably read everything since the invention of moveable type. Surely Hemingway and Faulkner and Scott Fitzgerald have seeped in, too.

I have no unpublished work. The first thing I wrote, *Godwulf Manuscript*, was published by the first publisher I sent it to.

I know that's annoying, but what can I do?

As for my peers (if any), I never miss Elmore Leonard. Other than that I don't read much fiction any more. I tend to look at it like carpenters look at houses and it distracts me. I read some non-fiction. I recently read Jonathan Lear's *Open Minded* (Freud and the classical philosophers), and am currently reading *Rembrandt's Eyes* by Simon Schama. I don't understand any of it, of course, but it makes for such a good answer to the what-are-you-reading-these-days question.

The issue of violence rears endlessly. I have no approach to it. I have no problem with it. I pay no attention to it. I don't think about how much, how little, how graphic, etc. I think only of making my story in the best way I can, which may, or may not, require violence. And may, or may not, require a lot, or a little. I do not very much attend to the monkey see, monkey do, theory of literary influence.

As for the matter of sexuality. Again, I simply don't think that way. I guess in life I would come down firmly in favour of it. In the practice of story telling I use the amount necessary to make the novel good. As a practical matter, it is very difficult to depict sex graphically without sounding dopey, so I tend toward the "they embraced the next morning" approach.

Having covered violence and sex, I turn to politics. My political credo is "don't vote – it just encourages them". I have no political agenda in my writing, but since my writing is the result of experience filtered through imagination I assume it is not devoid of attitude. How the reader reacts to that attitude, would, I assume, depend on his own attitudes. This, it seems to me has always been so, and to that extent all writing is, and always has been, political as opposed to apolitical.

To accomplish all this magic, I write five pages a day, every day, on a word processor. The pages are adjusted to be about one-to-one with the final printed page so that a 300 page manuscript will produce a 300 page book more or less. I revise in process. But what I have at the end of the day is, essentially, what you see in the book. I don't do a second draft. I normally work at an office in my home from maybe 9.30 to maybe 2.30. First I do five pages on the current novel. Then, normally after lunch, I work on the current other project (most usually a screenplay, usually with Joan). Then I take a nap, go to the gym, and the day is done. I feed Pearl, eat supper, and watch baseball. Once a year I do a book tour. Fifteen cities in thirty days. And for maybe a week or more each year I am on

location with whatever film we're making (the last one was *Walking Shadow*, which we shot in Vancouver, and which aired in the USA on A&E cable). I do a read through with the cast and director, shoot my cameo (in *Walking Shadow* I play a janitor, and brilliantly), eat some donuts and come home.

I am often asked the principal appeal of the fiction I write. I have always contended that it is my picture on the back, but if that answer isn't satisfactory, I suppose one might argue that I present in relatively linear and comprehensible fashion a world in which a protagonist finds love and is not defeated. Modesty forbids that I comment on how well I do that. But were that same world presented by someone else it might not be as appealing.

I am not particularly au fait with film (though I very much enjoyed *Shane*). On the other hand, one cannot be writing now without having film's narrative techniques imposed on one's consciousness (montage, lap dissolves, etc. etc.). Music is very much a factor however. The writing of prose seems to me very much akin to the writing of music (which I don't know how to do), but I seem to choose one combination of words rather than another on the basis of how it sounds. And I like books partly because they sound good. And I dislike books partly because they sound bad. Simon Schama, for instance, sounds terrific. And so does Elmore Leonard.

I suppose I have imagined the central characters before I conjure a plot. In fact I don't outline, or plot ahead. I start with the simplest of story ideas (Spenser and a group of associates from past novels go west and tame a town – *Potshot*) and begin. When I write the first page, I don't know what the second page will say. Or how the book will end, or what I'm going to write tomorrow. This is hard on the psyche unless you are confident, but I've written about forty books, all of them published, so I assume that probably I can do another one. For the new writer, however, an outline might be comforting. Of course a distinction between plot and character is, finally, an artificial distinction. Henry James once said (something like) what is plot but the illustration of character. What is character but the determinant of plot?

I live in Boston, so I find it easier to write about Boston, and I'm more comfortable there because I have lived there for more than fifty years. That said, there is no place where creative juices flow or don't flow. Indeed if one is a professional writer one probably shouldn't spend too much time waiting for the creative juices. They start to flow when they are called upon. Indeed, I suspect, one reason people are writers is because they flow all the time anyway. You're not, probably, creative because you write. You write, probably, because you're creative, willy nilly.

I am perfectly happy with my publisher and editor. I think they treat me kindly, pay me appropriately, market the books well. I like the people at Penguin Putnam Inc. I don't get a lot of editing (mostly it's the copy editor who cleans up after me), but what I get is intelligent and I like my editor personally, too.

I don't think about the reader when I write. Or the editor, or the movie deal, or the advance, or even my picture on the back. I am simply focused on making this story, and getting it right: the only question I ask is, is it any good?. Once I'm done

and it's being published, then it becomes product, and all future questions are rooted in economic gain.

I have no idea about the current state of literacy. I think that the transfer of image and information can take place in a variety of ways, and as long as it does take place, I'm not sure I know if the particular medium matters. In the same vein, I think a writer, within the limits of temperament, should be what he or she needs to be in order to do his or her work. I also suspect that what a writer is would be connected to what the person is. So the world and monastic isolation are equally acceptable as a condition for writers.

In the same way I don't think religious conviction matters in literary terms. If you are religious it will affect your writing. If you are not, it will affect your writing. You write out of yourself, and don't have much choice in that. I see no harm in religion.

I have touched on my feelings about the commercial aspects of writing above, but I think it is fair to say that if no one would pay me, I would have to do something else. The world of non-commercial publishing (i.e. vanity press and academic publication) does not seem to produce better writing. As you doubtless recall, Dr Johnson once said something to the effect that only a block head, sir, writes for anything but money.

And, finally, I am on page 200, today, of the next book about Spenser, which is called *Widow's Walk*, and will be published in USA next spring. It's grand.

Robert B. Parker's Perish Twice *is published in the UK by No Exit Press.*

PICK OF THE PUBLISHERS

Brian Ritterspak

An occasional look at publishers with a particular commitment to crime fiction: this issue: No Exit Press.

KC CONSTANTINE

From Chandler onwards, the calling card of top practitioners in the crime genre has been razor-sharp dialogue. But few have handled it as well as Constantine, whose *Blood Mud* is the latest in a prestigious – and highly enjoyable – series featuring Mario Balzic, retired police chief of Rocksburg, Pennsylvania. Balzic is hired by an old friend to track down the arsenal stolen from a gun shop. Irresistible stuff.

SPARKLE HAYTER

Her admirers know that Sparkle Hayter's brand of sassy humour and quirkily inventive characterisation is quite unique in the field. *The Chelsea Girl Murders* could be the book that makes many more readers aware of what a phenomenally entertaining writer she is. Sardonic TV newswoman Robin Hudson braves guerrilla artists, brooding poets, art forgers and various other larger-than-life characters to sort out the truth behind an apparent suicide.

GEORGE V. HIGGINS

All the more cherishable for being the final book of one of the greatest talents the genre has ever known, *The Agent* is not entirely typical of the protean talents of its author, but this tale of skulduggery in the world of American sports still has all the Higgins fingerprints: brilliantly observed dialogue, ruthlessly pared-down descriptive prose and plotting quite unlike anything else in crime fiction.

MARK TIMLIN

Unassailable in his position as the king of the British hard-boiled thriller, Timlin's battered sleuth Nick Sharman encounters even more bloody mayhem than usual in *All the Empty Places*, one of the most seductively nasty entries in a highly consistent series. Once again, Timlin pulls off the nigh-impossible: transplanting a jaded Chandlerian sensibility into the mean streets of East London. Robbery with violence, sexual betrayal and a grisly climax in a tunnel: Timlin enthusiasts could ask for no more.

FRED WILLARD

Always tricky to bring off, the comedy thriller is the most fraught of genres. For anyone but Willard, that is – and *Princess Naughty and the Voodoo Cadillac* is vintage stuff, with the same kind of acidic wit and high octane narrative that marked out *Down on Ponce* as one of the finest hard-boiled début novels. The usual Dickensian monikers (Ginger Loudermilk, Peanut Shoke) decorate a dazzling tale of deception, torture and sudden death.

Brian Ritterspak

"Richly atmospheric, haunting, utterly compelling, the Lew Griffin novels are magnificent."
– Frances McDormand

JAMES SALLIS GHOST OF A FLEA

£14.99
ISBN: 1 84243 041 6
www.noexit.co.uk

SALLY EMERSON

The hero of my latest novel *Broken Bodies* (Little, Brown) is a young American historian who body-guards in his spare time. The heroine is a rival, a more established young British historian involved with a man who deals in stolen art treasures. The novel is in part about their fight to discover, through the diaries of Lord Elgin's wife, the where-abouts of a hugely valuable missing part of the Elgin Marbles (the statues Elgin took from the Parthenon in Athens in the early 1800s). The dealer badly wants it for all the wrong reasons.

I want the readers to be gripped from the beginning, be in a magical and unique world as they read, and be startled and sat-isfied by the end. I think every writer writes what he or she wishes to read; we all try to produce our own ideal book. For me it is a book which is short and power-ful and expands in the mind after its fin-ished. The influences on my work include the writing of Hans Christian Anderson –

in particular a powerfully macabre and dramatic collection I have illustrated by Helen Stratton – the work of Borges, espe-cially the stories in *Labyrinths*, with their

Sally Emerson

BROKEN
BODIES

From the author of HEAT

Sally Emerson writes like a dangerous angel
DOUGLAS ADAMS

sense of mystery, of something terrifying beneath the surface. Muriel Spark is a great writer, and one of my favourite books is her *Memento Mori*. Raymond Chandler, too, has that sense of wickedness and intense pleasure in words. If you close a book and stop thinking about it, then the writer has failed. I want to read and write books which I'm still thinking about days later, weeks later, ideally even years later. Sometimes it's a rawness which makes a book powerful, and I am often drawn to first novels for that reason – Truman Capote's *Other Voices, Other Rooms*, Joyce's *Portrait of the Artist as a Young Man*. Maybe they lack the accomplished, sandpapered quality of later works but there's an exuberance, a sense of amazement, and of course all childhood and adolescence is funnelled into the paragraphs. Though of course it's not a first novel, I love the rawness of Graham Greene's *The End of the Affair* too; it has an anger, and sense of incompleteness.

I have no problem with a certain level of violence. In my novel *Separation* a child kills the stepmother she hates. In *Fire Child* the heroine kills the man she hates by making love to him again and again and again. There is violence, and arson. *Heat* ends with a violent rape and a shooting. When I read a novel I want things to happen – I don't want the story to melt away. After all, these are stories. We don't read newspapers for bland nothings. We want action, energy. But I haven't read *Silence of the Lambs*. I don't want my mind to be *changed* by extreme violence and cruelty. As for sexuality, I was always infuriated by books which took you to the brink then drew a polite veil. The great thing about

novels is that they allow you into private worlds, and they should do, they help to make individuals feel less alone and to understand themselves better. I want to know how people behave, how these characters behave in bed. I don't want to know who put what where exactly – but I want such scenes to be sexy, and I certainly intend my novels to be sexy.

My next novel deals with politics to some extent, in that the heroine's husband is a politican. I am interested in power, its uses and abuses, but not in the minute details of politics. In *Heat* there was a political background partly because it was set in Washington DC.

My bodyclock is not well designed for the life of a writer. I should like to wake up briskly, write for three hours like Graham Greene used to do, then play tennis in the afternoon and be out all evening, However, I tend to prowl round in the day and my most creative times are the evening and the night. I find the night magic, always have. There's a banality about the day – all that bright lighting. I can't understand how people can write a word. While I work I play loud music, the type of music depending on the scene I'm writing or the stage the book is at. The right music gives me the rush of adrenaline, or anyway the rush, I used to get when I took the first cigarette of the day. Richard Thompson's music is my favourite creative surge-music at present. It has an erotic energy and danger about it, which is what I hope my novels have at their best.

I find I like writing on a computer less and less, which is exasperation. I don't find that direct relationship between my mind, the pen and the paper that I have when writing long hand. There's a magical quality to each fountain pen I use. At the moment my favourite pen is a gold Cross pen, but it could just as well be a cheap child's Parker with a top from another pen. When I write good scenes with one pen I get suspicious about it – like a dress that always brings the wearer a good time – and won't write with any other for a while, until the spell gets broken. I like different inks too – brown and purple and blue – and the way my writing changes as the scene gets exciting. Whereas on a computer the words all look so formal and polished and identical without the drunken quality of handwriting. It's all part of the alchemy of writing.

The principle appeal of my fiction is I think its tightness, its pleasure in words, and I hope its originality. A review of my new novel in *Publishing News* called it "mysterious, compelling and strangely erotic – clever mixture of thriller and passionate love story which holds the reader spellbound."

Films do influence me but more in their technique than their subject matter. The fast frames of films are reflected to some extent in my use of short chapters in *Broken Bodies*. Although writers probably are aware of what is being watched, what is in the air, there is an argument which says that the writer should be beyond that. Some of the best books are written by those who just go ahead and write without worrying about what's going on elsewhere; the Brontes were not exactly au courant with the latest fads of London. My books all come out of a central image that comes to me first. In the case of *Broken Bodies* it's of the hero and heroine standing in front of the Elgin Marbles. The plot and characters come afterwards. First comes the image, then the mood, then the characters and plot together, as though they are tangled up with each other from the beginning. Very strongly drawn characters can in some novels, though not in mine, almost take the place of plot. Capote's *Breakfast at Tiffany's* is an example; Holly is such a fascinating character you hardly need a coherent plot.

The sea inspires me, but cities do too. Certainly London and Paris. But Washington DC especially interests me, and I wrote *Heat* based there after I lived there with my family in the early 1990s. The place is a living parable, a mixture of comfortable, suburban living on the outside and an underworld of natural life, vast insects and racoons, and of areas that are a wasteland because of crack. It isn't at all what it seems at first, like a book which at first you think is one thing but it turns out to be something quite different, like *Memento Mori* or the stories in *Labyrinths* or some of the Father Brown stories, which have another dimension. Some of the greatest books hanker after some kind of greater, almost religious, understanding, even if in Jane Austen maybe it's the pleasure in human beings, the comedy and warmth of living. Of course many writers write in order to create something lasting in an unstable world, a way of trying to dam up time, your time. And of course they write because they like it, they like the security of entering daily into an imagined world. When a book is finished, it is devastating to lose that world. That's why we start all over again.

Sally Emerson

NO EXIT PRESS

ROBBERS

Christopher Cook

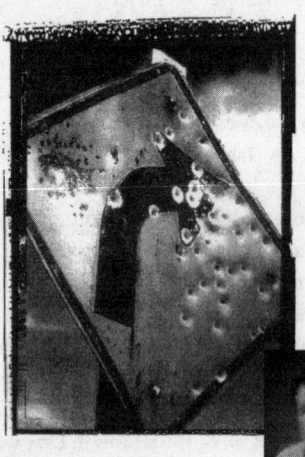

Two aimless Texas drifters, Ray Bob and Eddie, find themselves on the run after an impulsive act of violence escalates into more. They are joined by Della, a young working class woman who's had to leave town when a casual pick-up in a hotel bar has unexpected and lethal consequences. The trio are pursued by Rule Hooks, a Texas Ranger who follows his own lonely code, and breaks it.

In this fast-moving southern noir that marries poetry to action, the story flows over terrain from the Texas hill country through coastal swamps into the lush East Texas riverbottoms as each flawed character seeks his own secret redemption. *Robbers* is a literary thriller of the first water.

ISBN: 1-84243-016-5 £6.99 Paperback 400pp

TONY STRONG
DECOYS AND DECEPTIONS

Mark Campbell

Tony Strong was educated at Winchester and Oxford and went straight into the advertising business. Writing in his spare time, he produced the chilling psycho-frightener The Poison Tree in 1997 ("A début to die for," said Marcel Berlins of The Times). He followed it with the equally well received The Death Pit. Now he's taking the reader on another nightmare journey with The Decoy, a book that scales the heights of the thriller genre in its graphic tale of an actress hired as a decoy to a killer. I spoke to him recently about his books and just what it is that makes them so successful.

What made you want to write psychological thrillers?
Well, the biggest influence was probably Ian McEwan, because his short stories showed that evil, obsessive people are actually just like the rest of us, only a bit more so. Then there's people like Thomas Harris, for showing that serial killers can turn the traditional murder mystery into

something more closely resembling a thriller. And a bunch of writers in the 1990s who took the crime novel and tried to do something more interesting with it – Donna Tart, Peter Hoeg, Minette Walters, people like that. Oh, and of course Hitchcock. He was the first one to spot that love stories can so easily become twisted.

Was it hard to get *The Poison Tree* published?
Funnily enough, no. I had a friend in publishing who gave me the names of a few agents. But in fact she showed the manuscript to an editor who offered to publish it even before I had an agent.

Was a follow-up more difficult than the debut? Or had you planned it already?
I hadn't planned it, no. And in fact the book I wanted to write was turned down by my US publisher. It was set in a prison, with the hero being a cop who was inside for murder,

but it was just too dark for them. After that, *The Death Pit* just popped out of nowhere.

Plot and characters, the whole shebang?
More or less. I had the character Terry from *The Poison Tree*, who's kind of an off-on lesbian, and I thought witch trials might be an interesting thing to get her involved with, because so many of the aristocratic 'witches' were actually strong women, rebellious women, even some lesbians, who were being cut down to size. Then I discovered that witch trials were more a feature of Scotland than England, so that gave me my location. The present-day Wiccan thing then seemed fairly inevitable. And the pig-farming stuff was because my wife was, at the time, a pig-farmer. I found it much harder to sort out the plot for *The Decoy* though, partly because it's a more plot-driven book and partly because I was dealing with Hollywood as well as publishers. It's just been bought by Arnold Copelson, the producer who made *Perfect Murder*, *Seven*, and *The Fugitive*.

How does that feel?
Great, except that I've been given absolutely no indication whether or not the project will actually happen. But yes, I kind of wrote the book with a film in mind – not just because films are where the money is, but also because it's a very visual story; by which I mean that you never know what's really going on in the characters' heads, you have to guess from their actions. Usually, of course, books tell you what a person's thinking as well as what they're doing but in this case that would have given too much away. That's partly why it's written in the present tense – it's less reflective, more action-orientated.

How important to you is to grounding the plot in reality?
Well, I have a tendency to go horribly over the top! For instance, with hindsight the ending of *The Death Pit* should have been a little less melodramatic. But with *The Decoy* I actually tried to keep all the sex and violence out, at least to begin with. I wanted it to be very mainstream and accessible. But the story just seemed to demand a certain amount of darkness, so I added most of the sex scenes in the last few drafts. I did take out a lot of irrelevant poetry, though!

So tell me about your writing process – early morning starts, a set word count every day?
Well, I have a day job in advertising and a young family to support, so I only write one day a week. But I set aside a couple of mornings where I get up early and make notes for an hour or so. That's why I only produce a book every few years.

Ever wanted to chuck in the day job and write full-time?
Not really. I couldn't bear to sit at home all day and stare at a computer screen, week in, week out. Advertising is full of bright, likeable people who really care passionately about doing something good – honestly! Although, admittedly, it can get a bit tiresome having work rejected for stupid reasons. But I'd like to have more time to write than I do now -currently I work at advertising agency Abbott Mead Vickers four days a week. And I'd also like to write in different genres – I've written a comedy film script that's been optioned, for example. In my day job, comedy is what I do most – stuff like Utterly Butterly, Walkers crisps etc.

How long did it take you to write *The Decoy*?

It took six months to write the synopsis, nine months to write the book, and a year to rewrite it. I did about fifteen drafts, and I cut out nearly as much as is in the finished book. I decided it was going to be action and nothing else. Every scene, every description, every line that wasn't essential got stripped out. I even re-translated *Les Fleurs du Mal*, using a shorter meter and condensing whole verses of Baudelaire into single lines. Purists will probably kill me.

What comes first – characters or plot?

In *The Poison Tree*, it was definitely the former – I created this woman character who I loved, but then found a lot of people disliked her. She's an academic – her subject is detective fiction! – and she's actually quite arrogant intellectually, she's convinced she's right even when all the evidence says otherwise. But she's also gutsy and passionate. When the book starts, she's divorced and has somehow drifted into a gay relationship with an old friend, which she's busy extricating herself from. So she buys a little house in Oxford which is going cheap, and then later she discovers that it's cheap because a student was murdered there. I had no idea when I started writing where that plot idea was going to take me. But in *The Decoy*, it was the idea. How do you catch a serial killer with a decoy? Would you tell the decoy everything or would you manipulate her? How do you get round the problem that covert taped material is inadmissible? What sort of person might agree to become a decoy in the first place? So I worked back from there to this young actress in New York – Claire – struggling to make ends meet by acting already as a decoy for a detective agency. I know a few actresses and they're interesting people – quite neurotic sometimes, even needy, but also brave and impulsive and watchful. Again, not everyone liked Claire. After I'd written the book, my US publishers turned it down. They didn't like her or any of the other characters enough; they said she wasn't someone you could cheer for. I don't agree. I think you cheer more for someone who's a bit mixed up. So I decided to leave her as she was. Which was quite an expensive decision!

In *The Decoy*, the whole notion of pretence is fascinating – no-one is quite who they seem. What made you choose this as a theme?

Again, the idea came first and then everything else followed. If the central idea is deception, then what can be done with that in the subplots, in the minor characters, in the individual scenes? So, starting with the opening, almost every major scene has some kind of twist or deception in it. Maybe there are too many – there's a great big twist at the end of the book that would probably have had more shock value if I hadn't bombarded the reader with so many other twists. But I liked the idea of the construction echoing the central idea. I think of it as being like a series of Russian dolls – each revealed plot seems entire of itself, but is just one step closer to the truth. But the reader doesn't have to think about that, of course. Hopefully, they'll just sense that the writer is in control of his material and they can relax and enjoy the ride.

Mark Campbell

IN A CLASS
OF HER OWN

Val McDermid *is in a class of her own. The grittiest of all British women crime writers, her recent books have taken her into areas of dark psychology that even her breakthrough earlier work had not prepared readers for. And it's an uncomfortable place to be, as she told* CT...

My latest book, just out in paperback, is *Killing the Shadows* (HarperCollins). It's a serial killer thriller with a twist – the victims of this killer are themselves the writers of serial killer novels. There are some fairly grand guignol moments along the way, but there's a serious intent at play here too. There's been a lot of debate about the effect of violent films, books, TV programmes and computer games on society as a whole, and I was interested in exploring the notion of the writer's responsibility, of the relationship between writer and reader, of the morality of writing about violent crime. And I was also interested in writing about a different kind of offender profiling from the usual behavioural analysis. So my central character, Dr Fiona Cameron, is an academic psychologist who is somewhat contemptuous of what she calls the 'touchy-feely' approach

to profiling. Instead, she uses computer programs to develop crime linkage, identifying clusters of crimes with the same probable offender, then goes one step further with geographical profiling to narrow down where the offender may be found. This is fairly leading edge stuff; it's actually being tested in the field by various

A PLACE
OF EXECUTION
VAL
McDERMID

A STUNNING PSYCHOLOGICAL THRILLER FROM THE GOLD
DAGGER AWARD WINNER

police forces, including our own, and this sort of analysis is clearly going to play an increasing role in practical investigations in the future. I wanted to get in ahead of the game!

I've never understood novelists who say they don't read much fiction. It's always seemed to me that the only way writers can advance their craft, apart from sheer hard work, is to absorb what's already been done well and aspire to that level and beyond. I learned storytelling from writers as diverse as Enid Blyton, Robert Louis Stevenson, Agatha Christie and Margaret Atwood. From Sara Paretsky, I learned the blinding truth that it was possible to write crime fiction set in a contemporary world I could recognise, and with a defining edge of social politics. From Ruth Rendell, I learned to seize the challenge of writing more than one kind of book. And from poets-turned-novelists like Andrew Grieg, Anne Michael and Jackie Kay, I learned to try not to waste words.

I've always read widely in the genre, and outside it, and for me, the main criterion that I search for is good writing. That means never missing Reginald Hill, Ian Rankin, Denise Mina, Laurie King, John Straley, Liza Cody, Sara Paretsky, K. C. Constantine or James Lee Burke. Outside the genre, I eagerly await the new Ian Banks, Jeanette Winterson, Sebastian Faulks. The trouble with lists is all the names you leave out and kick yourself over.

Writing about violence is a vexed issue, and I feel we have a duty to write about it directly and honestly. We shouldn't trivialise or glamorise it, and we should never lose sight of the damage violence does to everyone touched by it. That doesn't nec-essarily mean anatomising every graphic detail of a violent act, but it does mean giving thought to the message we're sending. It's easy to be glib about violence, to turn it into a cheap thrill. But good writing isn't about what's easy.

On issues of sexuality, we all have the right to be as open or as private as we want to be in respect of our own lives. Personally, I don't see any reason to hide who I am, and in the interests of making life easier for those who come after us, I'd advocate such candour. But I don't have the right to take that decision for anyone else, and I know others whose reasons for their discretion seem to them at least as valid as my own choices do to me. As far as the characters of fiction are concerned, what possible point can there be in coyness with the readers? In my experience, they're often a lot more clued in than I am about the big bad world out there.

I grew up in the generation that believes the personal is the political, so I find it hard to comprehend how one can write any kind of novel without it being rooted in a world governed by moral, economic and political systems. How our characters behave is affected by external factors as well as internal ones. I don't see how it is possible to be apolitical and live in the world, and one's personal world view inevitably informs what one writes. But I'm always amused by the fact that it's only when the obvious politics of a book are to the left of centre that it's described as political. Shore up the status quo, lean to the right, and nobody ever accuses a writer of having a political agenda.

My working methods are theoretically disciplined and methodical. I always outline a novel in some detail before I begin, though as I progress through it I have to write supplemental scene-by-scene outlines so I don't lose my way. These days, I tend to spend the mornings doing admin, research, figuring out details of plotting, writing the occasional short story or working on new ideas. In the afternoons, I write. I try to do between 1,500 and 2,000 words a day. But inevitably, when deadline approaches, all order and method disappears and I write all the hours god sends, going flat out to try to get the book done on time. It doesn't matter how long or short a time I have to write a book in, the last three to four weeks are always manic. And I am horrible.

What I'm writing must, first and foremost, entertain. If I don't give the readers a good time, they're not going to stay with me. I think I offer novels that are tightly plotted, with characters the reader can care about, and that deal with wider themes and issues than the mere solution of a series of crimes. However, the story is what always comes first with me; I often don't even see the themes and issues myself until the book is well and truly finished.

I blame Manchester for my career in crime. When I moved here in 1979, it seemed to me to be a city that was screaming to be written about. It's a vibrant place with a strong sense of itself. It's a small enough city to walk around and to hold in your head, but it's big enough to have a lot of different things going on. A lively cultural life, the best football team in the world, a social melting pot, interesting politics and a fascinating history. Not to mention great places to eat and drink and make

merry. It's also a city that's gone through seismic changes in the past twenty years. What's not to get excited about?

I never think about readers when I'm writing a book. The person I need to satisfy is myself, and if I do that, then I think I've got a chance of pleasing others. There's no point in writing anything other than what's in your heart and head, and tailoring that to what you think might be the whims of others is a recipe for disaster.

A writer has to be a sort of schizophrenic. We need to be able to live inside our own heads in a world of our own making for large tracts of time. But we also have to remain plugged into the world outside our window or our work ultimately becomes sterile and disconnected. Other people are the raw material of our cannibalistic activities, and if we don't eat, the work gets starved.

My next book is the third Tony Hill/Carol Jordan novel. It takes place mostly in Germany and Holland and there are two central plot strands. Carol is working on a dangerous undercover operation against a major organised criminal when she learns about a possible serial killer operating across the borders of the EU. She persuades Tony to return to fieldwork from his new life in academe, with terrifying results that will change their lives forever. It's called *The Last Temptation* and it will be published next February. Along with the first two Hill/Jordan novels, *The Mermaids Singing* and *The Wire in the Blood*, *The Last Temptation* is being adapted for ITV starring Robson Green as Tony Hill. Filming begins this autumn, and the series is scheduled to be shown next spring.

Val McDermid

PROFILE

JAMES SALLIS

Mark Thwaite

It is not midnight. Nor is it raining. But, somehow, I feel it should be. James Sallis does that to me. Gets under my skin. Changes my mood. Changes me.

Paul Duncan (in his excellent Pocket Essential *Noir Fiction*) calls Noir, "all those things we fear in the back of our minds, the parts of ourselves we want to block out because they make us feel uneasy... [noir is] about the people... writhing, aware of the pain, aware of the future pain to come." Often so closely associated with the crime genre as to be inseparable from it noir has, in fact, a different heritage and its lineage is a great one: Dostoevsky, and I would argue Knut Hamsun, Conrad, Ralph Ellison, Willeford and others, all investigated the existential crisis of the immobilised, invisible man. And Lew Griffin, the black,

New Orleans, part-time heavy, part-time private investigator of James Sallis' most renowned work is part of this tradition. Pain for Sallis, and Lew Griffin is often in pain, seems to bring a kind of ongoing epiphany: each time Lew gets battered by life, or some criminal thug, he stumbles, sometimes falls again and falls hard and, later, the essence or meaning of his crisis opens up to him – and through him to the reader. The medicine that Lew now requires, in the early years it was often simply another drink, is love. Sallis' skill is to make this potentially banal truism revelatory throughout all the novels.

A crime writer's crime writer, Sallis' star keeps rising. Recently we've been given the fourth novel in his series of works on the life of Lew Griffin, *Bluebottle*, and the latest in the series is due out in a few months – *Ghost of a Flea*, the final Griffin novel, was delivered to the publishers in February. A second collection of Jim's poetry, *Black Night's Gonna Catch Me* is also forthcoming in Ireland from Salmon Publishing in 2001. Last year saw the appearance of his collected essays *Gently into the Land of the Meateaters* (an excellent collection badly in need of a decent introduction to contextualise the work) and his collected short stories (two volumes in one book: first half sci-fi, second half crime) *Time's Hammers*. This mounting body of work is worthy of the highest praise and Sallis, the man of letters, is beginning to be talked about as, in the words of Harlan Ellison, "one of the significant ones".

Born in 1944 in Helena, Arkansas, Sallis' writing career began with poems in *Ann Arbor Review* and *Transatlantic Review*, he published his first short story collection in 1976 and for a short while was editor of Michael Moorcocks' *New Worlds*. He has also published a number of remarkable science fiction stories but it was not until 1990's *Long Legged Fly* that Sallis began to establish a name outside the sci-fi milieu. *Fly* is the first of the Lew Griffin novels and, superficially, the most complex in structure. It is a fine novel (and my favourite) because of how insignificant the awful brutalities within the story truly are – the importance is Sallis' character study of Griffin.

The title for *The Long Legged Fly* comes from a poem by Yeats – this is typical of Sallis. Genre fiction this may well be but mired from his early reading in avant-garde literature (note his well received translation of the French classic *Saint Glinglin* by Raymond Queneau) all Sallis' work is highly allusive. Lew himself is a voracious reader: books themselves are regularly name-checked and name-dropped in the works. Lew, contemplating his life, aware of the gaps and silences, watches time flow away from him and tries to make some sense of its, and his, drift. Set in 1964, 1970, 1984 and 1990, *Fly* begins as a pulp novel and develops into something far denser and more complex. Who is actually writing *Fly*? Who exactly is Lew?

Hugely gifted as a writer, Sallis' compelling work is increasingly placing him as heir to the great crime masters, not least of whom is Chester Himes whose life Sallis so wonderfully reconstructed in his magnificent biography (released earlier this year). This wasn't Sallis' first non-fiction work – the primer he edited on the works of the important early sci-fi writer Samuel R. Delaney *Ash of Stars* is highly regarded and his essential *Difficult Lives* contains wonderfully insightful essays on Jim Thompson, David Goodis and Chester Himes (and I would agree with Paul Duncan that the piece on Goodis is absolutely superb). Highly intelligent and hugely literate, Sallis is one of those writers who is wholly aware that writing is often only rewriting, and that we are all in debt to those who have written before us. He produces spare, dark, existentialist novels: novels that base their concern on the daily struggles Lew has as he works, worries about what he should be doing and should have done, and tries to do the right thing. The books only concern themselves tangentially with 'crime': the novels are about Lew and his ghosts.

Crime, then, is only marginal to the concerns of Sallis' writing. His books are not mere pulp fodder, not neat whodunits and, whilst the reasons for the events under investigation unfold under Sallis' masterful control and fine pacing, throughout each work the final unmaskings (when and if they come) are not nearly as important as the route through to the conclusion. Lew has once again loved, lost, found, learnt. And we have too. Indeed Sallis says in his introduction to *Time's Hammers* that his interest in the marginal literatures of first sci-fi and now crime was an interest in a medium that could interrogate the metaphysical concerns of ordinary readers. Sallis believes that science fiction and mystery have much in common, they are "edge literatures, dealing with people in extremis… those who by choice or circumstance… have lit out for the territory". Because they deal with the individual set against society they always have something wild, untameable and transgressive about them. Just because ordinary folk read (and wrote) crime fiction did not mean it could not share the highest concerns of all literature to investigate the why of human existence and the how of the compromises of human communication.

Griffin is a compelling, fully rounded character – indeed one of the finest fictional creations around – a tough from the mean streets. Books, alcohol and failed loves have all bedded in and matured to produce a tough, bourbon swilling PI (an archetype we all recognise from Chandler on) whose humanity shines through. These are not moralistic works however – the denouements are often bathetic, barely existent: someone damaged by society damages other folk and Lew tries to do what little he can to ease the hurt. These

are crime novels because we all live in a world where crime and violence can touch and mar us. We all live in a world where crime is inevitable. And Griffin works as a character because, despite his flaws, he is an enviable hero. His heroics are often small, his fuck-ups often large, but Lew is attractive nonetheless: humane, passionate, flawed, learned, kind… and hard.

Sallis has said that the novels are essentially plotless. What this means is clearly illustrated in *The Eye of a Cricket* in which Lew, on yet another missing person case, stays put in his supposedly unknown home to which a string of visitors come, share coffee or more, and quietly move the narrative forward. Mostly we get Lew/Sallis's musings on life and love. And whether it is Lew or Sallis is part of the playfulness of the work. At the end of *Fly* the reader, knowing now that Lew is a novelist, is not sure whether what she has just been reading is actually one of Lew's book, a book about him, or a story at yet another remove. Whilst *Bluebottle*, the last Griffin novel, is arguably the straightest of the stories, refusing to play the intertextual games, the whole series plays on the conspiracy between reader and writer, and requires from the reader an attention to detail that these slight seeming novels seem to belie.

Sallis superb 'spy' novel *Death Will Have Your Eyes* which, when it came out in 1997 Michael Moorcock called his 'best novel', is key to the understanding of Sallis' project. As we'd expect this is not a typical spy novel. Our hero, primed to find an ex-colleague from what seems like another lifetime, starts to travel the country. Instead of attempting to find him, he makes it known, by running, that he wishes to be found. The spy becomes the hunted who hopes soon to see his predator drawn out into the open. The novel becomes an existential (that word again) road movie of motels and waiting and the most limited 'action'. On one very important level nothing very much happens and this is key: exciting, dangerous people like spies are not at all Sallis' concern whatever his characters' jobs may be. One of the characters in *Eye of the Cricket* says that once you are off the drink you have to get used to the grey of the quotidian: ordinary lives, good lives, are not, in this stained, battered world, exciting. Most of us wait about, hoping something might happen, it doesn't, and then we die. And what's the journey been about? The same for me, you or a spy presumably…

The 'avant-garde' sci-fi novel *Renderings* is not normally considered to be central to Sallis' work (although I would urge any Sallis fan to read this beautiful book), especially not for his crime fans, but even here we see all the themes that play so fully and well in the Griffin novels. And slight though *Renderings* is, barely a hundred pages, lots of white space, it does throw yet more light on the other books. Central to *Renderings* is a concern about the stories that we tell about ourselves – as well as an abiding sadness and search for meaning through love. All the way through the Griffin stories, Lew's concern both with his lost year (the year the *Bluebottle* fills in) and lost time in general boils down to a concern about how we orientate ourselves in this world. Like Paul Auster, Sallis is an American writing European novels: accessible yet literary self-aware works con-

cerned about the nature of being and explored via, and with, the stories we tell about the stories we tell about ourselves.

Sallis doesn't like to think of his novels in terms of trendy deconstruction – although, interestingly, his brother John, a philosopher and expert on Heidegger, is a friend of the French thinker Jacques Derrida who has taught us all so much about how a text can work against itself, go places the author did not intend. But he does see them as extending the genre. Sallis knows that every reader brings something new and different to every book they read and that once a book is published each reader fills in the blanks and reads it however they wish (Sallis tells of his surprise when his first fan mail for *Fly* took the book as a 'straight' crime novel). And he extends the genre through his love and knowledge of it and other literatures. Apart from the fact that it annoys publishers, why shouldn't genre fiction treat its readers as intelligent, perspicacious, literate peers with whom it can discuss the issues that are the loftier concerns of literature within pages devoted to a gritty, hardboiled realism?

"I tend to think of [deconstruction] as a certain kind of self-awareness of the text: a recognition that, yes, we are playing a game called literature." And this game, this set of metaphors and tropes piled on top of and lying beneath, working through and working against the straight story of Lew the PI/heavy/debt collector/teacher/narrator/writer is the depth that makes Sallis' work some of the most important the genre has recently produced.

Man of letters? Too damned right.

Mark Thwaite

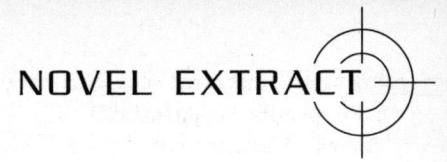

THE HOUSE OF DEATH

Paul Doherty

Chapter 1

"When the next campaigning season started,
Alexander left Antipater in charge of affairs…
and marched for the Hellespont."
Arrian, _The Campaigns of Alexander_,
Book I, Chapter 11

The time had been chosen by Aristander, soothsayer and keeper of the king's secrets: the rising of the star Arcturus in the forty-second year of the Olympiad. Alexander of Macedon stood in the middle of a circle of twelve stone altars erected in honour of the gods of Olympus. The sacred ring topped a small hillock a few miles from the city of Sestos, overlooking the steel-blue, fast-moving currents of the Hellespont.

Despite Aristander's preparations, the auspices were not good. A cold evening mist curled in from the sea, a sombre cloud which threatened to shroud the fires which flickered on eleven of the altars. Alexander lifted his hand. The trumpeters raised their salpinxes and blew a long, deafening blast which carried across the water and back over the Macedonian camp, which seemed to stretch to the far horizon. All now fell deathly silent. The troops, congregated around the hill, stared up at the sacred place where royal bodyguards protected the place of sacrifice. Those who had arrived first peered through the stockade, eager for a glance of their king. Alexander of Macedon, garbed in the full dress armour of a commander of the Royal Brigade, waited patiently, head slightly tilted back, staring up at the dark, forbidding clouds which hid the dying sun and threatened to obscure the paltry light of moon and stars. A gloomy, windswept night was promised.

Around Alexander were grouped his companions. There was tall, dark-haired Hephaestion with his sharp, sombre face, moustache and beard: some whispered how Alexander's "shadow" looked more like a Semite than a Macedonian. Next to him Ptolemy, sunburnt, clean-shaven, hair cropped. A cast in his right eye, together with his broken nose and slight harelip, gave him a perpetual sneering look. Then there was Nearchus, the small Cretan, concerned with the catapults, mangonels and other machines of war. Finally, Seleucus, tall and thick-set with heavy-lidded eyes, who dreamed of becoming an Asiatic potentate.

On the left of their king was a group of priests, led by the balding, spindle-legged Aristander with his bulbous eyes and ever-dripping nose. He looked the part everyone assigned him: warlock, magician, seer and fortune-teller. A priest who knew the secret rites and had been despatched by Olympias so that his mastery of the black arts could assist her son. They all watched him as the milk-white bullock with gilded horns, a garland of flowers round its neck and carefully drugged, plodded into the sacred enclosure. The royal page leading it stopped before Alexander. The king, using a small knife, sliced some of the hairs from between the horns and, going up to one of the altars, sprinkled these over the flames. Aristander handed him a gold goblet of Chian wine. Alexander poured this onto the fire and stepped back. The bullock was led closer to the altar where no fire burnt. At Aristander's signal, the priests grouped round it. One raised the ceremonial axe and brought it down in a slicing cut, strik-ing the bull expertly at the back of the neck. It bellowed with fear and its forelegs crumpled beneath it. Another priest, straddling the animal, pulled back its head and, in one deft stroke, drew a scythe-like knife across its throat. The bull's bellow was echoed by the bystanders, even as its lifeblood gushed into the silver bowl to be taken up to the sacred fire.

Alexander watched carefully. As he did so, the Delphic Oracle came back to haunt him: "The bull is prepared for sacrifice. All is ready. The slayer awaits." Words which prophesied his own father's death. Had Philip been sacrificed? Had his mother Olympias been the priestess? And why had the sacrifice taken place? To protect Olympias or Olympias' beloved son? And was he innocent of his father's blood? Or would Philip's shade come wandering back from Hades to mock and taunt him in the early hours of the night?

The priests had now lifted the bull's carcass onto the altar. Alexander tried to dispel his gloomy thoughts as the priests cut open the belly. He pulled up the hood of his war cloak and lifted his hands in prayer to Zeus the all-seeing. The bull's entrails slopped out. A sudden horde of flies, noisy in their buzzing, came to hover over the pool of blood. A bad sign. Alexander's heart skipped a beat. Were they sent by the Furies? A sign of impending displeasure and punishment by the gods? Of all of them? Or just one? Apollo perhaps? Hera? Or Poseidon whose permission Alexander needed to hurl his arms across the Hellespont. Surely the other signs would be good? The bull had been carefully chosen, Aristander given strict and secret instructions. The king recalled the letters he had received from Olympias. Was all this the workings of a god or the machinations of men? Every prince was surrounded by traitors and assassins, but to fail now, even before he started?

Aristander, his arms deep in the bull's belly, groped and seized the still warm liver full of the bull's rich lifeblood. He placed it on the altar and stared down; turning to his master, he shook his head slightly. Alexander had his reply. The auspices were not good. The liver was still vital but he could tell by Aristander's lopsided smile that it was blemished, unacceptable to the gods. Alexander pushed back his hood and grasped Hephaestion's arm.

"Useless!" he whispered. "It's sullied, tarnished! I give it to the gods and the gods send it back. Tell the assembled men, the signs are still not clear enough."

"And?" Hephaestion asked.

"Oh, clear up the mess!" Alexander snapped, and walked off.

He left the sacrificial enclosure, walking down the avenue between the troops. He tried to smile and was relieved when his parasol-carrier, hurrying behind him, tripped and fell to the amusement of the soldiers.

"A good sign!" Alexander shouted, helping the man to his feet. "The gods know I need no protection! I have you and I have them. What more does Philip's son need?"

His words, carried and repeated, were greeted with roars of approval. Alexander walked on. He felt a sudden chill down his left side and paused. Was that his father? A ghost? A premonition? Alexander felt vulnerable. He had walked from the sacrificial enclosure – no one was here to protect his back. On either side were his Macedonian pikemen, but any one of them might be an assassin. Alexander resisted the urge to hurry. Instead, he crossed over to a group of Thessalians and began to tease them about their long hair, recalling their exploits during previous campaigns. Some Alexander recognized by name and asked about their families, all the time fending off the same questions. When would they march? When would they cross the Hellespont?

"We will march soon enough," Alexander reassured them, hiding his own unease. "And believe me, within a year you will all be clothed in silk. You will feast on gold and silver cups and platters while the ladies of Persia cater for your every need."

"Every need?" one wit retorted.

Alexander pointed a finger at the speaker and winked playfully. "In your case, there may be one or two exceptions!"

A roar of laughter greeted his reply. Alexander passed on. He heaved a sigh of relief as he reached the royal enclosure, ringed by carts and the trophies set up to commemorate former victories, guarded by an elite unit from the Royal Brigade. Alexander had a few words with the captain of the watch and passed through. In the centre stood an altar, strewn with wet, bedraggled flowers. Alexander went across and, picking up a wild lily, crushed it between his fingers. Hadn't Olympias, or was it Aristotle, warned him about the juices of this flower? Wasn't it poisonous or . . .? Alexander looked towards the royal pavilions set up in the shape of a "T". The crossbar was his council chamber, the upright his personal quarters. At the entrance thronged a group of physicians. Perdicles the Athenian, tall, broad-browed, his black hair cropped close. Slanting eyes, a thin nose above prim lips. Next to him, Cleon of Samos: small, blond-haired, moon-faced and fussy, a man of secrets, close to Alexander's right hand. Leontes of Platea, brown as a berry with mischievous eyes and a slobbery mouth which seemed to ever hang open. Finally Nikias – where was he from? Ah yes, Corinth. Dry-eyed, dry-faced with a dry wit. A shock of unruly grey hair crowning an old man's face, furrowed and deep-set. The physicians were exchanging hot words with the officer who blocked their entrance – they didn't realize Alexander had arrived until the soldier came smartly to attention.

"Is he here, sire?" Perdicles called. "We heard a rumour. . ."

"You heard a rumour and I know the truth," Alexander teased. "Yes, you may meet him, but not now."

He winked at Cleon and pushed by them into the first part of the tent, the waiting chamber, where the royal pages lounged. Alexander handed his cloak to them and lifted the partition which led to the inner chamber containing his table, chairs, treasures and personal possessions. The page-boy, tending an oil lamp, spun round.

"Get out!" Alexander ordered.

The boy, wiping his hands on his tunic, hastened to obey. Alexander caught him by the shoulder and spun him round. He stared down at the smooth, olive-skinned face.

"You are a good boy." Alexander smiled. "I am just tired. Tell the others to keep quiet."

Alexander ignored Telamon whom he'd glimpsed sitting on a stool to his far left between two coffers. Instead he went across to the desk and sifted among the papers which littered it.

"The secretariat is always busy."

"Aren't we all?" Telamon coolly replied.

Alexander glanced at him sharply and began to undo the straps of his corselet.

"Oh, for the love of Apollo, or whatever god you believe in, Telamon! Don't sit there. Come over and help an old friend."

Telamon obeyed and, crouching down, unloosened the strap just beneath the armpit.

"You've changed," Alexander commented.

"So has the world, sire."

Telamon undid the strap, narrowing his eyes as he loosened the buckle.

"You've been out in the sun too long, Telamon. Your eyesight is not so good."

"Just the same, sire – near-sighted."

"You used to call me Alexander."

"And a lot more, sire," Telamon quipped.

"How's Mother?"

"Deadly as ever."

"Did she threaten you?"

"No, just those I love."

Alexander took off the corselet and threw it on a stool. "They are safe. Don't worry about her, Telamon. Your name and those of your family are on my list."

Alexander unloosened the war kilt, sat on a stool and undid his marching boots, then removed the sweat-soaked tunic. He stood naked except for a loincloth and spread his hands.

"Do I pass muster, physician?"

Telamon studied the rosy-white skin marred by old wounds and bruises, the darkened areas burnt by the sun. Alexander's legs and thighs were thick and muscular, his stomach flat.

"A healthy mind in a healthy body, eh, Telamon?"

"The body passes muster, sire."

Alexander's smile faded. He crossed to the chest, took out a white purple-edged tunic and pulled it over his head.

"You haven't changed at all, Telamon – tart and cynical as ever."

"Life is short, science so long to learn," Telamon replied. "Opportunity is elusive, experience is dangerous, judgment is difficult."

"Euripides?"

"No, sire, Hippocrates."

The king walked across, hand outstretched. Telamon clasped it. Alexander pulled him close.

"I wish you'd come sooner," he said fiercely. "As Euripides says, 'The day is for honest men, the night for thieves.' Do you still enjoy the playwright, Telamon?"

"One of his phrases in particular," Telamon replied. "The sacred fragment: 'Those whom the gods wish to destroy they first make mad.'"

Alexander felt his erstwhile friend tense as if expecting a blow. The king kissed him gently on the cheek and stepped back.

His head went to one side, his finger close to Telamon's face. "I wanted you here, because I need you. Because I trust you. However, if you don't want to be here, I can fill your purse with gold and send you back."

"I'd love to accept." Telamon smiled. "But I can't for two reasons. First, there is no going back. Second, you have no gold left."

Alexander grabbed him by the arm. "But I do have work." He glanced towards the entrance to the tent, face solemn, eyes worried. "Some men in this camp, Telamon, wish me dead. Others want to see me fall. I have just sacrificed the third bull in two days, the prime cullings of my herd. Like the rest, its liver was blemished. I don't know which is going to run out first: bulls for sacrifice or my patience with the gods." He paused. "There's something else I want

to show you."

Alexander slipped on a pair of sandals. He tapped the leather satchel which Telamon had slung over his shoulder. "You brought your medicines?"

"A soldier carries a sword, a physician his potions."

"You may need them."

Alexander lifted the tent flap and they went out through the antechamber into the cold night air. They were immediately surrounded by the other physicians – Telamon knew them of old. Perdicles grasped his arm, his face bright with pleasure.

"I heard rumours but I didn't think you'd come."

The others would have joined in but Alexander called across a guards officer to be an escort and they set off through the gloom, walking carefully between the tents and pavilions, wary of the guy ropes and tent pegs. Some tents were large, some were small but placed close together – not only for security, but to prevent a night attack. Enemy infantry or cavalry would find such narrow alleyways as great a hindrance as any ring of guardsmen.

"What are you smiling at?" Alexander asked, ignoring the chatter of the other physicians behind him.

"Our youth." Telamon smiled back. "Black Cleitus taking us out into the hills, showing us how and where to pitch camp. By the way, where is the great brute?"

"In Sestos buying wine. You'll sup with me tonight, Telamon?"

Alexander paused as a cowled figure stepped out of the darkness. The officer half-drew his sword but relaxed as the man pulled back his hood.

"Our man from Tarsus!" Alexander

exclaimed. "The tent-maker. Is all ready?"

The tent-maker nodded.

"And the fire?" Alexander asked.

The man shook his head. "I don't know. All I can say," he added mournfully, "is that one good tent has been demolished. Leather and cord are very precious."

"I know. I know." Alexander waved him away. He grasped Telamon's hand as they used to do when they were boys. "It was your tent," he whispered. "You have one for yourself. Both chambers went up in flames, only the poles and cords remained. It's a good job you were not in it."

"An accident?"

"Perhaps," Alexander replied.

Telamon glanced away. The cold night breeze chilled the sweat from his brow. He was tired after his long journey from Macedon and he idly wondered why his tent had burnt to the ground. Such fires were common but usually caused by someone being careless inside. He was about to ask further when Alexander stopped before a large, square-like tent, its roof rising to a peak. It had a cloth front, the rest consisting of stretched leather skins lashed to poles and kept taut by ropes and pegs. The guardsman outside lifted the flap. Alexander led Telamon in, the other physicians following behind.

The tent was not divided into two, but stretched like a small hall. A capped brazier stood in the centre. There were woollen rugs strewn on the ground, cushioned seats and polished small tables. At the far end were beds, coffers, chests and a high-backed chair and stools around a trestle table. A young woman, dressed in a simple dark-red tunic, sat at the table staring vacuously before her. Three women, talking quietly among themselves at the far end of the tent, rose and came forward. All three were dressed in the light-blue tunic and mantle of priestesses of Athena. Their leader carried a white, crooked shepherd's staff. A small bronze owl of Athena hung from a chain round her neck and her rings were emblazoned with the same symbol. Her two companions were mere striplings, dark-haired and pale-faced. The priestess, who introduced herself as Antigone, was striking in both looks and poise: sea-grey eyes in a long olive face, high cheek-bones, full red lips. She fleetingly reminded Telamon of Olympias and seemed unabashed in Alexander's presence. He paid her every courtesy, bowing slightly and spreading his hands like a suppliant in a temple.

"Why, my lord," Antigone's voice was soft but vibrant, "you promised to bring a physician, but not a gaggle."

She ignored Perdicles and the rest, and coolly studied Telamon with a slow appraising look, searching his face as if she were trying to recall him. Alexander made the introductions. Telamon felt slightly embarrassed and overawed – he wondered if Antigone was truly curious about him or quietly mocking.

Antigone stretched out a hand for Telamon to kiss. He did so. Her fingers were long, cool and perfumed.

"You look tired." Antigone clasped his right hand, her thumb gently stroking his wrist. "I know you, the famous physician!"

Telamon, embarrassed, looked at Alexander who was thoroughly enjoying his discomfort.

"Antigone, priestess of Athena," Alexander declared. "Serves the goddess at their temple in Troy. She has crossed the Hellespont to greet me. Honour enough! She also brought guides."

"Guides?"

Alexander made a cutting gesture with his hand. "I'll tell you later. First, the patient!"

Antigone stood aside. Alexander ushered Telamon towards the table.

'My lady, perhaps you can tell our physician the young woman's story."

Telamon stared down at the doll-faced, empty-eyed girl who still sat, lips soundlessly moving. Now and again she blinked or pulled a face and flinched as if from some unseen enemy. Telamon felt her pulse. The blood beat quickly through her wrist. He stared into her eyes: her dark pupils were enlarged and her breathing was shallow.

"She is in a trance," he declared. "But one brought on by fever."

He gazed up at Antigone. The priestess was playing with one of the heavy rings bearing the owl of Athena.

"Who is she? One of your temple maidens?"

Alexander sat on the edge of the table, arms crossed, staring down at the floor.

"She is what is left of a legend, Telamon. The curse of Cassandra!"

"Cassandra raped by Ajax after the fall of Troy?"

"The warrior," Alexander agreed, "took Cassandra prisoner and ravished her. The legend developed that his descendants, the hundred noble families of Locri in Thessaly, had to pay reparation. Cassandra, the prophetess, had been sacred to Athena. The hundred families were to send two maidens a year to serve in the goddess' temple at Troy."

"But that's legend!" Telamon protested.

"It was until about five years ago. My

father Philip wanted to make his landing at Troy successful. He wished to appease Athena, so he persuaded the Thessalian chieftains to reinstate the practice. Every spring two maids were to be taken across to the Hellespont, landed on the shore and told to make their own way to Troy. At least, that's the theory."

"Aspasia and Selena were the first." Antigone gestured at her companions. "None of the rest ever arrived. I wrote to Philip myself but he could do little – the western shore of the Hellespont is ravaged by brigands and outlaws. Two maidens would fetch a high price in the slave markets."

"It's barbaric!" Telamon exclaimed.

"It's happened before," Alexander explained. "This year was no different."

Telamon glanced at him quickly. Was Alexander lying? He caught the glance between the king and the priestess, a faint smile as if they were fellow conspirators.

"The practice will end now." Alexander sighed. "We have no further need for sacrifices. This unfortunate was found wandering on the outskirts of the ruins at Troy."

Telamon studied the girl's head, sifting her luxuriant hair. He felt lumps, a healing scab. Her face had been carefully painted to hide the fading cuts and bruises. He ordered a lamp to be brought closer.

"We have examined her," said Perdicles, coming forward with the other physicians.

"She's witless," Cleon lisped.

"There's nothing we can do," Nikias declared gently, "except hand her back to her family."

Telamon, crouching by the girl, grasped her hand, which was cold and clammy. He pressed his ear against her chest and, gesturing for silence, picked up the quick heartbeat.

"I can cure her," he declared.

Leontes guffawed. He came and stood behind the girl, glaring down at Telamon as if he was responsible for the young woman's injuries.

"Are you a miracle-worker, Telamon? Will you smear toad fat on her skin and perform a dance round her?"

"I'll make you eat the same fat!" Telamon snapped.

Alexander snorted with laughter and stood up. "Nothing worse than a gaggle of physicians arguing over a cure," he taunted.

"I'll not argue." Telamon got to his feet, face flushed with anger. "I have seen such trances before. They are brought on by a deep terror."

Alexander apologized with his eyes. "What do you recommend?"

Telamon cupped the girl's chin in his hands, turning her head. "What is it?" he asked softly. "What are you frightened of?"

"The darkness."

The woman's lower lip trembled. Her voice was guttural but Telamon could understand her tongue. During his exile he had worked for a while in Thessaly.

"What about the darkness?"

"Furies lurk deep inside. Monsters, they coil like snakes up my skin." She pressed her hand against the side of her face. "And the screaming. That and the spurting blood. A monster's claw stretches out to catch me. And the . . ." She closed her eyes and sniffed. "The pit, grotesque sights, foul smells."

She lapsed into silence, staring down at the tabletop.

Telamon took the satchel off his shoulder and undid the buckles. He searched among the phials carefully placed in the small pockets and straps within. He took

one out and squeezed the girl's hand.

"I am going to put you to sleep," he said. "And you will sleep for a long, long time."

"What will that do?" Alexander asked, curious.

"It will allow the body and mind to rest. Free the phantasms in her soul. Sometimes she will awake screaming but go back to sleep again."

"A woman's remedy," Leontes muttered.

"No, far from it." Telamon pulled out the stopper and sniffed it carefully. "In fact, it's a soldier's remedy. My lord," he turned to Alexander, "you have met soldiers whose wits have been turned by the shock of battle?"

"Lunatics," the king agreed. "Not fit for anything."

"They are lost in the maze of their terrors," Telamon explained. "They go round and round searching futilely for the way out. Sleep escapes them and the faster they walk, the more desperate they become and the worse it gets."

"I have heard of this," Perdicles broke in. "They call it the sleep of Aesculapius, the dream of forgetfulness."

Telamon agreed. "I have seen men sleep for weeks, sometimes months, that's all they do: sleep, eat and drink."

"Are they cured?" Leontes didn't sound so arrogant now.

"In some cases yes. In one or two I admit'. . ."

"Sleep is the brother of death," Antigone broke in. "They never regain consciousness."

"Precisely, my lady. Now, if I could have some wine?"

Antigone went deeper into the tent. She brought back a goblet emblazoned with Athena's owl and filled it with wine. She tasted it and, winking at Telamon, passed it over as if it were a loving cup. Telamon sipped the wine and sniffed: it was rich and dark.

"From the vineyards of Chios," Antigone explained.

Telamon tasted the wine again. He quietly resolved that if he was involved in Alexander's madcap campaigns and the killing and wounding began, such wine should be preserved to ease pain and cleanse wounds. Watched by the others, he poured the powder into the wine and stirred it with an ebony stick taken from his satchel. He picked the goblet up and tried to make the woman sip. She refused.

"Let me try," Antigone declared, taking the cup.

Telamon moved away. Antigone sipped the wine to give reassurance. She tried again but the patient recoiled, shaking her head. The priestess put the wine back on the table. Others also tried, but failed. Telamon crouched down, turning the woman's face gently with his fingers.

"Close your eyes," he urged. "Think of going home."

A faint smile appeared on the young woman's lips.

"This wine will take you home. It's magic wine, it will make you better."

Telamon took the cup from Antigone, and this time the girl sipped. Telamon placed the goblet down before her.

"We can do no more," he said.

Alexander was impatient to go. Antigone murmured something about a funeral. Telamon placed the phial back in his medicine satchel and did up the buckles. They all made to leave the tent.

At the entrance, Telamon stared back.

The young woman was now holding the cup between her hands, staring into the wine as if it contained the waters of Lethe, the river of forgetfulness.

"Will she drink it?" Alexander asked.

"She'll drink it," Telamon declared. "And fall asleep like a child with her head in her hands. Or she might go back to bed."

He gazed around the deserted tent and smiled to himself. Even here, in this military camp, he could tell this was a place of women: cleaner, fresher, the little items placed here and there, the tidiness. He recalled Analu's sun-filled chamber in the temple of Isis and his smile disappeared.

"Will she be safe?"

"She will be safe," Alexander assured him. "The tent coverings are tied tight – not even a worm could crawl underneath. The entrance is guarded."

They joined the rest. Perdicles and the other physicians were muttering among themselves. They raised their hands, shouting farewells. Alexander turned to talk to Antigone. The royal bodyguard now circled them, fierce and sinister in their Corinthian helmets with starched, horsehair plumes running from the crown of their helmets to hang down between their shoulder-blades. In the darkness they looked like creatures of the night, faces almost hidden by the broad nose and cheek guards. They stood silently, their presence only betrayed by the chink of metal.

"I want you to come with us, Telamon!" Alexander called across. "I must pay my respects at a funeral."

"What is this funeral?" Telamon asked, pulling his cloak tighter against the cold night air.

"My lady Antigone," Alexander said,

grinding the heels of his sandals into the rain-drenched earth, "brought me scouts from across the Hellespont. Once we have reached Troy, we will march down the coast, keeping in contact with our ships. You have crossed the Hellespont?"

Telamon nodded. He recalled the open windswept plains, the dark forest of fir and oak, the rushing rivers, a landscape gouged by deep ravines.

"A place of ambush," he said.

"Father said the same." Alexander peered up at the sky. "We will go along the coast, Telamon, and strike inland. I don't want to be ambushed."

He grasped the priestess' hand. Behind Antigone her two acolytes stood like shrouded statues.

"My lady brought me scouts led by Critias, a former soldier in the Persian army. He knows the lie of the land, the location of the wells, where rivers can be forded, which ravines and gullies can hide an enemy. Critias will draw maps and his men will guide us. They will be our eyes and ears."

"And this funeral?" Telamon insisted.

"The Lady Antigone arrived with these guides some days ago. Yesterday evening one of them was found on the rocks below the cliffs, his corpse drenched by the sea."

"An accident?" Telamon couldn't make out Alexander's face in the darkness but he sensed his uncertainty.

"No, a dagger thrust between his ribcage, up to his heart. He must have been dead before he fell to the rocks."

Alexander abruptly marched away. Antigone came up beside Telamon as he began to follow the king.

"The king has great trust in you, physician." She walked elegantly, her hand rest-ing on his arm. Telamon was pleased by her touch. Antigone reminded him of Analu: her serenity, the laughter in her eyes, her blunt speech and lack of guile.

"Do I know you?" he asked.

"Perhaps you do, Telamon. A traveller once came to our temple from lands further east across the Hindu Kush. He was a Brahmin, one of their holy men. He claimed we were all trapped on the Wheel of Life and came back to it time and again."

"The teaching of Pythagoras?"

"Something similar," she agreed. She dug her nails gently into his wrist. "Perhaps we met before, Telamon. They say that when we come back, the souls are the same but the relationships different. Perhaps, last time, I was your sister?" She laughed softly. "Or your mother?" She leaned closer and whispered in his ear: "Or even your lover?"

For the first time since he had arrived in Sestos Telamon laughed. Alexander looked over his shoulder but walked on. The royal enclosure still lay quiet. On leaving it the smells of the camp greeted them: woodsmoke, burnt peat, the stench of wet leather and horse dung. News of the king's arrival spread. Men left camp fires to toast him with their beaker cups, but the ring of bodyguards kept such well-wishers away. They made their way up between a row of tents and stopped before one. Telamon recognized the usual sleeping place for a detachment of eight soldiers. A makeshift brazier blazed in front of the entrance. On either side of this, pitch torches sputtered in the wind. From a rope hanging above the entrance to the tent hung a water stoup, the symbol of mourning, so that visitors who came to visit the dead might, on departure, cleanse themselves of pollution.

The tent was guarded. A sentry lifted the flap and Alexander entered. The makeshift funeral bier stood in the centre of the tent. The corpse lay in a circle of vine branches, feet towards the door. A slave stood by the head, waving a spray of myrtle to keep away marauding flies. Around the low-slung bier crouched the other scouts. They were all garbed in dark clothes, a sign of mourning. Their hair was freshly shorn, their faces covered in white chalk and garish streaks of paint. They made no attempt to rise as the king came in and their accusing glances showed that they blamed Alexander for their companion's death.

A burly, thick-set man, better dressed than the rest in tunic and mantle with a white cord round his waist, greeted them. He had deep-set eyes and weatherbeaten cheeks; his white hair was close-cropped like a soldier's. He grasped Telamon's hand.

"I am Critias." His light-blue eyes were friendly. "You must be Telamon – the king said you would come."

Telamon didn't understand why Alexander should be telling anyone about his arrival. He muttered his condolences and stared at the corpse, which was swathed in bands of linen and covered with a makeshift pall. Alexander demanded a cup of wine. He took this, stood at the head of the bier and dramatically lifted the cup like a priest making an offering above an altar.

"I have prayed," he declared in a strong voice, "that this man's shade will not be troubled in his journey across the river of death. I will supply the honey cake to satisfy the hunger of Cerberus. I will pay for Charon's ferry and I, Alexander of Macedon, swear that I will seek justice for his blood. I pledge this in the presence of the priestess of Athena and my vow is sacred!"

Alexander's gaze shifted. Just for a moment Telamon glimpsed his sardonic humour. "My own personal physician, Telamon, son of Margolis, a Macedonian by birth and upbringing, will investigate the cause of this man's death."

Alexander lowered the cup, took a deep gulp and passed it to the first mourner. While the cup was passed round, Alexander produced a purse, shaking out silver coins which winked in the light of the oil lamp. He placed these at the side of the corpse's head.

"My lord." An officer, ignoring the obsequies, had raised the tent flap. "You'd best come quickly!"

Alexander strode out. Telamon, Critias and the priestess followed. Alexander took the officer to one side, an arm across his shoulder, listening carefully as the man whispered in his ear. The king snapped his fingers at Telamon and hurried off. They re-entered the royal enclosure. The flap to Antigone's tent was pushed back, the entrance thronged by soldiers. Telamon followed Alexander as he thrust his way through. The young woman they had left sitting at the table now lay slumped on the floor in an untidy heap. Perdicles and Leontes sat on stools staring down at her.

"Is she dead?" Alexander demanded.

"Poisoned," Leontes replied, glaring spitefully at Telamon.

Telamon ignored him and hurried over. He picked up the wine cup. It was empty. The young woman lay in a huddle and yet, even as he felt her arm, Telamon recognized the stiffness was unnatural. He pulled the corpse over. Her face was a livid white with strange blotches high on the cheeks. Telamon searched for a blood pulse but it was futile. The skin felt cold and clammy and the rigidity of her muscles was testimony enough. He stared pitifully at the half-open eyes, the lids slightly purple as if the blood was bursting to break through. Her lips were bloodless, almost white, her jaw firmly clenched.

"What is it?" Alexander whispered.

"Poison." Telamon got to his feet and rubbed his face. "She has been poisoned. Socrates' death, some potion like hemlock. Paralysis, tightening of the limbs, an inability to breathe."

"Your first patient here," Leontes murmured.

Telamon picked up the cup and sniffed at it. "Someone must have come into this tent after we left."

"That's impossible!" the captain of the guard protested. "I have spoken to the sentry. Look around you. No one has been in here! The guard heard a movement, followed by a clatter. When he lifted the tent flap, the young woman was sprawled as you find her."

Telamon went across and examined the wine jug, but it was only pretence, a way to hide his confusion at the speed and cunning of the assassin.

Chapter 2

"Alexander was asked: 'Where, O King, is your
treasure?' 'In the hands of my friends,' he replied."
Quintus Curtius Rufus, *History*,
Book 2, Chapter 3

"Are you sure it's poison?" Perdicles asked.

Telamon sat in his colleagues' tent and shook his head disbelievingly. Alexander had left, ordering the corpse to be removed, shouting that Telamon's new tent, close to his, was to be prepared. Antigone's two companions, Selena and Aspasia, agreed to dress the body so it could be taken out with the guide's corpse to the large funeral pyre built on the cliff top. Telamon scrupulously checked the wine, the cup and the tabletop but could

find no trace of any noxious powders. The goblet had been drained; the odour of wine and the opiate was so strong it masked anything else. He glanced across at Perdicles. The Athenian stared sadly back.

"It's hardly a good introduction, is it?" Telamon murmured. "Leontes has it right: my first patient here dies within the hour. But how?" He got to his feet and strode round the small tent. "The priestess poured the wine. I saw her carry the cup. Others touched it but, if there had been any powder from a hidden ring or secreted in the palm of a hand, it would have been noticed. Yet she's dead." He whirled round. "Are you sure no one entered that tent after we left?"

Perdicles shook his head. "The king himself questioned the guard. The young woman just sat there, drank the wine and mysteriously died. How much spotted hemlock would it take?"

Telamon pulled a face. "Poisons are like wines, they have different strengths. But a few grains, not much more than your fingertip, if it was pure ground powder. Spotted hemlock, well, as you know, it freezes the limbs. The victims can't breathe. They choke to death very quickly. Of course," he added wistfully, "the opiate I gave would only heighten the effect."

He came and sat down on the small leather chest which Perdicles had mockingly introduced as "his finest chair".

"It could have been suicide," the Athenian remarked.

"No." Telamon, restless, got to his feet. "Antigone answered that. She offered to have her tent searched. Moreover, where would a poor distracted thing like that have the wit and cunning to find such a powder and then use it? She was terrified but not suicidal." Telamon beat his hand against his thigh. "We questioned everyone! I sipped the wine. Afterwards the victim sat in a closely guarded tent, its leather sheets lashed tightly together. Only a ghost could get through that."

"Have you ever dissected a corpse?" Perdicles asked.

"On a number of occasions in southern Italy. In this case it wouldn't prove anything. It would simply confirm our diagnosis. The poor woman has suffered enough. Alexan-

der will have to explain it to the family."

Telamon was angry. He had been depicted as a fool, slyly and subtly threatened. He went deeper into the tent. Cleon lay fast asleep on his cot bed snoring like a pig. Telamon sat down on the other bed. He removed Perdicles' heavy woollen cloak, which was spattered with mud along its hem, and picked at the fat barley husks stuck to the wool. He stared moodily down at the mud-caked sandals thrown into a far corner. He rolled a barley husk between his fingers. Perdicles, rather agitated, came and sat down next to him. The Athenian gestured across at Cleon.

"I envy you, you have a tent to yourself. I share with him. I've never seen a man sleep for so long, like a babe without a care in the world."

Cleon rolled over on the bed and squinted at both of them.

"I heard that. If you'd drunk the wine I drank…" He stretched. "Ah, the sleep of Dionysius!"

Telamon wiped his fingers on his robe.

"Why are you here, Telamon?" Cleon asked sweetly. "With your marvellous reputation and strange cures? Why don't you just bugger off and leave us all alone?" He pulled himself up. "By the way, I've heard your theory about bandaging."

"Why am I here?" Telamon snapped, ignoring the jibe about his medical skill. "I am beginning to ask myself that. I don't really know."

They heard shouts at the entrance to the tent. A pageboy came bustling through with all the arrogance of a successful general. He sketched a bow and pointed at Telamon.

"Your tent is ready, your baggage is stowed and the king wishes you to join him at supper. You'd best come now!"

"How can I refuse?"

Telamon got to his feet and followed the page, deliberately walking like a woman, swinging his hips, tunic flouncing above his bottom. Cleon called out something sarcastic about having friends in high places; Telamon ignored him. Outside, the camp was coming to life. The routine tasks had been completed, pickets set up, patrols despatched, sentries and guards in position. Loud neighs from the horse lines carried through the clang and clatter of the small smithies where the armourers, sweaty and black-stained in the light of their fires, worked late into the night. The army had finished its evening meal, the air carried the scent and flavours of different foods. Soldiers were returning to their units to sleep or sit chatting round the camp fires. Telamon heard a mixture of different tongues: the leisurely drawl of Greek mercenaries, the high-pitched chatter of Thessalian horsemen. Orders were being posted up, officers shouting for men, trumpets braying. They entered the royal enclosure. The page gestured at a large box-like tent with dyed cloths hung over the leather sheets.

"That is yours," he declared hoarsely. "You'll find everything there."

He sauntered off into the darkness. A guard lounged outside warming his hands over a dish full of charcoal. He smiled and nodded as the physician walked by him and around the tent. It was very similar to the one where the young woman had been murdered. He lifted the drape and studied the leather sheets beneath. These were pulled tight, the holes along the edges reinforced with rings. Twine, or cord, looped through them, kept the leather lashed

smartly to the ash poles, at least a dozen along each side. The knots were tied expertly like those on a ship's rigging. Telamon crouched down. The base was similar, the holes larger for the guy ropes, tied tight to pegs driven into the ground. Telamon pulled at the bottom of the sheet, taut as a bowstring.

No one, he reasoned, could get under this, and it would take an age to undo the cord. Surely someone would have noticed? Then the assassin would have to kill, leave, and re-tie the sheets with the same knots used by the tent-riggers.

"Is everything all right, sir?" The guard was on his feet, staring curiously at him.

"Everything's fine." Telamon grinned through the darkness. "Where are you from, soldier?"

"Father owns a farm just outside Pella. I am one of the Foot Companions. I'll be here for four hours, then I'll be relieved."

Telamon thanked him, lifted the flap and went inside. The tent was divided by a cloth into a living chamber and sleeping quarters. Telamon was grateful at Alexander's thoughtfulness: woollen coverings lay strewn on the floor; the camp bed had a feather-filled mattress and bolster; chairs, coffers and stools stood about. There were four oil lamps, one of them lit, and even a sealed jug of wine and an earthenware goblet. Telamon heard a sound and glanced round. The pageboy stood in the entrance, a red ribbon round his black, curly hair.

"What do you want?"

"To serve you, master." The page gazed cheekily back.

Telamon moved across to his travel bags which had been placed against a chest. He crouched down and examined the buckles.

They were loosened – someone had been through them. Telamon glanced at the pageboy.

"Piss off, boy! I don't like people with noses bigger than their brains! I'll find my own assistant."

The page flounced out. Telamon heard the guard laugh. He went and sat on the edge of the bed. Why had Alexander, he wondered, brought him here? What on earth did he want with him? And, more importantly, why had he truly come? He got up, filled the goblet with a mouthful of wine and rinsed his mouth out. He returned to the bed and dozed for a while. He was roughly awakened and found himself staring up at the sly, watery-eyed face of Aristander.

"Ah." Telamon rubbed his eyes. "The keeper of the king's secrets, seer of the future'. . ."

Aristander gestured to the servants behind him. "Fresh water! Up you get! You've got to change and be in the royal pavilion within the hour!"

Aristander swept out. Telamon watched him go. Had Aristander given instructions for his possessions to be searched? He sighed, got to his feet, washed his hands and face, rubbed oil into his hair and beard and dressed in his best tunic and mantle. He kept his marching sandals on but carried his slippers. A page, waiting outside, led him across to the royal pavilion.

The banquet had already begun, the guests lying on long low couches, small tables set before them. The pavilion was long, poorly lit but rich with a perfume which mingled with the less pleasant odour from the earthenware oil lamps. Alexander lorded it from a lion couch at the top of the pavilion. In the shadows behind stood two guards officers.

"Welcome, physician." Alexander gestured with his cup. He turned to his companions. "All hail to Telamon!"

The toast was taken up with a roar. This was one of Alexander's famous drinking parties. Only the closest and dearest were invited to lounge drunkenly on couches. This time, however, an exception had been made. On Alexander's left the priestess Antigone, lying like a queen, sipped carefully from a goblet. She winked slyly, telling the physician that she was the only sober person present. Next to her was Hephaestion, and then Ptolemy with his mistress, a Greek prostitute who insisted on dying her hair a deep red. Seleucus, already deep in his cups bawled at Nearchus and Aristander. The king's sword-master, Telamon's former tutor at the military academy, was also present: Black Cleitus, with his dark, lined features and cropped head, the sword slash which had taken out his right eye making his face look twisted. Alexander loved the sword-master, the king's personal bodyguard, dearly. Black Cleitus' sister had been Alexander's wet nurse.

"You haven't changed at all, Telamon!" Cleitus' one eye glared.

"You look as ugly and dangerous as ever!" Telamon shouted back.

Cleitus, who always insisted on wearing his black cloak lined with bear fur, threw his head back and bellowed deeply, wiping his mouth on the back of his hand.

"You are late, Telamon," he jibed. "Still frightened of swords, are we?"

"Aye, just as frightened of you, if the truth be known!"

Ptolemy giggled noisily. Black Cleitus glared at the physician.

"And d-d-do you, do you still st-stutter, Telamon?"

"Only when I meet someone as ugly as you."

Cleitus would have lurched to his feet but Alexander clapped noisily.

"Telamon, join me! Come!"

Alexander sprang to his feet swaying slightly. He gestured to the couch on his right. A pageboy led Telamon round. Alexander clasped the physician's hand, then pulled him closer, kissing him on each cheek. "Watch your tongue!" he warned. "They are all deep in their cups. I am not as drunk as I pretend." He laughed, pushed Telamon away and returned to his couch.

Telamon made himself comfortable and stared round. Most of the royal companions looked as if they had come straight from the drill ground, except for Alexander who was as clean and tidy as ever. His blond hair, carefully combed and oiled, was parted down the middle, the fringe lying flat against his sweat-soaked forehead. He was dressed in a snow-white, knee-length tunic edged with purple. He had gold sandals on his feet and the rings on his fingers glinted in the light. Telamon stared at the beautiful amethyst hanging on a silver chain round the king's neck.

"A present from Mother," Alexander explained. "She says if I put it into wine, it will show if there's poison."

"I could have used it earlier," Telamon retorted.

"Mother sent messages," Alexander continued blithely. "She wasn't too happy with her conversation with you. But, there again, as the poet says: 'The only joy of a woman is to have her sorrows ever on her lips'." He toasted Telamon with his cup.

"Let's thank the gods Mother is far away, eh? I love her dearly but her moods change as quickly as she moves her eyes."

"What are you whispering about?" Ptolemy called over. "Telamon, where have you been? Why did you leave the groves of Mieza? Why didn't you grow up with us all and become a warrior? Wouldn't you like to be a warrior, Telamon?"

"Wouldn't you?" Telamon retorted.

Ptolemy would have replied but the servants bustled in. The meal was not a banquet – nothing more than a drinking party. The food was second-rate: barley broth, pilchards, black pudding and roasted hare with fairly hard bread and unripe fruit looted from the local orchards. Cleitus protested loudly at the foul Euboean wine, so Alexander ordered it to be replaced with Thasian. Olives and nuts were served. The fruit girl also handed each guest a wreath of myrtle. She then took out a flute, struck up a tune and Ptolemy led them in a raucous sing-song. Telamon glanced across at Antigone. She lounged gracefully, ignoring Cleitus' lecherous glances, like an elderly aunt indulging a group of rowdy young boys. Telamon nibbled at the food and drank the undiluted wine. Antigone smiled at him; he toasted her back. Alexander was shouting something down the tent. Telamon seized the opportunity to whisper across to the priestess.

"Be careful what you drink," he urged. "These parties go on until the early hours."

"I heard that," Alexander said, falling back on the couch. He called across a servant. The large ceremonial goblet on the table in front of him was filled with wine. Alexander shouted for silence, calling upon the god of good fortune. Alexander grasped the goblet and spilled a few drops of wine on the floor as a libation. He drank as the rest chanted a verse and then the "cup of kindness" was passed round. This was the signal for the serious drinking to begin. A huge mixing bowl was placed in front of Alexander – a gorgeous piece of Samian ware depicting a horde of satyrs chasing anxious maidens. The dice were brought. Hephaestion won, throwing two sixes and a three, and he now took command as Lord of the Feast.

"Two and one," he said.

The measure was decided for the evening. Two stoups of wine for a portion of water were poured in the mixing bowl. The cups were filled. Hephaestion gave the toast and Telamon, like the rest, emptied his in one gulp. This was the signal for the guests to relax and talk among themselves. Alexander, however, took out a dagger and tapped it against the mixing bowl, the sign for silence.

"I welcome my friend, Telamon," he began. "And the Lady Antigone, priestess of Athena, from her temple at Troy. When the auguries dictate, the crossing will take place. The main army will meet General Parmenio at Abydos. I will first march south to Elaeum."

"What's there?" Ptolemy called.

"The tomb of Protesilaus."

"And who's he?"

"Telamon?" Alexander asked.

"The first Greek killed in the Trojan War."

"Clever bastard!" Ptolemy bawled.

"We will cross to Troy," Alexander continued matter-of-factly. "Make sacrifice and organize the army into battle array. We will then march south following the coastline. Critias is drawing his maps and, thanks to the Lady Antigone, we have guides enough."

"And when will all this happen?" Seleucus drunkenly brayed.

Ptolemy paused from nuzzling the neck of his mistress, and the whole tent fell silent.

"When?" Alexander queried, turning his head sideways. "Why, only when the sacrifices are pure and the gods accept our gifts."

"But it will be summer soon," Ptomely protested. "The wells and rivers will dry up. What if Darius and that bastard Memnon refuse to meet us in battle?"

"What if? What if?" Alexander turned ugly. He glowered around. "We know the Persian fleet is putting down a revolt in Egypt. What if the stars fall from heaven? Or the sea begins to boil? Haven't you forgotten the signs? The night I was born the Temple of Artemis at Ephesus was consumed by fire. I intend to spread that fire to the ends of the world."

Alexander was singing the same hymn of glory as he had as a boy, and it always entranced them. Even the cynical Black Cleitus was listening intently.

"How did Socrates describe us Greeks?" Alexander asked the throng. "We sit like frogs croaking round the pond." He laughed. "Well, the frogs are loose. We'll march to the edge of the world and bring it under the sway of Macedon." He lifted his cup. "To glory!"

They replied with a roar. Alexander, as if tired, lounged back on the couch and winked at Telamon.

"Do you think I'm telling the truth?" he whispered.

"Aristotle said truth was only an idea which can be divided and pared down. When you reach the part which is indivisible, you have arrived at the truth."

Alexander glared back. "What are you saying, Telamon?"

"I keep asking myself, sire, why I am here? But, of course, the real question is why are you here?"

"Do you believe I am the son of a god, Telamon?"

"If it makes you happy, sire."

Alexander pulled himself back up on the couch. "Do you believe?"

Telamon noticed how the contrast between the king's eyes was now quite definite: the left a deep blue, the right a dark brown. His face was slightly flushed, lips purple-stained as if he had supped deep of blood.

"Don't you believe Olympias conceived me by a god?"

"If she believes that, sire."

"Alexander! My name is Alexander!"

The king looked round. His companions were staring at him. He tapped the end of his nose. "Continue with your talking. Well, Telamon?"

"If you believe that, Alexander, and Olympias believes the same, then that's your truth. Philip believed differently. Is that why we are here, to prove that you are a god? Or that you are a better man than your father? Or is it for glory? Or what I heard travelling here, to bring the whole world under the sway of Greece?"

"I don't know," Alexander murmured. "I just don't know." He paused, sipped at his wine and smiled. "You never married, Telamon?"

"We have a great deal in common, Alexander."

"Sleep and sex," Alexander slurred, "remind me that I am mortal."

He pulled himself further up the couch, his face still full of contention. The physician studied his boyhood friend. You are a leopard, he thought, a master of ambush. Your moods are as shifting and as sudden as your mother's.

"I asked for you, Telamon…" Alexander paused to reply to one of Ptolemy's jibes. "I asked for you," he repeated, lounging back, "for many reasons." Alexander's face softened. "Do you remember when we were boys at Mieza? Cleitus would kick us out of bed long before first light. What did he say?"

Both chorused the call Cleitus would make. "A run before breakfast gives you a good appetite while a light breakfast gives you a good dinner!"

"What was that?" Cleitus called down the pavilion.

"Go back to your wine, old man," Alexander retorted. "Telamon and I are making up for lost time."

Alexander held his cup out for a servant to refill, reminding him of the measure to be used.

"I've drunk too much wine," Alexander continued. "Do you remember, Telamon, a white marble statue glistening in the early morning sun? The inscription carved on the plinth, how did it go? 'I AM AN IMMORTAL GOD, MORTAL NO MORE'."

"Is that how you see yourself?"

"Never mind that!" Alexander snapped. "We'd pray, wouldn't we? To god the father, to his son, born of the horned servant." Alexander closed his eyes. "May they guide and protect us all the day long." He opened his eyes. "I was happy then. I was free. I was the beloved son of the king and his wife. It was all a stage," he murmured. "And, as I became older, the shadows stretched across the stage to engulf me. Mother and Father closed in. First in small things. One day at Mieza I was riding a horse; it vaulted a wall. There was a slave girl carrying grapes. She was using her tunic as a basket; long golden legs and hair the colour of ripe corn. I teased and I flirted with her. We lay together in the cool shade of a holm oak tree."

"Oh, I remember this," Telamon replied. The wine had made him relax and the memories came flooding back. "The wood nymph'…?"

"That's right!" Alexander agreed. "The wood nymph! She was a beautiful girl. We lay on a bed of crushed grapes. The next day I went looking for her but someone had told Mother, hadn't they? The girl had been sold and Olympias informed me that I'd probably encountered a wood nymph, a gift from the gods. Do you know, Telamon, I believed her." Alexander's face turned ugly, a far-away look in those strange eyes. "That was Mother's first real lesson: there was only to be one woman in my life and that was Olympias. She began to sing her siren hymn, of how I was sacred, chosen by the gods. How Hercules and Achilles were my ancestors. Of course, I thrilled to this. The second verse was more cruel: that, perhaps, I was not Philip's true son but the off-spring of a god. I was confused. Do you remember how sad I became, Telamon?"

"I told you to speak with Aristander."

Alexander laughed abruptly. "Out of the pot into the fire, eh? Aristander of Tele-mus." He turned and toasted his keeper of secrets who was lounging morosely at the far end of the tent. "He hummed the same song as my mother, but he told me the hard truth." Alexander glanced down, and when he looked up his eyes were full of tears.

"He said that Philip and Olympias loved each other to distraction. When they first met on the island of Samo-Thrace, Philip believed he had been visited by a goddess; that he would never love another woman." Alexander sighed. "Of course, Philip drunk was different from Philip sober. He'd mount a goat, and probably did when he was drunk. Olympias never forgave such infidelities. You remember, Telamon? When we were boys and visited Pella, you stole into Olympias' bed chamber?"

Telamon repressed a shiver: sometimes his own nightmares came creeping back.

"Your mother's room was full of ivy," he said quietly. "There was a vine tree embed-ded in the outside wall with twisting branches of luxuriant leaves."

"And the snakes?" Alexander asked. "The snakes curling in and out? No wonder the story spread, how Olympias lay with a snake, a disguise for the god Apollo. She began to hint to Philip that I was not his true son; he retaliated with more women. Yet I did love him. The day I tamed Bucephalus," he went on, referring to his beautiful black warhorse which took its name from the brilliant white blaze on its forehead, "Philip hosted a banquet and toasted me. 'Here, he proclaimed, is my son the horse tamer!'" Alexander blinked quickly. "I have never been so proud in my life. He made me drink wine. I begged him to remain faithful to my mother. He became angry so I retorted: 'The way you sire bastards I'll have no kingdom to inher-it!'" Alexander leaned over and grasped Telamon's tunic. "He grabbed me like that, and pulled me close. 'If you are half the man I am,' he replied, 'you'll win your kingdom and keep it!' Of course, Mother heard all about it and took me into her confidence. She described how, when I was conceived, the night wind rushed through her room, the very stars were dimmed while the house was rocked by thunder and lightning. Mystical flames filled her bed chamber, and so on and so on." Alexander rubbed the side of his face. "Mother against Father, Father against Mother. Philip was a good general. He decided to take Olympias literally. If I was not his son he would marry again. So he wooed Attalus' brat. He divorced Olympias and gave Eurydice a son. Only the gods know how the battle would have gone if he hadn't been killed."

"Were you guilty of that, Alexander?"

The king glanced away. "No, no, I don't think so."

"And Olympias?"

"I'm not too sure. I thought that was finished." Alexander continued softly, "The Persians claim I did kill Philip. They argue no son could kill his true father so ergo, Philip is not my father. So, I am both a usurper and a bastard."

"But that's your enemies," Telamon reassured him. "You are Captain-General of Greece, holy vengeance against Persia."

"I am still Alexander!" The king's reply came as a hiss.

He would have continued, but the noise in the tent died as Ptolemy sprang to his feet and shouted: "Let's play kottebos!"

A servant brought a pole and drove it into the ground in the centre of the couches. A plate was balanced on top. Ptolemy stumbled to his feet. He drunkenly toasted his companions.

"Here is to my love!" he bawled, draining his cup and throwing the dregs in the direction of the plate. When he missed, he loud-

ly cursed and slumped back on his couch. Others staggered to their feet to hoots of derision. Antigone lay quietly, lolling against her couch, eyes half-closed. Telamon couldn't decide if she had been trying to listen to their conversation or was studying these wild Macedonian chieftains.

"I am still Alexander," the king continued. "Philip's dead and Olympias is back in Pella but their spirits haunt me. Olympias told me before I left that I must go to the Oasis of Siwah in the Egyptian desert where Amun-Zeus would reveal the true secret of my parentage."

"And Philip's ghost?"

"Ah, the man of iron. Sometimes I have nightmares about him. I am back on the battlefield at Chaeronea. The dead are piled high. The Sacred Band lie like a row of felled corn. The place is littered with shields and spears. The cries of the dying are shrill as night birds. An army of dead hoplites confront me, dressed and armed in their great plumed helmets, corselets, shields and spears. Their eyes and mouths are filled with blood. They stand between me and Philip. I fight through them." Alexander waved his hand. "I lay to the left and the right, pushing with my shield, thrusting with my sword. Eventually I am through, but Father's gone."

"Only nightmares'. . ."

"No, no, listen."

Alexander swallowed hard, his face heavily flushed, eyes glittering. Telamon noticed how his brow was soaked in sweat. Is this man sane, he wondered? When he had first arrived, Alexander had reminded him of his boyhood friend. But now? Was that only a mask he wore? Alexander clinked his goblet against Telamon's.

"You are secretive as always, Telamon. I want to tell you why you are here. I am surrounded by enemies, by traitors, by spies."

As if on cue Telamon glanced around. Ptolemy, ignoring the raucous noise of his companions, was staring across at them, a heavy-lidded glance, slightly mocking, as if he knew what Alexander was saying but didn't care.

"Listen!" Alexander stretched across and clutched Telamon's arm. "Darius and Memnon. I know their tactics."

"You have a spy close to them?"

"Of sorts. The Persian king will not challenge my crossing of the Hellespont. He hopes to draw me into his vast territories, exhaust my army, starve it, surround and kill it, but that's for the gods to decide. What concerns me is the spy they have close to me. Is it you, Telamon?"

"Nonsense! I wouldn't be here if you hadn't sent for me!"

"Why did you send away that page?"

"I don't like pretty bum boys. I'll choose my own assistant, as I do my friends."

"Get someone you trust," Alexander ordered. "Have you been down to the slave pens? We still have a few Thebans left to sell. You may find someone there."

"You were talking of a spy?"

"I don't know who it is." Alexander shook his head. "The only name I've been given is Naihpat."

"Naihpat?"

"Nonsense, isn't it?" Alexander made a face. "Naihpat – Apollo knows what it means." He pointed down the tent. "I have my keeper of secrets, Darius has his: a mysterious figure called after one of their gods, Mithra." Alexander stretched out his hand, fingers curled. "How I would love to

trap him and all his secrets: all those in Greece who furtively received Persian gold. I'd show no mercy, Telamon. I'd crucify them all."

"Who's your spy?" Telamon asked abruptly.

"Well, I think it's Lysias, one of Memnon's cavalry commanders. He sent me a secret message: he wants to meet me at Troy."

"For what purpose?"

"I don't know. He simply asked to meet me there and then tell me why."

"So, what do you fear, Alexander? Secret assassination? Betrayal?"

"No, I fear Philip."

"He's dead!" Telamon's voice rose.

"No, listen. Do you remember that line?" Alexander screwed up his eyes, a favourite gesture when he was a boy at the academy. "The one from Book Nineteen of the Iliad. How does it go? 'The liver was plucked from its place and, from it, the black bile drenched the front of his tunic.'"

"What has that got to do with Philip?"

"Do you remember the Delphic Oracle?" Alexander asked. " 'The bull is prepared for sacrifice, all is ready, the slayer awaits.' Father thought it was a reference to the Persian Empire; only after his assassination did people realize it was about him." Alexander paused. "I need a pure sacrifice, Telamon, before I order my troops to embark. Every bull I sacrifice is tainted. The portents augur badly, so we shelter on this headland and my army waits."

"Ignore the signs!" Telamon snapped. "Bring your fleet in and sail!"

Alexander shook his head. He put the wine goblet on the ground and, crossing his arms along the headrest, leaned his chin on his wrists, studying Telamon intently.

"Look around, physician mine. Is anyone watching us? Do you think anyone can hear?"

Telamon obeyed. Seleucus was now talking to Antigone. Aristander was feeling his crotch; the prostitute and Ptolemy were embroiled in some argument. Servants had now withdrawn, the flute girl had disappeared. Through the half-lifted tent flap, the physician could make out the shield and spear of a guard.

"Do you remember that scout whose corpse is to be consumed by fire?" Alexander continued. "The one who was found on the rocks below the cliffs? The only people who know the truth are Critias and Aristander. The rest think his death was simply the result of a camp fire brawl. The dagger was still embedded in the guide's body, in his hand a small scrap of parchment." Alexander's gaze never wavered. "The dagger was winged, of Celtic origin." Telamon flinched. He didn't know whether it was the cold night breeze or Alexander's soulless eyes. "The same sort of dagger," Alexander whispered, "which killed my father."

"But Pausanias was a madman! We all know the story," Telamon comforted. "Such daggers can be bought in any marketplace."

"Can they really, physician? And what about the piece of parchment thrust into the dead scout's hand? A note bearing a message: 'The bull is prepared for sacrifice, all is ready, the slayer awaits.' Do you realize what is happening, Telamon? Is father going to stop me?"

"Don't be ridiculous. You are as superstitious as an old woman."

Alexander moved his arms and smiled, his face transformed. "I am glad you came back, Telamon." He beat his first against his chest. "Olympias, Philip and all the might of Persia will not stop me. Nothing will stop me!"

"Is that why you levelled Thebes?"

"Just before you left Mieza," Alexander replied, "we fought with wooden swords. I kept lashing out until Cleitus intervened."

"You apologized. You talked of a red mist before your eyes."

"That's what happened at Thebes." Alexander bit his lip. "People should know when they are defeated. Time and again Thebes would meddle, conspire, start whispering campaigns throughout Greece. I remember standing before the Electra Gate watching the Sacred Band deploy. We drove them back. The red mist came down. I thought: this time, this time, I will settle matters once and for all. Never again would Thebes challenge Macedon. I gave the order, 'Take no prisoners! Leave not one stone upon another!'" He smiled crookedly. "Apart from the temples and the house of the poet Pindar. We killed all their fighting men. I took thirty thousand slaves and made a fortune out of their sale." He lifted a hand. "Never again will Thebes challenge me!"

"But someone is?"

"Yes."

Alexander coughed and swung his legs off the couch. He sat, speaking over his shoulder at the physician.

"And so we come to why you are here."

Alexander put the wine cup on the table. Telamon glanced down: the edge of the rug covering the ground near the king's couch was deeply tinged with wine. Alexander had indeed not drunk as much as he pretended. He had taken sips, the occasional gulp, but a lot of the wine had been secretly poured out.

"Look around you, Telamon. My hungry companions, they all want to be kings and princes and ride through Persepolis in glory. As long as I am faster, stronger, fiercer, more cunning, more fortunate, I am safe. As long as the pack feeds well, I'll be their leader. The same goes for the boys outside. They don't really want to leave the black soil of Macedonia but they dream of the soft, plump women of Darius' harem, of digging their arms elbow-deep into caskets of pearls and precious gems. If I realize those dreams, I am their king, their god-saviour. They wouldn't care if I proclaimed myself to be Apollo incarnate."

"You have Hephaestion, a true friend."

"Yes, I have Hephaestion, and I have Telamon. I thought long and hard about you. The day you left Mieza, riding behind your father, going down that white dusty trackway, the cypress trees on either side whispering goodbye. All Telamon wanted to be was a physician – not women, glory or gold. That's the first reason you're here."

"And the second?"

"In all my days, Telamon, I never met a pair of eyes like yours, sharp as a falcon's! You used to sit staring, missing nothing. There's the man I want, I thought: it's time Telamon came home. I heard about your little trouble in Egypt. The Persian territories are closed to you." Alexander shrugged and pulled himself up on the couch. "You can't go to Persia. No Macedonian is welcome in Greece, not really, so why don't you join your friends? Mother's threats helped you along the way. You are here, Telamon, because there is nowhere else to go and, above all, you are curious. Your curiosity would get the better of you. What better place to learn your trade and improve your skill? Before the year is out you will have patients enough." Alexander stretched across and tousled Telamon's hair. "But really, I want you to be my eyes, Telamon. I want you to dig out this spy Naihpat. I want to know how that young girl and the scout died."

Seleucus called something across to them.

"Shut up!" Alexander bawled back. "I am talking!" He turned back to Telamon. "Do you remember Homer's Iliad? You used to quote it line by line. I still keep a copy under my pillow. How many wounds does Homer describe?"

"One hundred and forty-nine."

Alexander snapped his fingers and smiled. "How was Eurypylus wounded?"

"By a poisoned arrow in his leg: the arrow was removed, the poison sucked out."

"By whom?"

"Achilles' great friend, Patroclus, in Book Eleven. He washed the wound with warm water, then smeared it with the bitter-sweet root of some plant."

Alexander drew closer. "No one else knows this," he hissed. "I have had two messages left scrawled on a piece of parchment. The first is from Book Nineteen of the Iliad: 'The day of your death draws near.'"

"And the second?"

"From Book Twenty-one, slightly changed: 'Die an evil death till all of you pay for the death of Philip.'"

The House of Death by Paul Doherty
Published by Constable in hardback
£16.99   ISBN 1 84119 302 X

CRIMEFILE
HENRY CECIL

Biography

Judge Henry Cecil Leon was born in Norwood Green Rectory near London in 1902. In 1923 he was called to the Bar and between 1949 to 1967 he served as a county court judge. He developed his writing skills while serving with the British Army during the Second World War, telling stories to officers to keep their minds off alcohol while sailing on 'dry' ships. These formed the basis of his first collection, *Full Circle*, published in 1948. Thereafter the law and official functions provided the main source for many of his stories and plays. Cecil had an extraordinary ability to examine the law in both a humorous and a more serious, analytical way, providing a series of thought provoking works. The titles being published by House of Stratus include some of his best-known work, many of which have been filmed, notably *Brothers in Law* and *Alibi for a Judge*. Though his books deal with the legal system many have more than an element of the mystery/thriller genre about them. Cecil was a hugely influential writer – providing stimulus for both those taking up a law profession and writers themselves, e.g. John Mortimer (Rumpole). Hitchcock, too, was an admirer, and planned to film *No Bail for the Judge* with Audrey Hepburn

---

Titles available in re-issue (House of Stratus)

According to the Evidence	Friends at Court	Portrait of a Judge
Alibi for a Judge	Full Circle	Settled out of Court
Asking Price	Hunt the Slipper	Sober as a Judge
Brief Tales from the Bench	Independent Witness	Tell You What I'll Do
Brothers in Law	Much in Evidence	Truth with her Boots On
Buttercup Spell	Natural Causes	Unlawful Occasions
Cross Purposes	No Bail for the Judge	Wanted Man
Daughters in Law	No Fear of Favour	Ways and Means
Fathers in Law	Painswick Line	Woman Named Man

According to the Evidence
(ISBN 1-84232-048-3)

Alec Morland is on trial for murder. He has tried to remedy the ineffectiveness of the law by taking matters into his own hands. Unfortunately for him, his alleged crime was not committed in immediate defence of others or of himself. In this fascinating murder trial you will not find out until the very end just how the law will interpret his actions. Will his defence be accepted or does a different fate await him?

The Asking Price (ISBN 1-84232-044-0)

Ronald Holbrook is a fifty-seven year old bachelor who has lived in the same house for twenty years. Jane Doughty, the daughter of his next-door neighbours, is seventeen. She suddenly decides she is in love with Ronald and wants to marry him.

Everyone is amused at first but then events take a disturbingly sinister turn and Ronald finds himself enmeshed in a potentially tragic situation.

Hunt the Slipper (ISBN 1-84232-055-6)

Harriet and Graham have been happily married for twenty years. One day Graham fails to return home and Harriet begins to realise she has been abandoned. This feeling is strengthened when she starts to receive monthly payments from an untraceable source. After five years on her own Harriet begins to see another man and divorces Graham on the grounds of his desertion. Then one evening Harriet returns home to find Graham sitting in a chair, casually reading a book. Her initial relief turns to anger and then to fear when she realises, that if Graham's story is true, she may never trust his sanity again. This complex comedy thriller will grip your attention to the very last page.

Natural Causes (ISBN 1-84232-058-0)

When megalomaniac proprietor of the Clarion Newspapers Ltd, Alexander Bean is humiliated in court by judge Mr Justice Beverly, he swears revenge. He engages the services of Sidney York to find a way to blackmail the judge. The situation gets out of hand when Sidney dies in a mysterious accident. The judge and his family fall under suspicion. Thus Alexander Bean becomes involved in a story that runs out of control for all those involved until it reaches its final unexpected conclusion.

No Bail for the Judge
(ISBN 1-84232-059-9)

A dour and highly respected High Court

Judge finds himself on trial for the murder of a prostitute. He has no recollection of the events leading up to the murder so believes he may be guilty. His daughter, however, is convinced of his innocence, so she enlists the help of a petty thief to help solve the complex mystery. Hitchcock always wanted to film this novel.

Tell You What I'll Do
(ISBN 1-84232-065-3)

Harry Woodstock is a lazy but amiable criminal who would rather live by fraud than by working. He is very comfortable in Albany Prison, Isle of Wight where a clergyman visits him in an attempt to reform his character. When he is out of prison he stays with a friend in Albany, Piccadilly and tries to avoid a violent criminal who is convinced Harry defrauded him out of £60,000. Understandably, Harry feels safer in prison so, when not dodging his enemy, he spends his time thinking up ways to get himself inside again. His amusing story ends with an ingenious solution for them all.

Unlawful Occasions
(ISBN 1-84232-067-X)

Mrs Vernay and her husband live in a flat above the Chambers of Brian Culsworth QC in the Temple. One day Mrs Vernay receives a visit from a Mr Sampson and she gets the impression that he is a blackmailer. She then immediately seeks advice from Mr Culsworth in his chambers below. Mr Culsworth's client, a Mr Baker, is bringing an action to recover his share of a win on the pools. The story of these people becomes inextricably linked in a brilliant novel of suspense and humour.

The Wanted Man (ISBN 1-84232-068-8)

When Norman Partridge moves to Little Bacon, a pretty country village, he proves to be a kind and helpful neighbour and is liked by everyone. Initially it didn't seem to matter that no one knew anything about his past or how he managed to live so comfortably without having to work. Six months before John Gladstone, a wealthy bank-robber, had escaped from custody. Gradually, however Partridge's neighbours begin to ask themselves questions. Was it mere coincidence that Norman Partridge had the build and features of the escaped convict? While some villagers are suspicious but reluctant to report their concerns to the police, others decide to take matters into their own hands...

henry cecil

Brief Tales From the Bench

CRIMEFILE
PETER MAY

After accumulating more than 1,000 television writing credits in fifteen years, Peter May has returned to his first passion – writing novels. Now, as an honorary member of the Chinese Crime Writers' Association, the Scotsman has been winning praise for his outstanding China thrillers.

Scottish Young Journalist of the Year in 1973, he had his first novel published at the age of twenty-six. He then left journalism and became one of Scotland's most successful and prolific television dramatists. By the age of thirty he had created two major TV series, *The Standard* and *Squadron*, for the BBC. During his time as storyliner and script editor on Scottish Television's *Take the High Road* in the 1980s, the popular drama serial achieved record audience figures. In the 1990s, as producer and creator of the highly-acclaimed *Machair*, he led a seventy-strong crew and cast to film in the remote islands of the Outer Hebrides. The ground-breaking Gaelic drama serial which, with English subtitles, achieved a remarkable 33% audience share, made it regularly into the top ten in the ratings in Scotland where only 2% of the population are Gaelic speakers.

During this time, he was still writing novels and being published. He wrote *The Reporter*, based on the BBC TV series, *The Standard*; *Fallen Hero*, a novelisation of the Granada TV series of the same name; *Hidden Faces*, a political thriller set in Brussels (published as *The Man With No Face* in the US); and *The Noble Path*, a very human story played out amidst the ruins of Pol Pot's Cambodia.

Drawn back to the East, May quit television in 1996 to concentrate full-time on writing novels. The first of his China thrillers, *The Firemaker*, was published in 1999 in the UK. Taking the reader on a vivid journey through the backstreets of Beijing and behind the scenes of the Chinese police system, May received outstanding critical acclaim. His follow-up, *The Fourth Sacrifice*, was published in January 2000, featuring the same winning combination of Beijing detective Li Yan and Chicago pathologist Margaret Campbell. *The Killing Room*, was published in paperback in May 2001. The latest, and most highly praised of the series to date, was selected in December 2000 as one of the "best original titles in hardback", confirming May's growing reputation in the genre. *Snakehead*, the recently completed fourth book in the series, is scheduled for publication in early 2002.

May – whose writing has been described

as "Cruz Smith meets Cornwell" – travels annually to China and the USA to research his books, and acknowledges the help given to him by the extraordinary network of contacts he has made through the internet, and the unprecedented access they have secured for him behind the scenes in both China and the US.

C R I M E F I L E
JOHN BAKER

John Baker is the creator of Sam Turner, a gritty northern private eye working out of York. The series includes: *Poet in the Gutter, Death Minus Zero, King of the Streets* and *Walking with Ghosts*, all currently available. His latest novel, *The Chinese Girl*, introduces ex-con Stone Lewis. *The Chinese Girl* is set in Hull and is a novel about masks, violence and exploitation and the necessity of confronting the past.

John Baker is a director of the CWA and a regular reviewer for the magazine *Shots* and the Internet's *Tangled Web*. He is also one of the seven members of Murder Squad, a collective of northern crime writers who promote the genre through workshops, panels, readings and lectures. John spent many years living in a community with handicapped people on the North Yorkshire moors. By way of a change he moved with his family to a barn in the south of France, and later spent two years in Norway, based in Oslo. He has worked in a variety of jobs at one time or another in the wholefood business, the computer industry, wines and spirits ("Ah, those were the days..."), as an operative in the aircraft industry, and as a milk delivery man.

He has published short stories in English and Scandinavian publications, and has twice been the recipient of a Yorkshire Arts Association writers' bursary. He has now settled in York, where he lives with his wife and family.

Bibliography

The Chinese Girl: Gollancz 2000
Walking with Ghosts: Indigo 1999
King of the Streets: Indigo 1998
Death Minus Zero: Indigo 1996
Poet in the Gutter: Indigo 1995

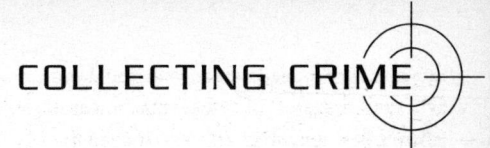

SEX AND THE HOLLYWOOD DETECTIVE

Mike Ashley

Mike Ashley has written and/or compiled nearly sixty books covering a wide range of subjects from science fiction and fantasy to mystery and horror and to ancient history. He has a keen interest in the history and development of genre fiction, particularly in magazines, and has a collection of over 15,000 books and magazines. Amongst his mystery anthologies are The Mammoth Book of Historical Whodunnits, The Mammoth Book of Historical Detectives, Shakespearean Whodunnits, Shakespearean Detectives, Classical Whodunnits, The Mammoth Book of New Sherlock Holmes Adventures, Royal Whodunnits and Impossible Crimes. His biography of Algernon Blackwood, Starlight Man is published by Constable.

It does seem remarkable that an author once dubbed 'one of the worst writers in the history of the pulps' by no less an authority than William F. Nolan, should find his way into the pages of an anthology published by such an august body as the Oxford University Press. Thirty years ago it would have been unheard of: even twenty years ago there would have been sharp intakes of breath. But go look in *The Oxford Book of American Detective Stories* edited by Tony Hillerman and Rosemary Herbert, and you'll find him – Robert Leslie Bellem.

Bellem is undergoing something of a rediscovery. His stories are being reprinted at last after having been neglected for nigh on fifty years. The author dubbed the Great Unknown of the pulps twenty-five years ago is now being recognised for his remarkable story-telling abilities. I touched on him briefly in my last column, but the sexual theme of this issue allows me to revel in the delight of Bellem's prose and look at the man of whom it has been said that his work is what would happen if P.G. Wodehouse turned to hard-boiled detective fiction. Let's give you a taster of what that means: Bellem's best known character – indeed the longest running detective series ever written – was Dan Turner, the Hollywood detective. The Turner stories are loving pastiches of the hard-boiled crime story, and, although Bellem wrote them with a twinkle in his eye, their verve, style, language and exuberance trap you from the start. Just consider some of these early lines:

> I opened the package and a human head rolled out into my lap. A man's head – with a bullet-hole between the eyes.

> I don't like to be shot at, especially on my birthday.

> The scream was she gender and harsh as a saw-toothed bayonet rasping through your eardrums all the way to the brain: high-pitched and penetrating, shrill with hysteria, freighted with terror and dripping despair from every decibel. Nobody but a dame in dire agony could possibly give vent to such an unearthly screech; and the instant it reached me I figured I had arrived too late.

Bellem threw himself into the action from the first line and just kept running. There is no attempt at sophisticated character building or scene setting and certainly no 'political correctness'. Who needed it? Bellem's readers just wanted slash-bang action and wow-bang sex, and that's what Bellem gave them. There are always plenty of delicious females in his stories, though Dan Turner has no qualms over how he deals with them.

> She had on some sort of filmy negligee. I could see through it. With the light behind her, I could see the silhouette of her body. She was a knock-out. Her legs and thighs were absolutely perfect. Her body wasn't too slender. Her breasts were firm without being boyish. Just nice handfuls. Her hips were rounded and feminine. I reached out and grabbed her. I put one hand over her startled mouth so she couldn't yell. Then I tripped her. She squirmed. I got her flat on the floor and rolled over on top of her. I mashed her hard breasts flat with my chest. I said, "Are you going to be good or shall I slap you silly?"

Well, at least he asks first. That's Turner for you. Male chauvinist to a fault. Sadistic – well, not totally, but he didn't mind who he bopped, dropped, squeezed or mashed if it served his purpose. But he has a sense of humour as well. Take the following:

> As a Hollywood private dick, I've heard of nudists and seen plenty of nuts. But nudists usually do their nuding in the good old summertime. They don't ordinarily go running across a rain-drenched strip of deserted beach in the middle of December, minus every stitch of clothing. Not even in Southern California… Therefore, I decided, the dame who came racing stark naked toward me through the storm-soaked twilight must be bughouse.

Mind you, what starts as amusing rapidly turns serious. After Dan Turner has ogled the girl for a while – "Naked Oriental women racing across deserted beaches aren't exactly numerous; and I've got my share of natural curiosity." – he gets out of his car to help her. Although naked she wears a necklace which starts to glow. Soon he smells burning flesh. He rushes to help her but is too late. "Before I could reach the girl, the blue-crackling necklace was an eye-blinding circle of luminous fire. The girl went down writhing. And then her head fell off." All that comes from *Death's Bright Halo*, definitely one of the more grotesque Dan Turner stories published in *Spicy Detective Stories* for October 1935. If you want to read the whole story and see what Turner does when he finds the beautiful Lorna McFee with a similar necklace round her neck, you'll find the story reprinted in issue 35 of *High Adventure* (September 1997), an American magazine, edited by John P. Gunnison, that specialises in reprinting from the pulps.

So who was Robert Leslie Bellem and what's the story of Dan Turner? Bellem started his career as a newspaper reporter in Philadelphia, where he had been born on 19 July 1902. His father was a policeman working on the local railroad. Bellem later recalled an incident from his childhood when he took his father his sandwiches one evening down at the local freight yard. When Bellem's father saw the boy coming he yelled at him to duck. The next second a gun was fired and Bellem's father staggered, clutching his side. He disappeared on the other side of a freight car. Moments later he reappeared clutching a freight thief. Bellem's father had a bullet crease across his ribs, and the thief had a broken jaw. "Dad was always handy with his fists", Bellem remarked.

From then on Bellem worshipped the police. "Guys who fought through to victory with their brains backed up by knuckles were supermen", he said. In fact Bellem wondered why he had not become a cop like his father. Instead he served as a journalist for newspapers right across America

throughout the 1920s. He ended up in Pasadena, where he also turned his talents to writing advertising copy and working in radio. He settled in Los Angeles in 1928. By then he had sold his first pieces to *Argosy, Brief Stories* and *Real Detective Tales*. In fact his first sale was a poem, and his delight with the English language – well, his version of it – is one of the treasures of his fiction. His fascination was always for adventure, mystery and detection – oh, and sex. He began to sell regularly to the saucy sex magazines, especially *Snappy, Broadway Follies* and the like, and this brought him in touch with New York publisher Frank Armer. In 1933 Armer had just established a new company, rather jokingly called Culture Publications, and had launched a brace of magazines all with 'Spicy' in the title – *Spicy Detective, Spicy Mystery* and *Spicy Adventure*. Bellem began to write for them,

and didn't stop for the next sixteen years.

It has been said that Bellem produced around 3,000 stories. I don't know the basis for that figure, but all of Bellem's papers are housed at UCLA, so maybe someone's counted them. But it's quite possible. Bellem was very disciplined, as you'd expect from a newspaperman of fifteen years experience. He would commute to his office in downtown Los Angeles, and put in a solid eight-hour day, five days a week. He would almost always produce a short story or novelette every day – that's twenty or so a month, enough to fill three or four magazines. He seldom wrote novel-length stories, though there are a few, and those probably took him all week! Even if we allow him just four completed stories a week, and grant him time off so that he worked, say, forty-five weeks a year – after all he did travel and was a film extra some of the time – that's still 180 stories a year for sixteen years. Which totals 2,880. Allowing for a few extra stories each year and the stories he wrote earlier and later in his career, 3,000 is not unrealistic. But it's treadmill. Bellem had to keep at it, rain or shine, regardless of how he felt. His output peaked in the late 1930s/early 1940s when he was frequently writing entire issues of *Spicy Detective* himself. He later had a magazine devoted almost totally to his stories – *Dan Turner, Hollywood Detective*. But it had its rewards. Although these pulps paid the worst of all magazines, usually one cent a word, but sometimes only half-a-cent, if you could pound out the stories, the cents mounted up. Bellem apparently wrote under contract to Frank Armer, so he probably wasn't paid by the word, but he would've made sure his contract didn't mean he ended up with less. His stories are usually around 5,000 words – sometimes longer, but let's keep to the lower figure. 180 of those a year gives you 900,000 words. In fact Bellem was rated amongst the million-a-word pulpsters, joining the elite that included Lester Dent, Walter Gibson, Bob Hogan, Arthur J. Burks, Norvell Page, Frederick Faust and H. Bedford-Jones. A million words at one cent a word is $10,000. Back in the 1930s that was equal to about £2,000 a year, which is today the equivalent of about £75,000. During the American Depression Bellem was one of the rich kids.

Having said all that, I don't know where these 3,000 stories all appeared. Bellem had about 600 stories under his own name in the detective and crime fiction magazines, plus another hundred or so in *Spicy Adventure*. Most of these magazines were published by Culture and its sister company Trojan Publications. There are another 150 under his personal pen names Ellery Watson Calder, Harley L. Court and Jerome Severs Perry. But that still leaves another 2,000. There are untold numbers under house names —those are pen names used by a particular publishing house under which works by various authors might appear. That's how Bellem wrote entire issues. He even had stories under the name John Wayne! He only needed two other stories in each magazine under pen names and that's the full 3,000. And we shouldn't forget all his stories for the sex and sleaze magazines. No, there's little doubt that Bellem was one of the most prolific short story writers of all time.

His total output is complicated by the fact that his stories were frequently reprinted under new titles with different by-lines. In fact this led to a court case. Bellem's friend and occasional collaborator, Willis T. Ballard (cousin of the author Rex Stout), discovered what was happening. One year Ballard received notice from the American Inland Revenue for failing to report on $35,000 paid to him by Armer. Ballard had not sold Armer anything during that period. He checked with Bellem and discovered that he too was being billed for tax on far greater earnings than he had received. They discovered that the editors at Armer's outfit, Ken Hutchinson and Wilton Matthews, had been reprinting old stories under new titles and with bogus by-lines, drawing the cheques and cashing them themselves. In 1947 Hutchinson and Matthews were sent to prison. So, Dan Hunter really did send two dudes to the slammer.

Dan Turner first appeared in *Murder by Proxy* in *Spicy Detective* for June 1934. There would be a Turner story in every issue of that magazine (and its successor *Speed Detective*) for the rest of its life – its last issue was February 1947. That's 132 issues. In addition there were stories in all issues of *Hollywood Detective* (another fifty-nine). There were often three or four Turner stories in each issue, but several of these were reprints. Turner also turned up in *Private Detective*. I'm not sure of the total number of original Turner stories, but it's certainly over 200 and probably closer to 300. I believe that's the longest running series of detective short stories by the same author. I certainly haven't read all of them. I don't have that first one. Copies of those early *Spicy Detective* are getting harder to find at anything much less than £30 or £40 an issue, which means a full-run of *Spicy/Speed Detective* in good condition is going to set you back something like £3,500. *Hollywood Detective* is easier to find, and not quite as expensive, but you'd be lucky to get a full run there for much under £600, and more likely £1,000. All too little of Dan Turner has been reprinted – I've listed what I know about at the end of this article, enough to give you a taster – but if you want to acquire all of the stories, it won't be cheap.

Bellem's formula for the Turner stories was pretty basic. He was a detective regularly hired by people in the film business to sort out their problems – usually people gone missing, dead or kidnapped. Turner is thrust into the action right from the start, encountering beautiful scantily-clad women within the first few paragraphs. He slam-bangs it out with the baddies and

sometimes wins the dame at the end – though not always. On a few occasions he may have to use his brain and actually solve a problem, though that was seldom more than identifying a disguised dame by a mole near her navel, so the thinking seldom got in the way of the action. Sometimes he worked with Lieutenant Dave Donaldson from the LAPD Homicide Department. He smoked heavily and drank Vat 69. He used his own style of slang. A gun was usually a roscoe or rodney or sometimes a cannon. Cigarettes were gaspers. Women were called just about every male chauvinist phrase you can imagine – and plenty more – wrens or cupcakes were most common. Guns never fired, they usually went 'ka-chow'. But Bellem could weave this into some wonderful passages. Take this one from *Homicide Hunch*:

> Even as he swung on me, a roscoe sneezed: "*Ka-Chow!*" from the kitchenette doorway. Baldy toppled forward on his profile, slugging a dent in the carpet with his trumpet. He was deceased before he stopped bouncing.

Or this from *Homicide Highball*:

> The next couple of minutes were pretty blurry. I finally got my brogans unlimbered and made a wild dive for the exit. Maw and junior blammed after me, bellowing like a pair of halfwits. They almost caught up with me as I gained the front door; or at least junior did. This cost him three front teeth.

As the titles of these two stories show, Bellem loved alliteration. His story titles are full of them: *The Crimson Crone* and *Crimson Crises*, for example; *Mesa of Madness* or *Movie Mad – Murder Mad*; though he probably milked about as much as he could get out of *Killer's Clue*, *Killer's Cue* and *Killer's Cure*. He used such phrases deliciously in his stories – "The pooch yelped piteously as the porky slob's brogan booted him in the brisket" – is a particularly good one.

What I most enjoy about Bellem's prose are his inventive similes:

> Welch gasped like a leaky flue.
>
> He dropped on the grass and rolled over, as cold as an iced codfish.
>
> He was as dead as a cannibal's conscience.
>
> He was deader than the chicken in a hard-boiled egg.
>
> I tensed my muscles and pounced into the air like a pogo stick.
>
> The room was getting hotter than an opium-smoker's breath.

These just roll out with apparent effortless ease. Bellem delighted in the joy of writing and the wonder of language.

> When I broomed the joint with my torch, I saw other things so crazy they gave me the drizzling meemies.
>
> A bullet can give a man a terrific case of indigestion, frequently ending in a trip to the graveyard.
>
> He had dignified white hair, the clear waxen skin you get when you're no more than three leaps from the graveyard.
>
> Pelting buckety-gallop across the clearing, I plunged into a dense thicket and smacked against a tree that bounced me like a tennis ball. I went down on all fours like a groggy bear, crawled behind the tree that had thumped me.

Then she let me have it, smack on the think-tank. It was a hefty wallop and it rendered my brains into a mess of scrambled eggs. I felt myself sagging as my knees lost their starch.

He can keep this up for page after page. You can become exhausted just reading it. And that's not all. Let's not forget what Bellem was famous for.

She was drawing plenty of deep breaths; leaning forward excitedly, eagerly, with anticipation glittering in her greenish glimmers. Her skin was a lustrous marble-white, heightening the crimson vividness of her mouth, and her flaming tresses curled down around her shoulders in a long, inward-curving page-boy bob. She was trembling feverishly, like some magnificent cat-animal sensing the smell of fresh gore and impatient for it to spurt.

Her kissing technique was marvellous. I'm an old osculatory expert myself; but the Manerling number taught me some tricks... She didn't kiss with her lips alone; she tossed her whole damned framework into the job. It amazed me. She had a rep for being strictly untouchable... yet here she was feeding me a work-out that would have had the Hays office screaming for the scissors. The succulent sweetness of her labial pressure sent steam sizzling past my epiglottis; it was like a shot of high-powered voltage crackling through my capillaries.

In the darkness she slipped a little unwillingly into my arms. I crushed her against me so that her breasts jabbed into my chest. I kissed her hungrily, forcing her lips apart until her hot little tongue-tip fluttered. My mouth wandered to the hollow of her throat. She made no objection when I put my hands on her firm, warm breasts. I caressed them. She quivered a little, and her arms went about my neck, drawing my head down ...

Yes, it's about time those ellipses came in! Remember this is the 1930s. Little wonder these magazines are so collectable today and cost so much. Also little wonder that the noted humorist, S. J. Perelman (who used to script for the Marx Brothers) deified Dan Turner in his essay *Somewhere a Roscoe* by calling him 'the apotheosis of all private eyes', likening him to an offspring of Sam Spade and Ma Barker. Yet that makes it all the more surprising that for years Bellem's name was pretty much forgotten except amongst the few die-hard pulp collectors.

I wanted to know more about Bellem himself. Was he the hard-drinking, thug-thumping, womaniser like Dan Turner, or was he meek and mild and hid himself away in his office? It seems he was a bit of both. Will Murray has referred to him as 'mild-mannered' and 'bespectacled'. He did tie himself to an office schedule and was known to leave parties to meet deadlines. However, his brother-in-law told Stephen Mertz that he was 'a gregarious, outgoing soul'. Apparently he loved everybody and liked to be the centre of attention. He could, at times, act the part and would sometimes shock the women at dinner parties with his liberal use of four-letter words, but he was always fun to be with. Yet there was also a sadness about him. Bill Pronzini tells the anecdote related to him by pulp writer Frank Bonham. Bellem and his wife, B.B., had no children and at meal times Bellem would place a toy stuffed panda bear in a highchair at the table and set a plate of eucalyptus leaves in front of it. Bonham thought it was a joke at first and then realised Bellem was serious.

Bellem rode the wave of the *Spicy* magazines for about ten years. Dan Turner wasn't the only detective he wrote about, but he was the most memorable. He never wrote a full-length Dan Turner novel, but occasionally he produced a lead story for the magazine that was longer than usual. He did write some novels. *Blue Murder*, published in 1938, could easily be a Dan Turner story if you just changed the name of the hero from Duke Pizzatello. There's the same mixture of fruity slang, helter-skelter action and steamy sex. It shows that Bellem could sustain his style over a complete novel. Thankfully that novel was reprinted in paperback by Dennis Macmillan in 1987 and is still easy to find. The original novel, from Phoenix Press, is highly prized and sells for £50 or more. Even more sought after is *The Vice Czar Murders*, which Bellem wrote with Cleve Adams (a friend of Raymond Chandler's) under the name Franklin Charles. It was published by Funk & Wagnall in New York in 1941 and you'll be lucky to find that in good condition, in its dust-jacket, for under £100. Almost equally prized is Bellem's *The Window with the Sleeping Nude*, the only other novel published under Bellem's own name. It was issued in paperback by Quinn Publishing in New York in 1950 as part of Quinn's Handi-Book series. Copies of that often fetch in excess of £40 today. The Dan Turner stories also appeared in comic strip form. In fact Henry Donenfeld, who was one of the managers behind Culture and Trojan Publications, was a pioneer of comic books – he was one of the executives behind the launch of *Superman*. Most issues of *Spicy Detective* and *Hollywood Detective* included a comic-strip version of the Dan Turner stories scripted by Bellem and drawn, usually, by Adolphe

Barreaux. These ran right through into the late 1940s and were later poshed up in colour for *Crime Smashers* in the early 1950s. There were also two Dan Turner films. *Blackmail*, released in 1947 from Republic, starred William Marshall as Turner. It was scripted by Royal Cole based on the story *Stock Shot* (*Speed Detective*, July 1944). More recently Dan Turner devotee, John Wooley, scripted a new story, *The Raven Red Kiss-Off*, released in 1990 with Marc Singer as Turner. Wooley also launched a short-lived comic book, *Dan Turner, Hollywood Detective*, which saw just four issues from March to September 1991, and featured new strips based on old stories.

By 1942 the writing was on the wall for the *Spicy* pulps. The New York mayor La Guardia had stamped down on them and got them to clean up their act. *Spicy Detective* became *Speed Detective*. The covers were tamer but much of the action was the same and Bellem never toned down his writing. He was now in full flow, not only writing for every issue of *Speed Detective* but also for his own magazine, *Dan Turner, Hollywood Detective*, which had been launched in January 1942 (its title was shortened to *Hollywood Detective* in September 1943). He even found time to work as writer and script supervisor on Boris Karloff's radio series *Creeps by Night* that ran from February to June 1944. But after the War the pulps began to fail, and the *Spicy/Speed* line came to an end in 1950. Like other old-time pulpsters, Bellem turned to the emerging television industry for his bread and butter. His talent for fast-paced, colourful, uncomplicated action was ideally suited to television. He became a scriptwriter on ABC's new *Dick Tracy* series. That only lasted a year but by then Bellem was writing for other ABC series, especially *The Lone Ranger* and *The Adventures of Superman*. He also worked on *Captain Midnight, Perry Mason, 77 Sunset Strip* and, towards the end, *Tarzan* and *Voyage to the Bottom of the Sea*. I suspect it would be quite revealing if someone could pull together a complete listing of Bellem's TV work.

He kept a hand in writing. He is known to have published at least two sex novels in the early 1960s under the name Anthony Gordon – *Doctor of Lesbos* (1963) and *The Sex Ladder* (1964), and there may be more hidden under pen names. He died on 1 April 1968 in Sherman Oaks, California, and was cremated at the Altedena Mortuary. He left behind a bizarre legacy that has only just started to be uncovered.

Mike Ashley

Bellem Checklist

(My thanks to Bill Pronzini, Ron Goulart, Victor Berch and Will Murray for their help with details in this article.)

(My thanks to William Contento for his help in the compilation of this list.)

Books by Bellem

Blue Murder, New York: Phoenix Press, 1938; reprinted Miami Beach: Dennis Macmillan, 1987

The Vice Czar Murders (with Cleve Adams as Franklin Charles), New York: Funk & Wagnall, 1941

Half-Past Mortem (ghost-written by Bellem for John A. Saxon), New York: Mill, 1947; London: Foulsham, 1949

The Window with the Sleeping Nude, New York: Quinn Publishing, 1950

No Wings on a Cop (completed by Bellem from story by Cleve Adams), New York: Quinn Publishing, 1950

Doctor of Lesbos (as Anthony Gordon), New York: Beacon Books, 1963

The Sex Ladder (as Anthony Gordon), New York: Beacon Books, 1964

[Note: it has been suggested that Bellem had a hand in writing *Dig Me a Grave* with Cleve Adams published as by John Spain, New York: Dutton, 1942]

Recently Compiled Collections

God's Gift to the Sherlock Business, Air Pirates, 1981. Contains *Star Chamber* and *Future Book*

Dan Turner, Hollywood Detective (edited by John Wooley), Bowling Green, Ohio Popular Press, 1983. Contains *Homi Highball, Off-Stage Murder, Dark St. Death, Homicide Spike, Drunk, Disor. and Dead, Hair of the Dog* and *Dumr Jackpot*

Three Dan Turner Stories, Winds of the World, 1986. Contains *Beyond Justice, Blackmail from Beyond, Cat Act*

Spicy Detective Encores #5, Winds of the World, 1987. Contains *Alimony League, Badger Bump, Killer's Cue*

Dan Turner stories reprinted in anthologies and magazines

The Crimson Flame in *Pulp Review*, May 1993

Crimson Quest in *Pulp Review*, December 1991

Dead Man's Bed in *The Pulp Collector* #18, Summer 1990

Dead Man's Head in *Pulp Friction* edited by Peter Haining (London: Souvenir Press, 1996)

Dealer in Death in *High Adventure* #25, January 1996

Death's Bright Halo in *High Adventure* #35, September 1997

Death's Passport in *The Pulps* edited by Tony Goodstone (New York: Chelsea House, 1976)

Diamonds of Death in *The Arbor House Treasury of Detective and Mystery Stories from the Great Pulps* edited by Bill Pronzini (New York: Arbor House, 1983) and *The Mammoth Book of Private Eye Stories* edited by Bill Pronzini & Martin H. Greenberg (London: Robinson Books, 1988)

Gun from Gotham in *Rue Morgue No. 1* edited by Rex Stout & Louis Greenfield (New York: Creative Age Press, 1946)

Homicide Highball in *Oxford Book of American Detective Stories* edited by Tony Hillerman & Rosemary Herbert (Oxford University Press, 1996)

Homicide Hunch in *Tough Guys & Dangerous Dames* edited by Robert E. Weinberg, Stefan R. Dziemianowicz & Martin H. Greenberg (New York: Barnes & Noble, 1993)

Killer Come Back to Me in *Pulp Review*, November 1992

The Lake of the Left-Hand Moon in *The*

Great American Detective edited by William Kittredge & Steven M. Krauzer (New York: Mentor, 1978)

Murder Mine in *Strange Worlds* #2, 2000

Murder on the Sound Stage in *Pulp Review*, July 1994

Murder's Messenger in *High Adventure* #27, May 1996

The Phantom Bullet in *The Saint's Choice, Volume 6*, edited by Leslie Charteris (The Saint Enterprises, 1946)

Preview of Murder in *The Mammoth Book of Pulp Fiction*, edited by Maxim Jakubowski (London: Robinson Books, 1996)

Reckoning in Red [4 stories] (Black Dog Books, 2001)

Televised Frame in *Strange Worlds* #2, 2000

Temporary Corpse in *Spicy Detective Stories* edited by Tom Mason (Newbury Park: Malibu Graphics, 1989)

Thug's Threshold in *High Adventure* #40, May 1998

BULLETS

Adrian Muller

Patricia Cornwell

Columbia Pictures are bringing out the big guns, enlisting *Saving Private Ryan* screenwriter Robert Rodat to adapt *Cruel and Unusual* from Cornwell's popular Kay Scarpetta series.

Free Magazine Offer

Sherlock Holmes – the Detective Magazine is bi-monthly covering all aspects of detective fiction and has a highly respected review section. Subscription for a year (six issues) is £20 (£22 Europe/ USA$40) For a FREE SAMPLE ISSUE send postal details to: PO Box 100, Chichester, West Sussex, PO18 8HD, UK. Fax: +44 (0)1243 576 456. E-mail: admin@pmh.uk.com

Nicci French: Drama Queen

Nicci French rules in drama adaptations this autumn. On the big screen comes *Killing Me Softly* starring Joseph Fiennes and Heather Graham. On the telly expect *The Safe House* with Geraldine Sommerville, Sean Gleeson and Robert Bathurst.

More Telly

Currently in production is a try-out pilot adaptation of Jill McGown's Lloyd and Hill series. Seen as a possible replacement for Morse, it stars Philip Glenister and Michelle Collins. Whatever happened to Collins' plans for playing Lauren Henderson's Sam Jones?

NEW BRITISH CRIME TITLES:

(author, title (series), publisher, price)

June (previously unlisted)

Tom Clancy: *Powerplay 5* (Roger Gordian): Michael Joseph, £5.99

Harlan Coben: *Tell No One*: Orion, £12.99

Nicci French: *The Red Room*: Michael Joseph, £9.99

Michael Meehan: *The Salt of Broken Tears*: Vintage, £6.99

July (previously unlisted)

Penelope Evans: *First Fruits*: Alison & Busby, £17.99

Anita Janda: *The Secret Diary of Dr Watson*: Alison & Busby, £17.99

Hugh Collins: *No Smoke* (debut crime novel): Canongate, £6.99

Liz Evans: *Barking!* (Grace Smith): Orion, £9.99/£16.99

Jonathan Gash: *Every Last Cent* (Lovejoy): Macmillan, £16.99

Patricia Hall: *Deep Freeze*: Alison & Busby, £17.99

Eoin McNamee: *The Blue Tango*: Faber & Faber, £9.99

Chris Paling: *Newton's Swing*: Vintage, £6.99

Henry Porter: *A Spy's Life*: Orion, £12.99

Michael Ridpath: *The Predator*: Michael Joseph, £9.99

Kevin Sampson: *Outlaws*: Jonathan Cape, £10.00

Joanna Traynor *Bitch Money*: Bloomsbury, £6.99

Kate Wilhelm: *The Deepest Water*: Robert Hale, £17.99

David Williams: *Criminal Intentions*: Robert Hale, £17.99

August

David Ambrose: *Coincidence*: Simon & Schuster, £12.99

Robert Barnard: *The Bones in the Attic* (Charlie Peace): HarperCollins, £16.99

Mark Billingham: *Sleepy Head* (debut crime novel): Little, Brown, £9.99

Matthew Branton: *The Hired Hand*: Bloomsbury, £10.00

Lizbie Brown: *Cat's Cradle* (Elizabeth Blair): Hodder & Stoughton, £17.99

James Lee Burke: *Bitterroot* (Billy Bob Holland): Orion, £16.99

Barbara Cleverly: *The Last Kashmiri Rose*: Constable, £16.99

Michael Cordy: *Lucifer*: Bantam, £9.99

Denise Danks: *Baby Love* (Georgina Powers): Orion, £9.99/£16.99

Leif Davidsen: *Lime's Photograph*: Harvill Press, £9.99/£15.99

Sarah Diamond: *Cold Town*: Orion, £9.99/£16.99

Tim Dorsey: *Orange Crush*: HarperCollins, £5.99

Marjorie Eccles: *Untimely Graves* (DS Gil Mayo): Constable, £16.99

Sylvia Hamilton: *The Pendaragon Banner* (Sir Ricahrd Straccan): Orion, £12.99

Mary Higgins Clark: *On the Street Where You Live*: Simon & Schuster, £16.99

James Humphreys: *Riptide*: Macmillan, £16.99

Greg Iles: *Dead Sleep*: Hodder & Stoughton, £17.99

Faye Kellerman: *The Forgotten*: Headline, £9.99/£17.99

Susan Kelly: *Killing the Fatted Calf*: Alison & Busby, £17.99

Michael Kimball: *Green Girls*: Headline, £10.00

Deryn Lake: *Death in the West Wind*: Alison & Busby, £17.99

Robert Ludlum & Philip Shelby: *The Cassandra Compact*: HarperCollins, £16.99

Hannah March: *A Necessary Evil* (Robert Fairfax): Headline, £17.99

Edward Marston: *The Repentant Rake*: Headline, £17.99

Maureen O'Brien: *Revenge*: Little, Brown, £16.99

Orhan Pamuk: *My Name is Red*: Faber & Faber, £9.99

James Pattinson: *Crane*: Robert Hale, £17.99

Kathy Reichs: *Fatal Voyage* (Tempe Brennan): William Heineman, £15.99

Lawrence Sanders: *McNally's Chance* (Archy McNally): Hodder & Stoughton, £17.99

Holden Scott: *The Carrier*: Robert Hale, £17.99

Lisa Scottoline: *The Vendetta Defence*: HarperCollins, £9.99

Gerald Seymour: *The Untouchable*: Bantam, £10.99

Robert Tanenbaum: *Enemy Within*: Simon & Schuster, £10.00

Marcel Theroux: *The Paperchase*: Abacus, £10.99

Donald Thomas: *Sherlock Holmes and the Running Noose* (Sherlock Holmes): Macmillan, £16.99

David Wishart: *Last Rites* (Marcus Corvinus): Hodder & Stoughton, £17.99

September

John Baker: *Shooting in the Dark* (Sam Turner): Orion, £9.99/£16.99

Jo Bannister: *Echoes of Lies*: Alison & Busby, £17.99

Adam Baron: *Superjack* (Billy Rucker): Macmillan, £9.99

Sally Beauman: *Rebecca's Tale* (sequel to Du Maurier's *Rebecca*): Little, Brown, £16.99

Ken Bruen: *London Boulevard*: Do-Not Press

Lorenzo Carcaterra: *Gangster*: Simon & Schuster, £10.00

Paul Charles: *Hissing of the Silent Lonely Room* (Kennedy): Do-Not Press

Stephen Coonts: *America* (Jack Grafton): Orion, £12.99

Robert Crais: *Hostage*: Orion, £12.99

Deborah Crombie: *A Finer Find* (CI Kincaid): Macmillan, £16.99

Judith Cutler: *Will Power* (Kate Power): Hodder & Stoughton, £17.99

Freda Davies: *A Fine and Private Place* (DI Keith Tyrell): Constable, £16.99

Linda Davies: *Something Wild*: Headline, £9.99

Jeffrey Deaver: *Shallow Graves* (John Pellam): Hodder & Stoughton, £17.99

Jeffrey Deaver: *Bloody River Blues* (John Pellam): Hodder & Stoughton, £17.99

Jeffrey Deaver: *Hell's Kitchen* (John Pellam): Hodder & Stoughton, £17.99

David Docherty: *The Killing Jar*: Simon & Schuster, £10.00

Frederick Forsyth: *The Veteran* (short stories): Bantam, £16.99

Kinky Friedman: *Steppin' On a Rainbow* (Kinky Friedman): Faber & Faber, £5.99

Martha Grimes: *The Blue Last* (Richard Jury): Headline, £17.99

Joyce Holmes: *Bitter End* (Fizz & Buchanan): Headline, £17.99

Maggie Hudson: *Looking for Mr Big*: HarperCollins, £5.99

James H. Jackson: *The Reaper*: Headline, £17.99

Bill James: *Split* (new series): Do-Not Press

Alan Judd: *Legacy* (Charles Thoroughgood): HarperCollins, £16.99

John Lescroart: *The Indictment*: Headline, £17.99

Frederick Lindsay: *Darkness in My Hand* (Jim Meldrum): Hodder & Stoughton, £17.99

Jenny Maxwell: *Bright Rooms*: Warner, £5.99

John McLaren: *Running Rings*: Simon & Schuster, £10.00

Marcia Muller: *Point Deception*: The Women's Press, £6.99

Bill Murphy: *Fractions of Zero*: Hodder & Stoughton, £17.99

Stuart Pawson: *Chill Factor*: Alison & Busby, £17.99

Anne Perry: *Rutland Place* (the Pitts): HarperCollins, £5.99

Anne Perry: *Come Armageddon* (Tathea fantasy sequel): Headline, £17.99

Elizabeth Peters: *Lord of the Silent* (Amelia Peabody): Robinson, £6.99

Jerry Raine: *Small Change*: Do-Not Press

Elizabeth Redfern: *The Music of Spheres*: Century, £15.99

Ruth Rendell: *Adam and Eve and Pinch Me*: Hutchinson, £16.99

David Roberts: *The Bones Are Buried* (Lord Corinth): Constable, £16.99

Simon Shaw: *Selling Grace* (Grace Cornish): HarperCollins, £9.99

Karin Slaughter: *Blindsighted* (debut crime novel): Century, £16.99

Veronica Stallwood: *Oxford Double* (Kate Ivory): Headline, £17.99

Sarah Strohmeyer: *Bubbles Unbound*: Headline, £9.99

Peter Tremayne: *Smoke in the Wind* (Sister Fidelma): Headline, £17.99

Margaret Yorke: *Cause for Concern*: Little, Brown, £16.99

October

John Baker: *Shooting in the Dark* (Sam Turner): Orion, £9.99/£16.99

Jo Bannister: *Echoes of Lies*: Alison & Busby, £17.99

Adam Baron: *Superjack* (Billy Rucker): Macmillan, £9.99

Lorenzo Carcaterra: *Gangster*: Simon & Schuster, £10.00

Stephen Coonts: *America* (Jack Grafton): Orion, £12.99

Robert Crais: *Hostage*: Orion, £12.99

Deborah Crombie: *A Finer Find* (CI Kincaid): Macmillan, £16.99

Freda Davies: *A Fine and Private Place* (DI Keith Tyrell): Constable, £16.99

David Docherty: *The Killing Jar*: Simon & Schuster, £10.00

Kinky Friedman: *Steppin' On a Rainbow* (Kinky Friedman): Faber & Faber, £5.99

John McLaren: *Running Rings*: Simon & Schuster, £10.00

Marcia Muller: *Point Deception*: The Women's Press, £6.99

Stuart Pawson: *Chill Factor*: Alison & Busby, £17.99

Elizabeth Peters: *Lord of the Silent* (Amelia Peabody): Robinson, £6.99

David Roberts: *The Bones Are Buried* (Lord Corinth): Constable, £16.99

Ace Atkins: *Leavin' Trunk Blues* (Nick Travers): Robinson, £6.99

Anthony Bourdain: *Bobby Gould*: Canongate, £9.99

Christopher Brookmyre: *A Big Boy Did It and Ran Away*: Abacus, £9.99

Jon Cleary: *Yesterday's Shadow* (Scobie Malone): HarperCollins, £16.99

Ann Cleeves: *The Sleeping and the Dead*: Macmillan, £16.99

Martina Cole: *Faceless*: Headline, £9.99/£17.99

Clive Cussler: *Valhalla Rising* (Dirk Pitt): Michael Joseph, £16.99

Clive Egleton: *One Man Running* (Ashton): Hodder & Stoughton, £17.99

Ron Ellis: *Grave Mistake* (Johnny Ace): Headline, £17.99

Ranulph Fiennes: *The Secret Hunters*: Little, Brown, £16.99

Clare Francis: *A Death Divided*: Macmillan, £16.99

Frances Fyfield: *The Nature of the Beast*: Little, Brown, £9.99

Jean-Christophe Grange: *The Stone Council*: Harvill Press, £10.00

Laurel K. Hamilton: *A Kiss of Shadows*: Bantam, £5.99

John Harvey: *In a True Light*: William Heineman, £16.99

Graham Hurley: *The Take* (Joe Faraday): Orion, £9.99

Alanna Knight: *The Dagger in the Crown*: Macmillan, £16.99

Bill Knox: *Deep Fall*: Constable, £16.99

Stephen Leather: *Tango One*: Hodder & Stoughton, £17.99

Roy Lewis: *The Nightwalker*: Alison & Busby, £17.99

David Lindsey: *Animosity*: Little, Brown, £17.99

John Malcolm: *Simpson's Homer*: Alison & Busby, £17.99

Shane Maloney: *The Brush-Off* (Murray Whelan): Canongate, £9.99

Andy McNabb: *Last Light*: Bantam, £16.99

Chris Mooney: *World Without End*: Simon & Schuster, £10.00

Carolyn Morwood: *A Simple Death*: The Women's Press, £6.99

Reggie Nadelson: *Sex Dolls* (Artie Cohen): Faber & Faber, £9.99

James Patterson: *Violets are Blue* (Alex Cross): Headline, £16.99

Ridley Pearson: *Parallel Lies*: Orion, £9.99/£16.99

Maureen Peters: *Goodbye Holly Jane*: Constable, £16.99

Peter Prince: *Bubbles*: Bloomsbury, £6.99

Richard Rayner: *The Cloud Sketcher*: HarperCollins, £6.99

Lynda Robinson: *Murder at the God's Gate*: Alison & Busby, £6.99

Jean Saunders: *Deadly Suspicions*: Robert Hale, £17.99

David Scofield: *The Pegasus Forum*: Simon & Schuster, £12.99

Barbara Seranella: *Unwanted Company*: Robert Hale, £17.99

John Smolens: *Cold* (debut crime novel): Flame, £10.99

For further information on the above titles, or to order books, contact:

Crime in Store

14 Bedford Street, Covent Garden, London WC2E 9HE

Tel: +44 (0)20 7379 3795, fax: +44 (0)20 7379 8988

Email: CrimeBks@aol.com   Website: http://www.crimeinstore.co.uk

Murder One

71-73 Charing Cross Road, London WC2H 0AA

Tel: +44 (0)20 7734 3483, fax: +44 (0)20 7734 3429

Email: 106562.2021@compuserve.com   Website: http://www.murderone.co.uk

Post Mortem Books

58 Stanford Avenue, Hassocks, Sussex BN6 8JH

Tel: +44 (0)1273 843066, fax: +44 (0)1273 845090

Email: ralph@pmbooks.demon.co.uk   Website:

http://www.postmortembooks.co.uk

CONSPIRACY THEORIES

The Essential Conspiracy Theories

by Robin Ramsay

Do you think the X-Files is fiction? If so, you must be one of those deluded fools who think Elvis is dead, and believe that the US actually went to the moon, and don't know that the ruling elites did a deal with the extra-terrestrials after the Roswell crash in 1947…

Boy, it really is getting strange out there. At one time, you could blame the world's troubles on the Masons or the Illuminati, or the Jews, or One Worlders, or the Great Communist Conspiracy. Now, in addition to the usual suspects, we also have the alien-US elite conspiracy, or the alien shape-shifting reptile conspiracy to worry about – and there are books to prove it as well!

Conspiracy Theories? They are all in here – but not just lined up to be ridiculed and dismissed. OK, there is some of that, but the author also tries to sort out the handful of wheat from the choking clouds of intellectual chaff. For among the nonsensical Conspiracy Theory rubbish currently proliferating on the Internet, there are important nuggets of real research about real conspiracies waiting to be mined.

This book has done the mining for you. Fully sourced and referenced, this is both a serious examination of Conspiracy Theories and the Conspiracy Theory phenomenon, and a guide to further explorations of the subject.

ISBN 1903047307 £3.99

Pocket Essentials are available from bookshops or ring 020 7430 1021
www.pocketessentials.com

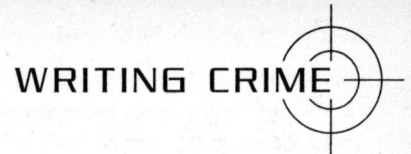

WRITING CRIME

SEX AND CRIME

Natasha Cooper

CT prides itself on the number of top crime writers who are happy to write for these pages – and here's Natasha Cooper (aka Clare Layton), regularly to be found as reviewee at the back of CT for her Trish Maguire crime treats, talking about the crime writer's life...with a thought or two on this issue's theme...

Ideas are like bacteria. They can't spread in an inhospitable environment, but once conditions are right they can take over the world. Women's suffrage was like that. Before the First World War campaigners fought, suffered and sometimes died to get the vote for women and failed. Only after the war had both decimated the young male population of the British Isles and shown that women were an essential part of action at the front, nursing, driving ambulances and so on, did the campaign succeed. Much the same happened with rape. Before women had reliable control of their own fertility and the ability to choose where, with whom and when they mated – as well as the economic power to feed their offspring without the help of a male – it was impossible for campaigners to persuade a sceptical,

smirking establishment of the full seriousness of the crime of rape. "Every woman fantasises about rape", blokes used to say at parties in the 1960s, or, "More women ought to resist, you know. It's their fault. If it were more difficult, men would stop. And not many women would be killed." Intelligent male judges could talk about contributory negligence or comment on the degree of trauma the victim had suffered, basing their assessment only on her demeanour in the witness box, so that if she put up a good front she would be assumed to have 'got over it'. That, in turn, was taken to mean it couldn't have been too bad after all. And other women would snigger if an unpopular 'friend' claimed she'd been the victim of what would now be called date rape.

So deeply have the campaigners driven home their crucial message that there is nothing remotely funny about rape, and that 'no means no', that attitudes have changed in line with women's increasing social and economic power. Indeed they have changed so much that there has been something a backlash. There has also been the (to me) ludicrously exaggerated suggestion that a woman has been raped if she was so drunk that she didn't object to what was happening at the time and only subsequently decided she hadn't liked it. That seems to me to be like changing the law retrospectively. No should definitely mean no in any circumstances, but yes last night (or even the lack of no) can't possibly be turned into no next morning just because you've had second thoughts. So-called date-rape drugs are a different matter. Administered covertly, they are tantamount to the kind of violence that few women are physically powerful enough to resist. Hearing one victim of the kind of date rape that involves physical violence describe the moment at which she realised she was not strong enough to prevent him doing whatever he wanted was both stomach-churning and unforgettable. No one listening could have believed she had in any way asked for what happened or contributed to it when she accepted an ordinary invitation from a sober and thoroughly respectable man of the kind she'd been going out with for years.

But passions are easily aroused on this subject and can flare into uncontainable fury in an instant. The oddest recent conflagration was the one that was lit by scientists suggesting that there was once an evolutionary advantage to rape, as though they have in some way expressed approval of the crime today. That's absurd – and dangerous too. Pointing out that a certain kind of behaviour had evolutionary advantages in the past has nothing to do with legitimising such behaviour *now*. Their suggestion arose partly out of the discovery that rape is statistically more likely to result in conception than unforced sex. It's not hard to see

the kind of advantage that might have had. In very restricted societies, genetic defects and genetically based illnesses are very much more common than in more widespread populations. For example, as Richard Dawkins has pointed out in *Unweaving the Rainbow*, most modern Afrikaaners are descended from a particular group of Dutch immigrants and therefore suffer more from genetic disease than other groups. He instances one disorder of the blood, porphyria variegata, which is rare in the outside world but apparently is found in about one in three hundred Afrikaaners. In the days before populations moved easily, or in societies that forbade marrying out, the risk of such genetic problems would have increased in every generation, unless of course they resulted in infertility. Rape by a stranger from a different tribe would have imported valuable new genes into the host tribe, while kidnap of a female and subsequent forcible mating would have done the same for the rapist's group.

Today primatologists have found that males of some bands of chimpanzees will march out of their own territory to kidnap and rape females of a neighbouring group – behaviour that almost certainly has advantages in enlarging their gene pool. Such benefits haven't necessarily been confined to whole groups. Individuals who were unlikely to achieve consenting sex would have been able to pass on their genes only by rape. Again looking at the animal kingdom, there is the phenomenon of the 'sneaky fucker'. This is the young or slight male, too low in the hierarchy to challenge the silver backs, the great bulls or the alpha males of the herd. He takes advantage of his seniors' distraction in fighting over the best females to sneak in and impregnate them. There have been suggestions that stranger-rapists today are subconsciously motivated by that drive. Unattractive or socially inadequate, they are unlikely to achieve sex with a desirable woman in any other way. This is the kind of man who, after the rape, will tell his victim how special she is to him and turn sick-makingly kind, even in one reported case calling up a cab to take her home and asking the driver to take extra special care of her.

This theory does not, of course, address the question of why some men rape elderly women, an act of barbarity that could not possibly result in conception and has not yet been explained by any evolutionary biologist, as far as I know. Nor does it deal with the fact that today stranger-rapists are in fact rarer than men who rape women known to them. Their crime may well have more to do with power – and straightforward violence – than sex. There is plenty more work to be done before the phenomenon is properly understood and therefore – perhaps – controlled. Prosecutions for date rape are much rarer than reported incidents, and convictions are rarer still. Perhaps in some of the many cases where serious violence is involved, victims should consider suing in the civil courts for assault rather than trying for a chancy criminal conviction of rape. Perhaps, to turn the 1960s blokeish comment on its head, if more men were forced to pay substantial damages to the women they've beaten up in order to have forced sex with them, the men would give up. I'm not, by the way, suggesting that any amount of money could make up for being forced to undergo that kind of horror. I'm suggesting that the fear of being forced to

pay large financial penalties might provide some kind of deterrent, but I could of course be wrong.

As a crime writer, I found my own particular interest in this painful and difficult subject was sparked by the discovery that rape results in conception more often than unforced sex. I began to wonder about the children who were born to rape victims. They can't all be given up for adoption or put into care. So what kind of relationship could their mothers have with them? There are enough tensions between freely consenting women and their families without adding the need to watch features and characteristics of your rapist developing in your growing child. You would have to be a saint to be unaffected by that or to let it have no effect on your treatment of the child. How would you cope? And how would the child cope? Would you tell him or her? How would you find the words to make such knowledge bearable? Questions like that began to obsess me and provided the seed of my latest Clare Layton novel, *Those Whom the Gods Love*, which will be published by HarperCollins in December. I have come to no conclusions – I'm only a writer of fiction after all, not a scientist or a jurist – but I have explored the consequences of a rape on a particular group of people about whom I came to care a great deal. As I wrote, more and more questions emerged and with them the familiar crime writer's urge to find out why some people are capable of destroying other people's lives, and how much they know of what they do. The selfish gene may be one answer. Pure selfishness another. But there must be plenty more.

Natasha Cooper

AUDIO CRIME

Brian Ritterspak

Macmillan continues to issue a good selection of crime and thriller material in the audiobook medium, and the choice of readers remains exemplary. Rennie Airth's *River of Darkness* is given an intelligent and well-paced reading by Nathaniel Parker, and this tale of golden age mystery has been very skilfully abridged. The latter is not an art to be sneezed at: Simon Callow's reading of Conrad's *Victory,* for instance, was ruined by the clumsy excision of a key subplot that left gaping holes in the narrative. Similarly, Michael Maloney's reading of Clare Francis' *Red Crystal* fits neatly into the three-hour running time, and while Nick Ryder of Special Branch may be a protagonist cut from very familiar cloth, the plotting here is (for the most part) well up to standard. If Wilbur Smith's *Warlock* is less successful, this is not down to Robert Powell's highly professional reading, which makes a strong case for the book. Smith appears to have lost the golden touch of earlier years, and this one often comes across as a parody of his vintage work, with unconvincing supernatural elements grafted onto the narrative. Nevertheless, Powell makes the best possible case for it.

Brian Ritterspak

THE SCREEN SEEN AT CRIME SCENE

Michael Carlson *takes in the film side of Crime Scene 2001*

Crime Scene 2001 is a combination film festival and mystery convention, and sometimes the two halves of the programme seem to exist separately. Separate but equal wasn't a problem, however, as the NFT's season of films and interviews attracted a wider audience, and the rest of the July schedule at the NFT, with its classic film noir on offer, made it a month of murder on the South Bank.

Still, my favourite of the films in the Crime Scene programme was a small but taut Dutch thriller called *Leak*. Based on true stories of police corruption in the face of Holland's burgeoning drug trade (Dutch police allow drug dealers to thrive in the domestic market with soft drugs, in return for the promise of tip-offs about bigger export deals), director Jean van de Velde and co-writer Simon de Waal have constructed a tale of paranoia and betrayal which gets one rather hapless cop (Cas Jensen) caught between undercover narcs, his uniformed colleagues, and the dealers, one of whom is his childhood friend, Jacky, played with great elan by Victor Low. The film plays with ambiguity, and its great virtue is that nobody is entirely good or bad (except perhaps for the cop's wife, played wonderfully by Ricky Koole as a kind of earth-bimbo). That sets off the film's very punchy violence against a background of uncertainty worthy of the best film noir. Despite being made on a budget of less than $2 million, the action scenes convince, but what keeps the action moving is a very real sense of tension from start to finish.

The high-profile end of Crime Scene was Steve Buscemi's *Animal Factory*, which, along with his Guardian interview, was a guaranteed sell-out, and the NFT Green Room was teeming with celebrities ranging from Paul McCartney, father of the famous fashion designer, to Chrissie Hynde, former pop journalist. I reviewed *Animal Factory* in CT23, after it played the London Film Festival, but hearing Buscemi's take was fascinating, particularly on the issue of the script, and what he saw in the film. Buscemi, of course, worked with Eddie Bunker on *Reservoir Dogs* (and the highlight of the interview was Buscemi's incredible imitation of Quentin Tarantino, illustrating the difference between the hard-boiled Eddie Bunker-style script for *Dogs* which he'd been sent and the high-pitched video geek voice of the writer which he first heard on the phone line, asking if he'd liked it!). Buscemi and Bunker had lost touch after *Reservoir Dogs*, but Danny Tajo had passed him the screenplay while working with him on *Desperado* and *Con Air*. Buscemi's work on the screenplay of *Animal Factory* was mostly designed to get back to the feel of the Eddie Bunker book. He shot the film in an empty prison in Philadelphia, worried that going to Canada, as his financiers wanted, wouldn't allow him the right ethnic mix of prisoners. He was taken to another prison where the warden made a pitch to the convicts, asking for extras – they had just screened *Con Air*, making Buscemi flavour of the month on the cell block. They used between fifty and 150 real convicts each day, and he said at first they were confused or simply bored, but once they got into it they helped give *Animal Factory* its undeniable air of realism. What appealed to Buscemi about the story, and what is still the key to accepting the film, is the love story. Earl (Willem Dafoe) wants a relationship with someone intelligent, something deeper than the prison sex you would expect him to take from Ed Furlong. And, of course, Mickey Rourke was a surprise as a drag queen, but his agent put him up for the role. Rourke was so into the part he actually wrote his own monologue, which Buscemi edited into two separate scenes, and he showed up on set in drag his first day. "Steve, you never want to fly from LA to Philly in drag", was all

Rourke would say.

Under the gentle probing from NFT/ Crime Scene boss Adrian Wootton, Buscemi concentrated on the difference between his acting in character parts in big money films, and his continued work acting and directing in independents. As well as directing *Animal Factory* and *Trees Lounge* (from his own original screenplay), Buscemi has also directed episodes of HBO's two top crime series, *Oz* and *The Sopranos*, as well as the late, lamented *Homicide*. "TV is stylistically very different", he said. "I was glad to have done features, because you have to work so fast: I did a one-hour show in seven days. Then there's very little pre-production, you basically pick locations and start shooting. Then I called for rehearsal, and all the actors stopped. I said, "You've been doing this show for seven years and you still don't know what to do?!"" For Buscemi, acting is the key to his films. He spoke of trying to create a collaborative feel for everyone on the set, to be able to listen to ideas, and to have the confidence to be able to give the actors direction, rather than have to struggle with visuals and technical problems. He mentioned auditioning for the Coen Brothers for *Miller's Crossing* (I read the part faster than anyone else!) and how the Coens work together in perfect sync, often laughing with each other behind the camera as the scenes play out in front of it. Although as an actor/director he enjoys improvisation, he said there's little room for it in the Coen Brothers works because the scripts have such an improvisational feel.

Improvisation is also important to Tom DiCillo, who started out as a standup, and whose very accomplished *Double Whammy* (no relation to the Carl Hiassen novel) was a Crime Scene premiere. Denis Leary plays cop Ray Pluto, whose cartoony name perhaps signals the kind of Wile E. Coyote experience he will have through this story of attempted murder and bungling. Buscemi plays his partner, and Elizabeth Hurley plays the chiropractor who realigns Pluto. Throw in a vengeful Puerto Rican teenager whose father won't let her get a tattoo, and a pair of wannabe Tarantinos trying to write their first authentic tough-guy independent film thriller, and you have a knowing and affectionate tongue-in-cheek thriller that moves confidently through its mood swings – again, much like a cartoon. Leary manages to keep the sad-sack tone that is necessary to make the part work, and his double act with Buscemi is itself worth the price of admission. Victor Argo as his tough lieutenant and Chris North as the slick star detective Chick Dimitri present a real change from the *Law & Order* precinct house! Under the skilled prodding of Adrian Wootton, who like everyone else wanted to know first about Elizabeth Hurley's participation, DiCillo opened up more and more as the interview went on, being particularly enlightening on the sea-change among American independent filmmaking. It took him three years to get the financing for *Double Whammy*, and his tales included one involving the estranged wife of one of the potential backers which itself was right out of Charles Willeford.

I say this because another of the festival highlights was *The Woman Chaser*, Robinson Devor's adaptation of Willeford's classic Hollywood novel, which originally was titled *The Director*. The Willeford short story, *Selected Incidents* (part of *The Machine*

in Ward 11, reviewed elsewhere in this issue) might have been a blueprint for the character of Richard Hudson, a slick car salesman who needs to express himself artistically, and manages to sell a studio on a B-movie which he writes and directs himself. The hard part about adapting Willeford is that his narrators are notoriously unreliable: Hudson's pathology must necessarily influence what he's telling you, as much as it does the picture he eventually gets made. Patrick Warburton as Hudson works hard to convey the sort of coldness which allows him to approach his fellow humans as a means to an end – in this he reminds me of Richard Stark's Parker at his early hardest. Devor works just as hard to keep the tone of both pictures consistent, and basically it works. The picture has been made in both colour and black and white. I saw the colour version, which is very LA in its bright light and washed out colours, but seems somehow too easy, as if it's intent is for the TV screen (where it has been seen in America). I'd like to see if the black and white version is harder and maybe bleaker, more in line with Willeford's own version. I don't doubt that it will be, because this is a finely judged adaptation from start to finish.

Chuck Parello's *Ed Gein* is also well judged. There can't be more than a couple of scenes in the whole film where the tone of almost gentle ordinariness is lost, and one supposes they were necessary simply to show what else Eddie was getting up to. This telling of the Gein story is really a dissection of small-town 1950s America as much as of that decade's most notorious sociopath. Parello, who worked on *Henry Portrait of a Serial Killer* and wrote and directed *Henry II,* deals with the story in a straightforward fashion, and is helped by two outstanding performances from Steve Railsback as Gein and Carrie Snodgrass as his mother. Railsback in particular imbues Gein with a sympathy that Parello admitted was not in his original conception of the character. "I saw Ed as an evil person, but Steve said people don't want to sit through such a one-sided portrayal. I didn't set out to make them feel sorry for him, but I'm happy if that's the case." Only two shots in the whole film might be seen as exploitative: one where Gein dreams of a bare-breasted Nazi woman, and another where he cavorts in his 'woman' identity, wearing parts of corpses. The former shot would be understandable to anyone who grew up in the 1950s reading the downmarket 'men's' magazines, with Betty Page-type models in underwear posed inside. *I Was the Nazi Lust Lord's Slave of Sin* would be a typical feature story, and it's not farfetched to see Ed feeding his imagination with such things (though buying them in his small town is another matter). As to the dancing, which recalls both *Psycho* and *Silence of the Lambs,* the two best-known of the films that draw on the Gein legend, Parello saw it as humorous. "It's a moment of liberation for him, and you feel the same joy that he does", grins Parello. Well, almost. "It's what's happening in his mind, and Ed's mind is funny as well as sick." Most of Ed's work, of course, was done with corpses he'd resurrected from the local graveyard. He killed only two women that we know of, and in both cases the film portrays them as typical small-town characters, with excellent performances by Carol Mansell as the mother-substitute and Sally Champlin as the brassy barmaid who is Ed's first victim. Their contrast with the tightly controlled intensity of Carrie Snodgrass' performance is excellent. This is a film that almost wants to toss itself into the exploitation cauldron, but Parello and his cast keep it simmering at a more thoughtful and entertaining level.

Thoughtful is a good word for the Italian mystery film, *The Impossible Murder,* which is an old-fashioned thriller which begins with a popular Sardinian prosecutor dropping dead of poisoning while he has a morning caffe with his mistress (herself a magistrate and married to another one). Piero, the procurator called in from Palermo to investigate, appears to have been chosen by Head Prosecutor Pani because he thinks he will be able to direct the investigation to his own ends, which involve ruining one or both of his colleagues. Of course things do not go that way, and Carlo Cecchi (Piero), as is the norm in such stories, appears to gather strength as the investigation goes on. What makes Antonello Grimaldi's film so interesting is that the plot, the mystery and the clues are all developed visually, with no cheating and with a beautiful subtlety. Thus the solution actually combines two elements that have been carefully shown, and a sharp audience may have picked up on both without necessarily putting the two together. There's a fine malevolent performance by Ivano Marescotti as Pani, and the whole thing is nicely shot by the aptly named Paolo Camera, who makes the interiors appropriately moody and threatening, while the Sardinian exteriors remind one of paradise. It's an intelligent thriller worthy of early Chabrol, and that's high praise indeed.

THE BIG WRAP UP

*Current films reviewed by **Michael Carlson***

Mike Hodges' slick little film *Croupier* took a while to be released in this country, with Film Four strangely lukewarm about promoting it, before it finally appeared in 1999 and died a death. But it became a hit last year in America, and has returned to these shores to meet critical acclaim and some box office success. (See the interview with Hodges by Charles Waring in CT22 for more background.) *Croupier* is the story of Jack Manfred (Clive Owen), a would-be writer who goes back to his former trade, dealing in a casino, and finds that the pressures of that job unblock his creativity. Those pressures relate to his relationship with his father (Nicholas Ball) back in South Africa, and are increased considerably by his strained relationship with his girlfriend (Gina McKee) – a security officer in a department store – and with an exotic South African woman (Alex Kingston) who tries to enlist Jack in a scheme to rip off the casino. The story is laced beautiful-

ly with big and little betrayals. Cheating at the tables, cheating with relationships. Dealers are forbidden to see each other off duty, but Jack winds up befriending one dealer and then having a one-night stand with the enigmatic Bella (a superbly underplayed Kate Hardie). Hodges does a great job of showing us the malleable forms of those relationships: this is a cramped film, full of shadowy interiors, mirrored surfaces, and distorted viewpoints, which echo the dual viewpoints of the film's story and the story which Jack is writing. The sense of randomness which you'd expect in a gambling context is drawn out brilliantly: this is the kind of 1950s pulp novel obsession you'd expect to read in Charles Willeford (see elsewhere in this issue) or David Goodis. Owen has that wonderful ability to appear both knowing and helpless, exactly the kind of deluded bozo who gets taken for a ride in these sorts of tales. And, of course, as a narrator he is not always the most reliable voice to follow. Since every character in the film may or may not be living fictions of their own, this makes for an intricate clockwork of a script, which Hodges manages to keep from going over the top to melodrama, even when a girlfriend shows up dead. The film's surprise, however, is pretty much telegraphed from the beginning, and is made even worse by the weird casting of Kingston, who makes it neither as femme fatale nor as South African. Still, with Jack's book success, and the almost fictional Bella moved in, we sense that this is, like the best film noirs, merely another turn of the wheel. There's a touch of class in this one.

The major issue raised by *Blow* has nothing to do with cocaine. The question is basically why anyone felt it necessary to remake *Goodfellas* from the point of view of the average guys who aren't mobbed up. This is basically the story of how working stiffs can become criminals too, and still cleave to their suburban values. Remember how Ray Liotta complains at the end of *Goodfellas* about how boring burb life is? In *Blow*, Liotta gets to show what life would have been like had he not started running for the local hoods. I'm sure he got a kick out of it, and, honestly, his performance is one of the highlights of a film in which everyone gets to do what they want to do, except the audience, who never really get to enjoy themselves once the film leaves the Swinging Sixties. On the other hand, isn't that the point of the move from psychedelia to the coke fuelled disco era? Who *did* enjoy themselves as much? Rachel Griffiths gets to play the mother of an actor who's probably older than she is, and transform her antipodean

accent into a Bahstan one, and her performance carries all the emotional resonance of a laboratory experiment. Penelope Cruz must be sick of playing ethereal beauties, because she clearly relishes the opportunity to play a hot mama in red and do Lorraine Bracco coke tantrums too. And Johnny Depp! Depp gets to wear a fake belly (so does Liotta) and walk with an unconvincing shuffle, as well as mix drug dealer and family man in a thoroughly sensitive new man performance. Hah! Those fake bellies challenge the fake beards of *Gettysburg* as modern cinema's least convincing make-up effects. The best thing about the film is its portrayal of the easy world of drug pushing in those glory days of the 1960s. And the analysis of the rise of coke as the drug of choice: "We'll get the movie and rock stars, and the rest of America will follow!" And that was before celebrity dominated the news. Speaking of celebrity, this film attracted a fair group of non-film-reviewing journo-celebs to its press showing, where I was struck by the separated-at-birth resemblance of one of them, Charlotte Raven (who parlayed the notoriety of a spell under Julie Burchill into a newspaper column), to Paul 'Pee Wee Herman' Reubens (who parlayed an arrest in a porn theatre to a new career as an actor). Pee Wee steals the show, playing the dope-pushing hairdresser who gets Johnny Depp into the drugs business and who later, like everyone else, betrays him.

Isabelle Huppert is the show in *Merci Pour le Chocolat,* Claude Chabrol's study of a Swiss spider-woman. There's not much subtlety about it, leading up to the final shot where the spider-web of a lace throw outlines Huppert, in case we've missed the point. If there was one to miss. Not much about this film (called *Nightcap*, which may be a better title, in English) makes sense, but I have the feeling the real point here was to satirise the Swiss, and that Chabrol feels Swiss society is so secretly bizarre that nothing really has to make sense. Nothing much really does. This has the feel of the outline of a Chabrol film, with none of the characters or the plot lines really developed fully. Huppert's performance, as a result, sometimes seems to be assuming things the audience just can't know, and few of the supporting cast are able to keep up with her intensity, because, frankly, they aren't aware that it's there. Writing that on the page, it seems to make perfect sense, if you're making a film about a psychopath whom nobody realises is gone, but on the screen it's not quite that simple. And there never is a real answer to the question of why Huppert would deliberately give herself away by spilling the eponymous hot chocolate. This time Chabrol has given us a bonbon without bothering to fill in the centre.

FILMS ON THE PAGE

Michael Carlson

Steven Spielberg by James Clarke: Pocket Essentials, £3.99, 1 903047 43 9

Red River by Suzanne Liandrat-Guiges: BFI Film Classics, £8.99, 0 851708 19 6

Natasha: The Biography of Natalie Wood by Suzanne Finstad: Century, £17.99. 0 712677 00 3

Blaxploitation Films by Mikel J. Koven: Pocket Essentials, £3.99, 1 903047 58 7

James Clarke makes a very accurate assessment of Steven Spielberg early on, when he says, "What Walt Disney was to Spielberg's generation, Spielberg was to the generation which grew up on his films." Clarke doesn't take it any further, but he has hit on a much-overlooked point. Disney didn't draw audiences to the cinema, he drew the youngsters of the 1950s to *television*, and not only has he been a role model for Spielberg, who indeed drew youngsters back to movies, but he has also been a remarkable stylistic influence. The remarkable consistency of Spielberg's childlike point of view is another of Clarke's observations, but the Disney I'm talking about is not so much the one who made silly movies for kids in the late 1950s/early 1960s, but the one who made adult-style historical dramas (*Davy Crockett, Swamp Fox, Johnny Tremaine, Dr Syn*) for children. In this sense, the director who may have been the biggest influence on Spielberg was Robert Stevenson. Clarke spends too much time trying to establish unnecessarily auteur credentials for Spielberg, whose skill as a filmmaker and whose personal style have never really been in doubt. The question has generally been whether he trusts his audience (whom he usually places in a child's viewpoint) to get what he is doing, and the answer is that he usually doesn't. Hence the embarrassing bookending of *Saving Private Ryan*, a device which had worked in *Schindler's List*, certainly the one Spielberg film which changes the POV to that of an adult. Of his other films, the most successful are probably the straightforward pulp adventures of Indiana Jones. *Ryan*, for all its bombast, works as a battle film, but fails as a study of men in war. He just can't do the guys in the squad sticking together through hostile territory. Families, not buddies, are Spielberg's primary concern.

Group bonding, not families, was Howard Hawks' theme, and *Red River* is one film where he gave a specific familial context to that issue. Matthew has to prove himself as a man, as part of the trail drive, before Dunstan will accept him as a part of his family. Suzanne Liandrat-Guiges' study of *Red River* is packed with interesting background (occasionally misleading, as she appears to place the 1850s cattle trade in Texas *after* the Civil War) and trenchant observation, but she also seems to get lost in critical theory, often leaving it unexplained. She describes one of the characteristic features of a Hawks western as 'a certain deployment of the *mise-en-scene*', without even hinting at what that deployment entails. This is particularly telling in her dealing with the issue of the film's title, where she veers suspiciously into literary thematic analysis, rather than '*mise-en-scene*'. Having quoted another French critic as saying all Hawks films are concerned with a horror of age and time, and its 'inscription' on the face, she also says violence is 'inscribed' in Hawks films by means of water. Well, it is and it isn't. The beauty of the title *Red River* is that it not only suggests violence (a river of blood) but also a geography, and a crossing (which of course is symbolic). The line of cattle on the drive is another red river, but the most important one is another river of blood, that which flows between Dunstan and Matthew. This is the river that the brand will come to symbolise and it's hard to miss that, even within Hawks' *mise-en-scene*. Hawks' heroines were always part of the group bonding that occurs in his films; the best of them are equals of the men.

Natalie Wood never played those sorts of women. It was probably unfair to Wood that the Harvard Lampoon named their worst actress award after her. She may have lacked range, but she certainly had a presence on screen, and in the hands of directors able to highlight the vulnerability of her expressive sexuality, she turned in some memorable film performances. Of course, she mailed in far more that justified the Lampoon's satirical faith in her. Wood grew up as tabloid fodder, so it's no surprise that this first full-scale biography of her is so schlocky. Suzanne Finstad is, according to the book jacket, 'the author of several previous literary works and possesses a law degree'. The literary merit of this book make the use of 'previous' in that sentence highly questionable, but the style of its prose never rises above the level of that sentence, not once in more than 400 pages. The book is also billed as putting 'an end to the mysteries' but it does no such thing. It draws no conclusions about Wood's mysterious drowning, and generally pulls its punches about her life as well. Instead, what we get is a combination of Enquirer-style tittle-tattle and Oprah-style victim uplift – a perfect five-minute tabloid TV piece blown into a book. Even the major revelation, that Wood was brutally raped while still a teenager by a Hollywood star she idolised, fails to identify the star, and amounts to no more than self-serving hearsay. Meanwhile Finstad's Wood bounces back and forth between sexual victim and sexual predator. Her lovers meander into the book in passing, out of sequence, to the point where if you go back to count you realise that any 'meaningful' relationship was going on simultaneously with half a dozen less meaningful ones. None of this interrupts Finstad's building the temple of Wood's victimisation. There's no meaningful discussion of her work, her strengths and weaknesses as an actress, the effect of her early affair with Nicholas Ray, nor even of the deadening effect on her talent of her marriage to Robert Wagner. Wood did little of note in the field of crime, yet she could've been a stunning force in any number of 1950s contexts… but that wasn't what her career was about. Finstad at least recognises the obvious comparison to Elizabeth Taylor, but Wood never had the presence to be able to carry a Tayloresque vehicle. Which is a shame. Natasha Zakharenko called her mother 'Mud'. This bio deserves a similar nickname.

Wood was at her best in small pictures, which suggests she might have made a great B movie mama, a white Pam Grier maybe? Grier is one of the stars of Mikel Koven's study of Blaxploitation. That we've reached the stage where these movies are receiving homage (*Jackie Brown*) and parody (*I'm Gonna Git You, Sucka*) signals that the time is right for a study, and Kovan is particularly good on the immediate roots of the genre – films like *Across 110th Street*, *Cotton Comes to Harlem*, and *Sweet Sweetback's Badass Song*. He's also right to suggest that, awkward as the last of those is as a movie, the fact it made money signalled the viability of other films. The growing presence of black actors in white action movies, and even on TV (Bill Cosby, say, in *I Spy*) was another contribution to the explosion in the early 1960s, as was the crossover of black music to white audiences in the same time period. Koven's analysis of films is solid – I just wish he'd found space for *Action Jackson*, a Carl Weathers throwback movie which may have been the last of the straightforward genre. But Koven is good on the influence of Blaxploitation in the current run of black and action (and black action) movies. I wonder if we could call Bruce Willis, or Keanu, or Nicholas Cage, or the *Lethal Weapon* series Whitesploitation in homage?

Michael Carlson

YOU'LL TAKE IT AND LIKE IT:
SEX IN THE CRIME FILM

Mike Paterson

Vivian: *Speaking of horses, I like to play them myself. But I like to see them workout a little first, see if they're front runners or come from behind, find out what their whole card is, what makes them run.*

Marlowe: *Find out mine?*

Vivian: *I think so.*

Marlowe: *Go ahead.*

Vivian: *I'd say you don't like to be rated. You like to get out in front, open up a little lead, take a little breather in the backstretch, and then come home free.*

Marlowe: *You don't like to be rated yourself.*

Vivian: *I haven't met anyone yet that can do it. Any suggestions?*

Marlowe: *Well, I can't tell till I've seen you over a distance of ground. You've got a touch of class, but I don't know how, how far you can go.*

Vivian: *A lot depends on who's in the saddle.*

Bacall to Bogart, *The Big Sleep* (1946).
Dialogue by William Faulkner and
Leigh Brackett.

Sex and violence, those two dominant survival instincts, figure higher in the crime film than any other genre. Sometimes separately, sometimes together, but never far apart. In human society the underworld of crime can be split into the desire to illegally acquire material goods or the incitement to transgress provoked by sexual impulse. Translated to the crime film this can read: heists, bank jobs and stick-ups or revenge killings, crimes of passion and lovers on the run. Either way, behind the smoking gun there is usually a smoking femme fatale.

The representation of sex in most art media is largely from the male perspective and, even today in current mainstream cinema, there are very few exceptions to this. The changes in the political and cultural climate in the last century have gradually allowed a more inclusive viewpoint but, still, the dominant image of sex in the cinema is a stereotype. Essentially we are a selfish species so it is only natural that self-interest prevails when it comes to depicting desire. In a male society this is reflected in the portrayal of sex and the hierarchy of sexual power. Unlike the crime novel where there is a tradition of independent female voices and successful women writers, crime cinema is a testosterone arena. Granted it is frequently dowsed by a Bette Davies, Gloria Graham or a Kathleen Turner but, largely, subtlety is clubbed into submission by hot-flushed rampancy or double-entendres so blatant they become single.

Take a film such as *Bound* where the twist on the story is that the kept moll is saved by a quick-witted, blue collar woman and swept, fairy-tale style, into the arms of an alternative lifestyle escape (lesbianism). Even here it is impossible to escape the jerking hand (however right-on) of the male fantasist. As written by the Wakowski brothers, Gina Gershon's Corky, despite wardrobes full of dungarees, is always an unreal, pouting überbabe. If you want realism you go to gay film festivals, if you want lesbian fantasies you watch *Bound* (however brave an attempt it is). Women such as Leigh Brackett and Katherine Bigelow are the exceptions that prove the rule. It's a man's world.

Taken as read that the separate issue of gender roles in fiction is an enclosed bubble, occasionally stretched but never pierced, we can view the depiction of sex in crime films within the context of the genre without recourse to microscopic academic, cultural and political scrutiny. Yeah, right.

The Hay's Code

Hollywood is a trip through the sewer in a glass-bottomed boat:

Wilson Mizner, screenwriter and wit

All stories have a romantic element. In reflecting the human condition they articulate what we aspire to and desire. To overlay romance (or its modern equivalent, sex) onto the crime film, somebody is going to have to die. Probably horribly. In jealous rages. In Hollywood, while romance was played out in escapist musicals or screwball comedies of manners, the more earthy stuff was the domain of the crime film. In 1920s America the high life came with glamorous women and every gangster had his moll. Distilled to their elements, the fantasy hero gets the girl, the villain gets their comeuppance and the detective solves the case. The best and most interesting films are the ones that twist these elements into unexpected shapes and take us into more challenging territory. A film's treatment of its sexual theme is an indicator of the prevailing moral culture. The peak of the Hollywood crime film was the noir period of the early 1940s to mid 1950s where American culture was straining against a changing demographic of women coming out of wartime employment and power rankings of political paranoia. Within this culture, increasing affluence and consumerism were allowing more leisure time. More entertainment product equalled a diversity of style. The pre-war Hays code was still in place however, and any liberalism that may have been growing in society was not necessarily being played out on screen unless in coded form.

The silent film era in America was rife with sex and nudity (all female); mostly in tasteful, classically-themed pictures (D. W Griffith's *Intolerance, Dante's Inferno, The Tree of Knowledge*) but also in underground stag movies and 'What the Butler Saw' penny reels. The European importing of sexually progressive product such as Czech film *Extase*, where a pre-Hollywood Hedy Lamarr (that's Hedy not Hedley) writhes orgasmically in scenes of wanton nudity, did not provoke mass panic in the streets. Yet there was still a hangover of Victorian prudery amongst the state censorship boards that ineffectually oversaw the growing cinematic mass entertainment. As with the instant explosion of pornography on the Internet the new visual media rapidly became a playground of male desire.

In 1934 US Postmaster General, Will H. Hays (a man with a strange facial resemblance to Nazi propagandist Joseph Goebbels) set up a code of practice for the Motion Picture Producers and Distributors of America that effectively stifled the explicit representation of sexual themes in cinema for thirty years. His aim was the "establishment and maintenance of the highest moral and artistic standards in motion picture production" and his power in the implementing of this was the imposition of a $25,000 fine on a studio for any script transgression. He decreed that "no picture shall be produced which will lower the standards of those who see it. Hence the sympathy of an audience should never be thrown to the side of crime, wrongdoing, evil or sin." Hollywood complied. Ironic given its culture of decadence and hypocritical status as an arena of mass excess where studio heads acted as pimps and leading men lorded over female extras like mediaeval princelings. Actresses progressed from stag film to casting couch to the girl-next-door role. Similarly in Britain the British Board of Film Censors, acting on the instructions of a seventeenth century blasphemy law, vetted scripts, blue-pencilling every line with a religious zeal. Hay's

code demanded such prohibitions as "No licentious or suggestive nudity" and "No inference of sex perversion" while the UK had such bizarre proscriptions as "No women fighting with knives" and "No salacious wit". What is a crime scriptwriter to do? Be inventive.

Femme Fatales

Give me a kiss or I'll sock ya:

Lana Turner as Cora in
The Postman Always Rings Twice (1946)

With the restrictions of the Hay's (and later the Breen) Code, sex in Hollywood became a repressed affair; in anything other than a Norman Rockwell family context sex led to bad things. It was a cipher for weakness and criminality and its primal urges turned weak men bad. All of this was depicted within a framework of enforced allegory and symbolism. The power of suggestion being an enormous force compared to what is explicitly depicted, this implied sexuality ended up having greater impact. In the same way that the best horror films suggest evil by sounds and shadows of half-seen spectral figures, the most erotic films are those where a glance, pose or flirtatious word hint at an insinuation of something exciting but hidden.

In the minor-key melodramas of noir the pulpish pessimism was underscored by simple components of sex, jeopardy and revenge. In the translation of literature into film in the era of censorious restraints, it was never going to be possible to reproduce the primal sexuality of a D. H Lawrence or Henry Miller, but in the world of pulp a comic-strip trash sensibility demanded it at least try. Other films had love stories, noir had lust stories. Take the sex out of crime and all you're left with is misdemeanour. Crimes of passion are the stock in trade of noir. Scores of noir films and superior B Movies from this era have sex as their primary narrative impulse; *The Postman Always Rings Twice, Double Indemnity, Out of the Past, The Big Heat, The Blue Dahlia, In a Lonely Place, Mildred Pierce,* all films charged by the presence of sexually powerful women. The women's roles however were proscribed stereotypes (James Ellroy so detests the term he prefers 'Phlegm Fatale'). Women were either the devoted, virginal home-town girl or the scheming vamp in much the same way that the men were Bogart heroes, Elisha Cook Jr whining sidekicks or Jack Palance sadistic villains. The Fatales were Freudian castrators, all flaming cigarettes and arched eyebrows as powerful with the tongue as the men were with the gun. Misogyny often ruled in films of this time; a hero had to keep the dame in her place be it with a Bogart slap or a Cagney grapefruit in the face. In this man's world a woman who wanted to escape her restraints had to use her sexuality. By turns seductive, manipulative, vulnerable and vengeful, the noir anti-heroine played her men like a cat with a mouse. Bad girls just want to have fun.

There are so many exemplars of the noir heroine, but epitomising the power of women to siphon the weakness from men's will and lure them into committing murder were;

Barbara Stanwyck – in *Double Indemnity* (1944) – a cold-blooded blonde in fuck-me shoes who schemes to murder her husband for the insurance money in a classic plot of dumb-schmuck entrapment and duplicity. A template of the genre by way of James M. Cain, Billy Wilder and Raymond Chandler, it was so strong the US censor called it "a blue-print for murder".

Lana Turner – in *The Postman Always Rings Twice* (1946) – luscious Lana, ironically dressed in pure white, is a more blue-collar killer. This twist on the old "lovers kill the boorish husband and make it look like an accident" is as sweat-stained with desire as they come. The director, Tay Garnett, said of the shooting of the sexual content, "It was a real chore to do the film under the Breen Office but I think I managed to get the sex across. I think I like it better that way. I'm not a voyeur and I don't like all the body display you get in pictures nowadays. I think that it's just a crutch for untalented directors and writers." Obviously not a quote that Bob Rafelson had framed in his trailer while filming the Nicholson/Lange remake.

Gene Tierney – in *Laura* (1944) – the high society obverse of *Postman,* this is a criminologist's dream. A girl's death is investigated by a detective (Dana Andrews) who begins to fall in love with the victim as much in her death as the suspects did in her life. A true puzzle with heart-thumping traces of psychological conflict.

Joan Crawford – in *Mildred Pierce* (1945) – "Hot stuff coming through!" Giving it all she's got with both barrels Joan took the experience of her casting-couch ambitiousness and fired it into this story of a single-minded mother intent on luxury for her daughters at any price. Including murder.

Gloria Grahame – in *The Big Heat* (1953) – never an actress to be stereotyped she nevertheless was particularly skilled at playing victims, vulnerable women and bad girls – and she's a very bad girl in this film. So bad that Lee Marvin feels forced to throw scalding coffee in her face. No way to treat a lady.

Veronica Lake – in *This Gun For Hire* (1942) – often underplaying as the icy blonde who becomes the protective obsession of the hero. In this and *The Glass Key* she played opposite another underplaying icy blonde, Alan Ladd.

Lauren Bacall – in *The Big Sleep* (1946) – talking in innuendoes and taking flirting to new levels Lauren Bacall instantly became one of those rare celebrities who is globally known by their surname. Not until Kathleen Turner has an actress emerged who can come close to the insouciance, style and sheer class of Bacall. In *The Big Sleep* she is given lines to die for and delivers them with a verve that belies her young age. She and Bogart sizzle like static.

Grace Kelly – in *To Catch a Thief* (1955) – marginal in Hitchcock's canon of perversity and by no means a noir film it is notable for a performance of sheer, breathtaking sensuality by Kelly in one of her few crime film roles (the others also being by Hitchcock). In possibly the sexiest moment in cinema history, the unapproachable, chaperoned society girl, the ultimate ice-cool blond who has rebuffed all advances by Cary Grant's Riviera jewel thief unexpectedly grasps him in a hotel doorway, brings his head to hers and delivers a lip-licking kiss of screen-burning passion. Seminal is not the word.

Icons

While today scores of teenage boys splash out on posters of Britney Spears, in the 1940s the pin-ups were older, more demure but (ironic given today's standards) suggestive of a darker sexual promise behind the "pure as the driven slush" garb. The mass entertainment of Hollywood populated its product with a hierarchy of stars. Sex appeal was the prime selling point, so the bigger the star the stronger their sexual magnetism. But there were genuine male icons of sexuality also. With most heroes, their ability to effortlessly get the girl is often questionable, an indicator more of the fantasy of the writer than the reality of the performance. One man who could not only get the girl but scare them for a 100 mile radius was Robert Mitchum. Who needs charm when you have danger and mystery? No other actor (Lee Marvin, though one of the greats in the menace stakes, was never a sexual animal) could convey sexual menace the way Mitchum did in films such as *Cape Fear, Night of the Hunter* and *Out of the Past*. In his characters he is a bulldozing sexual vehicle capable of sneered threat or outright licentiousness. When casting *Night of the Hunter* director Charles Laughton contacted Mitchum describing, "There's a character in it who's a diabolical shit." "Present", drawled back Mitchum. For *Cape Fear* he invested vengeful ex-con Max Cady with a daring intimation of sexual predation on the underage daughter of lawyer Gregory Peck. This man is beyond the pale and Mitchum doesn't hold back from portraying it, where other more image-conscious actors would step back from that edge. Rather than epitomising the sex appeal that the Hollywood star system propagated, his sexuality was more sleazy then desirable. That other twentieth century archetype of male sexuality, Elvis Presley, always cited James Dean as his style model but he owes more of a debt of gratitude to Mitchum with his Southern Gothic danger and curled-lip, prison-yard cool.

Bleach-blonde, Hollywood High graduate Lana Turner was a jazz groupie, serial dater of gangster muscle and a woman who walked it like she talked it. Her life was one that imitated her art. Or possibly it was the other way around. Lana had affairs with Bugsy Siegel's mob buddy Stephen Crane, dated Frank Sinatra, and most melodramatically merged the worlds of noir performance and real life moll-dom with her relationship with small-time hood Johnny Stompanato. At one point Stompanato was deported from the UK after he attempted to strangle Lana in a jealous rage over her clinches with a young actor called Sean Connery while filming scenes in London. Lana's teenage daughter Cheryl was witness to constant hostilities. Beatings followed threats. Stompanato could "make them disappear". After one too many violent arguments Stompanato was stabbed to death. Both Cheryl and Lana claimed responsibility but it was Cheryl who was charged. As the abused fourteen year old daughter of a beaten mother in a relationship with a known gangster, she was eventually acquitted in a case of justifiable homicide.

Very occasionally film would suggest something more diseased in sexual desire than the portrayed norm. An intimation of this is Peter Lorre in Fritz Lang's *M* (1931), playing a sexual psychopath so chillingly effectively that he was forever typecast as a villain with suppressed sickness at his core. The image of Lorre, whistling *Peer Gynt* as he lasciviously leads little girls to their off-screen death is one isolated in cinema history. With an echo of reality that makes the blood run cold, child killer Fred West would play children's musical themes as he committed his foul acts

Sexuality is the foundational motive for all pleasure: Sigmund Freud

Films, like advertising, are selling a product and to do so have to appeal to their target audience in simple ways. Reduced to the basics, the psychological signal a sexually attractive movie star sends is a subliminal shorthand for a display of genetically superior mating material. Sex sells. As Hollywood hawks it, Mitchum, Bogart and Cagney are the alpha males dominating our subjugated pack instincts (women want them and men want to be them). Rita Hayworth, Grace Kelly and Jane Russell are the sexual attractors, flattering us into self-confidence. Our cerebral cortex may filter these signals through a higher artistic sensibility but essentially we are still in thrall to irrational animal instincts. What our chimp brain is seeing in a darkened theatre with sound system blaring and senses heightened is a simple focus of human emotions. Natural selection in the cinema.

Next Issue: necrophilia, deviancy, fetishism, cross-dressing, voyeurism, sadomasochism and homophobia; Hitchcock and Lynch rewrite the Kinsey report.

Mike Paterson

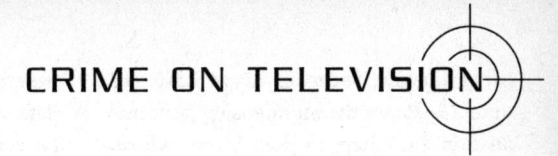

CRIME ON THE BOX
SEXUAL TEMPTATION

We've all been there… or have we?
Charles Waring *dons a dirty mac and investigates* The Vice

With his doleful eyes and lugubrious demeanour, the charismatic Edinburgh-born actor Ken Stott is fast becoming a familiar face in British television crime dramas. Recently seen playing a prominent role as a detective in BBC 1's excellent two-part gory thriller entitled *Messiah* – about a serial killer who believes he's Jesus Christ – Stott is better known to television viewers as Inspector Pat Chappell, the main protagonist in ITV's controversial drama series, *The Vice*. Devised for Carlton TV by executive producer Rob Pursey and former *The Bill* scriptwriter Barry Simner, *The Vice* first aired in January 1999 as a sequence of six feature-length ninety-minute episodes. Significantly, considering the frequent sexual nature of its subject matter, the show was broadcast after the nine o'clock watershed. Focusing upon the activities of the Metropolitan Police Force's Vice Unit based in Soho, *The Vice* is a gritty examination of London's seedy underbelly, taking the viewer into a dark, seamy world of pimps, prostitutes (often referred to in police parlance as "toms"), massage parlours and gaudy, neon-lit sex shops. Indeed, *The Vice* presents a facet of the criminal underworld that rarely makes prime-time viewing.

The series became an immediate hit with the British public, attracting a regular audience of over eight million viewers, and resulted in two further series, the last of which was broadcast in the early months of 2001. A fourth series is already in the pipeline. The main reason for tuning in to *The Vice* is the mesmerising performance of Pat Chappell (Ken Stott), whose complex, troubled character has progressively evolved over the duration of the show's twenty-two episodes. Chappell is a cop who doesn't go by the book. He also lets his feelings influence his decision-making, which sometimes results in potentially jeopardous consequences. In essence, Pat Chappell's a good man but also a seriously flawed individual who does a lot of soul-searching. In the recent third series he was tortured by self-doubt and a guilty conscience regarding his own romantic entanglement with a former prostitute – in one episode, he's also accused of having underage sex with a fifteen-year-old whore. Chappell maintains a precarious balance between his problematic private life and the high-pressure demands of his professional career. The series' co-creator, Rob Pursey, says this of the dour Scottish Inspector: "Chappell has totally immersed himself in the amoral world of vice, having sacrificed his own personal life. His uncompromising attitude often finds him at odds with his colleagues, and his isolation brings him uncomfortably close to the pimps and prostitutes he is investigating." Indeed, Chappell's moral ambivalence invests *The Vice* with a healthy realism – the series is not simply about a battle between the traditional moral absolutes of good versus evil but probes further into the darker realms of the human psyche. The programme illustrates that corruption can taint us all – even Chappell, who would like to be a white knight on a prancing charger, but whose character possesses

disquieting moral blemishes.

The show has been lauded for its apparent accuracy and verisimilitude. Arguably, then, one of the most important contributors to the programme has been the former West End Clubs and Vice Office Chief Superintendent, Michael Hoskins, as the show's police advisor. *The Vice*'s authenticity can be directly attributed to Hoskins' involvement – he brought his prodigious professional experience to bear on giving credibility to the programme's characters and story lines. Hoskins' presence in a technical capacity also facilitated the co-operation of the police, who allowed part of the programme to be filmed in Brentford police station. As far as the current crop of prime time crime drama goes, *The Vice* has been by far ITV's best offering this year. I can't wait for the next series.

The Cast

Inspector Pat Chappell (Ken Stott)

A middle-aged divorcee (though you could argue that he's actually married to the Vice Squad), Pat Chappell's life seems a perpetual struggle. Although his unorthodox attitude to prostitution (he tends to view the girls as victims rather than criminals) is frowned upon by some senior officers, Chappell's more sympathetic, protective and co-operative attitude to females in the sex industry often yields good results for the police force in its attempted suppression of prostitution. Pimps and punters, however, are rarely the recipients of Chappell's charity. The fact that Chappell's personal life dangerously intersects with his work (his old flame, Jane, an ex-prostitute, re-enters his life and goes on the game again) adds a further frisson of tension to the show. If Chappell has a haunted look about him it's not really surprising as ghosts from his murky past often revisit him.

DS Vickers (Tim Piggott-Smith)

The insidious Vickers is Chappell's nemesis. Vickers seems much more than the archetypal bent copper – this seedy character actually enjoys wallowing in a moral cesspool, luring innocent, attractive girls into his prostitution racket by posing as a talent scout for model agencies. Sliminess personified.

PC Cheryl Hutchins (Caroline Catz)

If your average WPC were as glamorous and good-looking as Cheryl Hutchins, criminals would be volunteering to be arrested! Besides her alluring, photogenic looks, Hutchins is intelligent, confident and trusts Chappell implicitly, though is not afraid to speak her mind. The nature of her work necessitates Hutchins getting involved in potentially dangerous undercover work – she's welcome to get under my covers anytime! If you think actress Caroline Catz's face is familiar, you'd be right: she appeared in *The Bill* a couple of years back as DS Rosie Fox.

Sgt Joe Robinson (David Harewood)

Robinson is still reeling from the break up of his marriage, which was prompted by devotion to his job in the Vice Squad. Unlike his boss, Chappell, Robinson is more cautious and prefers to go by the book.

PC Dougie Raymond (Marc Warren)

A bit of a would-be wide boy, this brash PC was seduced by the potential fringe benefits that working in the Vice Squad could offer to those who turned a blind eye to certain dubious activities. Given the push by the Met after he disclosed vital information about a covert pornography investigation to the wrong people, Raymond got embroiled with some gangsters and ended up in the morgue at the conclusion of the second series.

PC Kirsty Morgan (Rosie Marcel)

Morgan joined *The Vice* at the beginning of the third series as Raymond's replacement. She's diligent and enthusiastic but her inexperience has put her at risk in some situations.

The Vice Episode Guide

First Series – 1999

1. *Daughters* (Parts 1 & 2)
2. *Sons* (Parts 1 & 2)
3. *Dabbling* (Parts 1 & 2)

Second Series – 2000

1. *Home is the Place* (Parts 1 & 2)
2. *Walking on Water* (Parts 1 & 2)
3. *Betrayed* (Parts 1 & 2)
4. *Lovesick* (Parts 1 & 2)

Third Series – 2001

1. *Out of Mind* (Parts 1 & 2)
2. *Into the Night* (Parts 1 & 2)
3. *Forces of Nature* (Parts 1 & 2)
4. *Falling* (Parts 1 & 2)

Sources:
www.carltontv.co.uk/data/thevice
www.http://epguides.com/Vice/
www.polfed.org

Charles Waring

BACK TO THE VILLAGE: FRESH PERSPECTIVES ON THE PRISONER

Charles Waring

Time Travel

Rewind to 1967. In Britain, Harold Wilson's Labour Government is in power and appears to be harmoniously in tune with the times: industry is booming, the country is affluent and the public mood is one of buoyant optimism. Moreover, London is regarded as the hippest capital city in the world and perceived as the cultural epicentre of the gloriously hedonistic Swinging Sixties. In pop music, Liverpool's Fab Four have relinquished their teeny bop image and acquired facial hair to signify their evolution into serious artists – they've also meditated with a Maharishi, dropped bucket loads of LSD and released the seminal *Sgt Pepper* album. Across the pond, rock icon Jimi Hendrix sets fire to his guitar and blows people's minds at the Monterey Pop Festival. It's the summer of love and a new holy trinity holds dominion – free festivals, free love and plenty of free drugs. In fact, it's a year when the denizens of the western world seem intent on liberating themselves from many perceived impediments – from the burden of the past, from authority, from orthodox aesthetics, from conventional sexual mores and ultimately, with the help of large doses of consciousness expanding drugs, from reality. Indeed, one of the more colourful axioms of the epoch was 'free your mind and your ass will follow'. But this navel-gazing idealism was tempered by the more sobering actualities of events like the ecological disaster resulting from the oil tanker, the Torre Canyon, which polluted Britain's shores with its seeping cargo of toxic black gold. In the Middle East, a belligerent Israel waged war against its neighbours, and in America, fomenting racial discord sparked riots in many of the country's inner cities. Meanwhile, the war abroad, in Vietnam, continued unabated despite a growing chorus of public disapproval. In truth, 1967 was a mass of contradictions: hippies wore flowers in their hair while industrial pollution sullied the landscape; in America (the so-called land of the free), dignified passive protest often met with bloody confrontation from trigger-happy cops. It was a precarious balance between democracy and totalitarianism, order and chaos, affluence and poverty, creation and destruction. You might say that it was no different from any other era in history but somehow in 1967 these polarities seemed more marked and therefore more disturbing.

This is only a fragment of the overall picture but it serves as a reminder of the turbulent, exciting time that was 1967. Significantly, it was this extraordinary political, social and cultural climate that gave birth to a television drama series which I believe mirrored the complexity and turmoil of the times. It was called *The Prisoner* and, despite being shown on the same channel as *Coronation Street*, reflected a new cultural paradigm in mainstream broadcasting resulting from an infiltration by experimental and underground aesthetics (including facets of psychedelia, pop-art and the avant-garde). With its grandiose sets, startling visuals and mind-boggling plot, *The Prisoner* represented an archetypal example of 1960's hubris.

This is its story.

Cult Status: The Prisoner's Enduring Appeal

It has not only been affectionately parodied in *The Simpsons* and analysed by academics but *The Prisoner* has prompted a global cult following of quasi-religious proportions. Indeed, since its first transmission at 7.30pm on Friday 30th September 1967, the seventeen episode series has continued to excite and confound TV viewers in equal measure. But thirty-three years on and with rumours of an imminent movie version, *The Prisoner* refuses to die – this is a considerable feat considering that it was a critical and commercial failure at the time of its initial airing. The recent release on DVD of the entire series confirms the extent of *The Prisoner*'s enduring public appeal. But what is mystifying to some observers is the nature of that appeal – is it really worthy of the attention it receives or has the effusive praise heaped on it by an obsessive minority prompted others to admire the show possibly because they believe it's hip to do so? Who knows and to be brutally honest, who cares? There will always be those who regard the series as pure genius and others who see it as pretentious garbage. However, true dyed-in-the-wool Prisoner zealots cite a multitude of reasons for the elevation of *The Prisoner* into a veritable goggle-box avatar – for some it's the charisma of its star, Patrick McGoohan, while for others, the main attraction might be the barmy story lines or even the aesthetically pleasing views of Portmeirion, the secluded Welsh coastal village which functions as the setting for the show. Above all, many fans believe that *The Prisoner*'s outstanding quality is its ability to provoke its viewers to exercise the grey matter and think for themselves – the brain is customarily disengaged for primetime TV shows, but *The Prisoner* offered drama that surpassed the usual entertainment parameters to provoke meaningful cogitation without seeming overly cerebral. This fact was probably a major turn-off for many viewers when the show was first transmitted, but has subsequently become its saving grace and the prime reason why it has entered the pantheon of television all-time greats.

A Brief History

The Irish-American actor, Patrick McGoohan, became a bona fide small screen star in the UK during the early 1960s playing the role of John Drake, a crime-busting, gunless, celibate security expert employed by NATO. The series began as an energetic half-hour show called *Danger Man* but interest from America resulted in the programme expanding to an hour and adopting a different title (*Secret Agent* in the States), which reflected Drake's new role as an employee of a covert government espionage department called M9. *Danger Man*'s popularity had spawned a host of similar shows in the early part of that decade (*The Avengers*, *Espionage* and *Man of the World* to name a few) but McGoohan had grown weary of his role in a programme that had in his view had become increasingly formulaic and stale. It is believed (though I confess this is an apocryphal tale) that McGoohan had made an appointment to see the chrome-domed, cigar-chomping TV mogul, Lew Grade (head-honcho at ATV) not only to state his desire to quit *Danger Man* but also to propose another series, an innovative new drama entitled *The Prisoner*. Apparently Grade was persuaded to accept McGoohan's outlandish idea because the actor had made it patently obvious that no amount of money could tempt him to stay tied to another series of *Danger Man* – also, McGoohan's star appeal guaranteed an audience and this prompted the TV tycoon to give the green light to the project by allegedly uttering the following: ÅgYou know, it's so crazy it might just work.Åh He then added: ÅgWhen can you start?Åh Significantly, *Danger Man*, then in its fourth season, was cancelled allowing *The Prisoner* to enter pre-production just a month before John Drake's final adventure was televised in April 1966. Originally, only seven episodes were scheduled for production but Grade demanded more to sell the series as a viable commercial package to the USA. Eighteen months later, McGoohan was reprising his role as a secret agent, but as his somewhat bemused fan base discovered, it was unlike anything else he had ever appeared in. In fact, *The Prisoner* was unlike anything ever seen on British television before or since.

Public reaction, which initially ranged from bewilderment and confusion in the first few weeks of *The Prisoner*, mutated into bitter disappointment and hostility when the climactic final instalment intensified the mystery rather than achieving any kind of explanation or fulfilling resolution. Consequently, following the concluding episode, ITV's switchboard was jammed by hordes of outraged callers. Also, a media furore erupted over the show, resulting in front page newspaper headlines. ITC issued a formal press statement though it did little to placate the angry mob. But the disaster didn't end there. Financially *The Prisoner*, which involved enormous production costs, was an abject failure, propelling Everyman Films (McGoohan's own company) to financial ruin. Not only did the company file for bankruptcy but it also owed money to the Inland Revenue. Patrick McGoohan's image was seriously tarnished by the apparent debacle and he was forced to go into hiding (he left Britain soon after, moving first to Switzerland and then later to the USA). Ironically, *The Prisoner's* cult appeal came much later when it was repeated in the 1970s (the last time it was aired on terrestrial television was in 1983 on a fledgling Channel 4).

Evolution

Controversy surrounds the genesis of *The Prisoner*. It is widely accepted that Patrick McGoohan was the guiding light and principal architect of the series – however,

detailed examination of all the available evidence reveals that the series began as a collaborative venture between McGoohan, producer David Tomblin and story editor, George Markstein (all of whom had worked on *Danger Man*). Everyman Films, a company formed by McGoohan in association with David Tomblin, handled production. Although McGoohan's input elevated him to the role of auteur on *The Prisoner* (he was not only the main star but functioned as executive producer, occasional scriptwriter and part-time director), the contribution of Tomblin (producer and production manager) and, in particular, Markstein was crucial. Indeed, it now appears that Markstein – who also worked as a script editor on *Danger Man* – was actually responsible for the original concept of *The Prisoner*. The main idea stemmed from Markstein's experiences as a journalist during the Second World War – he claimed to have discovered the whereabouts of a real-life counterpart to the Village where retired espionage agents went either to 'lie low' or else resided on permanent 'vacation'. As with the Village in *The Prisoner*, it was a self-contained, hermetically sealed community where its captive inhabitants lived in relative luxury and comfort. Indeed, some observers have gone so far as to identify that community as an internment camp based in Scotland called Invelair Lodge. Significantly, George Markstein was also responsible for proposing Portmeirion as a scenic location for the series – when he was working with McGoohan on *Danger Man* he'd read an article featuring the alluring Welsh village in a Sunday Times magazine supplement.

Despite his valuable input on *The Prisoner*,

an intolerable friction developed between Markstein and McGoohan. As script editor, Markstein's duties were onerous, attempting to direct the show's scriptwriters by maintaining thematic continuity and artistic coherence. A schism developed between Markstein and McGoohan over the show's direction – Markstein was in favour of a more conventional thriller format, as he once told a Radio Two interviewer: "What I intended, originally, was that McGoohan is held by people and he doesn't know which side he's working for." Increasingly, however, McGoohan used his star status to pull rank and began moulding the show to express his own artistic needs – consequently, he produced a programme that was the antithesis of orthodox drama, reflecting his own perceptions on the notions of freedom, reality, individuality and power. Disillusioned and embittered by what he perceived as McGoohan's megalomania, Markstein quit the show under a cloud – he believes that as a consequence of his departure, The Prisoner lacked a firm, controlling hand and became, in his words, 'silly'. Markstein left during a hiatus period after shooting the thirteenth episode – McGoohan took time off to star opposite Rock Hudson in the Hollywood version of Alistair McLean's thriller, Ice Station Zebra. When McGoohan returned to begin the proposed second series he discovered that not only Markstein but also other behind-the-scenes personnel were conspicuous by their absence. Indeed, the fact that many of the crew who had served on the first series of The Prisoner failed to return for the four episodes that constituted the truncated second series may give credence to Markstein's claim that many had become disaffected by the show's propensity towards absurdity. It is believed that the second series was also expected to run to thirteen episodes, but with mounting pressure on McGoohan (exacerbated by Markstein's departure) only four episodes were completed before ATV wielded the axe, thereby cancelling the show.

The Plot

On a superficial level, the basic premise of The Prisoner is a simple one – a disillusioned secret agent resigns from his post and is afterwards abducted by unknown assailants and held captive in an isolated village. Each episode depicts the former agent's attempts to escape and the efforts of his captors to extract a confession as to the real reason behind his resignation from the service. It all seems pretty straightforward, doesn't it? However, to make matters more complicated, no one knows the real identity of the secret agent, who he worked for and who his captors are – McGoohan's real identity (which is never ever divulged) is replaced by a mere number. Throughout the series he is simply referred to as Number Six. As Number Six, McGoohan endures all manner of psychological and physical torments at the hands of his inscrutable jailers. They use mind-bending drugs, electroshock therapy, advanced brainwashing techniques and even hire women to seduce the prisoner into confession. Number Six also seeks the answers to his own gnawing questions – about the true identity of his captors and the precise location of a village that appears to be bordered by mountains and sea. But his main prerogative is to escape and seek freedom from tyranny. The net result of this unusual and complex scenario is a challenging, innovative hybrid that utilises elements from many varied TV genres – these range from espionage, fantasy, sci-fi, action drama and the psychological thriller, all of which are seamlessly blended into a programme that transcends mere mindless armchair entertainment to become an enduring message of mankind's bid to maintain individual liberty in a world of restriction, conformity and oppression. Or so some would have us believe!

Deeper Meanings

The Prisoner has frustrated viewers as much as it has entertained them – the world it depicts is bizarre, surreal and often communicates its message by dint of cryptic symbols and nebulous metaphors. Although it has conventional action scenes, the programme undoubtedly operates on a deeper metaphysical level by examining the nature of individual liberty. Many theories abound regarding the true meaning of *The Prisoner* – some are carefully considered while others offer a more humorous interpretation. They range from the disturbing idea that the whole thing takes place in the lunatic mind of Number Six to the hilarious notion that the programme is a result of Number Six imbibing an unhealthy quantity of hallucinogenic substances resulting in an elaborate acid flashback (certainly consistent with the era!). Some even believe that the programme is a sequel to *Danger Man*.

What makes *The Prisoner* both intriguing and ultimately frustrating is the feasibility of all these theories, no matter how risible some may seem. The programme offers the dual possibility of being both profound and ridiculous at the same time. Sure, it could be accused of being pure hokum and taking its audience for a ride. But then again, who can say with any degree of certainty that it's not a profound statement on human life?

However, an overwhelming majority of observers perceive *The Prisoner* as an existentialist allegory depicting a Kafka-esque dystopia populated by characterless ciphers that enforce the will of a paranoid, totalitarian society. Certainly, in this age of ubiquitous surveillance cameras, this Orwellian Big Brother aspect is something that has a resonance for us all. Despite a plethora of conflicting opinion regarding the show's message (if, indeed, it has one) most commentators agree that at its centre is the theme of man's dehumanisation. In view of the fact that many of the world's human inhabitants are denied fundamental rights and still live in some kind of fearful bondage to despotism reinforces *The Prisoner*'s timeless relevance. It is as valid today as it was way back when, and is rightly regarded as a television classic.

Number Six

"I am not a number, I am a free man!" is arguably the most famous catchphrase uttered by Number Six in *The Prisoner*. But just who is this nameless individual? As stated earlier, there is a school of thought amongst some fans of the show that believes Number Six is no other than *Danger Man*, himself, John Drake. Patrick McGoohan absolutely refutes this theory: "Unfortunately people assume that *The Prisoner* is a sequel to *Secret Agent* because I began the project closely afterward. Number Six is a former secret agent which is why people maintain this false notion for the sake of continuity." Despite this, the theory that Number Six and Drake are one and the same has been given some credence by the programme's co-creator, George Markstein, who once stated in an interview that when the show was being planned, McGoohan told him that Number Six's character would be a continuation of Drake's, although this fact would be concealed from the public. Also deemed significant is the presence in *The Prisoner* of a character called Potter (played by Christopher Benjamin) who appeared as John Drake's contact in two episodes of *Danger Man*. Other evidence cited by those who cling to the Drake-Number Six connection includes the use of the phrase 'Be Seeing You', which was not only used by John Drake in *Danger Man* but is also uttered by Number Six in *The Prisoner*. However, as one observer has sagaciously noted, this may simply be an idiosyncrasy of McGoohan himself, who used those very same words when he appeared in an episode of *Columbo*. Any nexus between the two secret agents is very tenuous in my opinion but it certainly adds to the mystique of *The Prisoner*.

What we do know of Number Six is that he's a strong-willed, obdurate individual who would rather die than kowtow to the Village authorities. He repudiates every aspect of Village life, refusing to be assimilated into the herd-like community and concentrating all his energies on escape. Despite being something of a loner with a sober demeanour, Number Six can turn on the charm when he so wishes and possesses a sardonic sense of humour. Res-

olute, stoic and possessing unquestionable moral probity, over the course of seventeen episodes the viewer learns many things about Number Six. He was an honours graduate who joined the RAF in World War Two to become a crewman on a bomber. Following the war, he was recruited by the Secret Service but disillusionment led to his resignation and subsequent incarceration in The Village. Athletic and intellectual, Number Six is a veritable renaissance man who excels at boxing, fencing (he apparently represented Britain at the Olympics), sailing and shooting. He is also a classical music afficionado with an interest in serious literature (he's fond of quoting Shakespeare). The viewer also learns that despite an apparent distrust of women that manifests itself during the series, Number Six has a fiancée in London. As well as being a man of principle, Number Six is also a creature of habit and always has two eggs for breakfast and cocoa before retiring to bed.

Number Two

Number Two is in charge of the Village and as chief interrogator represents Number Six's nemesis. Although Number Two appears in fourteen of the seventeen episodes, the same actor plays the character on only two occasions – Leo McKern plays the part in *The Chimes of Big Ben* and *Fallout*, while Colin Gordon assumes the role in *A, B and C* and *The General*. There is tremendous pressure on every succeeding Number Two to erode Number Six's resistance and obtain that all-important confession – but the price of failure is replacement, hence the nine separate incarnations of Number Two (played by

Eric Portman, Guy Doleman, George Baker, Anton Rogers, Patrick Cargill, Peter Wyngarde, John Sharpe, Clifford Evans, Derren Nesbitt and Mary Morris, who plays a rare distaff version).

Number One

The head of the regime's hierarchy, Number One is an unseen god-like figure with absolute power who is everywhere and nowhere. However, in the somewhat crazed denouement of the final episode, *Fallout* (which resembles a bad acid trip!), Number Six finally confronts the masked figure of Number One and discovers a chimpanzee! But that, too, is a disguise – under the ape mask Number Six sees his own image. As a result, some fans of the show believe that Number Six is actually Number One and only realises it during the last episode.

Rover

It was only referred to by name in one episode, but the big, transparent white balloon that remorselessly pursued Number Six when he tried to escape provides one of *The Prisoner's* most enduring images. Rover was in fact a semi-sentient being that could change its size and adapt itself to any environment. Receiving orders from a control room, the Rover guarded the Village and was used to pursue escapees (it had the potential to kill but usually just stunned its prey).

The Butler

Played by Angelo Muscat, Number Two's diminutive, rotund, reticent butler could often be seen holding a black and white umbrella. His appearance usually signalled

a nasty surprise for Number Six.

The Village

Number Six is abducted and finds himself resident at a picturesque coastal idyll. Fenced in by mountains and the sea, the Village is remote, inaccessible and inescapable. With its shops, cafes, tropical plants and attractive scenery, it appears like a holiday resort. Indeed, many of its residents dress like holidaymakers in brightly coloured casual clothing, which includes the mandatory wearing of deck shoes and straw boaters. But behind the pleasant facade of seemingly happy, smiling faces there lurks much unpleasantness: torture, scientific experiments, drug-induced indoctrination, blackmail, subterfuge, deceit and relentless pressure on Number Six for him to capitulate and confess. "Why did you resign?" reverberates like a mantra throughout every episode. All the villagers are fellow prisoners and wear badges depicting the logo of an antique Penny Farthing bicycle overlain with an identifying number. The Village is presided over by Number Two, who is beholden to an unseen but omniscient Number One. Throughout the seventeen episodes, suggestions are made as to the whereabouts of the Village but these vary and merely add to the mystery – in *Many Happy Returns* it's hinted that the Village is located on an island off Morocco while *The Chimes of Big Ben* places it at a location somewhere in Lithuania on the Baltic Coast. Finally in *Fallout*, when Number Six finally escapes and makes it onto the A20 road heading towards London, it appears that the Village is located somewhere in Kent!

Village Slogans

❖ Of the people, by the people, for the people.

❖ Humour is the essential ingredient of a democratic society.

❖ A still tongue makes a happy life.

❖ Questions are a burden to others, answers a prison for oneself.

Portmeirion

Portmeirion proved an inspired setting for *The Prisoner* and has since become a place of pilgrimage for aficionados of the show. This unique village can be found where Snowdonia's vertiginous peaks meet the sea in North Wales, occupying a small rocky peninsula in a corner of Tremadog Bay (the nearest town is Porthmadog). It is often described as a pseudo-Italianate village (based on Portofino) though in truth its architecture and buildings reflect a wide variety of different European historical periods, influences and styles. It was specially created by the architect Sir Clough Williams Ellis (he was knighted in 1971) and opened in Easter 1926. Many of its distinctive buildings were created elsewhere, disassembled then transported to the site where they were reassembled. Hotel and toll roads were added to provide the village with a source of income. Portmeirion has played host to many famous literary visitors over the years, including George Bernard Shaw, Aldous Huxley, Ernest Hemingway and Noel Coward (who wrote the play *Blithe Spirit* there during a week's stay in 1941). Patrick McGoohan was no stranger to the village as the location had featured several times in episodes of *Danger Man* (including *View from the Villa*).

Patrick McGoohan

McGoohan was born in New York to Irish immigrant parents. Shortly after his birth, he and his family returned to the Emerald Isle. When he was seven, McGoohan's family moved to Sheffield in England. After contemplating joining the Roman Catholic priesthood, the young McGoohan nursed an ambition to be an actor. Juggling a succession of day jobs (in a rope factory, a bank and managing a chicken farm in Chesterfield), McGoohan participated in many amateur dramatics productions before landing a job as stage manager at the Sheffield Repertory Theatre. As fate would have it, one of the leading actors fell ill and McGoohan was forced to deputise. This serendipitous event was the lucky break McGoohan needed to spur on his acting career. It wasn't long before he had graduated to a starring role and was offered small parts in British films like *The Dam Busters* and *The Dark Avenger* in the mid 1950s. The Rank Organisation snapped up McGoohan in a bid to transform him into a movie star but the actor left the company to pursue stage work before appearing on television and winning Best Actor Award for his role in the TV drama *The Greatest Man in the World*. During this period, McGoohan also shot three family movies for Walt Disney before he was headhunted by ITC chairman, Lew Grade, to star in a half-hour adventure series entitled *Danger Man*. That was 1960, and after thirty-nine episodes the show concluded in the summer of 1961. However, the show's popularity resulted in it being resurrected some three years later – revamped and lengthened to one hour, the show was sold to an enthusiastic American market as *Secret Agent* (though it remained *Danger Man* in the UK). During this same period, McGoohan was actually offered and ending up rejecting the role of 007 in the debut Bond film, *Dr. No* – apparently, he turned it down because of his aversion to onscreen kissing (reflected in the paucity of romantic elements in both *Danger Man* and *The Prisoner)*! Later in the same decade he persuaded Lew Grade to sanction a costly adventure series shot in colour called *The Prisoner* that aired in 1967. Adverse criticism and financial difficulties prompted McGoohan and his family (he married the actress Joan Drummond in 1951) to leave Britain and work abroad. Films like *The Moonshine War* (based on an Elmore Leonard novel) and *Mary, Queen of Scots* followed in the early 1970s, but McGoohan was anything but prolific. He appeared in a couple of *Columbo* episodes in the 1970s and won Emmy Awards for both his performances. After appearing in the Gene Wilder/Richard Pryor film *Silver Streak* (1976), McGoohan played opposite Clint Eastwood (as a callous prison warden) in Don Siegel's *Escape from Alcatraz* (1979). 1980 found McGoohan starring in David Cronenberg's controversial horror flick *Scanners*, but after a few undistinguished movies in the 1980s (usually playing a villain), McGoohan appeared sporadically in TV films until his role as the nefarious Edward Longshanks in Mel Gibson's rewrite of British history, *Braveheart*. Other recent roles have included parts in the 1996 films, *A Time To Kill* and *Hysteria*.

Facts for Anoraks (Prisoner Trivia)

❖ Number Six drives a Lotus Seven Series II sports car daubed in a distinctive yellow and black livery (imagine a wasp on wheels!) and displaying the number plate KAR120C. Other vehicles used in the series include two hearses and white, canvas-roofed Mini Mokes functioning as the village taxis.

❖ Number Six's home address is 1 Buckingham Place.

❖ The original Rover was intended to be a wheeled vehicle.

❖ Only in the episode *The Schizoid Man* is the spherical entity referred to as the Rover.

❖ Four episodes had different working titles – *Checkmate* was also known as *The Queen's Pawn*, *Do Not Forsake Me Oh My Darling* was *Face Unknown*, *A, B and C* was *Play in Three Acts* and *Once Upon a Time* was *Degree Absolute*.

❖ For publicity purposes and prior to the series' initial transmission, a couple of episodes were made available for viewing by the press – these rough cuts differed from the finished article and featured dialogue, scenes and music (both the theme tune and incidental music) which was later excised from the official broadcast versions.

❖ Fenella Fielding's husky voice was used as the Village announcer whose catchphrase was 'It's another lovely day.'

❖ The Village newspaper was called *The Tally Ho*.

❖ Script editor, George Markstein, makes a cameo appearance as 'the man behind the desk' in the opening title sequence.

❖ In *Free For All*, the picture of Number Six's face which is used for an election poster is a publicity shot dating from Patrick McGoohan's *Danger Man* days.

❖ Only five episodes were shot on location at Portmeirion: *Arrival, Free For All, Do Not Forsake Me Oh My Darling, Checkmate* and *Many Happy Returns*. Interiors were filmed at MGM's Borehamwood studios in London under the direction of Don Chaffey with sets devised by Jack Shamper. Brendan J. Stafford filmed the series.

❖ Ron Grainer (1922-81) wrote the theme tune. An Australian who emigrated to the UK, Grainer wrote music for films such as *A Kind of Loving, To Sir With Love* and *The Omega Man*. His TV themes included *Tales of the Unexpected*.

❖ A penny farthing bicycle represented the Village logo – according to Patrick McGoohan it is 'an ironic symbol of progress'.

❖ Patrick McGoohan used the pseudonym Paddy Fitz as the scriptwriter of *Free For All*. He also wrote and directed *Once Upon a Time* and *Fallout*, but both of these are attributed to Patrick McGoohan in the credits.

❖ In *Do Not Forsake Me Oh My Darling* an address on a letter can clearly be read as Portmeirion Road.

❖ Veteran British actor Eric Portman was so forgetful that he had to read his lines from cue cards in *Free For All*.

Episode Guide

Series One:

1 – Arrival
2 – The Chimes of Big Ben
3 – A, B and C
4 – Free For All
5 – The Schizoid Man
6 – The General
7 – Many Happy Returns
8 – Dance of the Dead
9 – Checkmate
10 – Hammer Into Anvil
11 – It's Your Funeral
12 – A Change of Mind
13 – Do Not Forsake Me Oh My Darling

Series Two:

14 – Living in Harmony
15 – The Girl Who Was Death
16 – Once Upon a Time
17 – Fall Out

The Prisoner on Video and DVD

Carlton Video has issued the series on both DVD and video.

Sources

www.the-prisoner-6.freeserve.co.uk
    (the most comprehensive Prisoner website)
www.avalondreamtime.co.uk
www.csolve.net
www.netreach.net/~sixofoone/
    (web address of *The Prisoner* Appreciation Society)

Charles Waring

VIDEO

VIDEO REVIEWS

Paul McAuley & Barry Forshaw

Homicide: The Movie (Trimark/NBC Home Video DVD VM 9649D)

Homicide: Life on the Street was a true rarity – a challenging, tough-minded programme made for mainstream prime time American TV. An ensemble police procedural that prided itself on the realism with which it depicted the underside of inner city life, its format was inspired and informed by reporter David Simon's book, *Homicide: A Year on the Killing Streets*, based on the year he spent shadowing detectives of Baltimore's Homicide Unit). It was filmed entirely on location in Baltimore with documentary-style handheld camerawork and choppy editing, and its interwoven story lines refused to pander to lowest-common-denominator expectations. The focus was not on shoot-outs, car chases and criminal masterminds, but on intense sessions in the interview room, where the detectives manoeuvred suspects into confessions and tried to make sense of what were often senseless acts of violence. Although critically acclaimed, *Homicide*'s ratings were always low. Dubbed by *TV Guide* "The Best Show You're Not Watching", it was finally killed off by NBC at the end of its seventh season – the season Channel 4 bought but shamefully and quite unjustifiably never

aired after relegating the fifth and sixth seasons to irregular late-night slots. *Homicide: The Movie* is a one-off eighty-nine minute episode in which dangling plot lines are tidied up and every major character (including two who were killed off) takes a final bow. Al Giardello (Yaphet Kotto), formerly Homicide Shift Commander, is leading the electoral race for Mayor of Baltimore when he's shot at a political rally. While surgeons work to save his life, the Homicide squad is joined by former members in a redball effort to track down the would-be assassin. For much of its length, *Homicide: The Movie* is more nostalgia fest than satisfactory mystery; although fans will undoubtedly enjoy seeing old faces reappear in the squad room, most of the cast have little to do but make what they can of their brief cameos. But there's plenty of *Homicide*'s trademark biting dialogue and black humour, the motive of the gunman is nicely foreshadowed, the final confrontation between Frank Pembleton (Andre Braugher) and Tim Bayliss (Kyle Secor), for six seasons *Homicide*'s pivotal partnership, sparks with raw emotion, and in its final twist the movie not only evokes *Homicide*'s power to overturn convention, but provides a moving coda that evokes the show's most famous unsolved case. The region one DVD has the usual excellent sound and picture quality, but beyond a preview 'hidden' behind the Trimark logo on the main menu, there are no extras – not even a case card or booklet. Smart, innovative, often demanding but never underestimating the intelligence of its audience, *Homicide* will be missed, and reruns on cable TV in the US means that few episodes have made it to video or DVD. It's about time Channel 4 resurrected it on its late night schedule, and finally showed that missing last season.

Paul McAuley

The most reliable staple for the DVD genre (as it was for the video format) is, of course, the action movie. And as the omnivorous appetite of the medium for material continues to grow, we punters can now take our choice from the best action movies along with highly collectable material from television. *The Way of the Gun* (Momentum) had a mixed press, but this is the kind of film that really comes into its own on DVD (the surround sound effects are stunning). Directed by Christopher McQuarrie (who wrote *The Usual Suspects*, and who perhaps should have given this project to another director rather than helming him it himself), this is a blood-soaked action movie with much more on its mind than simply the discharging of guns. Sam Peckinpah's ghost hangs over whole thing, and is even invoked in the extra features by one of the actors, Benicio del Toro – but Sam did this kind of thing better. Diverting stuff, nevertheless, with a supporting cast to die for: James Caan, Scott Wilson, Geoffrey Lewis. Carlton's much-to-be-applauded reissue of vintage ITC material continues with

further episodes of *The Persuaders*, *The Saint* and *The Champions* (episodes eleven to fourteen of each). It's interesting to see the work of such top of filmmakers as 007-director Peter Hunt in these issues, but, as usual, it's the latest volumes of *Danger Man* that really are the cream of the crop. A warm welcome for the third and fourth volumes of Patrick McGoohan's John Drake thrillers; this admirable series continues to make available vintage episodes from one of the sharpest, most intelligent adventure series of the 1960s – however dated (in many ways) they are. Of course, the key appeal of these reissues will be for fans of *The Prisoner*, eager to study the prototype for that enigmatic classic. It's particularly interesting, then, that the first episode in volume three is called *The Prisoner*. But although Portmeirion and the paranoia of the later show appear in *Danger Man*, they are not in this episode, which is rather disappointing – it's a throwback to the mere efficiency of the earlier episodes. Generally, though, episodes fourteen to twenty show the same growth in ambition and accomplishment as the last box. However, I can't resist my usual plea to Carlton: don't forget that the hour-long later episodes are infinitely superior to these earlier shows, and would enjoy healthy sales to a *Prisoner*-fed audience. Finally, (from Mosaic), a video issue for the well written Trevor Eve TV series, *Waking the Dead*.

From Carlton, a Hitchcock classic: *The 39 Steps* is possibly the finest of Hitchcock's early British films made at Islington's Gainsborough Studios (although some might accord *The Lady Vanishes* that honour), and was a prototype for such later Hitchcock classics as *North by Northwest*. Absolutely unmissable. **Barry Forshaw**

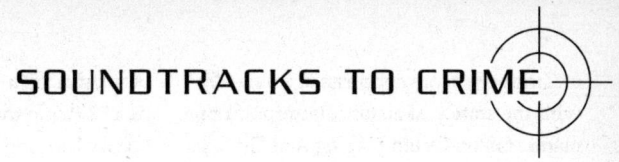
MUSIC

Charles Waring`

Hannibal: Original Motion Picture Soundtrack (Decca 467 696-2)
Unequivocally, the most memorable moment in Ridley Scott's lamentable movie version of Thomas Harris' *Hannibal* was Sir Anthony Hopkins' graphic demonstration of do-it-yourself brain surgery on a hapless Ray Liotta. It proved an appalling, almost nauseating sight – but more, I feel, for its unintentional absurdity rather than any gruesome, vomit-inducing qualities. Scott, in fact, proved more of a butcher than Lecter, transforming the finale of Harris' visceral thriller into something filched from the theatre of the absurd (minus the existential gravitas).

But I digress. Apart from Scott's eye-catching impressionistic shots of Florence, the best thing about *Hannibal* turned out to be the soundtrack. In the main composed by the German-born Hollywood stalwart, Hans Zimmer (*Pearl Harbor*, *Gladiator*, *The Thin Red Line*, *True Romance* etc.), the music for *Hannibal* largely consists of an atmospheric orchestral score. *Dear Clarice* features Anthony Hopkins' chilling narrative over a shape-shifting piece of music that begins eerily, then acquires the plaintive sound of choristers before mutating into a string piece of Mahlerian grandeur that concludes with a tinkling repeated piano figure. The density of Zimmer's score contrasts dramatically with the stately, skeletal counterpoint of pianist Glenn Gould playing *Aria De Capo* from Bach's *Goldberg Variations*. Hopkins again features on *Let My Home Be the Gallows*, with orchestral sonorities reminiscent of the great Bernard Herrmann's work, as does the cue entitled *To Every Captive Soul* whose elegiac string passages also invoke the late romantic spirit of Gustav Mahler's Fifth Symphony (the *Adagietto*). The score closes with a haunting operatic aria called *Vide Cor Meum* by Patrick Cassidy. An allusive blend of classical, romantic and atonal music, *Hannibal* the soundtrack is well worth investigating. Forget the movie – that was a dog's dinner. This, however, is a veritable feast. I advise you to tuck in.

15 Minutes: Original Motion Picture Soundtrack (Milan 74321 84668-2)

Taking its title from pop artist Andy Warhol's prescient quote about TV conferring instant but short-lived fame on potentially anyone, John Herzfield's taut thriller starring Robert De Niro, Edward Burns and Kelsey Grammar is accompanied by this ten-track soundtrack album. Consisting mostly of menacing, pounding, and occasionally atmospheric rock/dance/pop material like God Lives Underwater's muscular version of David Bowie's *Fame*, The Prodigy's *3 Kilos* and a hard-edged 'clubbed to death' remix of dance guru Moby's recent chart hit *Porcelain*, the soundtrack to *15 Minutes* contains material likely to bludgeon the listener into either submission or unconsciousness. For the most part, there's a remorseless intensity to tracks like Maxim's *Carmen Queasy*, Breakbeat Era's

propulsive *Ultra-Obscene* and Ballistic Mystic's *52 Pickup* that make this one hell of an uneasy listening experience. If you're of a nervous disposition, you'd best avoid this one.

The Godfather Trilogy: Nino Rota/Carmine Coppola (Silva Screen FilmCD 344)

Among the forty or so film scores written by the classically trained Italian composer, Nino Rota (1911-1979), his elegant and haunting *Love Theme* from the soundtrack to Francis Ford Coppola's 1971 landmark Mafia movie, *The Godfather*, has proved to be his most popular and enduring piece of music. Although Rota made his name collaborating with the legendary Italian film director Federico Fellini on movies like *La Dolce Vita*, Rota's *Godfather* music has exerted a more profound impact on the cinema-going public. Despite an impressive body of film work, Rota was never really regarded as Italy's premier movie composer, having been eclipsed by the younger, more adventurous Ennio Morricone. But like Morricone, Rota's music with its aching, delicate lyricism possesses a distinctly Italianate character – this passionate, Mediterranean quality is particularly evident on this new Silva Screen assemblage, a compilation of all three of *The Godfather* scores released to coincide with the initial movie's thirtieth anniversary. Performed by the City of Prague Philharmonic with conductor Paul Bateman at the helm, this surround sound digital recording proves to be a delightful rendering of Rota's original music for Coppola's trilogy. The strength of Rota's score is his utilisation of rural, folk music elements (including the use of mandolins and accordions) to add authentic ethnic colour. Also included are festive cues composed by Coppola's father, Carmine Coppola (1919-1991), who, after Rota's death, scored 1990's inferior second sequel, *The Godfather – Part III*, but also incorporated parts of Rota's original score. The music from *Part III* also includes the *Preludio* from Mascagni's opera *Cavalleria Rusticana*, which in the film has an important dramatic function as the plaintive musical backdrop to a scene of murder and mayhem. Paradoxically, for all the graphic violence and brutality of Coppola's cinematic depiction of an internecine Mafioso dynasty, this is never ever reflected in the music, which, for the most part, is spellbindingly beautiful. Here's a musical offering that you shouldn't refuse!

Get Carter: Original Motion Picture Soundtrack (Silva Screen FilmCD 348)

Get Carter: Music From and Inspired By the Motion Picture (Silva Screen FilmCD 347)

I have it on good authority that Stephen Kay's recent Hollywood remake of Mike Hodges's classic British gangster movie, *Get Carter*, isn't likely to win any awards – in fact, the film, which originally premiered Stateside in October 2000, received such a vicious mauling at the hands of US critics, that it is rumoured that its screening in the UK has been delayed due to fears of a similar fate befalling it here. It's no wonder when you've got the muscle-bound, monolithic, monosyllabic Sly Stallone in the role that Michael Caine played so effectively. Ironi-

cally, and to the disgust of some *Get Carter* aficionados, Caine appears in a cameo role in the new film, which also stars the British actress Miranda Richardson. Not having seen the film yet (which I am assured will be eventually released in the UK), I can't comment on the action – what we can explore though is the music, the release of which has preceded the film. In actual fact there are two soundtracks that you can buy – the original score by composer Tyler Bates, and a CD of songs 'from and inspired' by the film. The latter is largely comprised of rumbling, seismic dance floor 'tunes' (including Moby's *Memory Gospel*) and raucous slabs of thumping alternative rock. Far preferable (and easier on the ear) is Tyler Bates' atmospheric score, which features eighteen relatively concise music cues. To my surprise (and delight), Bates elects to modernise Roy Budd's main theme from Mike Hodges' original movie, complete with the pitter-patter sound of Indian tablas. In fact, what Bates does is simply inject a shot of musical testosterone into his arrangement, invigorating Budd's theme and bringing it up to date with the addition of rock and dance music elements. Even Budd's haunting four-note harpsichord motif is utilised as an introduction. The rest of the score is a mixture of plaintive, low key moments like *The Garden* contrasted with pulsating up tempo action cues – the best of these is *Christmas Tree Chase*, a virile, jazz-inflected piece that brings to mind the work of Lalo Schifrin. If we are to believe the reports that *Get Carter* is dire, at least the soundtrack, though modest, is almost beyond reproach. Perhaps the supreme irony of all though is that Tyler Bates is probably the only person to come out of Stephen Kay's film with his reputation actually enhanced.

Above the Rim: The Soundtrack (Death Row DROW102)

Gang Related: The Soundtrack (Death Row DROW104)

Gridlock'd: The Soundtrack (Death Row DROW105)

Just reissued is this trio of soundtrack albums to movies featuring the late African-American gangster rapper, actor and poet, Tupac Shakur. The shaven-headed LA based rapper was gunned down by an unknown assailant on Friday September 13th 1996, presumably in a revenge attack for the fatal shooting of the obese New York rapper Notorious B.I.G. (Christopher Wallace) a few months earlier. (Shakur was apparently not directly involved in Wallace's death but had exacerbated the animosity and fuelled the internecine rivalry between America's East and West Coast rap artists.). Shakur's martyrdom resulted in him being canonised as the patron saint of California's gangster rappers. His music (some of which is featured on these soundtracks) featured expletive dominated lyrics devoted to espousing the nihilistic 'thug' life philosophy and its attendant lore of gang warfare, sexual prowess, drugs and material gain. Incarcerated for sexual assault and living the gangster life to the full, Shakur saw himself as a modern day Jesse James or John Dillinger. Like James Dean, Tupac's early demise (he was only twenty-five when he died) has given him iconic status. Also like Dean, he made only a handful of films. The best of those was *Gridlock'd*, where Shakur played opposite Tim Roth in an offbeat, frequently humorous film about the exploits of a couple of heroin addicts. The soundtrack to *Gridlock'd* features fifteen hard-boiled gangster rap tracks, ranging from material by Tupac himself (*Wanted Dead or Alive* and the more sensitive *Never Had a Friend Like Me*) to other bleak ghetto fables from Nate Dogg, The Lady of Rage, Snoop Dog and Dat Nigga Daz. Released the same year as *Gridlock'd* was *Gang Related*, written and directed by Jim Kouf, whose other credits include *Stakeout* and its sequel, *Another Stakeout*. Here, Shakur plays – would you believe – a cop alongside James Belushi, Dennis Quaid and James Earl Jones in a tense action movie about police officers corrupted by drug money. The double CD soundtrack contains twenty-four songs with evocative titles like *Hollywood Bank Robbery*, *Greed* and *Made Niggaz*. Tupac supplies a couple of strong tunes as do fellow gangster rappers, Ice Cube (now an actor himself), Kurupt, Nate Dogg and Daz Dillinger. By far the best soundtrack Tupac contributed to was for his third movie appearance, *Above the Rim*, directed by Jeff Pollack, which focused on Kyle, an ambitious African-American high school kid (Duane Martin) who has aspirations of winning a college basketball scholarship (Shakur plays Birdie, Kyle's estranged gangbanger friend). This soundtrack is more varied, with softer, r'n'b-flavoured tracks sitting alongside some searing hip-hop moments. With this album in particular, it's easy to identify the attraction of gangster rap music – rolling, fluid rhythms and infectious hook lines imbue the music with an addictive, narcotic potency.

Coffy: Roy Ayers
(Polydor 314 529 777-2)

Here's a classic Blaxploitation soundtrack composed by the virtuoso jazz vibraphone player, Roy Ayers. *Coffy* starred the fabulously buxom Pam Grier as a vengeful nurse (Coffy) exacting payback on dope dealers in the lurid, violent 1973 movie written and directed by Jack Hill (director of other low budget cult classics including that other vehicle for Grier's ample pneumatic charms, *Foxy Brown*). Ayers' soundtrack not only boasts a memorable theme tune in the breezy *Coffy is the Color* but plenty more besides: a sultry ballad *Coffy Baby* is sung by the jazz vocalist Dee Dee Bridgewater, while male crooner Wayne Garfield handles the superlative *Shining Symbol*. For the most part, *Coffy* is composed of funky instrumentals like *Aragon*, *King George*, the wonderfully titled *Brawling Broads* and *Escape* (actually, the latter two tunes were borrowed by Quentin Tarantino for his *Jackie Brown* movie, though the songs failed to materialise on the official soundtrack CD). This wonderful remastered CD also includes a foldout movie poster. To quote the film's publicity blurb, *Coffy* will certainly 'cream ya!'

Hell Up In Harlem: Edwin Starr
(Motown 440 013 739-2)

Edwin Starr (real name Charles Hatcher) is a Southern soul singer with a powerful, husky voice. Starr's main claim to fame was as the original artist to record the anti-Vietnam protest song, *War* in 1970 – it was later covered, of course, by Frankie Goes to Hollywood. At the height of the Blaxploitation cinema boom in the early 1970s, Starr was asked to contribute to the soundtrack of the movie *Hell Up in Harlem*, written and directed by Larry Cohen. *Hell Up in Harlem* was, in fact, a sequel to 1973's *Black Caesar*, an ebony gangster flick which was originally intended as a vehicle for Sammy Davis Jnr but which ended up starring the tough guy black actor and former football star, Fred 'The Hammer' Williamson in the role of Tommy Gibbs (the film was originally released in Britain as *The Godfather of Harlem*). Williamson reprised his role as Gibbs in *Black Caesar*'s abject follow-up. Like many Blaxploitation movies, *Hell Up in Harlem* proved an execrable cinematic experience, redeemed only by its scorching soundtrack. With Starr the focal point of material written by cult producer and songwriter Fonce Mizell, this reissue proves to be a worthy addition to any soundtrack collection. Starr contributes his trademark stentorian vocal to the impassioned title track, though the best track, *Easin' In*, finds the charismatic singer in an uncharacteristically subdued mood, accompanied by a mellow, brooding bass groove. With its obligatory tense instrumental chase cue (*Airport Chase*) and maudlin ode to 'mama' (*Mama Should Be Here Too*), *Hell Up in Harlem* is littered with musical clichés but proves an enjoyable romp nonetheless. Hellishly good!

Charles Waring

NO EXIT PRESS

Straight From The Fridge Dad

A DICTIONARY OF HIPSTER SLANG

by Max Décharné

A PERSONAL VIEW

Mark Timlin

The creator of Nick Sharman (and crime reviewer for The Independent on Sunday*) gives CT the unvarnished truth (if he can just remember what happened last night)…*
(and check out www.nicksharman.co.uk)

Sex and crime, crime and sex, go together like… Well anything that rhymes I suppose. Lager and lime perhaps. The Duke and Duchess of Wessex maybe. No, maybe not. But whatever they do go together like, they seem to be inextricably linked. When the idea of this edition of *Crime Time* was first mooted, the editor Barry Forshaw called me up and said, "You've written some sex stuff haven't you?"

"Yeah", I replied.

"Anything with crime in it?"

"Yeah."

"So can we print some?"

"Suppose so", I said.

But. When I looked back at my dalliance in the field of crime and porn, I must admit it didn't exactly come over as my finest hour. So, I'm afraid you'll have to look elsewhere for the adventures of Marianne Champagne, girl detective who gets her man (literally), but keeps losing her knickers. Sorry Barry, but that's the way the ball bounces.

So what is it about sex and crime? When I started writing Nick Sharman novels way back in the dim and distant ninth decade of the last century, I thought I'd break all the rules and give the boy plenty of sex. So I did. But, as the series progressed, I found that the sex just got in the way of the story rather like all that sheet-covered pumping of couples gets in the way of the plot in so many contemporary films. Besides, my mum didn't like it. It embarrassed her. And I now know exactly what she means. In my other life as crime reviewer for the *Independent on Sunday* I have to read lots of books by people I know. It's a weird feeling at the best of times. But especially weird if they write in the first person using their hero/heroine as a mouthpiece. One has to work out if their protagonist is how they really are, how they'd like to be, how they want the world to see them, or what.

Recently I read a book by one of my dearest friends. First person, no problem. Then, suddenly, sex reared its ugly head. And not just missionary position type sex either. No, this was sex between the female lead character and a young man who – how can I put it? – preferred to be underneath if you get my drift. Suddenly there were lots of intricate knots and hot wax on the (male) nipples. Blimey. This woman is happily married with two teenage children. I've been to their house and broken bread with the family. Although I loved the book, I had to avert my eyes from that bit. So God knows what the kids would make of it. So now, in my books at least, I prefer to stop at the bedroom door and leave a bit to my reader's imagination. After all, most of them will hopefully have had sex at least once in their lives and have a good idea of what it's all about. But sex will always be with us. At least until that much vaunted replacement for men with some kind of machine which I read about in the papers from time to time when news is sparse, actually arrives, or until the human race dies out for one reason or another.

So do I enjoy sex in the crime novels I read? No, as it happens, I don't much. Not many crime novelists can actually write decent sex scenes. And I know, as I've written five porno novels myself, it's not as easy as it might seem. Even my favourite writers seem to have trouble when it comes to what goes on between the sheets. Let's face it, the act in itself is quite comical unless you're actively engaged in it, and there's always the temptation to make more of it than there actually is, especially when heroes or heroines are involved. So, maybe it's time for the CWA to launch a Bad Sex Dagger in their annual awards. The Used Rubber Dagger perhaps.

I once had a girlfriend whose salute when taking a drink was: "To crime and passion." Maybe that's what we need in our books when the characters do the wild thing together – less sex and more passion.

Mark Timlin

Timlin's Top Tips

Bad News by Donald E. Westlake – Mysterious Press (US)

Deal With the Dead by Les Standiford – Putnam (US)

Trans Am by Rob Ryan – Headline

Seepyhead by Mark Billingham – Little, Brown

West on 66 by James H. Cobb – Thomas Dunne Books (US)

People Die by Kevin Wignall – Flame

House of Correction by Doug J. Swanson – No Exit

Baby Love by Denise Danks – Orion

Cold Town by Sarah Diamond – Orion

Bitterroot by James Lee Burke – Orion

THE LAWRENCE BLOCK NEWSLETTER

His latest book in the UK is The Affairs of Chip Harrison (NEP). Here's the Lowdown from Larry…

I have much to tell you and little time to tell it, so let's Get On With It.

In keeping with this issue's theme, my most recent book is an anthology, *Speaking of Lust*, just out this month from Cumberland House. I picked a batch of outstanding stories by splendid writers, and wrote an original novella for the occasion, first of a new series, and entirely different from anything I'd done before. The anthology itself is the first of a series too, with each book devoted to a different deadly sin: volume two, *Speaking of Greed*, will be out in the fall. If you've picked up my two earlier anthologies, *Death Cruise* and *Opening Shots*, you know how attractive and well-produced Cumberland's books are. And speaking of *Opening Shots*, it was so well received that there's a sequel on the way: *Opening Shots 2*, coming soon.

There's a new Matthew Scudder novel

written. The title is *Hope To Die*, and it's due this October from Morrow in the US and Orion in the UK. I had a feeling while I was writing it that it was coming out nicely, but it's hard to see the picture while you're standing inside the frame. When I ran it up the flagpole, everybody saluted; my publishers are more enthusiastic than I've ever seen them, and plan a high-powered promotional campaign, a 100,000-copy first printing, and a sixteen-city tour. (As soon as I know the dates and cities, so will you.)

Some of you are familiar with my books for writers, the most popular of which has been *Telling Lies For Fun and Profit*. Instructional and motivational books seem particularly suited to audio, and I spent years wishing some audio publisher would pick it up. Last fall I decided the Little Red Hen was right and went ahead and did it myself. I've narrated and self-published a six-cassette, nine-hour audiobook of *Telling Lies*, beautifully produced and packaged, and priced quite competitively at $39.95. (If you can use five or more, the price drops to $24 a piece... and what fine gifts these make for your writer friends!) You won't find the audiobook in stores, but I've got plenty and would love to have your orders. See below for ordering information...

Tanner hardcover firsts. As you may know, Otto Penzler published handsome hardcover first editions of the first two Evan Tanner novels, *The Thief Who Couldn't Sleep* and *The Canceled Czech*. When a publishing merger shut down his imprint, the project was halted. This past October Subterranean Press brought out a handsome hardcover first edition of the fourth book in the series, *The Scoreless Thai*, and I want to thank you for the fine reception you've given it. The publishers went back for a second printing, and now that's gone too... but you're in luck! My deal with Subterranean called for payment in copies, so I still have signed firsts for sale at the original price of $30 ($18 each if you can use five or more). I also have a small stock of the slip-cased limited edition at $75 – no quantity discount on these. (I should add that *Thief* is completely sold out, but I have a few copies left of *Czech* at $50 while they last.) Next on Subterranean's agenda is *Tanner's Tiger*, due this summer, with the remaining titles to follow. And yes, I'll have copies.

Movie news... and plenty of it. First, I'm delighted to report that I've just completed a screenplay for *Keller*, based on my novel *Hit Man*. You know how I've said for years I have no interest in writing for the screen? Turns out I was wrong. Back in December, flushed with triumph from finishing *Hope To Die*, I heard from producer Richard Rubinstein that he and Jeff Bridges (who will star and co-produce) that they wanted to bring in someone new to rewrite the existing screenplay. What they both wanted, he explained, was someone who could make the script more like the original book. What a concept! Well, I didn't have to think too hard to figure out who might be suited to the task. Screenwriting turned out to be both harder and easier than I'd imagined. I found I couldn't keep at it for more than two hours a day, but that turned out to be enough to get the job done. I'm happy with the way it turned out – and, more to the point, so is everybody else. God willing and the creek don't rise, *Keller* may, before too long, be opening at a theatre near you. Two other films are still very much in active development. The folks at Jersey films and Universal Pictures are, I'm told, very enthusiastic about the screenplay for *A Walk Among the Tombstones*, and consequently have extended the option. And a screenplay's in the works at Warners for *Burglars Can't Be Choosers*, with George Clooney slated to star as Bernie.

Paperbacks. Avon's edition of *Hit List* won't be along until early next year. Sales of the Morrow hardcover topped everybody's expectations – the book reached number five on the *LA Times* bestseller list – and Avon decided to give their edition a better slot. If you can't wait, well, run out and buy the hardcover... Several titles in the Scudder backlist went into trade paperback in recent years, and they looked terrific, but it's clear trade's not a popular format for crime fiction. Most of you – readers and booksellers alike – seem to prefer massmarket size, so Avon will be reissuing all the Scudder titles in that format, with big displays planned to coincide with Morrow's October release of *Hope To Die*.

Early stuff. Not too long ago Crippen & Landru published a limited edition of *One Night Stands*, a collection of my previously uncollected early pulp fiction. The book, wonderful to look at if not to read, sold out in a hurry. Since then, a couple of readers/collectors have unearthed three novelettes which had somehow escaped, all of them featuring Ed London, the rather colourless star of my second novel, *Coward's Kiss* (aka *Death Pulls a Doublecross*). Doug Green of C&L and I mulled things over, and greed won out, as it so often does. Here's the plan: Crippen & Landru will publish the three novelettes as *The Lost Cases of Ed London*. It'll be a signed, limited

edition hardcover; then, sometime down the line, they'll issue a double volume of the two books in paperback for those of you who want a reading copy. CrippenL@pilot.infi.net for info...

Chip Harrison. All four titles are now out of print, although some stores may still have stray copies on the shelves. No Exit Press in the UK will bring out a four-in-one omnibus volume later this year. Booksellers in the States can probably order the book, or try No Exit's website, www.noexit.co.uk. You'll also find paperbacks there of most of the Evan Tanner titles, as well as the first Bernie Rhodenbarr novel, *Burglars Can't Be Choosers*, which is long gone on this side of the pond.

Travel schedule. We'll be doing a lot of it this year. Lynne and I took an Amazon River cruise on the Olympic Voyager over the holidays, and also went on a Cruise Works mystery cruise around Hawaii. (When we left the ship we continued on to – haul out your atlas – Guam, Pohnpei, Kosrae and Majuro.) May found us in Switzerland en route to Writers Week in Listowel, Co. Kerry (writersweek@tinet.ie) and in July we went on an Alaskan cruise. Then we're home until I go off touring for *Hope To Die*. We're closing in on full membership in the Travelers Century Club; our tally is ninety-three (or ninety-four if you count the Moldavian breakaway republic of Transdniester, which damn well ought to count – God knows Evan Tanner would count it) so we should hit the century mark before the year is out.

Be well. And I hope I'll get to see a whole lot of you on the fall tour.

Lawrence Block

TO THE MAX

Maxim Jakubowski

His own books have earned him the sobriquet King of the Erotic Thriller; he's one of the genre's premier editors... Mr Maxim Jakubowski.

Nightmare Town (Picador £16.99) is a welcome volume of previously uncollected stories by Dashiell Hammett, mostly from his early years of apprenticeship in the pulp magazines and the legendary *Black Mask* in the 1920s and 1930s. Hardboiled prose has never been tougher, as Colin Dexter perceptively points out in his preface, and the crystal-clear prose is a joy to behold in these tales of darkness full of men on the slippery slope to oblivion, and

the obligatory untrustworthy dames and colourful villains. As a bonus we are offered the first glimpse of the characters later to become famous in *The Thin Man*. Harsh lights and romantic black shadows: this is the heyday of American crime writing and has not dated at all. Another, later icon of the American hardboiled tradition was David Goodis. The reissue of the long unavailable *Of Tender Sin* (Serpent's Tail £6.99) presents another touching tale of paranoia and jealousy, in which everymen on the downhill road struggle hopelessly against the chains of fate and lust to little avail, losers all moving in top gear towards the gutter. Chilling. Another worthy resurrection is that of Newton Thornburg's *Cutter And Bone* (Serpent's Tail £7.99, with a new introduction by George P. Pelecanos) – as sharp an evocation of the angst of post Vietnam America as any, and a small, perfectly formed classic thriller which resonates to this day with its parade of idealists, alcoholics and macabre denizens of the American underbelly.

Undeterred by the weight of tradition, two young British authors tackle the negative side of the American dream and come up trumps. In Tony Strong's *The Decoy* (Doubleday £9.99), a British actress in New York without a valid visa is used by the police to snare a husband suspected of having murdered his wife. Soon she is drowning in a murky sea of sex and Internet manipulation, and discovers the true and ambiguous nature of her own sexuality as she falls for the seductive target. With many a surprising plot upset, this is an intelligent thriller about both the nature of acting and the negative side of human nature in which the conspirators stand on both sides of the law to disturbing effect. Rob Ryan's *Trans Am* (Headline £9.99) is the London travel writer's third venture into the US badlands, a breathless tale of a suburban New Jersey life whose tranquillity is shattered by the death of a child. The ensuing web of evil ensnares two families in a bid to replace the missing son of an evil businessman. Equally suspenseful is Harlan Coben's *Tell No One* (Orion £12.99), a breakthrough blockbuster by an author better known for his previous comic capers involving a sports agent. The premise is chilling: a doctor in mourning is contacted by e-mail by his dead wife with a message no one else could have written, and the whole weight of the past soon

returns in a slick race against time and an assortment of sharply-drawn villains. The plotting is a bit obvious and lopsided and the main character irritatingly touchy-feely but the pace never slows down and you can already see the movie on your mental screen as you read along.

Blue Lonesome by Bill Pronzini (Canongate £9.99) is the first book by one of American mystery fiction's hidden treasures to appear in the UK for ages. Pronzini, whose career already spans three decades, is truly the crime writer's crime writer: effective, melancholy, unshowy but never putting a foot wrong in this madly evocative blend of psychological thriller, whodunit and noir. Man meets woman at the Harmony cafe; woman rebuffs man and later is discovered to have committed suicide; man seeks to resolve the mystery of her sad life. The result is poignant and a peach of a novel. *Hollowpoint* by Rob Reuland (Jonathan Cape £10.00) is an impressive debut by a real-life Brooklyn homicide district attorney, a blackly comedic tale of a lawyer in a mission of redemption amongst the bleak world of crack addicts and the Brooklyn projects. Reuland knows the uncompromising territory all too well from personal experience and guides us through the cynical courtrooms and mean streets with assurance, cruel wit and pathos. An author to look out for.

The big guns slugging it out in the book corral come no bigger than Ian Rankin's twelfth Inspector Rebus novel *The Falls* (Orion £16.99). The murder of an art history student at the University of Edinburgh soon leads the hapless cop, now saddled with a new superior with a lack of tolerance for his drinking and unconventional methods, on a trail of Internet mischief and the customary riddles of the past in which the solution to today's criminal woes is buried. Once again, Rankin proves masterful in pulling all the varied strands of his fascinating plot together, and his home city of Edinburgh emerges as important a character as his floundering protagonists, while the author's sense of place casts a powerful shadow on this subtle tale of the recurrence of evil. With Inspector Morse's recent demise, Rankin and Rebus are now unopposed champions of the British police procedural field. But old masters always have new tricks up their sleeve and Reginald Hill's *Dialogues Of The Dead* (HarperCollins £16.99), the latest thriller to feature respectively cantankerous and suave cops Dalziel and Pascoe, comes up trumps with a witty demonstration of wordplay and uncommon detection by the Yorkshire pair. A man drowns while another dies in a motorcycle crash. Seemingly two accidents – but entries to a story competition in a local newspaper indicate otherwise. Soon Dalziel and Pascoe are playing a catch-up game with a sinister opponent known only as the Wordman. Confronted by a baffling multitude of clues, they end up fighting the word with the word. Hill, tongue firmly in cheek, spins clever variations on the traditional cop thriller and never ceases to surprise even on the seventeenth time around the block with his unique characters.

Another favourite is Donna Leon's Commissario Guido Brunetti and his investigation in *A Sea of Troubles* (Heinemann £15.99) sees him unsettling the peace of mind of the closely knit island community of Palestrina, a thin stretch of sand that separates the Venetian lagoon from the Adriatic. Two clam fishermen have died in a suspicious explosion and outsiders are decidedly unwelcome. When questore secretary Signorina Elettra visits, Brunetti (who has a gentle crush on her) fears for her safety and is quickly drawn into a morass of crooked local politics, pollution and secrets. The all too human character of Brunetti evokes the reader's sympathy as a tenacious underdog, and his journey through Italian venality and administrative woes is always rewarding. Advertised as a novel in two parts, *Candyland* (Orion £16.99) is a somewhat original collaboration between two of crime writing's biggest names, psychological thriller and sometimes mainstream novelist Evan Hunter and the classic author of the *87th Precinct* cop sagas Ed McBain. The joke is of course that they are one and the same man! Benjamin Thorpe is married, a father and a successful Los Angeles architect, but also a man obsessed. Alone in New York on business, he spends an empty night in compulsive search for female companionship. This leads to an early morning clash in a brothel and a subsequent self revelation. Heidi, a teenage hooker, whose path had crossed Thorpe's during the night, never returns to her apartment and is found murdered and mutilated in an alleyway the next day. Enter McBain and the cops for a painstaking investigation in contrast to the leisurely earlier unfolding of the plot and dissection of Thorpe's troubled soul. The resulting novel is a page turner and an ingenious way for Hunter/McBain to sharply demonstrate both sides of his enormous storytelling talents. At any rate, the collaborators never had to argue, I expect.

Maxim Jakubowski

THE VERDICT

Deadline by Campbell Armstrong
Corgi, 0 385 41070 0
Since bursting onto the thriller scene with his *Jig* trilogy, Armstrong has clearly been loath to sacrifice a winning formula for the sake of originality. Many books on, you'll still find him tapping into that same vein of high-octane thrills and look-behind-you shocks that made his first book so engaging. And there's nothing wrong with that, provided he can come up with engaging plots and fresh twists. *Deadline* begins with dedicated LA psychiatrist Jerry Lomax receiving a call from a mysterious stranger. The caller wants him to reveal all about a confidential counselling session he conducted with soon-to-be US Attorney General Emily Ford. Lomax refuses, but it's then that he's presented with a disturbing ultimatum – spills the beans or face personal and professional ruin. Lomax has until midnight to find his way out of a seemingly hopeless situation. *Deadline* may not be another *Jig*, but it's still pretty good. Despite the done-to-death plot device – in my mind, a count-down always smacks of desperation – Campbell's prose goes like the proverbial

express train (you'd expect nothing less) and the various tortuous twists and turns are excitably handled. We may have seen it all before, but it's still a classy read. And no, I'm not saying that just because we're related...

Mark Campbell

He Kills Coppers by Jake Arnott
Sceptre, £10, 0 340 74879 6
It's August 1966: the country swelters under a long hot summer as World Cup euphoria reaches massive proportions. But the mood changes when three policeman are shot in a West London street. The event may have a salutary effect on the national mood, but it is to change the lives of three very different men, inexorably connected with the event. And the final consequences of the killings are not to reach a climax until thirty years later. This is the intriguing premise of Jake Arnott's highly impressive thriller, and a powerfully organised plot is matched by a steely narrative control that pays out just enough information for the reader as it progresses to keep us on tenterhooks. Arnott's three protagonists, Frank, Tony and Billy,

He Kills Coppers

jake arnott

come from very different backgrounds (respectively, they're an ambitious detective, a tabloid journalist and a petty thief with a violent past). And the unfolding of their involvement in murder and over-up is deftly handled. There's a nice sideline, too, in pithy historic detail: from the psychedelic Sixties to the uncaring Thatcherite Eighties, the panorama Arnott conjures up is always authentic –and always at the service of his narrative.

Vic Buckner

Crossroad Blues by Ace Atkins
Robinson, £6.99, 1 84119 306 2

Crossroad Blues was recommended to me by no less a critic than Greil Marcus, and it's easy to see why he liked it, because the most intriguing mystery in this novel con-

cerned with lost recordings by Robert Johnson is Johnson himself, and we can never get too much of the bluesman who is arguably the first great icon of American rock'n'roll. But Marcus isn't a crime critic, and as a detective story, Nick Travers' search for the blues struck me as surface slick but strangely unaffecting, more Robben Ford than Robert Johnson. Maybe Atkins should consider selling his soul to the devil, as Johnson supposedly did. Part of the problem is Travers himself: he's an ex pro-football star, he's a detective, and he's also a professor of musicology. He's tough but vulnerable. He even smokes. This new definition of Everyman owes more to 'dirty-realist' novels written by and starring creative writing teachers than it does to Nick Charles or even Nick Stefanos. It gets worse when Nick goes off to the Delta to look for a missing blues scholar, and returns with a red-haired white blues singer, a Daisy Mae version of Bonnie Raitt. It reminded me of Kevin Costner in *Dances With Wolves*, managing to find a white woman with blow-dried hair in the middle of the Sioux nation. Atkins creates a couple of interesting villains, but never lets either grab enough of the focus to come off as a foil to Superbluesman Nick. It all ends in an unsatisfying sort of shoot-out that belies most of the build-up. For all Atkins bombast, this reminds me of Kinky Friedman, which means it may be popular, if not compelling. At least here the choice of music's better.

Michael Carlson

100 Bullets by Brian Azzarello & Eduardo Risso
Titan, £12.99
This much-acclaimed series appears in a

welcome second collection, and continues to widen the parameters of what is possible within the comics medium. Although this remains a sexy and exciting crime series, the real skills of the creators lie in the sharp and pithily drawn characterisations: we watch the characters torn apart by violence and marvel at how the once despised medium of comics can now be considerably more sophisticated than most TV soaps.

Barry Forshaw

Forty Words for Sorrow by Giles Blunt
HarperCollins, £12.99, 0 00 711571 7
"There is a town in North Ontario," sang Neil Young, and Giles Blunt has set an intriguing story in the fictional town of Algonquin Bay, where teenagers have been disappearing. When one of them finally turns up dead, Detective John Cardinal, whose persistence in trying to track down the missing kids resulted in his being

removed from the homicide squad, is called back onto the case. But his return is not without its own complications. A local drug kingpin has repeatedly escaped arrest, and someone on the job appears to be tipping him off. So when Cardinal is given a new partner, a French Canadian woman who has just transferred in from Internal Affairs, it is an open secret that he is being investigated. And though innocent of that crime, Cardinal, with a wife institutionalised with manic depression and a daughter studying art at Yale, has financial secrets of his own. Blunt weaves his two stories together deftly, and builds a strong bond between Cardinal's real but non-existent family, and the unreal but functional ersatz family that the killer builds around himself. The murders are solved with the requisite bit of action, which we might expect from a writer who has worked on TV's *Law & Order*, but more interesting is the way Cardinal's own dilemma is resolved. It works, but perhaps it's all too pat, and his wife appears to have undergone the world's simplest cure for manic depression. Still, this is an atmospheric and impressive debut.

Michael Carlson

Killing Pablo by Mark Bowden
Atlantic, £16.99, 1 903809 00 2
The skill with which Mark Bowden charts the rise and well-publicised fall of Pablo Escobar, one of the most successful (and violent) criminals in history, is quite remarkable. The author takes the reader for the first time into the massive covert operations by US Special Forces to track down this most dangerous of all drug traffickers. At the height of his success, Escobar's earnings

from his cocaine pedalling were so great that he even earned a listing from *Forbes* magazine as the seventh richest man in the world. But Bowden is equally fascinating in his descriptions of the members of the Special Forces who brought Escobar down. Every page of the book has the feel of exclusive access to highly classified intelligence documents, and makes for unputdownable reading.

Ingrid Yornstrand

Bad Timing by Molly Brown
Big Engine, £8.99, 1 903468 06 X
Molly Brown has long been one of the most idiosyncratic and distinctive of writers, dealing in fiction that frequently defies category (or more precisely, creates its own category). This beguiling collection is a demonstration that the short story is a particular

métier of hers, and the disturbing offerings here present a panoply of dark imagination. The title tale is a whimsical time travel piece, which gleefully explores (and explodes) most of the paradoxes and clichés of the genre. But with the *Feeding Julie*, Brown enters macabre territory that she is totally comfortable with (even if the reader will not be quite so comfortable after finishing this tale). Is it a crime piece? A horror story? Forget the categories – simply enjoy the fractured visions that Brown provides in this astringent collection.

Bitterroot by James Lee Burke
Orion, £12.99, 0 7528 4154 8
Burke's reputation as one of the finest writers in the US – in any genre – will be further consolidated by the powerful and involving novel. Ex-Texas Ranger (now lawyer) Billy Bob Holland is on a visit to his friend Doc Voss, still coming to terms with his involvement in the Vietnam conflict. Doc's daughter is savagely gang raped by bikers, and a miscarriage of justice means that the biker's leader walks free. Then the Doc is arrested – and Billy Bob finds that representing his friend is only one of the problems he has to face: a newly released killer is on his tail. As with previous Burke novels, this is American writing at its most the idiomatic and powerful, with dialogue and characterisation (notably the beleaguered Doc) as sharp as anything Burke has produced.

Eve Tan Gee

No Smoke by Hugh Collins
Canongate
No Smoke is the first part of a trilogy set in the Glasgow underworld that will span

twenty years – chronicling changing fashions, politics and innumerable scams and wrong-doings. In his autobiographical work Hugh Collins demonstrated a rare flair for dialogue and vernacular. And this novel brims with Glasgow patter that is utterly authentic – hilarious and dangerous. Barney is an old scammer – a gentleman outlaw who's roped in a couple of younger hoodlums who are prepared to use extreme violence at the slightest hint of trouble. Jake and Skud are helping Barney pull a fast one on two Pakistani brothers. Only, the brothers are scamming too – fobbing Barney and his boys off with forged notes. Celebrating their success in the infamous Woodside Inn, Barney and Jake's lecherous attitude and flamboyant spending arouse the suspicion of the bar manager – an ex-copper. Before he knows it, Barney is sitting with an

untouched pint and two seriously assaulted 'Untouchables' from the Strathclyde police – while Jake and Skud, still armed, are now on the run. In the meantime, Rashid the younger of the brothers has been picked up by the 'Untouchables' and has been beaten to death in a police cell... but by whom? With consummate plotting, a host of brilliantly drawn rogues and an uncanny sense of pacing, No Smoke is set to do for Glasgow what Ian Rankin did for Edinburgh..

Ralph Travis

Void Moon by Michael Connelly
Orion Books, £5.99, 0 75283 716 8
Breaking new ground, with no characters from his other books; using a criminal as the sympathetic character and the detective as the psychopath, Connelly skilfully weaves a plot of a lost loved one; a lost daughter; a crime caper and kidnapping on a theme of superstition. The start is a slow burning fuse with enough interest in what is exactly going on to maintain interest until the action takes off. Cassie Black is a Porsche salesperson with a few skeletons in the cupboard. Making a break from her dead end existence leads to big problems. The action takes place in LA and Las Vegas casinos where La Cuba Nostra — linking up the Mafia with Miami Cuban émigrés — are trying to get in on the act. The hotel room robbery is described in realistic detail as are the ingenious efforts of the private eye to track down the culprit. The questions keep coming back — such as how and why did Max go out of the window to his death? Twists and surprises keep this above the run of the mill story, although the ending is a bit too neat and tidy, if not a little too senti-

mental. A couple of characters are so well drawn it is a pity they are killed off and cannot be used again. With the kind of people involved death is a regular price and never far away. But there is a problem for fiction with psychopaths who needlessly kill people in that public and police attention is bound to be roused by the trail of death and expose the killer's identity. Connelly just about gets away with it here while with other writers, who depend on a supply of corpses to maintain interest, it breaks the spell and even becomes risible. Connelly is a former crime journalist on the *Los Angeles Times*, who uses his experience and skill to good effect and has made him one of the best American crime writers today. In *A Darkness More Than Night*, published this year, we meet Terry McCaleb again — the retired FBI agent, first encountered in *Blood Work*.

Martin Spellman

Layer Cake by JJ Connolly
Duckbacks, £5.99, 0 7156 3096 2
JJ Connolly's *Layer Cake* garnered a great deal of praise with its hardback release and, on reading the paperback, deservedly so. This is a compelling, fun read with a frantic pace and gloriously twisting narrative. It seems worth invoking comparisons to *Lock Stock and Two Smoking Barrels* and its follow up *Snatch*. The book shares these films' relish of a particular kind of cartoon London gangster life, their love of criminal patois (Connolly has a great ear for London street talk; his ear does, however, let him down a little when it comes to his Irish and Scouse characters), and their hectic, cut-up action. But even without these recent precedents *Layer Cake* stands up well: it is a

hugely entertaining romp with a heart. Our nameless hero ("My name? If I told you that you'd be as clever as me!") is twenty-nine and, by refusing to be flash, refusing to bait the 'Other People' (cozzers, fuzz, busies... police), has managed to make himself a tidy living 'in the powders game'. He'd always promised himself that by thirty he'd retire – but he's no mug: getting out of the business can be as tough as getting in and getting on. Two million pills need shifting: difficult enough but certainly not helped when a bunch of divvies called The Yahoos get involved. Then a Mr Big called Jimmy Price asks for a favour: his old friend Mr Ryder has a daughter, Charlie, who's gone missing. She has a drug problem and a lowlife boyfriend. Trouble is The Yahoos have gone and upset a bunch of German neo-nazi nutters and Tommy (aka Cody, aka Billy Bogus), who has gone looking for Charlie, has been arrested. And things only get more complicated here on in. Intricate, wonderfully plotted, at times serious, even sincere, this is a quality read: definitely worth taking a bite of the *Layer Cake*.

Mark Thwaite

Shock by Robin Cook
Macmillan, £16.99, 0 333 90280 7
Perhaps Cook is too productive a novelist for his own good, and it is certainly true that the appearance of a new novel by him no longer carries the charge that such riveting earlier books as *Coma* automatically guaranteed. But although we are in familiar territory, there's no sense of marking time in this latest thriller in which technology and personal greed collide. Deborah and Joanna are students and close friends. Spotting a campus newspaper ad that

offers the solution to their financial problems, they visit an upscale fertility clinic on Boston's North Shore to act as donors. Of course, they have never read any Robin Cook novels or they would realise that the disappearance of fellow donors should set alarm bells ringing. Soon both women have obtained employment at the clinic in an attempt to penetrate what they now see as its veil of secrecy. And (like many a Cook heroine before them) they are soon up against highly sinister doctors with malign agendas. Few surprises, but fans will not be disappointed.

Brian Ritterspak

Gallows Thief by Bernard Cornwell
HarperCollins, £16.99, 0 00 712715 4
When a writer is as successful as Bernard Cornwell, it is inevitable that the law of diminishing returns will kick in at some point, and a certain staleness may set in. There is always a remedy for this, although it is a risky one: write a different kind of book. Cornwell has accomplished this with real élan by setting *Gallows Thief* in the Regency period. This allows him to utilise his customary skills of characterisation and razor-sharp plotting against a vividly realised new backdrop. It is Britain in the 1820s. After the wars with France, with unemployment high and soldiers paid off, the government lives in mortal fear of social unrest. The solution is draconian punishment for any crime, and thousands die on the gallows. But despite this, it was possible to petition the King and instigate an investigation. Cornwell's new hero Robert Hawke is a hero of Waterloo struggling to repay his family debts when he becomes involved in the case of a man waiting to be

hanged in Newgate prison. Given the job by the Home Secretary of investigating the man's guilt or innocence, Hawke finds himself knee-deep in labyrinthine plots involving bribes, sedition and a massive conspiracy of silence. As this suggests, the contemporary parallels are never far away. The world Cornwell has conjured for us is as richly drawn as any in his distinguished career: gentlemen's clubs and taverns, haughty aristocrats, fashionable painters and their mistresses, and professional cutthroats; all this creates a heady melange that is just as impressive as anything in Cornwell's Sharpe series.

Judith Gray

Isle of Dogs by Patricia Cornwell
Little, Brown, £16.99, 0 316 85859 5
It has taken some while for the second strand of Cornwell's crime writing activity

(Judy Hammer and Andy Brazil of the Virginia State Police) to acquire the following of her more successful Kay Scarpetta novels. And there's no question that her best work is done in the more famous series. However, the Hammer/Brazil books are not to be dismissed lightly, and since *Hornet's Nest* and *Southern Cross* they show greater assurance and invention as Cornwell settles into the characters. This is the finest yet: an irreverent and strikingly characterised portrait of law enforcement at the mercy of politics. Judy Hammer and her right-hand man Andy Brazil are trying to protect the public from the politicians and vice versa. But the real mayhem begins when an island off the coast of Virginia declares independence, claiming that America's first settlers set sail from London's Isle of Dogs in 1607. Needless to say, this is a Cornwell that cannot fail to do well on these shores.

Judith Gray

Hostage by Robert Crais
Orion, £12.99, 0 7528 4182 3
Robert Crace has unerringly built a considerable reputation as one of the most ambitious and accomplished thriller writers working today. After *Demolition Angel*, there were amny making claims for him as the most impressive of current American thriller writers, and *Hostage* is likely to add more lustre to his name. When a convenience store robbery goes bloodily wrong, the teenage gang who perpetrated the crime tried to make a run for it. After a police pursuit, they crash into the suburban home of an accountant and take his family hostage. The armed siege that follows is very bad news for the local sheriff who left the force

Robert CRAIS
HOSTAGE

We can now add the name Crais to the pantheon of great American writers
SUNDAY TIMES

in LA because of the stress. But matters are complicated by the fact that the accountant of the gang had inadvertently chosen works for the Mafia and is the custodian of all the local families' financial records. And when the mob joins the scene, a grim three-way stand-off is in the offing. As this synopsis indicates, Crace continues to come up with individual and innovative plots that can appear totally fresh to the reader. That alone with marks him out in this era of endless repetition, but he matches his canny plotting with characterisation of a rare order.

Eve Tan Gee

A Spy by Nature by Charles Cumming
Michael Joseph, £9.99, 0 7181 4451 1
One might have thought that the espionage genre was thoroughly played out, particularly since the end of the Cold War. But now Le Carré has found a new lease of life, and with first novels as assured as Cumming's appear-

ing, it would seem that the genre is in rude health. Alec Milius leaves his dead-end job to make his way in the secret world of MI6. But soon the exhilaration of his new job is at an end: he finds himself caught in a lethal conflict between two sides, even obliged to keep his closest friends at a distance. Cumming's use of the same Christian name for his protagonist as the ill-fated hero of Le Carré's breakthrough novel *The Spy Who Came in From the Cold* is not accidental: this is a remarkably well-plotted piece that satisfyingly recalls the Master, with much of the latter's bitter moral ambiguity.

Vic Buckner

Valhalla Rising by Clive Cussler
Michael Joseph, £16.95, 0 7181 4417 1
July 2003. During its maiden voyage, the luxury cruise ship Emerald Dolphin is engulfed in a conflagration and plunges to the bottom of the sea. NUMA special projects director Dirk Pitt is assigned to find out why the alarms didn't go off and (more importantly) what was the connection to the revolutionary new engines that powered the ship. As he begins his investigation, Pitt is soon endangered by a bizarre series of monsters, both human and mechanical, ancient and modern. As in such books as *Atlantis Found*, Cussler is expert in taking us into worlds strange and forbidding. If at times this one reads rather like the blueprint for a movie, it is none the worse for that, and Cussler finds time (along with the colourful heroics) to instigate some radical changes in his hero's personality that raise the book over the level of a mere thriller. By now we've become used to the ludicrous name of Cussler's hero and time spent with Dirk Pitt is time well

spent. This is likely to do quite as well as other novels featuring Cussler's doughty protagonist.

Ingrid Yornstrand

Baby Love by Denise Danks
Orion, £9.99
Denise Danks was selected as one of the UK's best crime writers by *The Times*, and she's a favourite of the CT staff – this writer included. On the first day of December, a parcel bomb explodes in London's East End killing 'Gecko' Samuels, notorious womaniser and chief executive of the world's top games software company, and a young technology journalist, who turns out to be six weeks pregnant. For investigative journalist, Georgina Powers, holed up in her basement after a hit and run accident, it's a story she's got to do for the money. But she

A GEORGINA POWERS INVESTIGATION

DENISE DANKS

BABY LOVE

'Danks is the queen of techno-crime'
LITERARY REVIEW

has other things on her mind. Things that keep her from going outside… Like the faceless driver of the car that knocked her down. A list of thirteen women. A government computer contract. And an unsigned postcard of 'London by Night' on which someone has written three words – 'Be seeing you'. Danks at her considerable best.

Eve Tan Gee

Devil Take the Blue-Tail Fly

by John Franklin Bardin   Canongate, £5.99
Devil Take the Blue-Tail Fly is a complex, surreal psychodrama. Ellen, a world class harpsichordist, leaves a mental institution to go back to New York with her conductor husband, Basil. Once home she is tormented with paranoia that Basil is not only seeing another woman but also moving or hiding things to confuse her. After a lunch with her sister she meets a man from her past – a singer who had seduced her when she was a schoolgirl. Ellen is shocked to see the man, convinced that when she last saw him, he was dead. Slowly Ellen comes to understand that she has an alter ego called Nelle, who is as wild and dangerous as Ellen is calm and professional. Ellen begins to realise that it was Nelle who battered this man over the head, and it is Nelle who continues to create mayhem, as she becomes stronger and more corporeal as Ellen feels she is vanishing. Vivid, astringent writing.

Vic Buckner

Dead Famous by Ben Elton

Bantam, £16.99, 0 593 04804 0
Elton has won over far many more admirers as a writer of sardonic and sharp-edged novels than he ever did in his days as an irritating motor-mouth stand-up comic. And despite that irresistible tendency to show off, he demonstrates yet again that he has a finger on the current pulse in this murder tale set in the world of moronic reality TV programmes such as *Big Brother*. A group of unknown and unremarkable people submit themselves to the grim exposure of the televised docusoap *House Arrest*. As the public watches, wondering who will crack first and who will have sex with whom, there is a murder. But who could pull of the killing under the unremitting gaze of the thirty television cameras? What was the motive and (more pertinently) who will be next? This is Elton in the vein of his *Popcorn*, a bitterly funny and abrasive picture of modern society. It will do very well indeed.

Barry Forshaw

To Kill and Kill Again by Martin Fido

Carlton, £16.99
This is the history of British serial killers. It begins in the East End of London in 1888 with the Whitechapel Murders of Jack the Ripper, and goes on to record five other cases of British multiple killers, bringing us up to the present day. In addition, linking sections cover other serial killers, to build up a complete history of these horrific crimes. As well as documenting the crimes and the criminal investigations that led to the eventual capture of these British multiple murderers, the development of forensic science in relation to these cases is explored. Experts reveal how modern psychological profiling techniques can provide a surprising number of details about a suspect, from the type of car they drive, to the clothes they wear. The police and media interviews with the killers who offer their reasons for their crimes are

analysed and provide a fascinating insight into this aspect of detection. Not only does this book explore the motivation and madness behind the actions of the serial killer it also allows a unique insight into the minds of multiple murderers and those who attempt to stop them.

Ralph Travis

The Advocate by Marcello Fois
Harvill, £10, 1 86046 904 3
A truly masterly study of guilt and justice, distinguished by prose of elegance and precision. Set in a backward Sardinian community, Fois deals with issues of individual responsibility in his tale of a prosperous farmer shot dead in his olive grove. The victim's hired hand, a boy called Zenobi, is found guilty in absentia, and only Zenobi's mother considers him innocent. The lawyer Bustianu takes on the case – and confronts an implacable wall of silence. Essentially a novel of crime and detection, Fois subverts the rules of the genre at every possible moment, and the moral force of the book is strongly reminiscent of the now-neglected crime novels of Durrenmatt. The first in a series of crime novels, this bodes well for other books by the author, and deserves wide currency.

Barry Forshaw

The Nature of the Beast by Frances Fyfield
Little, Brown, £17.99, 0 316 85746 7
Why would someone who had survived the horror of a rail crash walk away from the scene and pretend to be dead? Such is the premise of Fyfield's new novel, which is every bit as accomplished as her much-acclaimed *Undercurrents*. Her protagonist Douglas is a man comfortable in his reputa-

tion as a *bon viveur*, and enjoying a superfluity of wine and women. Marriage and inheritance have given him a little stability, but his attempt to sue a tabloid newspaper is endangered when his wife (a key witness) is involved in a massive train crash and vanished, apparently dying in the ensuing fire. But there is no body. Why has she disappeared? In a mesmerising first-person narrative, Amy gradually reveals why she is unable to return to the home she loved and how childhood lies have cast a long shadow over her adult life. Fyfield's speciality has always been the psychology of her characters, and this facet of her writing took a particularly dark turn in *Undercurrents*. That trajectory is maintained here, and we are in a queasy, shifting world in which moral values are extremely equivocal. So many crime novels these days have a warmed-over feel, but Fyfield successfully avoids that trap here and comes up with a fresh narrative that cannily utilises recent events for the purposes of a highly effective thriller.

Barry Forshaw

For My Eyes Only by John Glen
Batsford, £16.99, 0 7134 8671 6
An absolutely fascinating first-person account from one of the most talented of all Bond directors (and possibly the finest editor in the whole Bond canon – remember *OHMSS*?). John Glen handled the much-underrated Timothy Dalton entries, and many Fleming aficionados consider these the truest in tone to the original novels. As with the same company's *Kiss Kiss Bang Bang*, this is an absolutely must-have purchase for 007 enthusiasts, and is likely to send you to the DVD store, cash in hand (in the unlikely event you haven't got such John Glen Bond movies as *For Your Eyes Only* and *Licence to Kill*).

Brian Ritterspak

The Stone Council by Jean-Christophe Grangé   *Harvill, £10, 1 86046 864 0*
Inevitably, publishers will always trumpet the virtues of a new author on their list. He or she is, of course, always the Second Coming, and both reviewers and the public have learned to take such claims with more than a pinch of salt. When Harvill instigated the hype for Jean-Christophe Grangé, we could all be forgiven for reaching for our salt cellars, but after *Blood-Red Rivers* and *Flight of the Storks* many of us have realised that Harvill were right: Grangé really is a bright new star in the thriller firmament, and his new book, *The Stone Council*, will do much to consolidate his

already growing reputation. Elegantly translated from the French by Ian Monk, this is a kinetic thriller that yokes elements of the macabre into its tale of mystery and detection. *The Stone Council* includes themes of telepathy, psychokinesis and hypnosis, stirring these into a mix of savage murder and state secrecy. His protagonist Diane was the victim of an assault as a child. By the age of thirty she is an ethnologist whose speciality is the study of predatory animals. She is also a considerable martial artist (the latter may be said to be one of the few missteps in the novel). She gives her life new meaning when she adopts a five-year-old Thai boy, but the boy has an accident and is declared to be brain-dead. Then a series of grisly murders force her to the realisation that her son is no ordinary boy, but is being pursued by sinister supernatural forces. What makes this

work so well is the cool verisimilitude that Grangé imparts to his outrageous tale, and although elements of the supernatural (while often fascinating when incorporated into non-genre novels) may sometimes sideline psychology, that is resolutely not the case here: all of the characters (Diane in particular) are rendered with skill and understanding. If the freshness and impact of *Blood-Red Rivers* is missing, it is more than compensated for by new levels of powerfully realised plotting (not to mention some striking set pieces).

Barry Forshaw

The Month of the Leopard

by James Harland   *Simon & Schuster, £10*

A woman's disappearance, the drop in value of an eastern European currency and a cold yet fanatical financier. How do these three things relate to each other – and to the destruction of the world's financial markets? Those are the key elements in James Harland's new thriller *The Month of the Leopard*. The story revolves around Tom Bracewell, an economist for an investment bank; when he comes home to find his Estonian wife has vanished, his world is turned upside down. Sarah Turnbull is a currency analyst who has just been headhunted for the Leopard Fund, one of the world's most powerful financial predators. Jean-Pierre Telmont heads the Leopard Fund. His past is blurred. As Tom investigates Tatyana's disappearance, he comes to wonder if he ever knew his wife – there are trips to Europe and massive Swiss bank accounts of which he had no knowledge. And, once he has met Sarah, the two of them begin to realise that Tatyana and the plans of Telmont are somehow linked. This realisation

leads them into deadly danger and helter-skelter chase across Europe. Finally, both Telmont and his fund show their true spots in attacks on the markets that threaten a global financial crisis. At the risk of death, Tom and Sarah must unravel the mysteries of the Leopard Fund and a plan that dates back over half a century. *The Month of the Leopard* is the first novel by James Harland, the pseudonym of a leading financial journalist. He has written a thriller that mixes the high adventure of Hitchcock chase movie with the fascinating machinations of the financial markets, which effect every one of us every day.

Brian Ritterspak

Dialogues of the Dead by Reginald Hill HarperCollins, £16.99, 0 00 225846 3
We're used to the hyper-intelligent criminal who delights in laying umpteen false trails

REGINALD HILL

DIALOGUES OF THE DEAD
THE NEW DALZIEL
AND PASCOE NOVEL

for the beleaguered protagonist, while creating a mystifying series of enigmas for the hero (and the reader) to crack. Hill, of course, does it better than most, and here, Hill's classic coppers Dalziel and Pascoe are joined by a young recruit who's called (believe it or not) Hat Bowler, and have to solve a rash of random killings. A series of bizarre conflicting accounts of these murders keeps appearing in the Mid-Yorkshire County library, and the arcane information in them points to them being the work of the killer. Characterisation is as quirky and eccentric as ever (notably a brash young TV personality called Jax and a sardonic city councillor destined for a bloody end), while the puzzle-packed structure adds a satisfying layer of intrigue that richly rewards the reader. As long as Hill is able to ring the changes as cleverly as this, the Dalziel and Pascoe series will continue to enjoy rude health.

Eve Tan Gee

A Rage in Harlem by Chester Himes
Canongate Crime, £5.99, 1 84195 024 6
Chester Himes' first book *If He Hollers Let Him Go* (1945) was written when he was in jail for armed robbery. Several books later, and still not receiving the recognition he rightfully deserved, Himes moved to France where he met the editor of Gallimard's famous Serie Noire, Marcel Duhamel. *La Reine des Pommes*, later *A Rage in Harlem*, went on to win the prestigious Grand Prix de la Litterature Policière (the first time it was won by a non-French author) and Himes began winning the acclaim and best-seller status he lacked back home in the US. He went on to write eighteen novels, eight in *The Harlem Cycle* all containing the won-

derful detective duo of Coffin Ed and Grave Digger. *Rage* keeps Ed and Grave Digger very much in the background and focuses instead on Jackson. An ingenue and a square, Jackson can't see through a scam purporting to turn ten dollar bills into one hundred dollar bills, and he can't see through Isabelle – his impossibly attractive but far from innocent girlfriend. Losing all his savings Jackson is forced to steal from the safe at the undertakers where he works and forced to gamble this 'borrowed' money playing on the crap tables. An ineluctable cycle of chaos and crime ensues. Himes' writing is, with the help of James Sallis' recent excellent biography, rightly being reassessed. A massively important voice, he justifies Sallis' assertion that within edge literature the huge talent and formidable intellect of a skilled craftsman can work with and against the limitations of the genre to produce something that supercedes its normally safe content without exploding its form. Himes shows Jackson, a resolutely Christian man forced, after a stupid error of judgement, into dangerous criminality, and he shows the paradoxical position of Ed and Grave Digger attempting to seek justice for their people from within the very system that forces them into criminality.

Mark Thwaite

Hot Springs by Stephen Hunter
Arrow, £6.99, 0 09 941497 X
When I reviewed Stephen Hunter's *Time To Kill*, I said its strength was the way it showed America's dark past in Vietnam remained unresolved. With this book, we might argue that Hunter is becoming the poet laureate of America's dark pasts. At

the same time, he writes thrillers that are complex and challenging, with characters who convince, and ties the personal, the plotting and the political subtext together in a package which is tied together, not with a ribbon, but more in the way that sticks of dynamite are bound together to make a bomb. Earl Swagger is the father of Vietnam sniper Bob 'the Nailer' Swagger, hero of *Time To Kill* and the earlier *Black Light*. Earl is a Medal of Honor winning Marine sergeant, who has survived the Pacific War, and who is recruited by an Arkansas DA who's putting together an elite force to clean up Hot Springs, an Ozark oasis of gambling and prostitution which forms a shiny buckle in the Bible Belt. It is based on a true GI revolt against corruption, similar to the one chronicled in Phil Karlson's noir film, *The Phenix City Story*. Hunter has integrated the Swagger family's legacy into this extremely Clintonesque setting (Bill Clinton, who claimed to come from Hope, actually hailed from that very same Hot Springs, part of his white-trash legacy which so infuriated the Washington establishment). Earl's own father was a legendary sheriff who inflicted extreme brutality on his family; Bob Swagger is named for Earl's brother who hung himself after one particularly fierce beating. Of course that family history turns out to be intimately connected with the very forces Earl is sent out to fight. Along the way, Earl single-handedly desegregates an Arkansas town, and we get a wonderful side view of Bugsy Siegel and Virginia Hill. We also learn everything there is to know about the Browning automatic rifle and the Thompson submachine gun, to the point where I felt like putting the book on the gun rack of my pickup truck, only to discover I have neither truck nor rack. No matter. More importantly, Hunter paints a picture of what soldiers returned to after World War II, a land of immense promise and also immense corruption, filled with a brutal, violent innocence. It is the real basis for what we now call film noir, or noir fiction, the conflict between the world of Hope these men fought and killed for, the world of Hot Springs they returned to. It is no coincidence that the children of these men rebelled against the Vietnam War, and that those who fought in it returned to an even darker corruption, one which no soldiers' revolt could touch. Hunter's books delve deep into the contradictions of the American dream, and they do it with style. Read them.

Michael Carlson

Death at Apothecaries' Hall by Deryn Lake
NEL, £5.99, 0 340 71861 7
John Rawlings, eighteenth century apothecary and friend of the 'Blind Beak' Sir John Fielding, is on the scene after a dinner at Apothecaries' Hall results in mass food poisoning. He helps one of the victims and seems to be succeeding with his cures when the man dies. Rawlings and Sir John investigate the poisoning and soon find themselves surrounded by suspects. The apothecary still manages to run his business, search for a house in the country village of Kensington and carry on an amorous affair while searching for a murderer. This is the sixth John Rawlings mystery and they show no sign of flagging in their inventiveness and rich evocation of the sights, sounds and smells of Georgian London. Deryn Lake does not let the mystery suffer for the sake of period detail, rather she makes the back-

ground seem so real that we easily accept it and the characters. Rawlings is a bit of a rogue and although he enjoys working in his apothecary's shop he welcomes the chance to help Sir John Fielding. He also spends time with other characters from the previous books, among them his mistress, and even manages to deliver a baby when the doctor is delayed! The central mystery seems to have an obvious solution but we are kept guessing as motives for other suspects gradually come to light. It is not until the end of the book that the murderer is revealed and even then there is a final surprising twist. It is very interesting to see how various diseases such as epilepsy and cancer were treated in the past and the use of real historical characters adds to the authenticity. May there be many more cases for John Rawlings!

Gun, with Occasional Music

by Jonathan Lethem   *Faber, £6.99*
"Okay," I said. "My name is Conrad Metcalf, and I'm a private inquisitor. You knew that. You read it somewhere and it gave you hope. Let me tell you now that it'll cost you seven hundred dollars a day to keep that hope alive. What you'll get won't be a new best friend. I'm as much of a pain in the ass to the people who pay me as I am to the guys I go up against." Sounds like standard hardboiled private eye stuff, right? Wrong: this is a futuristic spin on the genre involving the king of generic 'evolving' beloved of such writers as David Brin in books like *Sundiver*. Conrad Metcalf has been shadowing Celeste – the wife of an Oakland urologist – and when the doctor turns up dead, Metcalf realises he has problems. He finds himself caught between the heavy handed guys at the Inquisitor's Office, and a group of gangsters, including an evolved, trigger-happy kangaroo, all of whom are preventing him from uncovering the murderer. A mordantly witty science fiction noir mystery, this is Jonathan Lethem's début novel, published here for the first time in the UK. Lethem enjoyed much acclaim for the multi-award winning non-genre *Motherless Brooklyn*.

Vic Buckner

In a Strange City by Laura Lippman
Orion, £9.99, 0 75284 167 X
Lippman's growing reputation will be burnished by this latest outing for her doughty PI Tess Monaghan which combines the author's cool reporter's eye with a highly individual gift for labyrinthine plot-making. Lippman has long been careful to come up with something fresh in the plotting arena

(a difficult enough task in a painfully over-stretched genre), and she pulls that off again in a murky narrative involving fake identities, homophobic hate crimes and graveside murders. The plot impetus here is a man who has visited the Baltimore graveside of Edgar Allan Poe every year for the past fifty years – and the grotesque imagination of The Master has inspired Lippman to one of her strangest and most disturbing books.

Judith Gray

The Chill by Ross Macdonald
Canongate, £5.99

Macdonald at his very best. Lew Archer has been asked to look for Dolly, a missing wife, but while searching he uncovers other crimes and casualties that have been hidden for decades. *The Chill* covers Macdonald's favourite theme; how the sins of the father shall be visited upon the second and third

generations, and how a seed planted by an act decades earlier can sprout in the present, destroying those who are otherwise innocent. *The Chill* is extraordinarily chilling, with a conclusion that will stay with you long after you have finished. Ross Macdonald, pseudonym of Kenneth Millar, was one of America's best hardboiled crime writers, although his reputation does not match his achievement. Along with Hammett and Chandler, and is often credited in bringing the detective novel into the literary mainstream. Born in California in 1915, he was raised and educated in Canada, and wrote over twenty-five novels. He was particularly intrigued by personal identity, family relationships, childhood trauma, why men and women need to battle each other, how the past rises to confront the present, and the twisted secrets of the human heart. He died in 1983.
Vic Buckner

Whole Wide World by Paul McAuley
Voyager, £16.99, 0 00 225903 6

McAuley has built a considerable reputation as a purveyor of off-kilter meta-fictions that defy category (although SF comes as close as anything). His books transmute futuristic tropes into bizarre artefacts that illuminate darker areas of psychology. But he's best at vividly realised alternative societies that refract the more arcane aspects of our own. *Whole Wide World* partakes of the noirish thriller genre with a complex murder-cum-conspiracy theory mystery in a world where information is the key currency – and many kill for it. An InfoWar has destroyed society, with microwave bombs set off by terrorists in the City, while bank accounts run back to zero. McAuley's beleaguered narrator (nicknamed Minimum) gets by in the Information Technology section of the Met, despite a mortifying loss of status. But when a woman is bloodily dispatched in front of three webcams, Minimum is plunged into a nightmare scenario in which his every move is (apparently) controlled by malign, unseen forces. As ever with McAuley, this is heady, inventive and disorienting.

Barry Forshaw

Last Light by Andy McNab
Bantam, £16.99, 0 593 04617 X
Some find McNab uninteresting, but he has long proved himself to be more than a one hit wonder, and such books as *Remote Control*, *Crisis Four* and *Firewall* have shown that he has the necessary staying power in the thriller stakes. After aborting an officially sanctioned assassination attempt at the Houses of Parliament after he realises the identity of the intended target, Nick Stone ("deniable operator") of the intelligence services, is read the riot act by his bosses. He is to fly to Panama and complete the task or he and Kelly (the eleven-year-old girl he is looking after) will be despatched themselves. As Stone prepares for his mission in central America, he soon finds that the powerful enemies he has made have turned the hunter into the hunted, and Nick is soon embroiled in a massive conspiracy involving Colombian rebels and the US government. McNab fans know perfectly well what to expect from his writing: little subtlety, rudimentary characterisation, but bags of atmosphere, action and colour. As with previous books, the word page-turner seems coined for McNab's work, and while he may lack the subtlety and sophistication of a writer like Gerald

Seymour, he is his equal in kinetic action.

Brian Ritterspak

James Bond Movie Posters: The Official Collection by Tony Nourmand
Film Four Books/Boxtree, £25, 0 7522 2017 9
The James Bond series is the most successful film franchise ever established, and the interest in 007 memorabilia is at an all-time high, with auction houses such as Christie's mounting major sales. The highly distinctive posters are, of course, particularly cherished, and this is not the first collection between book covers. However, it is one of the best, with all the rare and highly collectable Bond film posters, ranging from the very first movie (*Doctor No*) to the 1999 release *The World Is Not Enough*. For many, the name of the highly creative illustrator Bob Peak (who virtually created the look of the Bond poster with his stylish graphic work) is unknown, even though his work is recognised throughout the world. This collection does full justice to his work, and also includes poster art in progress, interviews, and features on the creators behind the scenes and practical information on poster auctions and price guides.

Judith Gray

Walking on Water by Gemma O'Connor
Bantam Press, £9.99, 0 593 04719 2
This is Gemma O'Connor's fifth psychological mystery set in rural Ireland, and once again she dazzles the reader with her haunting prose and insightful characterisation. This is not so much a crime novel, more a novel that just happens to feature a crime. You feel that even if the priest doesn't stumble across the body in that desolate estuary, there'd still be enough here to

maintain interest. Touching on issues of faith, family ties and the burial of old secrets, this is an astoundingly lyrical read, suffused by a real sense of time and place. The narrative is more linear than her previous works; and far from detracting from the book it adds a strength and clarity that was perhaps missing before. Importantly, O'Connor manages to make you care about the characters and their environment as she slowly untangles the web of lies and half-truths that mesh the locals and newly mon-eyed outsiders together. Francis Recaldo, the detective charged with uncovering the murderer of Evangeline Walter – the body that appeared to be 'walking on water' – is a sublime creation. His unwillingness to get involved in something that has so many personal ramifications is entirely credible.

Mark Campbell

Total Recall by Sara Paretsky
Hamish Hamilton, £16.99, 0 241 14160 5
Devoted readers have followed Paretsky's beleaguered VI Warshawski through many pungently written investigations, and rarely has the author put a foot wrong in creating strikingly detailed adventures for the flinty heroine. The new book follows her on a road that stretches back more than fifty years and into a labyrinthine plot involving wartime lies and grim retribution. At a con-ference for the recovery of Holocaust assets in Chicago, a man tells an amazing story of a life shattered by the Holocaust. And VI's much-loved mentor, Lotty Herschell, soon has her protégé involved in a complex mys-tery more harrowing than any she has encountered. The plot here quickly signals Paretsky's interest in broadening the moral complexity of issues her protagonist has to

face, and it's a mark of her authority as a writer that never once do the serious issues involved appear to be trivialised by their treatment in a popular genre. Even more than the much-acclaimed *Hard Time*, this one represents a new level of ambition for the author.

Ingrid Yornstrand

Violets Are Blue by James Patterson
Headline, £16.99, 0 7472 6348 5
After the grotesque miscalculation of Patterson's move into mawkish *Love Story* territory with his last novel, it's refreshing to find Alex Cross back in the kind of book that Patterson's admirers are much more at ease with. This one features the sinister master-mind of *Roses Are Red*, who is keenly on Alex Cross' trail. The latter finds himself drawn into his most disturbing investigation: two San Francisco joggers are found dead,

THE No.1 INTERNATIONAL BESTSELLER

hanging by their feet, with the blood drained from their bodies. More savage killings ensue in California and on the East Coast. Cross finds himself reluctantly considering the possibility of modern-day vampires, although he initially prefers the idea of a religious cult. Teaming up with Jamilla Hughes, a sassy young woman detective from San Francisco, he is soon penetrating to the heart of a very dark mystery. All of the customary Patterson finger-prints are here, most notably the extremely brief, cliff-hanging chapters and the welcome refusal to linger over Alex Cross' private life. If Patterson has struck out in no new directions with this one, that's perhaps a good thing given the appalling mawkishness of his last non-thriller novel. Welcome back, Alex.

Eve Tan Gee

Nineteen Eighty by David Peace
Serpent's Tail, £15.99/£10, 1 85242 683 7/694 2
Having single-handedly carved out a new genre, 'Yorkshire Noir', David Peace continues in the third instalment of the *Red Riding Quartet* to journey further into the troubled psyche of Yorkshire with the Ripper still terrifyingly at large. December 1980, in the harsh northern winter the Yorkshire Ripper murders his thirteenth victim: Lauren Bell. Assistant Chief Constable Peter Hunter struggles ever deeper in a culture tainted with dark and sordid detail to solve one of the country's most hellish crimes and bring an end to this bloody rule. *Nineteen Eighty* is a tour de force of crime fiction which confirms David Peace's reputation as one of the most important names in contemporary crime literature.

Ralph Travis

Middle Of Nowhere by Ridley Pearson
Orion, £9.99
Ridley Pearson's nowhere is a dark space within the soul of Seattle cop Lou Boldt. Boldt's depression has been further heightened by his colleague's 'sick-out', and this unofficial strike puts exhausting pressure on him, and the few detectives still working. One of them is nearly murdered in what appears to be the latest in a string of robberies, but as Boldt investigates, and is attacked himself, he begins to fear criminals within the strike-torn department. As he investigates, Boldt is also thrown back, literally, into the arms of an old lover, a situation which may put his marriage, already under severe pressure from his overwork, and the usual problems a homicide cop brings home, into jeopardy. Boldt is the darkest cop this side of Harry Bosch, but

Pearson's prose lacks Connelly's drive. Like Deaver or Danks, he's researched techno-crime; here a clever criminal appears to control the entire mobile phone network in the Pacific Northwest, shutting large portions of it down at will. But the plot is the least interesting part. In resolving the story he bogs down in formula, introducing new characters, and meandering at times before finding an action-oriented solution. This book is most gripping when the conflict between crime and colleagues plagues Boldt, and Pearson's best writing is the way in which that conflict echoes those in Boldt's married life. I can't help but feel Boldt would be more effective in a shorter, punchier, and more straightforward context.

Michael Carlson

The Hard Shoulder by Chris Petit
Granta, £14.99, 1 86207 462 3
Petit has steadily been building a reputation as one of the most accomplished thriller writers in this country, and this lean and atmospheric piece will consolidate that reputation. Set in the grim world of Mrs Thatcher's Britain, Petit's antihero comes home from jail to Kilburn and struggles to recognise the place he left. His estranged wife is gone; his daughter is living with a wealthy record producer. Living in his sister's unprepossessing hotel, he is persuaded to undertake dangerous schemes against those for whom he took the fall. Petit's subject is the seedy criminal milieu of north-west London, with its Irish pubs and disenfranchised inhabitants. As a thriller, this delivers in no uncertain terms; as a character study, it's even more acute.

Judith Gray

A SPY'S LIFE

A Spy's Life by Henry Porter
Orion, £12.99, 0 7528 3859 8
Remembrance made it clear that Henry Porter was a thriller writer of considerable acumen, and this follow-up shows much of the same skill. Porter's particular speciality is the dark and devious world of the intelligence services, and he evokes that universe with maximum astringency. *A Spy's Life* has a British ex-spy finding himself pulled back into his old trade after a mysterious plane crash, and struggling with deceptive (and dangerous) allies and enemies. In narrative terms, we been here before – but the trick in a novel such as this is to render the materials fresh and invigorating. That Porter does at every opportunity, and his protagonist is characterised in an imaginative and adroit fashion. Another winner from an author to watch.

Eve Tan Gee

Adam and Eve and Pinch Me

by Ruth Rendell   *Hutchinson, £16.99*

Not the best book for those new to Rendell. But of all female crime writers, Ruth Rendell remains the one most prepared to tackle the dark and dangerous side of human psychology. Her books take the reader into a more sinister and threatening world than any of her contemporaries, and there is a reason why she remains non-pareil in this territory: a reason demonstrated with disturbing impact in her new book *Adam and Eve and Pinch Me*. Rendell's speciality is her ability to enter the psychopathology of her characters and make us not only understand their often murderous behaviour, but also vicariously participate. It's a skill that Hitchcock made his own in the cinema, but he rarely moved into such black waters as Rendell. This new book continues a trend initiated in earlier work by Rendell: the grafting of supernatural elements into a typical Rendellian tale of menace. And what makes the ghost in the new book so disturbing is the total avoidance of cliché: no grey, wispy phantom, this – it is disturbingly corporeal. Jock Lewis died in the Paddington train crash. Or did he? His fiancée Minty is coming to terms with both his loss and the loss of all her savings, which Jock vanished with. And there is Zilla, who had been married to a man called Jerry Leach. She also received a letter from the railway company telling her that her husband is dead. Other women, too, who do not know each other, have all had relationships with a dark-haired man who disappears from their lives. And when Jock's ghost reappears to Minty at her home and at her work, she begins to carry a knife... but if she stabs him, will he

bleed? Rendell has always been a writer who likes to take risks, and the danger here was that Adam and Eve and Pinch Me would end up as a smorgasbord of supernatural and crime elements, each cancelling the other out. But Rendell is far too assured a writer for this, and the balance between the different aspects of the book is always kept rigorously in place. So many writers fall into dull repetition; here, again, Rendell demonstrates that she's going from strength to strength.

Vic Buckner

Hollowpoint by Rob Reuland

Jonathan Cape, £10, 0 224 06154 2

Although Rob Reuland's work as a Brooklyn District Attorney is the main selling point of this novel, and its portrayals of the denizens of Brooklyn are its strength, *Hollowpoint* is much less an urban crime thriller than a novel of yuppie midlife crisis. Reaching his mid-thirties, Brooklyn ADA Andrew Giobberti is haunted by the accidental death of his daughter in a car crash, blaming himself for his carelessness. His carelessness has also resulted in putting at least one bad guy, wheelchair-bound dope dealer 'Pirelli' back on the street. In the aftermath of their child's death, his wife has left him, and his life is falling apart. Even worse, as a Brooklyn ADA still paying the rent on what was once his family's apartment, he's the world's most stunning anomaly, a lawyer broke in New York, which makes it hard to chase those gorgeous women who just naturally gravitate to the Brooklyn DA's office, and to him. When he's assigned the case of a fourteen year girl, shot dead in the projects in front of her baby while her crack-whore mother and aspirational older sister slept in the next room, it all seems open and shut. Of course it isn't. Forget the crime. Yuppie lawyer in dead-end job finds responsibility of children and marriage too much, and now seeks to make amends for his life in a way that will earn him 'closure' and maybe get him out of the DA's office too. That isn't a plot summary, it's an analysis of the result, and basically, it's all too uninteresting. Reuland writes the crime well. His portrayal of the criminals and victims, of the other nation of Brooklyn which moves beneath Manhattan's radar, has the ring of authenticity, and picks up more resonance from his weary, cynical, and sometimes hopelessly mediocre parade of city employees, fighting a losing battle against the tide of uncaring. Where the book drifts away is its following of Gio's decline, a sort of 'After Hours' form of urban and personal nightmare in which a subway ride is a descent into hell. In fact, I kept seeing New York movies flow past, Al Pacino losing it in front of judge and jury. But that's unfair. It's a nicely structured story, which just can't make its protagonist as interesting as its story. We simply can't care enough for Gio. He lets the book down in the same way he does the people in his life.

Michael Carlson

The Cure of Souls by Philip Rickman
Macmillan, £16.99, 0 333 90623 3
In this series of supernatural mysteries featuring the Reverend Merrily Watkins in her role as a diocesan exorcist, Rickman has virtually created a new genre, combining crime with nicely judged supernatural elements. He is also particularly good at conjuring up the detail of the rural settings, counterpointing them cleverly with the grim, eldritch happenings that are centre stage. High summer in north-east Herefordshire and dark shadows gather – literally – round a converted hop kiln where the last owner was brutally despatched. The local vicar pooh-poohs claims that the place is haunted, but the story is taken up by Sunday newspapers, and Merrily Watkins is assigned by the Bishop of Hereford to diffuse the situation. She already, however, has her hands full dealing with a woman's claim that her adopted teenage daughter is possessed by an evil spirit. Merrily's initial scepticism towards both events is sustained in the face of some strange happenings, notably an exorcism that produces unhappy results. Her career is now on the line, but she attempts to discover the dark secrets of Knight's Frome, a village with a sinister past. And soon she is up against a horror from beyond the grave. This is highly entertaining stuff, delivered with a panache that we have come to expect from Rickman.

Eve Tan Gee

A Crown of Lights by Phil Rickman
Macmillan, £16.99
The occupational hazard of crime writing is not that it's entertainment literature but that it tends toward the formulaic. What makes Phil Rickman's novels so refreshing is the fact that they are unlike almost anything else in the genre. This is the third of his 'spiritual procedural' novels, a series which centres on the activities of the Rev. Merrily Watkins, the 'diocesan deliverance consultant' of Hereford. The job title means exorcist, but *A Crown of Lights* is not a horror novel. Merrily, a heavy smoker who agonises over her teenage daughter, has her feet firmly planted in an entirely secular

reality. Here she collides with paganism – both on primetime TV and in a lonely farm on the Welsh borders. She also collides with Christianity, in particular with an Evangelical priest who does not consider tolerance a virtue. Then there's the man in the same parish who will not accept that his wife is dead, together with any number of people pursuing the tangled threads of their own devious lives. Last but not least, at the very heart of the book, is Radnor Forest, a forest now in name but not in fact, the home of a slumbering dragon. But there is a rational explanation – you can take it or leave it as you choose – for almost everything that happens. This is not a book 'about' religions, or indeed about things that go bump in the night. It is a highly sophisticated crime novel that happens to have a priest as its protagonist, some religious ingredients and a pervasive, disturbing sense that life isn't quite as simple as it seems. Its complex narrative grips like a clamp. Rickman makes us care about his characters; he is good at establishing a sense of place, brilliant at dialogue. Sometimes he even makes us laugh.

Andrew Taylor

Run by Douglas E. Winter
Canongate Crime, £6.99, 1 84195 100 5
Douglas E. Winter's much vaunted *Run* deserves all the praise it has so far garnered and with this new Canongate Crime paperback is bound to win new readers and convert them into big fans. Frantically but beautifully paced, intricately plotted and exhibiting a fine ear for dialogue that reproduces, at times, the street rhythms of hip-hop (Winter, by all accounts, is a big rap fan and the righteous anger of this urban

poetry shines through) *Run* is a blazing and intelligent debut. Burdon Lane is told by his boss CK that Mr Berenger wants him and his best-friend Renny Two Hand to act as back-up on a weapons deal. Burdon is suspicious about the run especially when he hears that the U Street Gang – a bunch of dangerous, black street criminals – are coming along to give some sort of credibility and insurance to the sale of the guns to another gang The Bravos. With plots and counter plots abounding nobody is quite who they seem: not even the author. The book opens with a quote from the Second Amendment, "...the right of the people to keep and bear arms shall not be infringed", but, despite its authentic hardboiled scenarios, goes on to show – often quite graphically – what actually happens when a culture bases itself on gun ownership. Contrary to the characters' explicit and stylised gun fetishism (detailed cataloguing of differing types of guns and ammo and their uses) the book's heart is wonderfully humane. A key moment at the end of the novel comes when Jinx, Burdon's unwanted partner, throws away his gun, "I don't need this anymore." Without preaching, and by producing a blisteringly good, frantic, highly visual Tarantinoesque thriller, Winter has managed to write something quite special. He gets right to the heart of his racially riven underground and explores how perverted the relationships between people get when based on the acquisition of money, drugs and guns. And he does this without sacrificing any of the momentum and drive of his irresistible narrative. Run is an absolute triumph.

Mark Thwaite

Strangers in Town: Three Newly Discovered Mysteries by Ross MacDonald edited by Tom Nolan
Crippen & Landru, $37, 1 885941 51 X

Preferring to work on the more expansive canvas provided by the novel form, Ross MacDonald wrote a mere nine stories during his lifetime featuring his seminal creation the hardboiled private investigator, Lew Archer. The publication of *Strangers in Town*, which consists of three hitherto unavailable mysteries, thus represents a literary event of some importance. This volume also contains a meaty and informative introduction by Tom Nolan, MacDonald's biographer, as well as a separate preface (also by Nolan) to each story. The first story in the collection, *Death by Water*, was written in 1945 while MacDonald was serving on the Shipley Bay in the Pacific during World War II. The protagonist of this tale is one Joe Rogers, the author's first detective and a character who would eventually evolve almost directly into Archer. The story was a companion piece to MacDonald's first Rogers mystery, *Death by Air*. Both stories were entered into the prestigious 1946 Ellery Queen Mystery Contest. *Death by Air* was eventually published as *Find the Woman* and it garnered for its author a fourth prize in the competition. (*Find the Woman* was later rewritten as an Archer story and placed in the 1954 collection, *The Name is Archer*). In *Death by Water*, which was withdrawn from submission, Rogers investigates the apparently accidental drowning of an elderly eccentric who has been caring for his younger, but gravely ill, wife. Here we find in nascent form MacDonald's trademark preoccupation with the motivations of his characters.

Determining the actual circumstances of Henry Ralston's death becomes far less important to Rogers than coming to grips with the psychology of the case. As he puts it, "The trouble's all over... I'm just trying to understand it." The title story, *Strangers in Town*, is a Lew Archer novelette written in 1950. The piece was never published as MacDonald decided that its basic plot outline could be better utilised as the framework for a novel. Many readers will no doubt recognize here the skeleton of what was to become the 1952 novel, *The Ivory Grin*. The story begins as Archer is hired by an African-American woman. Her son has been accused, wrongfully she believes, of murdering the family's female boarder. Archer discovers that the victim, the vivacious Lucy Deschamp, is a young lady with a 'past'. That knowledge places the detective on the wrong side of the mob. The author's social awareness takes centre stage in this tale. From his African-American client and the family's Latino lawyer to the shady local doctor and the wealthy syndicate enforcer, the interaction between these individuals from such diverse social, ethnic and economic backgrounds makes for some compelling and provocative reading – all the more so in a genre short story! The seeds of the author's more mature work have clearly been sown here. The final offering in this collection is the 1955 story, *The Angry Man*. When the violent and paranoid Carl Heller bursts into Archer's office the detective quickly finds himself enmeshed in a web of jealousy, greed, deceit and psychosis. All the elements that mark MacDonald's best work are here in spades – the examination of the tension that often exists between moral responsibility and legal obligation, the psychological depth, the sharp dialogue, and the labyrinthine plot carried along by singularly fluid prose. *The Angry Man* was to form the basis for the 1958 novel, *The Doomsters*, one of the author's greatest achievements. Despite their eccentricities, these stories all hold up well in their own right and are worthy additions to the MacDonald canon. The real value of these tales, however, is that they foreshadow and place into bold relief the eventual accomplishments of one of the mystery field's true innovators. In ways sometimes dim and inchoate, they offer a gratifying glimpse of the creative process that ultimately gave birth to what the *New York Times* was to call "the finest detective novels ever written by an American."

James C. Clar with thanks to *Mystery News*

The Decoy by Tony Strong
Doubleday, £9.99, 0 3856 0228 6
This book confirms Tony Strong as one of the foremost exponents of the psychothriller this side of the Atlantic. He proved himself with his debut, *The Poison Tree*, consolidated his position with *The Death Pit*, and now with his third novel *The Decoy* he once again reminds us of how the genre ought to be tackled. His story of Claire Rodenburg, a talented British actress in New York who gets mixed up in an FBI surveillance operation, is sexy, dark and, above all, nerve-wrackingly tense. Claire is a method actress who slips into the role of a suspected serial killer's lover with ease. But how long can she sustain the act? And who will drop the pretence first – her or the killer? Twist piles on twist, and the reader is dragged helplessly along with no idea of what to expect next. If there's one too

many shock revelation to properly suspend belief, then that's a small flaw in a book that's otherwise perfectly crafted. But what impresses most is the clear, unfussy narrative. In a story brimming with subterfuge, dark secrets and the pleasures acquired from intense pain, Strong never allows the prose to become purple. Every chapter, every scene, is bared down to its vitals. Dialogue is stripped to the bone, description always tight and evocative, characterisation precise. Strong may chart familiar territory (debts are owed to Thomas Harris and Agatha Christie to name but two) but nonetheless he's carving out his own unique niche in the thriller genre.

Mark Campbell

Death's Own Door by Andrew Taylor
Hodder & Stoughton, £17.99
When the body of Rufus Moorcroft, a middle-aged widower with a distinguished war record, is found in his summerhouse, the verdict is suicide. But both reporter Jill Francis and her lover, Detective Richard Thornhill, approaching the case from different angles, discover there's more to it than that. The key to the mystery stretches back to a highly charged summer before the war, and back to another death. A local asylum plays a part, as do a moderately famous artist and his wife; Superintendent Williamson, now retired and loathing it; Councillor Bernie Broadbent – a man with more pies than fingers to put in them; a Cambridge don; an aristocratic unmarried mother, now gleefully drawing her old-age pension; and – to Thornhill's surprise and growing horror – his own wife, Edith. This is Andrew Taylor at his consummate best: spare, elegant and atmospheric.

Judith Gray

I Spit On Your Graves by Boris Vian
Canongate Crime, £5.99, 1 84195 104 8
Some novels recommend themselves to the
reader because of their history: the stories
that have become tied up with the book,
rather than the narrative itself, become the
focus and can't help but subvert and aug-
ment the reading experience. Vian's infamous *I Spit On Your Graves* is one such book.
Prefaced in unambiguously laudatory tones
by none other than James Sallis, Canongate
have brought us a gem of pulp fiction that is
as trashy, coarse and fascinating as ever it
was. But it is the story behind the novel that
makes its appearance particularly exciting.
Post WWII France was in love with all things
American and the French public were suckers
for the great film noirs banned by the Vichy
regime during the war. Following the success
of Marcel Duhamel's Serie Noire of American
hardboiled translations Jean d'Halluin wanted to launch his rival Editions du Scorpion
with a bang. The well-known jazz trumpeter
Boris Vian was approached and asked if he
knew of any suitably salacious novel that
would fit the bill. In ten days, on his family
holiday at Vendee, Vian wrote what was presented as a translation of a black American
writer Vernon Sullivan. A disturbing, brutal,
misogynist blast, Vian's novel tells the compelling, if appalling, tale of Lee Anderson.
Mixed-race Lee passes for white and manages a bookshop in Buckton. Ingratiating
himself with the local kids (he is old enough
to buy alcohol) Lee seems happy enough
working, playing a little guitar, and sleeping
with all the local girls. But Lee is out for
revenge – his kid brother was killed in a
racial attack and Lee's confused sense of justice means that a perfect pair of well-to-do
sisters are his ideal target for deflowering

and then dispatching. This really is a caustic,
unadorned, pitiless book – the reader is
never sure whether Vian's righteous anger at
America's racism is as important to him as his
brilliant mimesis of the hardboiled style. But
it is an essential read because of its fascinating history and the implicit contradictions
and complications of the narrative (white
man pretending to be black writes about a
black man pretending to be white) and also
because the adjective 'pulp' has never been
so fully embodied.

Mark Thwaite

Acid Row by Minette Walters
Macmillan, £16.99, 0 333 90748 5
Acid Row is the ironic name given to their
home by the luckless inhabitants of a sink
estate. Disenfranchised, dangerous youths
roam the streets and into this no-man's land
of one-parent families comes Sophie
Morrison, a young doctor visiting a patient.
But she is unaware that she is entering the
home of a paedophile known to the police.
Within the first pages of Minette Walters'
latest book, *Acid Row* clearly marks itself out
as a further step in the author's move into
the kind of crime novel in which social significance is every bit as important as the page-
turning imperatives of a thriller. Once again,
Walters is just as interested in the psychology
of the characters and the problems of modern life as in the dictates of the classic crime
novel. The use of the young Sophie as the
protagonist is a brilliant stroke. When
reports circulate that a disturbed child called
Amy has disappeared, Sophie finds herself
caught between dangerous vigilantes and a
man she dislikes intensely. And Walters
keeps the cutting-edge aspects of her narratives to the fore, cleverly wrong-footing the

reader at every turn: although we think we have decided how we feel about the endangered paedophile and the vigilantes, she never allows these aspects to overwhelm the nagging, disturbing power of her narrative. At heart, *Acid Row* is still a mystery. Is Amy, the supposed victim, really missing? This is probably Walters' most authoritative and compelling novel to date.

Brian Ritterspak

The Machine in Ward Eleven
by Charles Willeford
No Exit Press, £6.99, 1 84243 027 0

This is the book that should confirm Willeford's status, not only as a cult hero but as a great, indeed, visionary writer. The six stories here either connect or interact, to provide a portrait of man in the misery of life which recalls Philip K. Dick or John Franklin Bardin. Or Sartre's *No Exit*, in *Jake's Journal*, a memoir of a character manning a deserted airfield in Tibet, as punishment for killing his CO's dog. What no one knows is Jake actually killed the dog to disguise his killing of a native labourer in the Phillipines, an act he saw as kindness, putting the man out of the misery of his meaningless life. Jake is the same character who narrates the title story, which was published in *Playboy* in 1961. As JC Blake, he is a film director who has attempted suicide following a blow up with the star of the TV show he is directing. His perfectionism is dragging the show behind schedule, yet he finds himself unable to descend to hack levels. The machine of the title is an electroshock unit, to which a cold psychiatrist consigns JC. I don't know if Ken Kesey read this story, but its theme and its uncertain first-person narration certainly do suggest *One Flew Over the Cuckoo's*

Nest. That story leads directly to *Selected Incidents*, in which a movie producer digresses during a session with ghost writer to talk about Blake's suicide (or attempt) and explains his entry into the business. As an analysis of the business of Hollywood and the screenwriter's art, this is one of the most biting and accurate pieces of writing I've read; in the context of the other stories, it is devastating. Willeford couldn't sell it to *Playboy*: it appeared in the more downmarket *Gent*, entitled *The Sin of Integrity*. The echoes of Willeford's own career are obvious and chilling. This is a major book, and No Exit have published it complete with its original cover, reminding us of its very minor Belmont Books original edition. If you've wondered about Willeford before, wonder no longer. This is a must-read.

Michael Carlson

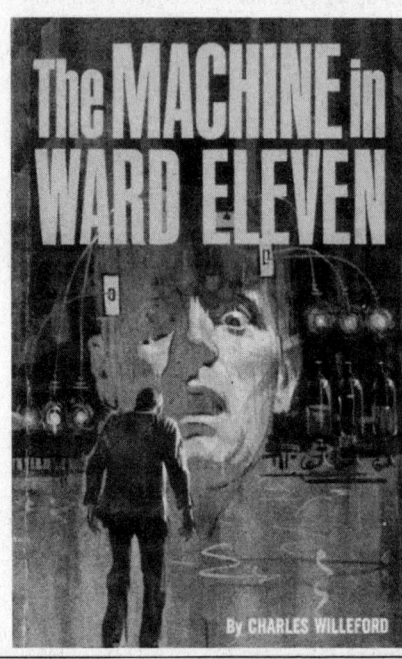

THE AU PAIR WRITERS

John Kennedy Melling

Musical duets are traditionally difficult, particularly if one singer is stronger or more devious than the other. When two writers collaborate on a book or play, they must establish the rules. When leading author and playwright Ian Hay collaborated with broadcaster Commander Stephen King-Hall to produce several very successful plays and comedies, one supplied plots and situations, the other the dialogue. Only once have I been a co-author, when international opera tenor John L. Brecknock and I wrote *Scaling the High Cs*, an account of his life and career. The incidents and explanations came from him, the writing from my side. In Monte Carlo recently when congratulating an authoress on her latest book, she remarked that I had been very helpful over the style and language, but had nothing to do with the plot, which was right, for it was editing not collaboration.

The most obvious and best known detection fiction partnership is the American cousins who wrote as, and about, Ellery Queen: Frederick Dannay (1905-1982) and Manfred B. Lee (1905-1971). Novels, short stores, anthologies and books of reference made up their vast output. That indefatigable French duo about whom I wrote in the previous issue, Boileau and Narcejac (Pierre Boileau (1906-1989) and Thomas Narcejac (1908-1997)) were versatile in every field of crime fiction. The first great French literary partnership was that of Pierre Souvestre and Marcel Allain, who created the legendary Fantomas in 1911, a character who appears to this day in films, television and comic strips. Comic strips are often produced by a partnership, an artist and a writer (as are musicals, with a writer and composer), although occasionally one brain copes with both.

Literary collaborations come in all shapes and sizes. Husband and wife? The American Lockridges: Richard (1898-1982) and Frances (1896-1963), his first wife. He created Mr and Mrs North and continued writing alone after his wife's death. The English academic pair of G. D. H. and M. Cole consisted of George Douglas Howard (1889-1959) and Margaret Isabel (sister of Raymond Postgate) (1893-1980) who created Superintendent Henry Wilson, a rather heavy-going series sleuth. Another married team was that of the Gordons. Mildred Gordon (1905-1979) and Gordon Gordon, born in 1906 and a former FBI agent, whose various detectives included the Undercover Cat.

Can brothers work together? And what about twins? 'Peter Antony' could! Anthony Shaffer, born in 1926 and a barrister whose second wife was actress Diane Cilento, and twin Peter, a critic. Their successes included plays like the hugely successful trick piece *Sleuth* and the wickedly subtle *The Case of the Oily Levantine*, later re-named *Whodunnit* (not to be confused with the earlier Abbott and Costello comedy film).

Two writers can work together, and an early example was a novel filmed by Hitchcock (who later directed the Boileau-Narcejac *D'Entre les Morts* as *Vertigo*) entitled *Enter Sir John* by Clemence Dane and Helen Simpson. Hitch re-named it *Murder!* The ladies wrote a second novel about their actor manager, Sir John Menier, based on the successful Sir Gerald Du Maurier, father of Daphne. Menier was the stage name of the hero, played by Herbert Marshall. Menier was, and still is, a famous

French chocolate! An interesting amalgam was 'Emma Lathen', two professional women in Mary J. Latsis, former economist, and Martha Henissart, a banker. A string of Wall Street crime and murder cases solved by banker John Putnam Thatcher started in 1961, all with clever titles. In 1968 writing as R. B. Dominic, they created another detective in Ben Safford. Presumably they chose this pseudonym to sound masculine, as did P. D. James and C. V. Wedgwood. A very involved American partnership was that of 'Patrick Quentin'. This started out as Englishman Hugh Wheeler (1912-1987) who wrote with American Richard Wilson Webb until 1952; their other pseudonyms were Q. Patrick and Jonathan Stagge. Their Peter Duluth novels had titles like *A Puzzle for Fools* and *Puzzle for Players*.

Sometimes a writer would work in partnership for just one book. Dame Ngaio Marsh (1895-1982) wrote *The Nursing Home Murder*, and adapted it for the stage under the same title, with Dr Henry Jellett; the book in 1935, the play three years later. Dorothy L. Sayers (1893-1957) wrote one book in collaboration: *The Documents in the Case*, 1930, was written with Robert Eustace and did not feature her famous polymath Lord Peter Wimsey. She wrote the play *Busman's Honeymoon* with Mildred St. Clare Byrne in 1936. It first starred the late Dennis Arundell as Lord Peter Wimsey whom she thought completely wrong in the part of the honeymooner; the film had elegant Robert Montgomery playing Wimsey.

We have covered only those partnerships where the work has obviously been shared, as has the credit, and naturally the royalties!
John Kennedy Melling